From Gods to God

UNIVERSITY OF NEBRASKA PRESS | LINCOLN

FROM
GODS
TO
GOD

How the Bible Debunked, Suppressed,
or Changed Ancient Myths & Legends

AVIGDOR SHINAN & YAIR ZAKOVITCH

Translated by Valerie Zakovitch

THE JEWISH PUBLICATION SOCIETY
PHILADELPHIA

Library of Congress Cataloging-in-Publication Data

Zakovitch, Yair.
[Lo kakh katuv ba-Tanakh. English]
From gods to God: how the Bible debunked,
suppressed, or changed ancient myths and
legends / Yair Zakovitch and Avigdor Shinan;
translated by Valerie Zakovitch.
    p. cm.
"Published by the University of Nebraska Press
as a Jewish Publication Society book."
Includes bibliographical references and index.
    ISBN 978-0-8276-0908-2 (pbk.: alk. paper)
1. Bible. O.T.—Criticism, Redaction. I. Shinan,
Avigdor. II. Zakovitch, Valerie. III. Title.
            BS1158.H4Z3413 2012
              221.6′6—dc23
             2012020072

Set in Arno Pro by Shirley Thornton.
Designed by A. Shahan.

Dedicated with affection and gratitude
to our many students in Israel and abroad.

*Much have we learned from our teachers,
more from our colleagues,
and from our students most of all.*

Contents

Acknowledgments

We would like to take this opportunity to express our gratitude to our academic home of many years, the Mandel Institute of Jewish Studies at the Hebrew University of Jerusalem, and to the Yitzhak Becker Endowed Chair in Jewish Studies and Father Takeji Otsuki Endowed Chair in Bible Studies for their support of our research throughout the years. Thanks are due also to Ms. Yael Shinan-Tzur for preparing the excellent glossary and to our dedicated research assistants, Ms. Esther Bar-On and Mr. Yochai Ofran, for their invaluable help.

Our translator, Ms. Valerie Zakovitch, served as a very sensitive and knowledgeable mediator between the original Hebrew edition of this book and its counterpart for an English-reading audience. Words cannot express our feelings of thanks and gratitude. We would also like to thank the Deborah Harris Agency for finding a good home for the book and the highly dedicated people at the Jewish Publication Society and the University of Nebraska Press, including Carol Hupping, Elisabeth Chretien, Sabrina Stellrecht, and Mary Hill, for their careful and wise handling of our book, "upon them the blessing of good will come" (Proverbs 24:25).

Translator's Note

All translators of literary works must choose which of the different meanings and nuances of the original text they will convey and which they will, out of necessity, silence. Translators of the Bible must continually choose not only between denotations and connotations of different Hebrew words but between a translation that conveys a more limited and immediate sense and one that preserves crucial intertextual relationships. I have generally relied on *Tanakh: The Holy Scriptures: The New JPS Translation According to the Traditional Hebrew Text* (1985) for all biblical quotations. The nature of this book, however, which often focuses on analyses of specific Hebrew terms or expressions, required that I sometimes adjust that translation to reflect other meanings present in the Hebrew. These changes were meant not as "corrections" but only to enable English readers to understand the interpretative possibilities of the original Hebrew that are being addressed by the authors.

From Gods to God

Introduction

When God Fought the Sea Dragons

The twenty-four books that constitute the Hebrew Bible were written over the course of roughly one thousand years, during which time they gradually reached their final form. The purpose of these books was to teach readers about themselves: who they were, where they came from, what their relations were with other nations. Most importantly, the Hebrew Bible aimed to persuade readers of the existence of one god and of their relationship with that god. The Bible was the manifesto of the revolutionary thinkers who were its writers: it was the manifesto of the monotheistic revolution.

Though the writers of the Bible may have lived hundreds of years apart, they spoke with one another through their writings, each adding his words to the growing canon. Indeed, the Bible is not merely a collection of books but a network of connections in which stories talk to poems and laws to prophecies. Two brief examples illustrate the phenomenon.

The genealogy of David's ancestry in the book of Ruth (written in about the fifth century BCE) supplies information that was missing from the (earlier) book of Samuel, which, when it introduces the youthful David to us for the first time, relates almost nothing about his ancestry except for the name of David's father. The writer of Samuel had his reasons for not describing David's background. For one thing, he wanted David to prove himself as a leader and so to be seen as a self-made king. But the writer of Ruth, who lived a few centuries after the writer of Samuel, did not share that point of view. For Ruth's writer it was unthinkable that we would not know the genealogy of such a figure and that David would not be the descendant of illustrious ancestors.

As a second example, a short prophecy in the book of Isaiah about the Days to Come (Isaiah 2:2–5) tells us how, in that wondrous future, "the Law [Torah] will come forth from Zion, the word of the LORD from Jerusalem." This prophecy actually converses with the Bible's paramount story about the giving of the Law on Mount Sinai in Exodus 19. That first Law was given only to the Israelites at the base of Mount Sinai when they were alone in the wilderness, in "Splendid Isolation"; on the other hand, in the Days to Come, according to Isaiah, the Law will be given to *all* the nations, and not on Mount Sinai but on the Temple Mount in Jerusalem. Isaiah's goal was peace, and he deemed peace to be attainable only if all the nations join together and communicate. Isaiah conveys the importance of communication by shaping his prophecy as a mirror image of the story of the Tower of Babel.

The Tower of Babel was another case where humanity united and sought to ascend (in that case, to ascend to heaven and challenge God). In Babel, however, God puts an abrupt end to the people's hubris by confusing their languages and scattering them to the ends of the earth. By using these two stories—about the giving of the Law at Sinai and the Tower of Babel—as the building blocks for his prophecy, Isaiah both reveals his disagreement with the ideology of separatism and gives humanity a second chance: again the people will join together, again they will speak and understand one another as they ascend the mountain of God—but this time with humility in order to learn God's ways and walk in God's path. This, in the prophet's view, will bring peace.

This web of connections between different writings is what we call "inner-biblical interpretation." It happens when one text expands, alludes to, or becomes reflected in another. It is worthwhile to consider this phenomenon that created layers upon layers of interpretation within the biblical corpus itself. As these ancient thinkers wrote their texts, whether historical accounts or psalms, legal texts or narratives, they planted them firmly into the already growing canon, incorporating them into already-established contexts or appending them to existing texts, and, by doing so, they introduced new ideas and interpretations. They didn't erase a text with which they disagreed; instead, through additions both slight and significant, they were able to alter our understanding by interpreting the text and thus influencing our sense of it.

An interesting example of this is found in Genesis 30, which recounts the story of Jacob being swindled by his father-in-law, Laban. Jacob wishes to leave Laban, having served him for twenty years, and the two agree that Jacob will take with him for wages "every speckled and spotted animal, every dark-colored sheep and every spotted and speckled goat." Before Jacob manages to remove the goats and sheep that are now his, however, Laban hands those animals over to his sons and sends them off on a "three days' journey." Wanting to secure his rightful property, Jacob resorts to magic. He peels off the bark from some fresh tree shoots and places them into the herds' drinking troughs: "[The goats'] mating occurred when they came to drink, and since the goats mated by the shoots, the goats brought forth streaked, speckled, and spotted young" (vv. 38–39). Jacob then positions the mating sheep in front of the streaked or totally dark-colored animals and thereby influences the color of the offspring to his advantage. In such a way, by his own initiative and power—and magic—Jacob manages to produce a flock for himself despite Laban's trickery.

At least one writer, however, apparently viewed as problematic the idea that Jacob used magic. For him, this notion—that a human could manipulate God's Creation—was mistaken and intolerable. Disagreeing with the story in Genesis 30 but unable to delete it, this writer managed to modify our understanding of it by describing Jacob in the next chapter as he recounts to Rachel and Leah what transpired: "As you know, I have served your father with all my might; but your father has cheated me, changing my wages time and again. *God, however, would*

3

not let him do me harm. If he said thus, 'The speckled shall be your wages,' then all the flocks would drop speckled young; and if he said thus, 'The streaked shall be your wages,' then all the flocks would [give birth] to streaked young. God has taken away your father's livestock and given it to me." Jacob's version manages to introduce God—who was entirely absent from the account in Genesis 30—into the original story. Jacob, it now seems, knew all along that it was God and not Jacob's fiddling with sticks that gave him his rightful wage. In this way, the second writer interprets the first story for us and changes our initial reading: it was not human magic but God's work that secured Jacob's payment. This is the power of interpretation.

Of course, the phenomenon of interpretation never ceased. New books continued to be written, and even the existing books continued to be changed. (We see evidence of this in the Septuagint—the Greek translation of the Bible that was used by the Jews of Alexandria—where we find not only that the books are ordered differently but that some, like Esther and Daniel, have been significantly expanded, and many new books have been added [e.g., Judith, Maccabees, Ben Sira].) This is because of the significant role that the Bible continued to play in society: in fact, it was precisely this process of interpretation that saved the Bible from becoming obsolete. The exegetical work of explaining and interpreting Scripture is known as "midrash." It reinvigorates old texts by breathing new life into them, maintaining their relevance over changing times by generating fresh meanings and ever-pertinent lessons. The exegetical work that so famously blossomed in extra-biblical literature, however, in the Apocrypha and Pseudepigrapha, Rabbinic literature, medieval commentaries, and so on, is found already within the pages of the Bible, in the careful maneuverings of those ancient writers who, by interpreting already established texts, sought to persuade readers of their views and opinions.

When did interpretation begin? Is the first written expression of a tradition necessarily the beginning of that tradition? Did a tradition come into the world only when it was first scratched onto a stone or tablet or written on a piece of papyrus or skin? The Bible is not like a book written by a modern author who sits behind a desk, wrinkles his or her brow, and imaginatively concocts new characters and plots. The writing of the Bible involved the recording of ancient traditions that had been passed orally for generations from teachers to pupils, from the society's elders to its youngest members—an idea expressed in Exodus 13:8: "And you shall tell your son." Indeed, this book is our attempt to recover the pre-biblical traditions and to offer a glimpse of the rich lives the traditions lived before they became molded into the written forms that we have inherited.

In fact, we often become aware that the official, written version of a story (i.e., the Bible's version) was meant to dispute views and opinions that were accepted when the story still made its way orally through the world. By fixing stories in writing, biblical writers aimed to establish what they deemed to be the "correct" tradition, the tradition that was worthy of preservation, and to eliminate traditions and viewpoints that they considered unsuitable or impossible to accept. For various reasons that we will soon discuss, many of these popular traditions were problematic for the biblical writers who censored them—by interpreting them—for their readers.

Uneasiness with the beliefs and worldviews of the ancient traditions tended to surface around a number of themes, four of which will be explored in this book: the world of myth; cult and sacred geography; biblical heroes and their biographies; and relations between men and women.

The World of Myth

Israel's break with its pagan past was hardly instantaneous and certainly not painless. Many stories carried their mythic foundations within them and spoke about gods and the progeny of gods and semidivine beings; these stories told of these beings' heroic antics and their involvements with humans. Such stories are familiar to us from Israel's neighbors, such as Sumer and Babylonia, ancient Egypt, and Canaan. The Bible, as we will see, did its best to resist these polytheistic traditions and to purify the religion of Israel and its Scripture from any and all mythological-pagan elements.

Cult and Sacred Geography

Cultic elements—customs, objects, and relics—that were legitimate in the context of one culture (e.g., a polytheistic one) naturally provoked anger in a different (monotheistic) culture and period. Moreover, a place that is holy to one population is not necessarily so to another, whose members might question and even challenge its sanctity. Disputes over the legitimacy of cultic sites often assumed a nationalistic dimension when antagonisms between tribes or kingdoms (e.g., the Kingdom of Israel and the Kingdom of Judah) became focused on questions concerning the sanctity and foundation of these sites. In a number of chapters we will see how the Bible sought to establish correct cultic behavior and to mark the sanctity of one or another site, often by fighting beliefs and ideologies that it refused to tolerate.

Biblical Heroes and Their Biographies

Controversies tended to gather around the status of heroes and historical figures who were admired by one or another group. Some heroes were depicted by the oral tradition in ways that were considered incompatible with Israel's sacred writings. A character, for example, whose mischievous pranks and schemes provided laughter-filled entertainment for a gathering of friends would hardly be appropriate in literature that aimed to refine the characterizations of the central figures in the history of Israel. On the other hand, when that character was a political or national opponent, traditions might be allowed to besmirch a reputation severely. And while oral traditions often reflected unbridled admiration for human heroes, the written Scripture of a monotheistic religion could not tolerate a human whose heroic stature might compete with God's, perhaps even outshine God. As we will see, the Bible's war against the threat of personality cults was constant.

Relations between Men and Women

Recording tales in writing necessitated also a change in the depiction of male-female relations. We will observe how writers eliminated sexual elements from oral traditions as they were incorporated into written Scripture in an attempt to preserve the more lofty tone that such a context required.

The writers of the Bible did not argue openly or directly with these unwanted traditions. Instead, the battle they waged against oral traditions was, for the most part, a covert one fought through interpretation. These writers presented a new or different version of a known story that did not openly oppose the views it disputed but, instead, interpreted them. The polemicist of this sort often finds himself between a rock and a hard place. On the one hand, if he wants his readers (who know the old version) to be willing to accept his rendition, he must reproduce faithfully, as much as possible, the popular tradition. On the other hand, he is committed to his beliefs and ideology, which require him to change the familiar tradition. The art of the biblical story can be found in the delicate balancing act performed by these writers, who tread carefully between the old and the new.

Our enterprise of detecting ancient oral traditions and lifting them from under their written versions is one that we call "literary archaeology." The archaeologist of this sort retrieves hidden treasures from the *literary* past. We have established three strategies for recovering these ancient traditions. Each can be used alone, or, as is always preferable, two or more can be used together.

1. Identifying Duplicate Traditions within the Bible

We find many cases where the written tradition (i.e., the Hebrew Bible) includes more than one version of a tradition. A careful comparison of these duplicate versions will often betray a conflict between the more ancient, problematic elements and those that were intended to challenge, obscure, or even replace them. At times we find the older, unwanted version in the Bible's margins, banished to the textual periphery far from the primary recording of the tradition. Sometimes a tradition's double is found outside the main body of biblical historiography in some other of the Bible's literary genres, such as prophecy or psalms. In this way, for example, a polemic that in the biblical narrative was handled covertly may become overt in a prophetic context, an occurrence that certainly facilitates our identifying the polemical elements in the narrative. Another useful source can sometimes be found in parallel traditions that relate the same story about different characters; with both in hand, the older tradition can often be reconstructed.

2. Considering Traditions from the Pagan World

We have an abundance of sources from the ancient Near East, on whose soil Israel's culture was born, and from the classical world, cultures that were both separated from and connected to Israel by the Mediterranean Sea. Both of these vast reservoirs of traditions—from cultures in which Israel grew and was in contact—can help us identify elements that the biblical writers endeavored to disown.

3. Reading a Story's Subsequent Renditions
in Post-Biblical Literature

A rich literary world was erected on the foundations established by the biblical stories: Jewish-Hellenistic literature, the Apocrypha and Pseudepigrapha, the writings of the Dead Sea sect, Aramaic Targumim (translations), Rabbinic literature in all its various expressions, ancient liturgical poetry (*piyyutim*), and even traditions related to the Hebrew Bible that are found in Samaritan writings, the New Testament, and the Qur'an. This enormous corpus preserves more than a few remnants of ancient traditions that the Bible barred from its pages but that continued nonetheless to be told and retold, transmitted orally until much later. When they were no longer deemed threatening to anyone's beliefs or ideologies, they reemerged and were recorded. Here we notice what distinguishes literary archaeology from its more physical cousin: a "real" archaeologist must dig deeper and deeper through layers of dirt and stone in order to unearth the earliest strata, whereas the literary archaeologist is likely to find ancient elements specifically in the later and younger literary texts.

Let us present one example of our methods as an appetizer of what is to come. This is a case where we have been able to reconstruct a pre-biblical story that was rejected from the Bible's central narrative stream. The example we've chosen was first studied by Umberto Cassuto, a professor at the Hebrew University of Jerusalem.[1] Cassuto wanted to show how the Bible's Creation story (Genesis 1:1–2:3) was an attempt to dispute another account of the Creation that was then prevalent in the ancient Near East: that the world had resulted from a war between gods, a battle fought between the chief god of the pantheon and the god of the sea and his allies, the primeval marine creatures. Cassuto reconstructed the ancient story by using all the methods that we have mentioned: traditions from the ancient Near East (Babylonian and Canaanite), echoes of the rejected tradition that he found inside the Bible, and later retellings of the story from post-biblical literature.

Cassuto showed how the story that welcomes us into the Bible presents a restful, quiet, and orderly Creation in which, with mere utterances, God creates the world in a wondrous progression over the course of seven days. Light/day and darkness/night, heaven and earth, vegetation, heavenly bodies, marine animals and birds, land animals and humans, male and female: God creates one after the other over six days of productivity, which are followed on the seventh with the Creator resting from all that work.

The creation of the animal and plant kingdoms is presented in Genesis using general categories: "seed-bearing plants of every kind, and trees of every kind bearing fruit with the seed in it" (day three); "and all the living creatures of every kind that creep, which the waters brought forth in swarms and all the winged birds of every kind" (day five); "wild beasts of every kind and cattle of every kind, and all kinds of creeping things of the earth" (day six). Amid these general designations of plants and trees, creeping creatures and flying birds, beasts and cattle, one phrase draws our attention. It describes the creation

---

1. Umberto Cassuto, *A Commentary on the Book of Genesis: From Adam to Noah*, trans. I. Abrahams (Jerusalem: Magnes Press, 1961); *Biblical and Oriental Studies*, trans. I. Abrahams (Jerusalem: Magnes Press, 1973–1975).

of a specifically named animal type that was created on the fifth day: "God created the great sea dragons" (v. 21).

Cassuto argued that the particular identification of the sea dragons in the context of the Creation was polemical in nature. It was meant, he proposed, to remind the reader that these enormous creatures were created beings like all others: they were not divine, nor were they mythical creatures with powers to challenge God, the Creator. The polemical nature of these few words will become evident when we examine the three groups of sources that we mentioned above. They will help us to reconstruct the very Creation story that the writers of Genesis sought to deny.

The peoples of the ancient Near East—the Babylonians and the inhabitants of the Kingdom of Ugarit (a large Canaanite city in what is today Syria whose rich library of inscribed clay tablets was discovered only during the twentieth century)—knew many stories about the great war between the gods at the world's beginnings. According to the Babylonian myth *Enuma Elish*, the god of the heavens, Marduk, waged war against Tiamat, the goddess of the sea, and defeated her. Marduk then created the world from Tiamat's corpse (notice the word *tehom* in Genesis 1:2, "with darkness over the surface of the deep [*tehom*]," suggesting that this mythic figure left her mark here as a physical term). According to an Ugaritic myth (which will now occupy most of our attention), Baal, the god of the heavens and the head of the pantheon, battled Mot, the god of the netherworld. Mot's allies included the "prince of the sea" along with Leviathan the Twisting Serpent, Leviathan the Elusive Serpent, and the sea dragon (or dragons). The people of Ugarit told how the seas challenged Baal at the earth's beginnings: how the sea and the rivers, along with their allies, the great sea creatures, aspired to conquer the world and how they rose up. Baal appeared against them in a great tempest, amidst lightning and thunder, and loudly denounced them; he launched an attack against the rebellion and won. The disgraced oceans were quieted and found themselves confined by shores, while the creatures that had joined the insurrection were either trapped or killed by Baal.

No trace of this story is evident in the first chapter of Genesis (except for the brief mention of the sea dragons). But it seems certain that the people of Israel told a similar story about their own god—we find no reason to believe that the ancient Israelites were not like the other nations in whose midst they lived—and we find allusions to it in many of the Bible's other books. This is because traditions that the Pentateuch tried to suppress did not disappear entirely from Israel but found their way into writing, probably when the ancient myth no longer posed a threat to the burgeoning monotheistic religion. We'll illustrate this with a few of the many possible examples.

A war that God waged against a multitude of challengers—the deep, the sea, Rahab the sea monster, the rivers, Leviathan the Twisting Serpent, Leviathan the Elusive Serpent, and the sea dragons—is referred to in the psalms, the prophecies, and other writings. We find, for example, in Isaiah 51:9–10: "Awake, awake, clothe yourself with splendor. O arm of the LORD! Awake as in days of old, as in former ages! It was you that hacked Rahab into pieces, that pierced the Dragon. It was you that dried up the waters of the great deep [*tehom*]." The prophet pleads with God to repeat the great wonders of the past—God's killing of Rahab and the sea dragon, God's defeat of the sea and of the "great abyss"—in the prophet's own day, the period of the return to Zion from Babylonian exile. The same can be seen in the psalmist's words: "You rule the swelling of the sea; when its waves surge, You still them. You crushed Rahab; he was like a corpse; with Your powerful arm You scattered Your enemies. The heaven is Yours, the earth too; the world and all it holds, You established them" (89:10–12). So, too, in the words of the prophet Nahum: "He travels in whirlwind and storm, and clouds are the dust on His feet. He rebukes the sea and dries it up, and He makes all rivers fail" (1:3–4). Again, the psalmist:

> Smoke went up from His nostrils, from His mouth came devouring fire; live coals blazed forth from Him. He bent the sky and came down, thick cloud beneath His feet. . . . Then the LORD thundered from heaven, the Most High gave forth His voice, hail

and fiery coals. He let fly His shafts and scattered them; He discharged lightning and routed them. The ocean bed was exposed; the foundations of the world were laid bare by Your mighty roaring, O LORD, at the blast of the breath of Your nostrils. (Psalm 18:9–16)

These are but a few of the biblical verses that describe the great battle at the beginning.

A number of verses speak about the sea dragons that participated in this war and that were defeated by God, such as these words in Job 7:12, where Job bewails his fate: "Am I the sea or the Dragon, that You have set a watch over me?" In Isaiah's vision of the future we hear a request to repeat the events of the past: "In that day the LORD will punish, with His great, cruel, mighty sword, Leviathan the Elusive Serpent, Leviathan the Twisting Serpent; He will slay the Dragon of the sea" (27:1). We find the sea dragons also in a poet's praise of God's actions in Psalm 74: "It was You who drove back the sea with Your might, who smashed the heads of the dragons in the waters; it was You who crushed the heads of Leviathan, who left him as food for the denizens of the desert" (vv. 13–14).

The pre-biblical sources from Ugarit that we mentioned above, along with the biblical texts that we have just cited, provide more than sufficient evidence to argue that the verse "God created the great sea dragons" was not a trivial detail but a sharp riposte aimed at overthrowing, in one swift parry, an entire complex of mythological beliefs. Still further evidence can be culled from post-biblical sources where, though some traditions were created in order to interpret these same verses, others clearly preserve pre-biblical traditions.

An example of this can be found in the apocryphal Prayer of Manasseh, whose writer turns to God with the epithetical, "You who made heaven and earth with all their order; who shackled the sea by your word of command, who confined the deep and sealed it with your terrible and glorious name" (vv. 2–3). The writer of the book of Revelation, in the New Testament, used the ancient tradition in order to describe the future Apocalypse. He tells of an angel descending from heaven who "seized the dragon, that ancient serpent . . . and threw him into the deep and sealed it over him" (20:2–3).

Numerous indeed are the sources in Rabbinic literature that tell of the sea's rebellion or of the uprising of the "prince of the sea" and of the war between God and the rebellious forces that brought their defeat at the creation of the world. We bring here but a few examples.

> At the time when the Holy One, blessed be He, desired to create the world, he said to the angel of the sea, "Open thy mouth and swallow all the waters of the world [in order to reveal the dry land]." He said to him, "Lord of the Universe, it is enough that I remain with my own." Thereupon He struck him with His foot and killed him, for it is written, "By His power He stilled the sea; by His skill He struck down Rahab" (Job 26:12). (B. *Bava Batra* 74b)

> The Holy One blessed be He, said, "The dry land appear." The waters said, "Behold, we fill the entire world, and until now we've been constrained: where will we go now?" The One Whose Name is blessed trampled on the ocean and killed it. . . . When the rest of the waters saw how He had trampled the ocean, to the sound of [the ocean's] screams, . . . [they] fled. As it is said, "They fled at Your blast" (Psalm 104:7). And they didn't know to where they were fleeing. . . . He struck them and said to them, "I told you to go to the place of the Leviathan. . . . 'You set bounds they must not pass' (v. 9)." (*Exodus Rabbah* 15:22)

> When the Holy One blessed be He created the sea, it went on expanding, until the Holy One blessed be He rebuked it and caused it to dry up, for it is said, "He rebukes the sea and dries it up" (Nahum 1:4). (B. *Hagigah* 12a)

Rabbinic literature also contains references to the war that God fought against the sea dragons. Rabbi Yohanan explicitly identifies the Creation story's "great sea dragons" as "Leviathan the Twisting Serpent" and "Leviathan the Elusive Serpent" (B. *Bava Batra* 74b). The Talmud goes on to relate, in the name of Rab, that God "castrated the male" sea dragon and "killed the female" in order to prevent their mating with one another and destroying the world with the force of their sexual act. In the future, according to the apocalyptic description of the End of Days, when there will be a sort of return to the beginning of history, a number of years are set aside for "the wars of the sea dragons" and others for "the war of Gog and Magog, and the remaining [period] will be the Messianic era" (B. *Sanhedrin* 97b). The identification of the sea dragons with the Leviathan, another great sea creature, resulted in a whole group of traditions about God's victory over that threatening creature, with which God "plays" (see Psalm 104:26; Job 40:29) or which God kills, using the meat to feed the righteous in the future (e.g., B. *Bava Batra* 85a; Aramaic Targum to Psalm 104:26).

Cassuto's work demonstrates how the verse in Genesis that states "God created the great sea dragons" represented but the tip of an iceberg that tried to hide an entire bustling world of other, competing traditions. Explicit references to these can be found in pre-biblical literature, in the Bible itself, and in post-biblical literature. Revealing these traditions restores the full and powerful significance to the short phrase in Genesis.

Now that we've exemplified our methods and reconstructed an ancient tradition, we should probably emphasize that *the act of revealing ancient traditions has nothing whatsoever to do with recovering historical facts.* This rule will be confirmed in every chapter of this book. Uncovering historical and biographical facts about figures from the past is not within our powers, nor are we interested in reconstructing them. By recovering traditions that relate to such personalities and events, however, we are able to contribute to the understanding of the history of ideas and the history of culture. It is unimportant, in our opinions, whether or not (for example) the Exodus from Egypt, as described in the Bible, actually took place. It is enough that, as Jews read every year in the Passover haggadah, "every generation must see itself as though it went forth from Egypt." The Exodus is charged with ideological and symbolic meaning for the Jewish people and for the people of the Western world generally, even while that meaning may change and assume directions that were unimagined by the ancients. Our inquiry is not into what actually occurred. Rather, our interests lie in knowing what people told about the history of their world, their people, and their heroes. All that we have done is to search for those traditions that were excluded from the Bible or that were reported only faintly. In this volume we examine thirty biblical stories and try to reveal the more ancient traditions hidden behind them using the tools we have mentioned: inner-biblical parallels and allusions, traditions collected from cultures that surrounded the society that produced the Bible, and later retellings of stories from post-biblical literature in all its various expressions. (We should note that, with regard to Rabbinic literature, we usually bring only the most complete version of a tradition without referencing all of its many parallels.) We are not certain that we succeeded in uncovering the hidden tradition in every case. But even if occasionally we have made mistakes or have fallen short of our goal, we are nonetheless confident in the correctness of our methodology and certain that it is in the power of the literary archaeologist to recover intriguing chapters in the cultural-literary heritage of the people of Israel.

It is our hope that this book will enable readers to peer between the lines of the Hebrew Bible and discover a bit of the great wealth of traditions that preceded the present shape of Scripture. We have wanted to offer a bit of the tremendous intellectual satisfaction that our research has given us along with the thrill of peeking "behind the curtain" at ancient culture. From here on, we hope, readers' appreciation of the Bible—even of the many stories that we have not dealt with—will be less naive and all the more profound.

1

The World of Myth

1

Eden's Winged Serpent

The very first creature we meet once the world has been created is the serpent: "Now the serpent was the most cunning of all the wild beasts that the LORD God had made" (Genesis 3:1). The polemical nature of the verse is clear: the serpent, this verse teaches, is only one more of God's creatures. Job says this specifically in the course of his sketch of the creation process: "His hand created the elusive serpent" (26:13). Genesis 3:1 disputes the belief that the snake was an independently divine being whose battle with God marked the beginning of the Creation. An echo of that ancient myth (as we saw in the introduction) can be found mouthed by the prophet Isaiah: "In that day the LORD will punish, with His great, cruel, mighty sword, Leviathan the Elusive Serpent, Leviathan the Twisting Serpent; He will slay the Dragon of the Sea" (27:1).

Placed at the very beginning of the Torah, the story of the Creation and the Garden of Eden teaches us how nothing preceded God's creating the world and that the snake, who was created by God, sought to ruin God's plans by tempting the first couple to eat from the Tree of Knowledge so that they would become "like God who knows good and bad" (Genesis 3:5). The serpent's deed provoked God's punishment and established that animal's physical form and most identifying characteristic: "On your belly shall you crawl and dirt shall you eat all the days of your life" (3:14). This image of the snake and its punishment became the symbol of the enemy who was forced to capitulate, as we hear when the prophet Micah speaks about the enemies of Israel: "Let them lick dust like snakes, like crawling things on the ground!"

(7:17). An allusion to the same characteristic is found also in another prophet's promise to Israel—"Kings shall tend your children, their queens shall serve you as nurses. They shall bow to you, face to the ground, and lick the dust of your feet" (Isaiah 49:23)—as well as in Psalm 72, which speaks of the king, "Let desert-dwellers kneel before him, and his enemies lick the dust" (v. 9).

But what was the snake's appearance before its divine punishment, before it was reduced to slithering on its belly? In order to answer that question, we must first address a different issue, one whose relevance will only later become clear, concerning the relationship between the primeval Garden of Eden and the Temple, the House of God in Jerusalem. Isaiah, for example, in his prophecy concerning the future "shoot" from the "stump of Jesse" (chapter 11), envisioned an idyllic image of a return to Eden, of a period of peace and tranquility between all God's created beings. The serpent's role in this reincarnated garden will be as a tamed pet for a child's amusement: "A babe shall play over a viper's hole, and an infant pass his hand over an adder's den" (v. 8). The snake will no longer cause harm; indeed, "in all of My sacred mount nothing evil or vile shall be done" (v. 9). Isaiah 11:9 makes it clear that this new Garden of Eden will in fact be the Mount of the Lord, where the Temple stands. Another prophecy, in Isaiah 65, quotes from the picture drawn in chapter 11 and strengthens (even accentuates) the connection between the story of Eden and that of the future Garden/Temple: "And the lion shall eat straw like the ox, and the serpent's food shall be dirt. In all My sacred mount nothing evil or vile shall be done" (v. 25).

Recognizing the relationship between the Garden of Eden, the serpent, and the Temple may teach us something about the appearance of the serpent in the Temple, which may then help us determine its previous appearance in Eden. In Isaiah's inaugural vision in chapter 6, in which he accepts the prophetic mission, Isaiah carefully describes the divine entourage: "Seraphs stood in attendance on Him. Each of them had six wings: with two he covered his face, with two he covered his legs, and with two he would fly" (v. 2). Seraphs, then, have wings, legs, and even hands, as we learn later, in verse 6: "Then one of the

seraphs flew over to me, and in his hand was a live coal, which he had
taken from the altar with a pair of tongs."

But what, indeed, is a "seraph"? We find the answer to that question
also in Isaiah: "For from the stock of a snake there sprouts an asp, a
flying seraph branches out from it" (14:29), and also "of viper and flying seraph" (30:6). From these verses it becomes clear that seraphs
were in fact flying serpents: the temple envisioned by Isaiah was filled
with serpents with arms, legs, and wings, and it seems likely that this
was the tradition that Isaiah knew regarding the primeval serpent in
the Garden of Eden, before God transformed it into a dirt-slithering
animal. Indeed, this is the image of the paradisiacal snake that we find
in the pseudepigraphic book *Life of Adam and Eve*. Here, when God
curses the serpent, God says, "You shall crawl on your belly, and you
shall be deprived of your hands as well as your feet. There shall be left
for you neither ear nor wing" (26:3).

Other ancient sources also represent the pre-sin serpent as having
legs, hands, or wings. So we find in the Jewish historian Flavius Josephus's *Jewish Antiquities* (1.1.4) and in a number of different Rabbinic sources, for example, *Genesis Rabbah* 20:5 ("When the Holy One
blessed be He told him 'on your belly you shall crawl,' the ministering
angels came down and cut off its hands and feet") and *Targum Pseudo-
Jonathan* to Genesis 3:14. This same winged serpent with arms and legs
can be found flying about in texts from the ancient Near East, Egypt,
and Mesopotamia.

The presence of a snake in the Temple during the time of Isaiah or
King Hezekiah, a king who reigned Judah at that time, is mentioned
in the book of Kings in the course of a description of the cultic revolution that Hezekiah instituted: "He abolished the shrines and smashed
the pillars and cut down the sacred post. He also broke into pieces the
bronze serpent that Moses had made, for until that time the Israelites
had been offering sacrifices to it; it was called Nehushtan" (2 Kings
18:4). When Hezekiah decided to eradicate all cultic practices from
the Temple in Jerusalem, practices offensive in his eyes, he destroyed
the bronze serpent that had previously been perceived as something

intrinsically divine (if not, the Israelites would not have "offered sacrifices to it").

The writer of Kings, who refers to Hezekiah's actions, explicitly links the serpent to Moses. At least on the face of it, he seems to refer to the serpent that Moses created in the wilderness (as described in Numbers 21) after the Israelites had been attacked by a swarm of serpents and God had directed him to make a seraph, a copper image of a snake: "Moses made a copper serpent and mounted it on a standard; and when anyone was bitten by a serpent, he would look at the copper serpent and recover" (v. 9). On the other hand, the tradition in Kings may refer to a more ancient tale, against which also the verse in the book of Numbers is directed, according to which the sculpted image of the snake represented a divine being or a member of the divine assembly. The Torah, alarmed at the image of the people of Israel sacrificing to the serpent in the Temple, makes it clear in the story in Numbers that the bronze snake does not represent any divine, mythological being but was only a device, an object determined by God and fashioned by Moses—a mere human—for the purpose of healing snake-inflicted wounds. The story in Numbers 21 is therefore the beginning of a process whose end is reflected in Hezekiah's act: the story from Numbers did not stop the people from worshiping the snake, and so Hezekiah felt the need, finally, to forcefully remove and destroy it.

The idea that the snake in the Garden of Eden was a seraph with legs, arms, and wings suggests that also the story in Genesis was part of the polemic against the serpent-seraph that was installed in the Jerusalem Temple. The story in Genesis remarks that, with the expulsion of Adam and Eve from the Garden, God stationed cherubim—also winged creatures—"to guard the way to the tree of life" (3:24). It seems that in the course of the cultic revolution in the Temple in Jerusalem, these winged cherubim—explicitly linked with the Ark of God in Exodus 25:18–22 and other places—replaced the winged serpents as the official flying guards in the divine entourage (see also, e.g., Ezekiel 10:2).

Returning to the story in Genesis, we find that though the account of the Garden of Eden admits that the snake was "the most cunning

of all the wild beasts" (3:1), to which no other creature could compare in its cleverness, nevertheless the snake's knowledge is that of
one of God's creatures: it is not divine wisdom. What's more, "cunning" ('ormah, from the root '-r-m) in this context is hardly a positive attribute of wisdom (as we find, e.g., in Proverbs 1:4, 8:5, 12) but
rather denotes evil scheming, as we find in Exodus 21:14, "when a man
schemes against another and kills him cunningly" (see also regarding
the people of Gibeon, who "resorted to cunning" [Joshua 9:4]). The
serpent in our story uses his cunning deceitfully when he tempts man
with his scheming words, all in order that man might win the sort of
knowledge that would position him to challenge God.

The primeval snake, according to this story, was able to converse
with humankind, speaking with his mouth and hearing with his ears.
The snake wreaks havoc with humankind by using his voice, his powers of rhetoric, and even when this avenue of deceit is denied him, he
continues to endanger his victims with his poisonous tongue: "He
sucks the poison of asps; the tongue of the viper kills him" (Job 20:16).
About evil men, writes the psalmist, "they sharpen their tongues like
serpents" (Psalm 140:4). Perhaps the words of Ecclesiastes—"If the
snake without utterance [lahash] bites [i.e., a snake against whom there
is no charm], then there is no advantage to the trained charmer [lit.,
One with Tongue]" (10:11)—should be understood differently, as a
rhetorical question: "Does the snake bite without [first] whispering?
Does the eloquent have no advantage?" The snake's hissing is here
credited with the power of first paralyzing the victim, thereby rendering him helpless, and the eloquent man is credited with a similar
capacity. Let us add that such riddles—equivocal sayings that were
meant to be understood in two different ways—are a common phenomenon in biblical literature. Be that as it may, the curse spoken by
Jeremiah aligns with the first understanding of the riddle: "Lo, I will
send serpents against you, adders that cannot be charmed, and they
shall bite you" (8:17).

According to Psalm 58, charms are powerless over snakes not because of the serpent's ample cunning nor because of any innate fac-

ulty for withstanding the enchanter's powers but merely because of its own deficiency, the defect to which it was condemned, meaning its lack of ears: "Their venom is like that of a snake, a deaf viper whose ear is closed so as not to hear the voice of charmers or the expert mutterer of spells" (vv. 5–6). We now recall the snake's punishment according to *Life of Adam and Eve*, which included also the snake's ears amongst the organs then denied him. The snake's deafness is also alluded to by Micah when he compares Israel's enemies to snakes: "Let nations behold and be ashamed despite all their might; let them put hand to mouth; let their ears be deafened; let them lick dust like snakes, like crawling things on the ground" (7:16–17). This depiction of the snake's deafness serves a double function, both mocking the snake's supposed wisdom and power while also casting doubt on the assumed powers of the spell-casters whose charms are powerless on creatures that cannot hear.

Aside from the physical appearance of the paradisiacal snake—with wings, arms, legs, mouth, and ears—this creature, in its pre-fall form, seems to have possessed one more significant characteristic. The serpent, like God, apparently lived eternally. Just as with the granting of knowledge, the snake gave to Adam and Eve what he himself already possessed—wisdom, insight, shrewdness—so it is possible that he also was about to grant them eternal life. The story of the Garden of Eden, it appears, was also meant to challenge that belief.

The immortal serpent as the source of life plays a role in the mythologies of the ancient Near East. In the Epic of Gilgamesh, for example (tablet 11, lines 289–301), the snake steals from Gilgamesh a special plant that has the power to reinvigorate, to retain one's youth, and so gains what he denies humankind: immortality. Perhaps this belief developed out of snakes' regular shedding of their skin and their re-emergence as though reborn. The Rabbis, unlike the ancient Babylonians, underscored what is not overtly stated in the Torah: the snake is mortal, and the excruciating pain that it experiences from shedding its skin is just one more of its punishments: "And [God] punished him that he will shed his skin once every seven years with great suffering" (*Pirkei de-Rabbi Eliezer* 14).

With God's curse, the serpent—who was the source of life before being punished—becomes, according to Genesis, a source of human mortality: "I will put enmity between you and the woman, and between your offspring and hers; they shall strike at your head, and you shall strike at their heel" (3:15). The story's ambivalence toward the snake—whose tongue contains the potential of both life and death—is hinted at also in the story we discussed above, the story of the serpent-seraphs through which God punishes the Israelites (Numbers 21:4–9). In that story the snake was the source of suffering, while its bronze image brought healing. Of course, according to the religious-monotheistic worldview of the Bible, God was the source of both the Israelites' punishment and mercy. Beneath the biblical narrator's words, however, it seems that we still hear the rush of older currents, of more ancient belief systems, in which the source of death and life was the snake.

The image from Numbers 21, of the seraph that is fastened to the pole, "and when anyone was bitten by a serpent, he would look at the copper serpent and recover" (v. 9), is familiar to us from a different source, from the tradition amongst the ancient Greeks about the god of medicine, Asclepius, son of Apollo, who knew the secret of resuscitating the dead. Images of Asclepius from the ancient world show him as a vigorous young man holding a staff on which a snake is curled.

The story in Genesis, we have found, actively argues against ancient traditions that were deemed unsuitable to the biblical writers for inclusion in their great work. The primeval snake, that mythological being who fought against the Creator before the creation of the world (see the introduction), is transformed into a creature like all other created beings after he springs a last-ditch attack on God by attempting to sabotage the harmony in God's created paradise. That divine creature, the winged serpent-seraph who had arms, legs, ears, and the power of speech and who occupied a prominent place in the Temple cult in Jerusalem, in our story is stripped not only of his limbs and ability to speak and hear but also of his immortality and is expelled both from Eden and the Temple. Even the snake's God-like wisdom becomes reduced to a mundane and even devious intelligence: "the most cunning of all the wild beasts."

Here again we have seen how pre-biblical traditions from the ancient Near East, along with echoes of a tradition that we found in the Bible and traditions about the story from post-biblical sources, can be brought together to re-create, in all its glory, an ancient story that—almost—disappeared.

2

When Gods Seduced Women

Tucked between the Bible's introduction of Noah and his descendants in Genesis 5:28–32 and the story of God's decision to flood the earth in Genesis 6:5–7 we find a short narrative about the "sons of god" (*benei 'elohim*) having relations with human women: "When men began to increase on earth and daughters were born to them, the sons of god saw how beautiful the daughters of men were and took wives from among those that pleased them" (6:1–2). God hastens to intervene. He denies immortality to the offspring of these unions and pronounces that their lives, like those of all humans, will be limited to 120 years (v. 3).

In its context, the episode serves to introduce the story of the Flood: this contamination between the upper and lower worlds provokes God to erase humankind from the face of the earth (Genesis 6:7). The story of the Creation, one remembers, prescribed fixed areas and boundaries that would separate light from dark, lower waters from upper waters, oceans from dry land, day from night. The disorder caused by an intrusion of upper beings into the lower world incites God to equally confound the order of creation. God inflicts a measure-for-measure punishment that erases the boundary between the upper and the lower waters: "On that day all the fountains of the great deep burst apart, and the floodgates of the sky broke open" (7:11). But the Flood, we understand from the end of our story, does not put a final end to these boundary-crossing events, since the divine beings will continue to come to the daughters of men and to father children by them, producing Nephilim, "mighty heroes," "giants": "It was then, and later too, that the Nephilim appeared on earth, when the sons of God cohabited with the daughters of men, who bore them offspring. They were the heroes of old, the men of renown" (6:4).

The intermingling of domains is a recurring transgression in the Hebrew Bible, one that inevitably brings God's quick response. For this sin were Adam and Eve expelled from the Garden of Eden when their eating from the fruit of the Tree of Knowledge provoked God to voice his apprehension: "Now that the man has become like one of us, knowing good and bad, what if he should stretch out his hand and take also from the tree of life and eat, and live forever!" (Genesis 3:22). The builders of the Tower of Babel were also punished—dispersed over all the earth—after they tried to cross another of God's boundaries by climbing to heaven (see chapter 6). Snug between these two tales of humanity's aspirations to become like God, our story relates a disturbance that originates from the other direction: divine beings descending to earth.

The story of the coupling of the sons of god with the beautiful mortal women reminds us of mythological traditions that were widespread in ancient cultures, including some that were Israel's neighbors. Canaanite literature (we've already mentioned the discovery of the rich archives in Ugarit) tells how the father of the gods, El, had relations with two women. Shachar and Shalem, the progeny of these unions, became gods themselves and joined the pantheon. Classical literature tells the tale of Zeus, the father of the gods, having relations with the mortal Alcamene and fathering Heracles, who ultimately gains divine status and immortality. This is how the Greek poet Hesiod recounts that great union in *The Shield of Heracles*:

But the father of men and gods was forming another scheme in his heart, to beget one to defend against destruction gods and men who eat bread. So he arose from Olympus by night pondering guile in the deep of his heart, and yearned for the love of the well-girded woman. Quickly he came to Typhaonium, and from there again wise Zeus went on and trod the highest peak of Phicium: there he sat and planned marvelous things in his heart. So in one night Zeus shared the bed and love of the neat-ankled daughter of Electryon and fulfilled his desire. (lines 27–36)[1]

These stories were not unfamiliar to the people of biblical Israel (see the description of the birth of Samson in chapter 21), but the Bible, the manifesto of the monotheistic revolution, could not easily embrace such pagan traditions. At the same time, biblical writers felt unable to ignore the stories, since doing so would allow them to continue to circulate unhindered. Instead, the Bible trod an intermediary path by telling the story in such a way that, while preserving most of the elements of the ancient tale, allowed a believer in one god to feel comfortable.

One senses that the story in Genesis reveals only the bare bones of the tale, as though the writer was unwilling to elaborate. The story's brevity, however, virtually cried out to readers for completion, for them to fill its narrative gaps, and this took place in post-biblical literature. There we find, for example, that "the angels that fell from their holy place in heaven saw the daughters of Cain walking exposed, with their flesh bared and eyes painted like prostitutes, and they strayed after them and took from them wives" (*Pirkei de-Rabbi Eliezer* 22). This and other later traditions enable us to recover many of the story's elementary details that were rejected by the writers of Genesis in their determination to throw out—or at least curtail—references to the heavenly beings' lust for mortal women.

Which were the changes made to the pre-biblical pagan story that enabled its ultimate inclusion in the Pentateuch? First, we should identify who or what are the "sons of god" that appear in the Canaanite epic. The designation *benei 'elohim* (lit., sons of god or sons of gods) evidently refers simply to gods: to members of the divine pantheon. We compare it, for example, to "sons of prophets" (*benei nevi'im*, found, e.g., in 2 Kings 2:5), a phrase that refers simply to prophets: the form "sons of *x*" indicates belonging to the general category of *x*. But in our

1. *Hesiod: The Homeric Hymns and Homerica*, trans. H. G. Evelyn-White (London: Loeb Classical Library, 1964).

case the Bible has preserved the vessel—the title *benei 'elohim*—while pouring into it new meaning. When we look at the occurrences of the term in the Bible, we find that it signifies God's servants (i.e., the divine entourage) and not other divine beings who were in any way equal to God in stature or status.

This relationship between God and God's attendants can be found in Psalm 29, which calls on the divine attendants to praise and serve God: "A psalm of David. Ascribe to the LORD, O sons of gods, ascribe to the LORD glory and strength. Ascribe to the LORD the glory of His name; bow down to the LORD, majestic in holiness" (vv. 1–2). The frame story in Job also mentions "sons of god" who appear before God and who are the members of God's council (Job 1:6, 2:1). Some early interpreters of Genesis 6 explicitly identified the "sons of god" as angels. So we find, for example, in 1 Enoch, "and the angels, the sons of heaven, saw them [daughters of men] and desired them" (6:3), and in a number of manuscripts of the Septuagint, where "sons of god" in our story has been replaced with "angels of God." The change in the meaning of the expression *benei 'elohim*, which lowered the beings' status in order to conform to a belief in one god, removed one of the more significant obstacles blocking the myth's admittance into the Hebrew Bible.

Another threat neutralized by the Bible's version of the story becomes apparent when God sets a finite life span for the offspring of the divine-mortal unions. God's declaration prevents the mixed-breed progeny from inheriting their fathers' immortality, one of the characteristics of divinity: "The LORD said, 'My breath shall not abide in man forever, since he too is flesh; let the days allowed him be one hundred and twenty years'" (Genesis 6:3). God establishes a limit of 120 years—the number of years reached later by Moses (Deuteronomy 34:7; see chapter 20, where we discuss the relationship between Moses's age at his death and the question of immortality).

While immortality will not be inherited, one paternal trait is nonetheless passed on: the offspring are giants, Nephilim, whose extraordinary size becomes clear much later, in the reports of the spies sent by Moses to the Land of Canaan. The spies relate, on returning to their brethren in the wilderness, that "all the people that we saw in it are men of great size; we saw the Nephilim there—the Anakites are part of the Nephilim—and we looked like grasshoppers to ourselves, and so must have looked to them" (Numbers 13:32–33). The physical description of the Nephilim fits with parallel traditions about the heavenly origins of Heracles (as we mentioned above) and Samson (see chapter 21).

Although the original meaning of the word "Nephilim" referred to the enormous size of these beings, already in the Bible we find evidence that it was understood as though formed from the root *n-f-l*, "to fall," and referred to the descent to Sheol, the underworld. The prophet Isaiah relates a satirical dirge that was also based on a myth of the fall of heavenly beings in which a Babylonian king sees himself as a divine being. In it, Isaiah rejoices at the failure of one who thought he could ascend to the heavens and thus achieve immortality:

> How are you fallen [*nafalta*] from heaven, O Shining One, son
>   of Dawn!
> How are you felled to earth, O vanquisher of nations!
> Once you thought in your heart, "I will climb to the sky;
> Higher than the stars of God I will set my throne.
> I will sit in the mount of assembly, on the summit of Zaphon:
> I will mount the back of a cloud—I will match the Most High."
> Instead, you are brought down to Sheol, to the bottom of the
>   Pit. (14:12–15)

The prophet Ezekiel also uses the term to denote the descent to the underworld: "O mortal, wail—along with the women of the mighty nations—over the masses of Egypt, accompanying their descent to the lowest part of the netherworld, among those who have gone down into the Pit. Whom do you surpass in beauty? Down with you, and be laid to rest with the uncircumcised! Amid those slain by the sword they shall fall [*yipolu*, from the root *n-f-l*]" (32:18–20, see also 22–24, 27).

And yet, despite the literary compromise that turned these beings into nothing more than God's attendants, many readers were still hard-pressed to admit any sort of miscegenation between mortal women and divine beings—God's attendants or not—which in their minds presented an intolerable notion. In this spirit, *Genesis Rabbah* relates a tradition about Rabbi Shimon Bar Yohai cursing anyone who, when translating our story into Aramaic—the vernacular of the period—translated *benei 'elohim* into the Aramaic "sons of god" (26:2). Indeed, Rabbi Shimon's ruling was accepted by the Aramaic translations to the Pentateuch (though in the margins of *Targum Neofiti* we find the phrase translated as "sons of angels"). Instead, these reader-interpreters, reluctant to grant divine status to the "sons of god," endeavored to find in that term a nickname for a particular group of mortals. As a result, some interpreted *benei 'elohim* as referring to sons of important people, sons of ministers, or just "great men," while Rabbi Shimon preferred to view them as "sons of judges" (*Genesis Rabbah* 26:2). In his commentary on the story, Rashi combined both interpretations: "sons of ministers and judges."

How, we should ask, did these early interpreters end up replacing "god" with "judges"? The key lies in the understanding of the enigmatic term *yadon* in our verse: "The LORD said, 'My breath shall not abide [*yadon*] in man forever.'" The word, traditionally understood and translated as "abide," could be understood as deriving from the root *d-w-n*, "to judge," and in midrashic literature many examples can be found where it was understood in this way, for example: "Rabbi Eleazar ben Parta says: Behold it says, 'My breath shall not judge [*yadon*] man . . .' (Gen. 6:3). Said the Holy One, blessed be He: I shall not judge them until I have given them their reward in full. As it is said, 'They spend their days in prosperity, but then they go down to Sheol' (Job 21:13)" (*Avot de-Rabbi Natan*, version A, chap. 32). And also (in the same source): "Rabbi Meir says: Behold, it says, '[My breath] shall not judge.' Said the Holy One, blessed be He: That generation declared, The Lord does not judge: there is no judge of the world; God has abandoned the world!'"

A number of verses in which God plays a role in the legal process—such as Exodus 21:6, "his master shall take him [the slave] before God," or 22:7–8, "the owner of the house shall depose before God"—gave force to the impulse to interpret *'elohim*, "god" (the word is a plural form in Hebrew: "gods"), in our verse as "judges." Thus did the "sons of god" become sons of judges: mortal beings of flesh and blood.

When did this interpretation of *'elohim* gain credibility? Quite possibly it was widespread already during biblical times. In Deuteronomy 25:1 we find: "when there is a dispute between men and they go to the court, and [judges] judged them declaring the one in the right and the other in the wrong." The phrase "they go [*nigshu*] to the court" reminds us of the verse cited above, from Exodus 21:6, which uses the same verb: "take him [*ve-higisho*] before God." According to this, the word "court" (referring to human judges) is an interpretation of "God" from the verse from Exodus.

The shift from understanding *benei 'elohim* as denoting divine beings to understanding it as referring to descendants of human judges can be seen in Psalm 82. The psalmist was aware of the interpretation of "sons of god" as judges, but he also wanted to include the other view, according to which "sons of god" are "sons of the Most High," that is, divine beings. This poet, whose psalm opens with a picture of the court—"God stands in the divine assembly; among the divine beings He pronounces judgment" (v. 1)—initially regards the judges as gods. According to the psalm, God, too, initially assumes these to be divine beings, "I had taken you for divine beings, sons of the Most High, all of you" (v. 6), and only the miserable behavior of the judges, who are utterly wanting in wisdom and knowledge, pushes God to recognize that they are mortals, not gods, and will die like all mortals: "But you shall die as men do, fall [*tipol*] like any prince" (v. 7; the phonemes *p* and *f* share the same letter in Hebrew, so that this writer, too, interprets our giants, the Nephilim, as having fallen to the nether regions).

The psalm declares that the judges were erroneously labeled as divine and that that designation was taken from them when their true identities became apparent. God is the sole high judge of this world, and the psalm's last verse restores the title to its true owner: "Arise, O

God, judge the earth, for all the nations are Your possession" (Psalm 82:8). The writer of Psalm 82 successfully dismantled the arsenal of the mythological ideology; the sons of god are judges but not divine. Merely human judges, they are both fallible and mortal.

It becomes clear that Genesis 6:1–4, the Bible's version of an ancient oral tradition about gods having intimate relations with women, did not succeed in cleansing the tale of its mythological origins. This failure is what stands behind the further interpretation of *benei 'elohim* as mortal judges, an interpretation that developed already in the biblical period and was recorded within the Bible's pages. The ancient, pre-biblical story was stronger, however, than both its rewritten version in Genesis and its other biblical interpreters. It returned along various paths and finally resurfaced in post-biblical literature, long after monotheism had become well established and tales such as this one, about gods descending to earth and seducing the most beautiful of the human women, could no longer pose any real threat.

3

Moses or God?

Who Split the Sea of Reeds?

The story of the parting of the Sea of Reeds and the Israelites crossing on dry land, as it appears in the book of Exodus, preserves a certain balance between the greater role played by God and that played by God's servant, Moses.

The Israelites, fearful of the Egyptian oppressors who nip at their heels, cry out to their God: "As Pharaoh drew near, the Israelites caught sight of the Egyptians advancing upon them. Greatly frightened, the Israelites cried out to the LORD" (Exodus 14:10). At the same time, they complain to Moses and hold him responsible for their suffering: "Was it for want of graves in Egypt that you brought us to die in the wilderness? What have you done to us, taking us out of Egypt? Is this not the very thing we told you in Egypt, saying 'Let us be, and we will serve the Egyptians, for it is better for us to serve the Egyptians than to die in the wilderness?'" (vv. 11–12). Moses's answer expresses his absolute confidence in God's salvation, and he attributes no role to himself in the people's deliverance: "Have no fear! Stand by, and witness the deliverance that the LORD will work for you today; for the Egyptians whom you see today you will never see again. The LORD will battle for you; you hold your peace!" (vv. 13–14).

God, however, gives Moses a role, "And you lift up your rod and hold out your arm over the sea and split it, so that the Israelites may march into the sea on dry ground" (Exodus 14:16), and Moses obeys—"Then Moses held out his arm over the sea"—but, the verse continues, it is

God who parts the waters: "And the LORD drove back the sea with a strong east wind all that night, and turned the sea into dry ground" (v. 21). When the time comes to restore the sea to its previous state (and drown the Egyptians), God again commands Moses, "Hold out your arm over the sea, that the waters may come back upon the Egyptians and upon their chariots and upon their horsemen" (v. 26), and Moses obeys: "Moses held out his arm over the sea and at daybreak the sea returned to its normal state." Again, however, the one who performs the miracle is God: "But the LORD hurled the Egyptians into the sea" (v. 27).

The remainder of the story attributes the glory almost entirely to God: "The LORD delivered Israel that day from the Egyptians . . . and when Israel saw the wondrous power which the LORD had wielded against the Egyptians, the people feared the LORD" (Exodus 14:30–31); Moses's promise of God's deliverance, from verse 13, is here fulfilled. Nonetheless, the final words of verse 31 grant Moses some distinction: "They had faith in the LORD and His servant Moses."

The cooperation that we find between God and Moses in this, the principal account of the parting of the sea, disappears in the tradition's various other formulations in the Bible. In the Song of the Sea, a poetic rendition of the parting of the sea that immediately follows the story, Moses and Israel praise God for their salvation and make no mention at all of Moses's role: "I will sing to the LORD, for He has triumphed gloriously; Horse and driver He has hurled into the sea" (Exodus 15:1). In the song, the waters pile up due to wind blown from God's nostrils (v. 8); God blows the great wind that plunges the Egyptians into a flood (v. 10); and the outstretched arm belongs not to Moses—whose arm extended out over the sea in the previous chapter (14:21, 27)—but to God: "You held out Your right hand, the earth swallowed them" (v. 12). Though sung by Moses, the song ascribes no role to him in the story of the crossing of the sea.

Indeed, Moses's role in the crossing of the sea is almost completely denied outside of the book of Exodus. Rahab, the prostitute from Jericho, voices her countrymen's fear of their Israelite conquerors who advance toward the Canaanite city when she tells Joshua's spies: "For we have heard how the LORD dried up the waters of the Sea of Reeds for you when you left Egypt" (Joshua 2:10). After crossing the Jordan River, Joshua himself tells the people, "For the LORD your God dried up the waters of the Jordan before you until you crossed, just as the LORD your God did to the Sea of Reeds, which He dried up before us until we crossed" (4:23). Much later, after the Judahites return from their Babylonian exile, the Levites bless the Lord for His many acts of benevolence toward His people, including: "You split the sea before them; they passed through the sea on dry land, but You threw their pursuers into the depths, like a stone into the raging waters" (Nehemiah 9:11).

A similar picture emerges in the psalms: "Come and see the works of God, who is held in awe by men for His acts. He turned the sea into dry land; they crossed the river on foot" (Psalm 66:5–6); "When Israel went forth from Egypt, the house of Jacob from a people of strange speech . . . the sea saw them and fled, Jordan ran backward. . . . What alarmed you, O sea, that you fled, Jordan, that you ran backward. . . . Tremble, O earth, at the presence of the LORD, at the presence of the God of Jacob" (114:1–7). The case is the same in the distinctly historical psalms, which, when describing the crossing of the sea, speak of God and God alone: "He split the sea and took them through it; He made the waters stand like a wall" (78:13); "He sent His blast against the Sea of Reeds; it became dry; He led them through the deep as through a wilderness. . . . Water covered their adversaries; not one of them was left" (106:9–11); "Who split apart the Sea of Reeds . . . and made Israel pass through it . . . who hurled Pharaoh and his army into the Sea of Reeds" (136:13–15).

Psalm 77 seems to be an exception. There, God's redemption of Israel is expressed in mythical terms:

By Your arm You redeemed Your people, the children of Jacob and Joseph. Selah. The waters saw You, O God, the waters saw You and were convulsed; the very deep quaked as well. Clouds streamed water; the heavens rumbled; Your arrows flew about; Your thunder rumbled like wheels; lightning lit up the world; the earth quaked and trembled. Your way was through the sea, Your path, through the mighty waters; Your tracks could not be seen. (vv. 16–20)

In the very last verse of the psalm, Moses and Aaron are suddenly credited: "You led Your people like a flock in the care of Moses and Aaron" (v. 21). The fact that verse 21 relates to none of the psalm's previous verses, however, suggests that it was added secondarily by an astonished reader who objected to the absence of Moses and Aaron from this telling of the Exodus. It may also have been appended in order to prepare us for the next psalm, Psalm 78, which also omits Moses from its account of the Exodus and the splitting of the sea. There, in verse 53, for example, we find: "He [God] led them in safety; they were unafraid; as for their enemies, the sea covered them."

The reader who comes upon these two psalms in the Psalter, one after the other, will naturally drag Moses, who is named in the last verse of Psalm 77, into Psalm 78. Nevertheless, even this added verse does not state unequivocally that Moses played a role in the splitting of the sea, and it also grants Aaron equal credit for leading the people. Even here, then, the status and scope of Moses's position has been kept in check.

All in all, our review of the story of the parting of the sea has revealed an obvious discrepancy between the significant role Moses plays in the narrative version told in the book of Exodus and his omission from all appearances of the tradition in the rest of the Bible. The removal of Moses from the story of the crossing of the sea was apparently aimed at discouraging the personality cult that had flourished around him (see our discussions of Moses's birth and death in chapters 18 and 20). The depiction of Moses splitting the sea on his own was a tradition that the Bible sought to minimize and even erase altogether, since it added a sublime dimension to Moses's character that encouraged not just admiration but, perhaps, deification.

The Bible's polemics against the glorification of Moses's character continued in Rabbinic literature, where we find similar attempts to diminish his role in the story of the splitting of the sea. An example is found in the *Mekhilta de-Rabbi Shimon ben Yoḥai*:

"Then Moses held out his arm over the sea . . ." (Exod. 14:21). The sea began to challenge Moses. To what can this be compared? To a mortal king who had two gardens, one inside the other. He sold the inner [garden], and left [to himself] the outer. The buyer came to enter, and the guard did not let him. [The buyer] mentioned the name of the king and the guard did not obey. He showed him a ring, and he did not obey. The king himself came. When the guard saw the king, he started to flee. [The buyer] said to him: "Why are you fleeing?" He said to him, "I do not flee from you, but from the king I flee." So when Moses came and stood at the sea, he said to him in the name of the Holy One, and [the sea] did not obey. He showed him the rod, and he didn't obey. But when the Holy One blessed be He appeared to him, "the sea saw and fled" (Ps. 114:3). Moses said to him, "I said to you in the name of the Holy One, and you didn't obey. I showed you the rod, and you didn't obey. Now, what alarmed you O sea, that you fled?" (114:5). He said to him, "Not before you, son of Amram, but tremble, O earth, at the presence of the Lord" (Ps 114:7). (*Mekhilta de-Rabbi Shimon ben Yoḥai* to Exodus 14:21)

An even more dramatic presentation of this tradition is found in an Aramaic *piyyut* (liturgical poem) embedded into an Aramaic Targum of Exodus 14:30 that was found in the Cairo Genizah. There we read:

And Moses went and stood by the sea.
And he said to the sea, "Depart from the presence of God."
The sea departed from the presence of Moses
when it saw in his hand the rod of miracles.
Rage and anger rose up in the sea.
Boasting [he refused] to retreat:
"You are wrong, son of Amram.
You do not control me, and you are not older than me.
I am three days older than you:
I was created on the third day, and you on the sixth."

When Moses saw that the sea refused and its waves taunted
   him,
God shouted and told the sea "Go away!"

. . . .

Finally, the sea said to Moses:
"Before a mortal I do not surrender."
Moses answered and told the sea:
"He who is greater than me and you will subdue you."

. . . .

The sea heard the voice of the Holy Spirit
that was speaking with Moses from the fire,
the sea stopped raging,
and the Israelites passed through it.

Both the *Mekhilta* and this Aramaic *piyyut* emphasize the unequivocal and absolute supremacy of God over Moses in the miraculous story of the splitting of the sea. Moses is but God's emissary, and even in that status he meets with such difficulties that his Sender must rescue him and perform the task that he was sent to perform.

Let us return to the Bible. The issues that the Bible encountered when it struggled to formulate Moses's role in the splitting of the sea become even more apparent when we look at how the Bible describes other biblical heroes who participated in similar miracles: Joshua, Elijah, and Elisha. The fear of encouraging a personality cult was significantly less with these three figures, so that it was possible to maintain the correct balance between the role of God and that of the human hero in the performing of the miracle (a balance that was successfully maintained in the narrative account of Moses's splitting the sea in Exodus 14, though not, as we said, in the other appearances of the tradition in the Bible).

Joshua's crossing of the Jordan River—when the people of Israel first enter their land—provides a fitting ending to the Exodus story, which began with the crossing of the Sea of Reeds. In this account, the priests, who carry the Ark of the Lord, perform wondrous acts:

"When the feet of the priests bearing the Ark of the LORD, the Sovereign of all the earth, come to rest in the waters of the Jordan, the waters of the Jordan—the water coming from upstream—will be cut off and will stand in a single heap." . . . But as soon as the bearers of the Ark reached the Jordan, and the feet of the priests bearing the Ark dipped into the water at its edge, the waters coming down from upstream piled up in a single heap. . . . The priests who bore the Ark of the LORD's Covenant stood on dry land exactly in the middle of the Jordan, while all Israel crossed over on dry land, until the entire nation had finished crossing the Jordan. (Joshua 3:13–17, see also 4:18)

Although the miracle is performed by the priests carrying the Ark—the Ark that represents the presence of God and essentially replaces Moses's rod from our story—the glory is not attributed to the priests but to Joshua, Moses's heir: "The LORD said to Joshua, 'this day, for the first time, I will exalt you in the sight of all Israel, so that they shall know that I will be with you as I was with Moses'" (Joshua 3:7); "On that day the LORD exalted Joshua in the sight of all Israel, so that they revered him all his days as they had revered Moses" (4:14).

Let us move to Elijah. The story told in 2 Kings 2:1–18 tells of two river crossings. First, Elijah divides the waters of the Jordan and crosses to its east bank, from where he ascends to heaven, after which his disciple Elisha repeats the actions of his master and returns to the river's west bank. The story is meant to teach how Elisha was Elijah's true heir and that "the spirit of Elijah has settled on Elisha" (v. 15). Of interest to us, in particular, is how, when Elijah strikes the Jordan with his mantle and divides the waters, God is not mentioned (v. 8): the narrative's spotlight illuminates what is entirely a human act. But when Elisha parts the waters of the Jordan we are told: "Taking the mantle which had dropped from Elijah, he struck the water and said, 'Where is the LORD, the God of Elijah he too?'" (v. 14).

The words "he too" make no sense. Most likely they are a secondary addition mistakenly inserted into the wrong place: they were probably meant to follow the words "and [he] said," producing the verse: "Taking the mantle which had dropped from Elijah, he struck the water and said, he too, 'Where is the LORD, the God of Elijah?'" With these two words a reader tried to "fix" the previous episode about Elijah parting the waters, in which God had played no role, by removing any doubt that Elijah would have performed the miracle without first turning to God. In other words, God's role in the miracle is mentioned in the story about Elisha, while, in our opinion, the words "he too" were added in order to insert God also into the previous scene about Elijah. In any case, God and man are partners in the splitting of the Jordan, according to the story about Elisha (and Elijah). The appellation "God of Elijah," which appears only here, assures the desired balance between the human and divine roles: the prophet performs the miracle, but the miracle is God's.

Back to Moses. We have seen how the story in Exodus contains two intertwined traditions, one that grants Moses a significant—albeit not exclusive—role in the splitting of the sea and the other that places the entire miracle in the hands of God. An echo from the first would seem to be heard by way of a sharp polemic against it in the story of Moses's name giving. The name *mosheh* (Moses) is an active verb that means "he draws out," "he pulls out," suggesting that Moses received his name because he drew his people from the sea. And yet Pharaoh's daughter, who names him, gives the opposite explanation, according to which Moses is not active subject but passive object: "She named him *Mosheh*, explaining, 'I drew him [*meshitihu*] out of the water'" (Exodus 2:10). The tension between the active form of the name and the passive meaning assigned to it was felt by the writer of *Midrash ha-Gadol* to Exodus, who wrote that "he should have been called *Mashui*, '[one who] was drawn from the water,' but she named him *Mosheh*, saying 'He drew himself [out of the water],' meaning that his own virtue caused him to be saved."

The continuation of this polemical voice, which blurs the characterization of Moses as the active savior, the one who pulled his people from the water, and depicts him instead as the one who is saved, who is himself drawn from the water, can apparently be found in Isaiah 63. Here it is God and not Moses who is called the *mosheh 'amo*, "The One who pulled His people out": "Then He remembered the ancient days, He who pulled His people out . . . who made His glorious arm lead to the right of Moses, who divided the waters before them to make Himself a name for all time, who led them through the deeps so that they did not stumble, as a horse in a desert" (vv. 11–13). These verses mention Moses only in order to make it perfectly clear that God—and not the human Moses—is the *mosheh*, the one who rescued his people. This is very different from *Midrash ha-Gadol*'s comment on Exodus 2:10, which states unambiguously that "due to [what he has done for] Israel [was Moses named], because he drew [*mashah*] them and brought them out of Egypt. . . . [T]hat's why he was named Mosheh, that he drew others."

A psalm that twice makes an appearance in the Bible (in 2 Samuel 22 and as Psalm 18) uses the imagery of the Exodus to express the extreme predicament of the sufferer, who likens his situation to that of the Israelites. Even here we find the polemic that opposed Moses's role as the savior who drew his people from the waters.

> He made darkness His screen; dark thunderheads, dense clouds of the sky were His pavilion round about Him.
> Out of the brilliance before Him, hail and fiery coals pierced His clouds.
> Then the LORD thundered from heaven, the Most High gave forth His voice—hail and fiery coals.
> He let fly His shafts and scattered them; He discharged lightning and routed them.
> The ocean bed was exposed; the foundations of the world were laid bare by Your mighty roaring, O LORD, at the blast of the breath of Your nostrils.
> He reached down from on high, He took me; He drew me out [*yimsheni*] of the mighty waters;

He saved me from my fierce enemy, from foes too strong
for me. . . .

He brought me out to freedom; He rescued me because
He was pleased with me. (Psalm 18:12–20; with slight changes also in 2 Samuel 22:12–20)

It is not only the general picture that is drawn—darkness and light (cf.
Exodus 14:20), the foundations of the world revealed, the drying up of
the sea (cf. v. 21) and crossing through it, being drawn out of the sea,
walking through waters on dry land (cf. v. 22), and being rescued from
enemies (v. 23 and following)—but even the specific terminology indicates how the story of the Exodus provided the psalmist's linguistic
reservoir. We can compare Psalm 18's "your mighty roaring, O LORD"
(v. 16) with "He roared against the Sea of Reeds; it became dry" (Psalm
106:9), and "at the blast of the breath of Your nostrils" (Psalm 18:16)
with "At the breath of Your nostrils the waters piled up" (Song of the
Sea, Exodus 15:8) and also with "You blew with Your breath" (v. 10).
The *Mekhilta de-Rabbi Shimon ben Yoḥai* long ago sensed the psalm's
connection to the story of the Exodus and, when portraying the Israelites as they stood on the shore of the sea, quoted extensively from it
(*Mekhilta de-Rabbi Shimon ben Yoḥai* to Exodus 14:13).

Of significance to our discussion here is how the psalmist, when
wishing to depict his own salvation, used imagery of being pulled from
the sea, and he attributed the act of drawing to God ("He reached
down from on high, He took me, He drew me out of the mighty waters"). This writer, it would seem, used some previous source that described the deliverance of Israel from the Sea of Reeds in a way similar
to what we saw in the book of Isaiah, where Israel's being drawn out
and saved was attributed to God alone.

There once was a mythical figure who possessed divine powers, who
divided the sea, and who drew his people from the waters. His name
was *mosheh*, Moses. That tradition, however, is almost entirely absent
from the Bible, which opposed it. Instead, it was replaced by the concept that God alone divided the sea in order that the people could pass

on dry land. The name etymologies that we've brought here reinforced for us an awareness that the tradition about the human Moses, *mosheh 'amo*, "he who draws his people," is what bothered the biblical writers and propelled them to shift the emphasis in the story of the splitting of the sea to God's acts. God is the *mosheh*, the "one who draws" his people, and Moses is but the *mashui*, the one who is delivered from the waters.

4

What Is Manna?

The Israelites express their ingratitude toward God at the very beginning of their wilderness journey. Rather than acknowledging and appreciating their recent rescue from the Egyptian oppressors, the Israelites instead complain and longingly recall the richly varied cuisine in their enemy's land. They bewail their predicament: "If only we had died by the hand of the Lord in the land of Egypt, when we sat by the fleshpots, when we ate our fill of bread! For you have brought us out into this wilderness to starve this whole congregation to death" (Exodus 16:3). The Lord hastens to reassure His disbelieving people, and Moses reports that "the Lord . . . will give you meat to eat in the evening and bread in the morning to the full" (v. 8). The "meat" to which Moses refers is quail; the "bread" none other than manna.

The promise of manna, however, comes with a test: "And the Lord said to Moses, 'I will rain down bread for you from heaven, and the people shall go out and gather each day that day's portion—that I may thus test them, to see whether they will follow My instructions or not'" (Exodus 16:4). The same instructions are repeated with the giving of the manna: "Six days you shall gather it; on the seventh day, the Sabbath, there will be none" (v. 26). Each day of the week the people are to collect only the manna that they will need for that single day; on the sixth day, Friday, they will gather twice that amount (for that day and the seventh day, the Sabbath), for on the Sabbath no manna will fall from the sky.

The daily gathering of the day's food constitutes a test: Will the Israelites place their trust in God, that He will indeed fulfill His promise and cause the manna to fall also the following day, or will their disbelief cause them to hoard it? The cessation of the manna on the seventh day provides the ultimate proof of the miraculous nature of its falling in the first place by underscoring how the manna does not belong to the natural order established at the Creation but represents an act of God, who manipulates the world according to the character of sacred time, the Sabbath.

The people of Israel neglect to observe the Sabbath and fail the test: "Yet some of the people went out on the seventh day to gather, but they found nothing" (Exodus 16:27). God is furious: "And the LORD said to Moses, 'How long will you refuse to obey My commandments and My teachings?'" (v. 28). This discouraging picture of the people's disappointing conduct is even more distinctly drawn in Psalm 78, one of the Psalter's historical psalms, where the roles of tester-tested have been reversed: "To test God was in their mind when they demanded food for themselves. They spoke against God, saying, 'Can God spread a feast in the wilderness? True, He struck the rock and waters flowed, streams gushed forth; but can He provide bread? Can He supply His people with meat?'" (vv. 18–20).

The people of Israel are nourished by manna for the entire period of their wilderness wanderings: "And the Israelites ate manna forty years, until they came to a settled land; they ate the manna until they came to the border of the land of Canaan" (Exodus 16:35). This continues until the day following the passover offering in the Land of Canaan: "On the day after the passover offering, . . . they ate of the produce of the country. . . . On that same day, when they ate of the produce of the land, the manna ceased. The Israelites got no more manna; that year they ate of the yield of the land of Canaan" (Joshua 5:11–12).

The manna will be remembered even after it ceases to fall. Moses commands Aaron, "'Take a jar, put one *omer* of manna in it, and place it before the LORD, to be kept throughout the ages.' As the LORD had commanded Moses, Aaron placed it before the Pact, to be kept" (Exodus 16:33–34). A similar act by which the memory of a miracle is preserved in order to teach the Israelites a lesson is found, for example, in the story of Aaron's sprouting staff: "The LORD said to Moses, 'Put Aaron's staff back before the Pact, to be kept as a lesson to rebels, so that their mutterings against Me may cease, lest they die'" (Numbers 17:25).

And still, until now the entire narrative has preserved the essential mystery of the manna—what was it? We are struck by the people's apparent unfamiliarity with the manna, as conveyed in the etymology of the word that is provided in the story of its first falling: "When the Israelites saw it, they said to one another, 'What is it [*man hu'*]?'—for they did not know what it was. And Moses said to them, 'That is the bread which the LORD has given you to eat'" (Exodus 16:15). The people's perplexity is discernible also in other verses that highlight the magnitude of God's miraculous and merciful act: "He subjected you to the hardship of hunger and then gave you manna to eat, which neither you nor your fathers had ever known" (Deuteronomy 8:3; we find a similar observation in v. 17, "who fed you in the wilderness with manna, which your fathers had never known").

Manna's appearance represents an anomaly in the context of the Bible's miracles, since miracles do not usually introduce previously unknown substances or creatures. Instead, they change the world by undermining the order of the various elements of Creation; they resemble (somewhat) a surrealistic painting in which the components, all common and borrowed from reality, achieve their fantastical effect by having been rearranged. Water is drawn from a rock, the earth swallows up human beings, humans ascend to heaven: these and other such miracles represent familiar ingredients that have been reorganized. Indeed, it is this act of rearrangement that constitutes the miracle. The deviation of the manna from this pattern, its being an entirely new creation, becomes clear by the Bible's various attempts to define, describe, and fathom it by comparing the manna with other, known phenomena: "When the fall of dew lifted, there, over the surface of the wilderness, lay a fine and flaky substance, fine like frost on the ground" (Exodus 16:14); "it was like coriander seed, white, and it tasted like wafers in honey" (v. 31); it "was like coriander seed, and in color it was like bdellium. . . . It tasted like rich cream" (Numbers 11:7–8). "Like frost," "like coriander seed," "like bdellium," and so on—each of these similes attempts to find something in the known world to which the manna can be likened.

In addition to the question of manna's essence, we can add one more query: Why did God solve the problem of the Israelites' hunger by raining food onto them from heaven ("I will rain down bread for you from the heavens" [Exodus 16:4; see also Numbers 11:9])? Why didn't He merely increase the availability of already-known foods that the earth provides, as He did, for example, for Elijah and Elisha with flour and oil (1 Kings 17:15–16) and oil or bread (2 Kings 4:3–6, 42–44)?

Answers to both questions—one regarding the nature of the manna, the other its heavenly origins—can be found by looking carefully at how the miracle of the manna is formulated in verses 23–25 of Psalm 78:

> So He commanded the skies above, He opened the doors of heaven [*shamayim*]
> and rained manna upon them for food, giving them heaven's grain [*degan shamayim*].
> Each man ate the bread of the mighty ones; He sent them provision in plenty.

The opening of the doors of heaven in verse 23 reminds us of the opening of the sky's windows to let the waters rain down in the account of the Flood (Genesis 7:11), though in our case we speak not about water but about food. An echo of the manna story, in which the sky's windows are opened in order to drop food during a period of famine, is found in a story told in 2 Kings 7 about the people of Samaria, in the Kingdom of Israel, who are under siege from their Aramean enemies. When the prophet Elisha nonetheless promises a plentiful food supply, the Israelite king's aide mocks him: "The aide on whose arm the king was leaning spoke up and said to the man of God, 'Even if the LORD were to make windows in the heavens, could this come to pass?'" (2 Kings 7:2). In the end, the besieged population receives ample food, though it does not fall from the sky but is provided in a more rational way: a great warlike clamor (induced by God) causes the Aramean army to flee, leaving behind a camp brimming with food and drink. Another echo of the tradition of heavenly food descending from the skies can be found in the words of the prophet Malachi: "Bring the full tithe into the storehouse, and let there be food in My House, and thus put Me to the test—said the LORD of Hosts. I will surely open the windows of heaven for you and pour down blessings on you" (3:10). Those who obey God's command and tithe their crops will be rewarded, and their food supply will be increased by food pouring down from heaven's windows.

In verse 24 the writer of Psalm 78 identifies what it is, in fact, that pours down from the sky through heaven's widely opened doors: manna is "heaven's grain." The epithet resembles that given in Psalm 105, another historical psalm that also recounts God's gracious acts toward Israel: "They asked and He brought them quail, and satisfied them with heavenly bread" (v. 40). Are we to identify the combination "heaven's grain/bread" that we find in these psalms with the "bread *from* heaven" that we found in Exodus 16:4 (the verse in Exodus is echoed in Nehemiah 9:15: "You gave them bread from heaven when they were hungry"), or is there a difference between the two?

Before answering, we should note that, in the Bible, the word *shamayim*, a plural noun that can usually be translated as "sky," "heavens," or "heaven," can also refer to heaven's inhabitants. This is apparent from the parallelism in Psalm 89:6: "Your wonders, O LORD, are praised by the *heavens*, Your faithfulness, too, in the assembly of holy beings"; and also in Job 15:15: "In His holy ones [this is the divine entourage] He puts no trust, the *heavens* are not guiltless in His sight." We can say even more. At the very end of Moses's song in Deuteronomy 32 (known as the *Ha'azinu*) we find a call to the foreign nations: "O nations [*goyim*], acclaim His people! For He'll avenge the blood of His servants" (v. 43). A fragment from a scroll of Deuteronomy that was found at Qumran and the translation of the verse in the Septuagint read *shamayim* in place of *goyim*, with *shamayim* conveying the meaning of "heavenly beings." From this we understand that the real meaning of *leḥem shamayim,* which we've read as "heaven's bread," is in fact the bread *of the inhabitants of heaven.* As we'll see in a moment, the related expression "bread *from* heaven" was used to obscure this meaning.

Psalm 78's next verse provides final clarification that, in the wilderness, the Israelites ate the food of the heavenly beings: "Each man ate the bread of the mighty ones [*'abirim*]" (v. 25). *'Abirim,* a plural noun, refers to heroes, strong and mighty beings. The singular form *'avir* (whose second letter, *bet,* is unaccented and therefore pronounced *v* and not *b*) is a common epithet for the God of Israel (and is found, e.g., in Genesis 49:24, "*Mighty One* of Jacob," and Isaiah 1:24, "the declaration of the Sovereign, the LORD of Hosts, the *Mighty One* of Israel").

It is important to remember that the distinction between *'avir,* "Mighty One," with an unaccented *bet,* and *'abir,* "mighty one," with an accented *bet,* is an artificial distinction that was conceived not by the biblical writers but by the grammarians who inserted vocalization marks into the biblical text (these are the vocalization marks in a Hebrew text and include the dot that distinguishes *vet* from *bet*). The sole purpose of omitting the mark, in our case, was to obscure the connection between God (*'avir*) and the primary meaning of the word *'abir/'abirim* as an epithet for bulls (e.g., Psalm 50:13: "Do I eat the flesh of *mighty ones* [i.e., bulls] or drink the blood of he-goats?") or stallions (e.g., Jeremiah 47:3: "at the clatter of the stamping hoofs of his *mighty ones* [i.e., stallions]") or any powerful hero (e.g., Lamentations 1:15: "The LORD in my midst has rejected all my *heroes*; He has proclaimed a set time against me to crush my young men").

When Psalm 78:25 refers to *'abirim* it means "divine beings," members of the heavenly entourage, and the Aramaic Targum to the verse confirms the divine identity of these beings when it identifies them explicitly as "angels": "food that descended from the dwelling-place of the angels." The verse appears similarly in all the ancient translations, including the Septuagint, Peshitta, and Vulgate, as well as in a paraphrase of the account in the apocryphal Wisdom of Solomon: "Instead of these things you gave your people food of angels, and without their toil you supplied them with bread from heaven, ready to eat, providing every pleasure and suited to every taste" (16:20). This is also the conclusion in Rabbinic literature: "Our Rabbis taught: 'Each man ate the bread of the mighty ones,' that is, bread which ministering angels eat, this was the interpretation of Rabbi Akiva" (B. *Yoma* 75b).

A midrash to Psalm 78 (*Shoher Tov* 78:4) explicitly identifies the *'abirim* as "angels": "'bread of the mighty ones' [by this] is meant that [the children of Israel] became as angels." We apparently find this meaning also in Psalm 103:20, which appears to be interpreting the word *'abirim*—without mentioning it—when it describes God's angels as *giborei koah*, "mighty heroes": "Bless the LORD, O His angels, mighty heroes [*giborei koah*], who do His bidding." Psalm 78:25 thus sets up the contrast between "mighty ones" and "man." Men were given the opportunity to eat the food of the heavenly creatures, the "mighty ones," and not only did the Israelites eat, but they ate and were satiated. In this way were their complaints about the great abundance of food in Egypt silenced, "when we sat by the fleshpots, when we ate our fill of bread" (Exodus 16:3).

It becomes evident that Psalm 78 preserves the more ancient tradition about the nature of manna, a tradition that accounts also for the manna raining down onto the Israelites from the sky. Indeed, according to Psalm 78 the miracle of the manna did not, in fact, differ from other miracles; its Maker did not create something from nothing. God showed compassion for His people, for the forty years of their wanderings in the wilderness, by nourishing them with the bread that was usually served to heaven's inhabitants.

This tradition was preserved in the Bible's margins—in psalms that mention the miracle of the manna only in passing—while it was rejected from the Bible's main narrative. No overt references to the tradition survived in the Pentateuch, since it still carries the scent of myth: it admits that heavenly beings (even if only the servants of God, his angels, and not God Himself), like humankind, required nourishment (though their fare may have been different, even superior to ours), food reminiscent of the ambrosia and nectar that we find in Greek and Roman mythology.

Another method for suppressing the tradition that we find preserved in the psalms can be glimpsed in two medieval Hebrew manuscripts of the Bible where, instead of "heavenly bread [*lehem shamayim*]" (Psalm 105:40; as we've shown, this should be understood as "bread of the heavenly beings"), we find "bread *from* heaven [*lehem mi-shamayim*]," as we saw already in Nehemiah and in the story in Exodus. The copyists of these two manuscripts removed what little was left of this mythological tradition and changed the word, apparently under the influence of the story in Exodus.

The Bible preserves additional remnants of the controversy over whether or not God's angels, like mortals, required nourishment. The angel of the Lord who appears to Gideon does not eat the food presented to him: "The angel of the LORD held out the staff that he carried, and touched the meat and the unleavened bread with its tip. A fire sprang up from the rock and consumed the meat and the unleavened bread" (Judges 6:21). The angel who appears to Manoah and his wife tells them outright: "If you detain me, I shall not eat your food; and if you present a burnt offering, offer it to the LORD" (13:16).

The continuation of the passage from the Talmud that we cited above (from Tractate *Yoma*) argues against Rabbi Akiva's opinion that the Israelites ate the angels' food: "When these words were reported to R. Ishmael he said to them: Go forth and tell Akiva: Akiva, you have erred. For, indeed, do the ministering angels eat bread? Was it not said long ago, 'I ate no bread and drank no water' [Deut 9:9]?" Rabbi Ishmael recalls the words of Moses in order to teach that if Moses, who was flesh and blood, needed neither food nor drink when he ascended to God, all the more would be the case with the angels. By the way, it is significant that Rabbi Ishmael (*Yoma* 75b) understood "bread of the mighty ones [*lehem 'abirim*]" by changing it to *lehem 'eivarim*, "bread of the [body] organs," "bread which was absorbed by the two hundred and forty-eight organs": a miraculous food that gets absorbed entirely by the body, leaving nothing to excrete.

Apart from the desire to avoid portraying heavenly beings as human-like, with human needs, the Bible also sought to sever once and for all any connection between upper and lower beings, an idea expressed well in the psalms: "The heavens belong to the LORD, but the earth He gave over to man" (Psalm 115:16). A portrayal of the Israelites eating heavenly food betrays a contamination between the upper and lower worlds, an event the Bible wished to avoid. It is enough for us to recall the story of the Garden of Eden when Adam ate from the tree that was forbidden to him, lest the serpent's words become fulfilled: "As soon as you eat of it your eyes will be opened and you will be like divine beings who know good and bad" (Genesis 3:5; see also chapter 2).

Before we leave the tradition of the Israelites eating bread of the divine beings in the wilderness, let's turn to another example—even more extreme—of the Bible's disassociation from it. Just as God sustained the Israelites in the wilderness by miraculously producing bread and meat, manna and quail, He also sustained Elijah with bread and meat while he was hiding in Wadi Cherith: "The ravens brought him bread and meat every morning and bread and meat every evening, and he drank from the wadi" (1 Kings 17:6).

In the Septuagint to this verse the prophet eats the meat once a day only: "The ravens brought him bread in the morning and meat in the evening." The Septuagint's version is very close to that of Exodus 16:8: "Who will give you meat to eat in the evening and bread in the morning to the full," but from the Elijah narrative the mythological element has already disappeared, and even the remaining miracle has been greatly curtailed, reduced to the identity of the messengers God sends to bring Elijah his food: ravens. It may be that an additional stage in the process of the story's disassociation from its mythical origins is found in one of two opinions expressed in the midrash, which declares that the messengers who brought food to Elijah were not ravens ('orvim) but the human inhabitants of a town named 'Oreb or were "Arabs" who were concerned for the prophet's sustenance: "Rabbi Judah said, 'This refers to a city in the district of Baishan [Beit Shean] whose name was Arbo.' Rabbi Nehemia said, 'This refers to real ravens'" (*Genesis Rab-*

bah 33:5), and also: "What is meant by 'the ravens'?—Rabina said, It means actually ravens. R. Ada b. Manyomi, however, suggested to him: May it not mean two men whose names were Oreb? . . . But perhaps they were so named after the town in which they lived?" (B. *Hullin* 5a).

Thus developed this polemical tradition, which gradually concealed every mythical remnant in the story of the manna. The bread that the Israelites ate in the wilderness, food of the divine beings that rained miraculously onto them from the heavenly kitchens, became transformed into simple bread and meat brought by some thoughtful townsfolk, kind and mortal, to the prophet Elijah.

5

The Hero Who Stopped the Sun

Joshua's stopping the sun and the moon in order to lengthen the day—and provide him with more time to complete his victory over the Canaanite kings—is one of the most spectacular of the Bible's miracles.

> Then Joshua addressed the LORD, on the day when the LORD routed the Amorites before the Israelites; he said in the presence of the Israelites:
> "Stop O sun at Gibeon, O moon in the Valley of Aijalon!"
> And the sun stopped and moon stood, while a nation wreaked judgment on its foes, as is written in the Book of Jashar. Thus the sun halted in mid-heaven and did not press on to set, for a whole day; Neither before nor since has there ever been such a day, when the LORD acted on words spoken by a man, for the LORD fought for Israel. (Joshua 10:12–14)

A close look at these verses reveals several distinct notions of what occurred. The bulk of the story attributes the miraculous act to God: Joshua turns to the Lord, who then performs the feat because He fights "for Israel," that is, on Israel's behalf. Joshua's greatness, according to this view, lies in the fact that God listened to his plea. A different idea, however, is found in the actual words that Joshua utters: "Stop O sun at Gibeon, O moon in the Valley of Aijalon!" (Joshua 10:12), which resemble not so much a prayer to God as a direct command to the sun to stop in its place and express Joshua's tremendous confidence in his own ability to control the workings of the heavens and the earth.

Let's look first at Joshua's command and identify the relationship between its two parts: "Stand still O sun at Gibeon," on the one hand, and "O moon in the Valley of Aijalon," on the other. Is this an example of what we call "synonymous parallelism," according to which the verb "stand" in the first part of the command controls also the noun in the second part, effectively saying, "Stop, O sun, at Gibeon, stop, O moon, in the Valley of Aijalon"? Or does Joshua's order to halt pertain only to the sun in order to enable the defeat of Israel's enemy, while the second part, lacking a verb, signifies that the moon can continue along its normal path and appear above the Aijalon Valley (a valley that lies, in any event, outside the battlefield)? Did Joshua stop both the sun and the moon or only the sun?

Once again, we find both viewpoints expressed in the story. One view clearly presents Joshua halting both heavenly bodies: "And the sun stopped and the moon stood" (Joshua 10:13). It should be observed that these words do not continue Joshua's pronouncement: they are not part of the command but rather affirm its realization. Indeed, it seems that this interpretation of Joshua's order as addressing also the moon is meant to conceal some special relationship between Joshua and the sun (as we will see in a moment) and that, in fact, this is the reason for the verse's insistence that the moon also stopped in its tracks and that Joshua said what he said to both heavenly spheres. The view that Joshua's command was directed only to the sun appears once more, in the continuation of verse 13: "Thus the sun stood in mid-heaven and did not press on to set, for a whole day." The sun did not hurry on its usual path, a phenomenon described, for example, in Psalm 19:6: "He [the sun] is like a groom coming forth from the chamber like a hero, eager to run his course," and compare Ecclesiastes 1:5: "The sun rises and the sun sets—and yearns to get back to the place it rises."

Evidence that an ancient tradition spoke of only the sun's stopping in its tracks can be detected in later accounts of the story. Ben Sira, for example, glorifies Joshua's heroism: "Was it not by his hand that the sun stood, so that one day became like two?" (46:4). According to Ben Sira, Joshua stopped the sun with his own hand—similar to what happened, according to the same author, when Joshua performed another wondrous act: "How glorious he was when he lifted his hand and brandished his javelin against the cities!" (46:2). Ben Sira alludes here to Israel's victory over Ai, in the course of which Joshua stretched out his arm and held out "the javelin in his hand toward the city" (Joshua 8:18).

The tradition about Joshua's stopping the sun (and, in some traditions, the rest of the heavenly bodies) with his hand is shared by Ben Sira and the midrash, which considers Joshua's holding out his hand a gesture accompanying invocation: "Joshua came and fought the battles of Israel. It was the eve of the Sabbath, and he saw the plight of Israel lest they might desecrate the Sabbath. . . . What did he do? He stretched forth his hand to the light of the sun and to the light of the moon, and he invoked upon them the [divine] Name, and each one stood for thirty-six hours in its place until the termination of the Sabbath day" (*Pirkei de-Rabbi Eliezer* 52).

Like Ben Sira, some midrashic traditions emphasize that Joshua stopped only the sun:

> Then Joshua addressed the LORD . . . "Stop O sun at Gibeon"—
> Joshua wanted to silence the sun. He did not tell it "Sun in
> Gibeon, stop [*dom*]!" but "be quiet" [reflecting a different meaning of the same word]. Why did he say "be quiet"? Because as long
> as the sun moves, it praises God, and as long as it praises God, it
> has the strength to move. That's why Joshua told it to be quiet, as
> it is said, "Quiet, O sun at Gibeon!" (*Tanḥuma Buber, Aḥarei* 14)

Also the Talmud: "Our rabbis have taught: Hillel the Elder had eighty disciples, thirty of whom were worthy of the Divine Spirit resting upon them, as [it did upon] Moses our master, thirty of whom were worthy that the sun should stand for them [as it did for] Joshua the son of Nun, [and the remaining] twenty were ordinary" (B. *Sukkah* 28a).

A different Rabbinic tradition refuses to leave Moses in Joshua's shadow and maintains that, whereas Joshua stopped the sun only once, "the sun stood for Moses twice, the first when he fought the war against Amalek . . . and the second in the war against Sihon and

Og" (*Shoḥer Tov* 19:8). The tradition that Moses stopped the sun is found also in a small passage that was found at Qumran. That fragment is from a much earlier text, a scroll scholars refer to as the *Apocryphon of Joshua* (4QapocrJosh^a), which, in relating Moses's achievements, specifies "great signs and he stopped the sun." The idea is found also in other midrashic traditions: "[Moses] said to [Joshua]—'May it be the will of God that the sun will stand for you as it stood still for me'" (*Shoḥer Tov* 19:8); and "for the sake of three the sun broke through [*niqdemah*; the meaning of the Hebrew is unclear], Moses, Joshua and Naqdimon b. Gurion" (B. *Taʿanit* 20a; even if the meaning of *niqdemah* is unclear, once again we see linked together Moses, Joshua, and the sun).

A psalm in the book of Habakkuk contains a particularly interesting reference to Joshua's miraculous stopping of the sun. The psalm, in Habakkuk 3, includes an unexpected addition at the end of verse 10 and beginning of verse 11: "[He] lifted his hand to heaven, Sun moon stood at its height." The words interrupt the natural continuity of the surrounding verses, which address God in the second person—"The mountains saw You and rocked" (v. 10), "By the light of your arrows they walk, by the brilliance of your flashing spear" (v. 11)—suggesting that they were added at a secondary stage. Moreover, when we compare the verses of the Habakkuk psalm with a parallel section in Psalm 77:17–19, we find no place for the added words.

The new words introduce an incongruous element into the proph-

Psalm 77:17–19	Habakkuk 3:10–11
[17]The waters saw You, O God, the waters saw You and were convulsed; the very deep quaked as well	[10]The mountains saw You and rocked,
[18]Clouds streamed water; the heavens rumbled;	A stream of rain came down; Loud roared the deep, [He] lifted His hand to heaven. [11]Sun moon stood at its height
Your arrows flew about; [19]Your thunder rumbled like wheels; lightning lit up the world.	By the light of Your arrows they walk, by the brilliance of Your flashing spear.

et's speech. If the sun and moon are providing light by standing motionless in the sky, why would the prophet say that it is the light of the arrows and the brilliance of the flashing spears that illuminate the battlefield? It seems likely that the addition was motivated by a desire to further glorify the picture of God's deliverance of His people (see Habakkuk 3:13: "You have come forth to deliver Your people, to deliver Your anointed") by incorporating an element taken from the ancient story about Joshua, an element that dramatically adds light to the battleground. Particularly interesting for us is that, in the added words, God is the subject: He is the one who stops the orbs by admonishing them: "[He] lifted His hand to heaven." (Compare God's words in Deuteronomy 32:40: "Lo, I raise My hand to heaven and say: As I live forever.")

Targum Jonathan ben Uzziel to the Prophets sensed the relationship between the Habakkuk psalm and Joshua and viewed the psalm as speaking explicitly about the miracle at Gibeon: "Also in Your performing miracles for Joshua in the Gibeon Valley, the sun and moon stood in their place; Your people, by Your word, overcame" (vv. 9–10).

The language of the addition in Habakkuk is particularly similar to that of the tradition about Joshua that is found in Ben Sira:

Habakkuk	Ben Sira
[He] lifted His hand to heaven.	Was it not by his hand that
Sun moon stood at its height	the sun stood. (46:4)

There is yet another remarkable element in Habakkuk. Not only do the two parts of the subject appear unconnected, "sun moon," but the verb "stood" is conjugated according to a singular subject, and the description of the place of the stopping, "at *its* height," relates also to a singular subject. All of this suggests that the original addition included only the words "sun stood at its height" and that a subsequent reader who noticed the connection between the verse in Habakkuk and the story in Joshua in its final, written form saw fit to complete the miracle of the stopping of the sun in Habakkuk by adding "the moon."

We have found, then, a number of clues that hint at an earlier tradition that related the extraordinary event of Joshua's stopping the sun; the addition of the moon to Joshua's feat was apparently made in order to suppress a particular relationship between Joshua and the sun. That relationship is found also in traditions about Joshua's property and the place of his burial, Timnath-heres: "Joshua son of Nun, the servant of the LORD, died at the age of one hundred and ten years. And they buried him on his own property, at Timnath-heres in the hill country of Ephraim, north of Mount Gaash" (Judges 2:8–9).

Ḥeres—a less common word for "sun"—appears in Judges 14:18 ("before the sunset") and Job 9:7 ("Who commands the sun not to shine"). Verses identical to Judges 2:8–9, which related Joshua's death and burial, are found at the very end of the book of Joshua (24:29–30), though the letters of *ḥeres* are there transposed into *seraḥ*—the same form that appears earlier, in the story of Joshua's receiving his inheritance: "At the command of the LORD they gave him the town that he asked for, Timnath-serah [in some Septuagint manuscripts the name is preserved as Timnath-heres, showing that this may, in fact, have been the original reading] in the hill country of Ephraim; he built the town and settled in it" (19:50). Here we find one more attempt to dissolve the connection between Joshua and the sun, this time by transposing the letters in *ḥeres* to form *seraḥ*. This switch was made in the central telling of Joshua's tale, in the book carrying that leader's name, since that is the book readers would naturally open for learning about Joshua's life and death. But in the periphery, in the book of Judges, the original name of Joshua's burial site has been preserved.

Despite these many efforts to remove the link between the sun and the place of Joshua's burial, we nonetheless find a clear vestige of the tradition in *Genesis Rabbati* in a midrash that links Joshua's burial place to the stopping of the sun: "'After the death of Joshua' (Judges 1:1). This can be compared to a man who chased a lion and defeated it. After some time, he died. . . . They made on his grave the shape of a lion and they said, 'Woe to him who defeated a lion and [nonetheless] lies here.' So did Joshua stop the sun, and here he lies, as it is said, 'and was buried on his own property, at Timnath-heres' (Judges 2:9)" (*Genesis*

Rabbati on Genesis 25:11). This tradition dodges any explicit assertion that an image of the sun was erected on Joshua's grave. It is reluctant to tell of a hallowed object, a relic, with such a mythological, pagan nature. But the parable of the man who kills the lion leaves no room for doubt that there was such an image on Joshua's grave—an image of the sun. By the way, notice how (once again) this tradition mentions only the sun in relation to Joshua and so is a further witness to the secondary nature of the moon element in the context of the war at Gibeon.

A more complete version of the midrashic tradition can be found in Rashi's commentary on Joshua 24:30, concerning the place-name Timnath-serah: "And in another place he calls the place Timnath-heres because an image of the sun was erected on his grave to say: this is the one who stopped the sun. And everybody who passes his grave says, Pity for him who did such a great deed and died." (Compare the similar explanation in Rashi's commentary on Judges 2:9.)

This ancient tradition, about the hero who enjoyed an unusual relationship with the sun and even controlled it, a tradition that related how Joshua commanded the sun to stand still or even stopped it with his hand, was stifled in the book of Joshua because of its mythical character: the attribution of divine powers to a mortal being. We have found three distinct methods that were used to silence this tradition: (1) the attribution of the miraculous act to God, who answers the mortal Joshua's prayer; (2) the addition of the moon to the heavenly bodies that were halted during the war in order to diminish the particular relationship Joshua enjoyed with the sun; (3) the alteration of the name of Joshua's gravesite from Timnath-ḥeres to Timnath-seraḥ, representing the removal of the overt reference to the sun.

And still, despite all these efforts, the mythical tradition that knew of the extraordinary connection between Joshua and the sun reemerged in later layers of our literature. A reader's addition in the book of Habakkuk gave voice to the submerged story, which resurfaced again in the words of Ben Sira and, after an extended period, in medieval midrashic literature.

2

Cult and Sacred Geography

6

....

The Wandering Gate of Heaven

The tale of the building of the Tower of Babel (Genesis 11:1–9) is a story of unbounded hubris. Humankind sought to build a tower that would cross the boundary between the human and divine worlds, a tower that would reach the heavens in order "to make a name for ourselves" (v. 4). Expulsion from Eden—after Adam crossed that boundary when he ate from the tree that granted him divine knowledge—was not enough to convince the people of the error of such endeavors. Also the breach between the realms of heaven and earth (this one initiated from above) when the "sons of god" came to the daughters of men (Genesis 6:1–4; see chapter 2) was a recipe for disaster and precipitated the Flood, yet humankind remained determined in its divine aspirations. Also, this time failure was complete, and punishment followed quickly: God disrupted the people's unity, dispersing the mortal builders throughout the earth and making communication between them impossible by introducing different languages. The story ends with an explanation of the name Babel, the place from which the people had hoped to climb to heaven: "That is why it was called Babel, because there the LORD confounded [balal] the speech of the whole earth" (Genesis 11:9).

The derivation of "Babel" from b-l-l seems to have originated as a response to the widely accepted Babylonian explanation of that place's name, Bab-ilu, "God's Gate," or Bab i-lani, "Gate of the Gods"—a meaning that, we'll soon see, was known in Israel. Indeed, the story of the Tower of Babel in its entirety polemicizes against a Babylonian tradition according to which the tower-temple in Babylon, which was dedicated to the god Marduk, was built as a tribute both to him and to the belief that Babylon was the earthly passageway between heaven and earth. According to ancient Babylonian belief, the tower in Babylon—Babel—was Heaven's Gate.

The temple of Marduk in Babylon was called E-sag-ila, "House of the Raised Head." Inside its compound rose the tower Etemen-an-ki, "Foundation of Heaven and Earth." The description of the building of Esagila, as told in the Babylonian Creation story *Enuma Elish*, can still be heard in the biblical tower story ("Come, let us make bricks. . . . Come, let us build us a city, and a tower with its head in the heavens" [Genesis 11:3–4]). In the Babylonian story we read:

> For one whole year they molded bricks.
> When the second year arrived,
> They raised high the head of Esagila equaling Apsu.
> Having built a stage-tower as high as Apsu [Apsu, something like "the freshwater deep," refers to the vast waters in the underground aquifers, the meaning here being that the tower was as high as the waters were deep]. (*Enuma Elish*, tablet 6, lines 60–62)

It seems that the biblical writer, unwilling to accept that Babylon—a pagan city—was the entryway to heaven, found various ways to counter this Babylonian tradition that was well known in Israel. First, he converted the story of the building into one of ultimate failure and human conceit. At the same time, though, he introduced an alternative story about the gate to heaven. This time the gate's location was in Israel, the Land of One God. This replacement story is found in Genesis 28: the story of Jacob's dream.

When Jacob escapes the wrath of his brother, Esau, and flees from Canaan to Haran, he stops to rest for the night in a place that will eventually be called Bethel (*beit 'el*), "House of God." There he dreams a dream: "He had a dream; a stairway was set on the ground and its head reached to the heavens, and angels of God were going up and down on it" (Genesis 28:12). The words "and its head reached to the heavens"

66

remind us of that attribute of the Tower of Babel, "with its head in the heavens" (11:4), especially since these are the only two appearances of this expression in the biblical narrative. (There are allusions to the Genesis Babel story in Job 20, where we find similar language: "Though he grows as high as the heavens, His head reaching the clouds, He perishes forever, like his dung; Those who saw him will say, 'Where is he?'" [vv. 6–7].)

Indeed, a close look at the two stories reveals how the tale of Jacob's dream—the story of the foundation of the cultic center in Bethel—represents an inversion of the Babel story.

- The tower, with its "head in the heavens," was the product of wrong-headed human initiative and resulted in failure, while the revelation of the stairway in Jacob's dream, with its "head in the heavens," is the manifestation of God's will. In contrast to the story of the tower, in which humankind sought to climb up to the divine realm, the story of the stairway depicts the mortal Jacob remaining on the ground while the angels of God ascend and descend, creating a link between earthly and heavenly realms.
- God's position is also depicted antithetically in the two stories. In order to see the human builders of the tower and punish them, God must descend from His place on high: "The LORD came down to look at the city and tower that man had built" (Genesis 11:5). When God addresses Jacob, however, and speaks words of promise and redemption, He remains on high, at the top of the stairway: "And the LORD was standing on it, and He said, 'I am the LORD, the God of your father Abraham'" (28:13).
- The builders of the city and tower in Genesis 11 used bricks: "Brick served them as stone" (v. 3). This is possibly an expression of wonderment—or even mockery—toward those who place their trust in the efficacy of manmade bricks. Jacob, for his part, uses real stone: "Taking one of the stones of that place, he put it under his head and lay down in that place. . . . Jacob took the stone that he had put under his head and set it up as a pillar" (28:18). That stone will be-

come the foundation for the House of God: "And this stone, which I have set up as a pillar, will be the house of God" (v. 22). The act of the tower's builders was antagonistic toward God, while Jacob's placement of the stone and the future building of the House of the Lord in the same spot were acts promoting God's glory.

- The builders of the tower began their initiative when they "migrated from the east" (Genesis 11:2). Jacob arrived at "the land of the Easterners" (29:1) after he vowed to erect the House of God on his safe return to his father's home in Bethel.

- The fears of the tower's builders, "else we shall be scattered all over the world," are realized in their punishment: "Thus the LORD scattered them from there over the face of the whole earth . . . and from there the LORD scattered them over the face of the whole earth" (Genesis 11:8–9). To Jacob God promises the opposite, to return him to his place of origin—"and I will bring you back to this land" (28:15)—a promise that is kept in the continuation of Jacob's story.

- In contrast to God's scattering of the people "over the face of the whole earth" (Genesis 11:8), we find God's particular promise to Jacob: "You shall spread out to the west and to the east, to the north and to the south" (28:14), signifying Jacob's descendants' inhabiting the entire land. In chapter 11 God's words were a punishment; here they are a blessing.

- The curse with which the tower story ends divides the earth's families, while the climax of the story of the stairway is Jacob's blessing: "All the families of the earth shall bless themselves by you and by your descendants" (Genesis 28:14).

- Both stories contain name derivations, but in contrast to the negative interpretation of the name Babel—"confound"—which reflects the curse on that place, the explanation of "Bethel" expresses the presence of God in Bethel, promising blessing and hope: "And he was afraid and he said, 'How terrifying is this place! This is none other than the house of God [*beit 'elohim*], and this is the gate to heaven'" (Genesis 28:17); "He named that site Bethel" (v. 19); "And this stone, which I have set up as a pillar, will be the house of God [*beit 'elohim*]" (v. 22). In Jacob's words, "this is the gate to heaven," we hear the polemic against those who located heaven's gate in Babel; his words declare that the gate is not there, in Babylon, but in the temple that is in Bethel.

The transfer of heaven's gate from Babel to Bethel, where it was God who showed Jacob its location, does not mark the end to the gate's wanderings. Bethel was located in the Kingdom of Israel and was the cultic center of that kingdom. Later, with the sanctification of Jerusalem in the Kingdom of Judah and the Judahites rejection of the sanctity of other cultic cities, the need was created to move heaven's gate to their kingdom's territory.

This need is expressed in one version of the story of the threshing floor of Araunah. This is the story of the sanctification of Jerusalem in the days of David, and it appears twice in the Bible (2 Samuel 24; 1 Chronicles 21). According to this episode, God punishes David by sending a destroying angel who sets loose a devastating pestilence on the land, but when it reaches Jerusalem God stops the angel, and David is commanded to erect an altar at the very place at which the pestilence was arrested. In the later version of the story, the version in 1 Chronicles, a verse was added that is not found in 2 Samuel: "David said, 'This is the House of the LORD God [*beit 'adonai ha-'elohim*] and this is the altar of burnt offerings for Israel'" (1 Chronicles 22:1).

In both the story of Jacob's dream and the Chronicles version of the threshing floor story, the speaker's response is one of fear—Jacob says, "How terrifying is this place" (Genesis 28:17), and David "was scared by the sword of the angel of the LORD" (1 Chronicles 21:30). The verse in 1 Chronicles appears to have been purposefully fashioned according to the form of the other (compare David's words in 1 Chronicles 22:1 with Jacob's proclamation in Genesis—"This is none other than the house of God, and this is the gate to heaven" [28:17]), conveying the notion that Jerusalem and Bethel, two cultic centers, are but alternative names for the same location. More accurately, Bethel is but another name for Jerusalem. This understanding is taken up later in a midrash that explicitly locates Bethel on Mount Moriah, which is Jerusalem:

"Jacob was seventy-seven years old when he went forth from his father's house, and the well went before him. From Beer-Sheva as far as Mount Moriah is a journey of two days, and he arrived there at midday . . . and tarried there all night, because the sun was set" (Gen. 28:11). Jacob took twelve stones of the stones of the altar, whereon his father Isaac was bound, and he set them for his pillow in that place. . . . Jacob rose up early in the morning in great fear, and said: the house of the Holy One, blessed be He, is in this place, as it is said, "And he was afraid and he said, 'This is the gate to heaven.'" . . . And Jacob returned to gather the stones, and he found them all [turned into] one stone, and he set it up for a pillar in the midst of the place. . . . What did the Holy One, blessed be He, do? He placed [thereon] His right foot, and sank the stone to the bottom of the depths, and He made it the keystone of the earth, just like a man who sets a keystone in an arch; therefore it is called the foundation stone, for there is the navel of the earth, and therefrom was all the earth evolved, and upon it the Sanctuary of God stands, as it is said, "And this stone, which I have set up as a pillar, will be the house of God" (v. 22). (*Pirkei de-Rabbi Eliezer* 35)

According to this Rabbinic tradition, the place where Jacob lay down and dreamed his dream was in Jerusalem. Genesis 28, which mirrors the story of the Tower of Babel and relocates the gate of heaven from Babel to Bethel, did not put an end, therefore, to the gate's wanderings. The Chronicler expresses the viewpoint that the gate has again moved, this time to the Temple on the Mount of the Lord.

Finally, it is likely that we glimpse an even earlier expression of this concept, that Jerusalem is the fitting substitute for Babylon, in the eighth century BCE prophet Isaiah's prophecy about the Days to Come:

In the days to come, the Mount of the LORD's House shall stand firm above the mountains and tower above the hills; and all the nations shall flow to it.

And the many peoples shall go and they say: "Come, let us go up to the Mount of the LORD, to the House of the God of Jacob; that He may instruct us in His ways, and that we may walk in His paths." For the Law shall come forth from Zion, the word of the LORD from Jerusalem. (Isaiah 2:2–3)

Isaiah shaped his prophecy according to the story in Genesis 11. The story of the tower opened with the image of humanity's unification after the Flood—"Everyone on earth had the same language and the same words" (Genesis 11:1)—and their departure for their common journey—"they migrated from the east" (v. 2). Isaiah's prophecy, in a mirror-image of that story, assumes the existence of different nations, all of whom depart from their various locations toward a common destination: "And the nations shall flow towards it."

In both story and prophecy, the people voice their initiative and encourage one another, saying, "Come, let us build us a city, and a tower with its head in the heavens" (Genesis 11:4); "Come, let us go up to the Mount of the LORD, to the House of the God of Jacob" (Isaiah 2:3). Both groups want to reach the uppermost point: the top of the tower that will touch the heavens, or the summit of the highest mountain that towers above the hills. But here we arrive at the enormous difference between the two endeavors: in Genesis 11 the people aim to make a name for themselves, to be like God; in Isaiah, the people wish to learn from God and walk in His ways.

The ambitions of the tower-builders were thwarted. Instead of their ascent to heaven, we witness God descending to scatter them. The intentions of those who ascend the mountain toward the new gateway that is in Jerusalem, on the other hand, are worthy and will be realized. Their ascent to the Mount of the Lord and their studying God's Law will produce peace and unity among all the nations of the world: "And they shall beat their swords into plowshares and their spears into pruning hooks; Nation shall not take up sword against nation; they shall never again know war" (Isaiah 2:4).

When the Rabbis took up the story of the Tower, they laid stress on the intent of the builders to build a tower "at the top of which [they] will set an idol holding a sword in its hand, which will thus appear to wage war against Him" (*Genesis Rabbah* 38:6), which resulted, finally, in disunity, with conflict and war breaking out between the people: "Thus one said to his fellow worker, 'Bring me water,' whereupon he would give him earth, at which he struck him and split his skull" (*Genesis Rabbah* 38:6). The tower's objective, which was to declare war, was therefore achieved. Indeed, the midrash's depiction of war breaking out among the tower-builders makes us wonder whether it perhaps sensed the connection between Genesis 11 and Isaiah's prophecy: whereas the prophecy speaks of renewed unity that brings peace, the story of the tower deals with the disintegration of human society, which yields war.

We have found two traditions, both reflection-stories that challenged a widely known story in the ancient world about the gate of heaven being located in Babylon. The tradition about Bethel located the gate in the Kingdom of Israel; the tradition about Jerusalem relocated it to the Kingdom of Judah. Each kingdom claimed that the gate to heaven was within its own territory, while the story of the Babylonian tower became, in the hands of the Bible's writers, one of derision and ridicule, a mockery of humankind's futile aspirations to be like God.

7

Seeing and Weeping

Managing the Story of a Divine Defeat

In ancient times, we imagine, there developed among the people of Israel a story (told orally, we assume) about a mighty battle waged between Jacob and a certain divine being. The match ended with Jacob's triumph and the defeated creature pleading to be allowed a safe retreat. This story did not survive, at least not fully. We are able to reconstruct it, however, by examining its various reflections and reincarnations in the biblical corpus and are assisted in our endeavors by traditions that opposed it. Many of these traditions, it turns out, are stories that purport to explain names of cultic sites (in either covert or overt etymologies), sites at which the battle was supposed to have occurred: Jabbok, Penuel, Mahanaim, and Bethel.

The most obvious and well known of the tradition's reincarnations, that which most preserves the components of the ancient story, is the story of Jacob's confrontation at the ford of the Jabbok River. The story relates how, on his return from exile in Haran to the Land of Israel and just prior to meeting his brother and enemy, Esau, Jacob wrestled with a man/angel. (On the interchange between the two terms, see, e.g., the story of the destruction of Sodom, where the messengers of God are called both "men" [Genesis 19:5, 8, 12, 16] and "angels" [19:1, 15].) At the story's end, the Patriarch receives a blessing, his name is changed to Israel, and he names the place at which the confrontation occurred Peniel (32:24–32).

The encounter takes place at the Jabbok crossing, and the name of the river, *yaboq*, is interpreted in the story as deriving from *'-b-q*, "wrestle," a root that makes its single appearance in the Bible in this episode: "Jacob was left alone. And a man wrestled [*va-ye'aveq*] with him until the break of dawn" (Genesis 32:25); "he touched Jacob's hip at its socket, so that the socket of his hip was strained as he wrestled with him [*be-he'avqo*]" (v. 26). The story preserves the more ancient elements in the conjectured tradition about a match between Jacob and a heavenly being, although even here we observe attempts to create doubt about certain details. For example, Jacob's adversary is a "man," not a divine being. To a certain extent we are compensated for this revision in the story's continuation when we read the etymology of Jacob's new name: "No longer Jacob shall your name be said but Israel, for you have striven with God and with men, and have prevailed" (v. 29; the verse connects between the name Israel, *yisra'el*, and the verb *sarita*, "you have striven," from the root *s-r-h*). Even this verse, for theological reasons, mentions also "men" alongside "God."

Although both the repeated appearances of the word "wrestled" along with the rare use of the term "striven" in the etymology of the name Israel allude to a real, physical conflict, a different etymology also appears in this tradition, this time involving the name of the city Peniel, adjacent to the Jabbok crossing, and it refers to a meeting involving visual contact only: "So Jacob called the place Peniel, 'For I have seen God face to face, and my life has been preserved'" (Genesis 32:31). Since this etymology of Penuel (reading it as *panei-'el*, "face of God") relates the name to an encounter involving only visual contact, the tradition is able to say that Jacob met God Himself and not a "man." Seeing God was dangerous enough, and one who survived such an event unscathed should offer a blessing. (Note Exodus 32:20: "For man may not see Me and live"; Judges 13:22: "And Manoah said to his wife, 'We shall surely die, for we have seen a divine being'"; and especially 6:22–23: "Then Gideon realized that it was an angel of the LORD; and Gideon said, 'Alas, O LORD God! For I have seen an angel of the LORD face to face.'")

Nevertheless, the tradition that associates Peniel with Jacob having seen God still manages to preserve traces of a physical struggle. The expression it uses to create the etymology, "seeing [a] face," is an equivocal one, an example of the ambiguous words and expressions that were commonly used by the Bible's writers in order to counter older, oral traditions. Granted, the most commonly found meaning of "I have seen a divine being face to face," which is the *peshat* (literal meaning) in this verse, involves nothing more than the act of looking. There exists, however, another, less common meaning of "seeing face." In the context of war, "to see face" can mean "to confront," and it was to this second meaning our writer alluded. (For this meaning of "seeing [a] face," compare 2 Kings 14:8–11: "Then Amaziah sent envoys to King Jehoash son of Jehoahaz son of Jehu of Israel, with this message: 'Come, let us confront each other [lit., see one another's face, *nitra'eh panim*].'... But Amaziah paid no heed; so King Jehoash of Israel advanced, and he and King Amaziah of Judah confronted each other [lit., and they saw each other's face] at Beth-shemesh in Judah.") It would seem that, in using the expression "seeing [someone's] face," the etymology manages to suggest that, while "seeing" did occur at Penuel, it was not a physical-confrontation type of "seeing" such as what was related in the ancient, oral tale but involved the Patriarch looking at God's face—itself an event involving great danger—and surviving.

Additional explanations of the name Penuel (as Peniel is now called) that contain echoes of the ancient man–versus–divine being physical struggle are found in other verses of Jacob's travelogue, this tale of a younger brother who fears an imminent meeting with his well-armed and more powerful sibling. These covert name etymologies come before and during the brothers' reunion, and they replace the story of Jacob's physical struggle with God with one about his fear of fraternal conflict. In this way, a bit of the older, well-known story was preserved, though the listener, hearing that Jacob dreaded a meeting with his brother, begins to doubt that this same Jacob could ever have confronted—let alone defeated—God.

The first of these covert name derivations for Penuel includes several elements from the overt explanation, that of "to see [one's] face." Here,

Jacob instructs his servant, "And you shall say, 'And your servant Jacob himself is right behind us.' For he thought, 'If I make amends with a gift that goes before me and only afterwards *look on his face* [lit., I will see his face], perhaps he will show me favor'" (Genesis 32:21).

A second explanation includes both elements that we hear in the name—*pan[im]*, "face," and *'el[ohim]*, "God"—making it more complete. This etymology elucidates the significance of the name Peniel while emphasizing that no meeting between Jacob and God took place there. Instead, it insists, there was a meeting between Jacob and his brother: "But Jacob said, 'No, pray, if I have found favor in your eyes, accept from me this gift; for to see your face is *like seeing the face of God* [*penei 'elohim*], and you have received me favorably'" (Genesis 33:10).

Seeing God's face, which Jacob compares with seeing his brother's, alludes to the offering one must make if one indeed sees God, as stated in the Law concerning the pilgrim: "And none shall appear before Me empty-handed" (Exodus 23:15, 34:20). This explanation, which apparently sought to cancel completely any notion of Penuel's sanctity, seems to declare that no actual seeing of God's face took place but only a metaphoric seeing: it was "like seeing the face of God."

The gradual diminishment of the tradition that told of a prehistoric battle between Jacob and God, a process that we've followed by examining the overt and covert name etymologies of Penuel, is again apparent in the explanations for the name Mahanaim, another city that Jacob passes through on his way to Penuel. The explicit explanation for this name tells that Jacob saw angels of God there after his meeting with Laban: "Jacob went on his way, and angels of God encountered him [*va-yifge'u bo*]. When he saw them, Jacob said, 'This is God's camp [*mahaneh 'elohim*].' So he named that place Mahanaim" (Genesis 32:2–3). According to this explanation, at Mahanaim Jacob saw divine beings, angels of God, and nothing more: no confrontation, no struggle of any kind, took place.

And yet it is no coincidence that we find here the word *va-yifge'u*. The root *p-g-'* carries two meanings: its simple meaning is "to encounter," to "come upon." (See Genesis 28:11: "He came upon [*va-yifga'*] a place and stopped there for the night, for the sun had set.") But another meaning, no less common, involves harm being caused, as in Judges 18:25: "Don't do any shouting at us, or some desperate men might *attack* [*yifge'u*] you, and you and your family would lose your lives," or 1 Samuel 22:18: "Thereupon the king said to Doeg, 'You, Doeg, go and *strike down* [*ufga'*] the priests.' ... That day, he killed eighty-five men." In other words, we find here another attempt to nullify the tradition about a fight between the Patriarch and God using an ambiguous term that lends itself to two different meanings—similar to what we found with the overt etymology of Penuel—as if to say, yes, an encounter did take place there, but it was only a simple meeting. (Another encounter-meeting between Jacob and God's angels was in the story of Jacob's dream, when Jacob, having fled Israel out of fear of his brother, Esau, saw God's angels ascending and descending a stairway [Genesis 28:10–12].)

When the angels meet/confront him, Jacob realizes that God must also be nearby and so he says, "This is God's camp," although no meeting will take place. Also here we find a similarity with the dreamed stairway, where Jacob saw the angels and, immediately afterward, God: "And angels of God were ascending and descending on it. And the LORD was standing beside him" (Genesis 28:12–13).

Just as the covert name etymologies of Penuel retained no remembrance of a struggle, we find the covert name etymologies of Mahanaim no longer carry the association of a battle or even a meeting with any divine being but of a simple meeting and an anticipated conflict with Jacob's brother, Esau. The covert explanation for the name Mahanaim is extremely important for the story of the meeting between the brothers. It reads the ending of the place-name as the dual-plural suffix *-ayim* and so interprets the name as denoting not one but two camps. Jacob, fearful of the expected battle with his brother, divides his property into two camps: "He divided the people that were with him, and the flocks and herds and camels, into *two camps*, thinking, 'If Esau comes to the one camp and attacks it, the other camp may yet escape'" (Genesis 32:8–9). One verse later, Jacob declares: "I am unworthy of all the kindness that You have so steadfastly shown Your servant: with my staff alone I crossed this Jordan, and now I have become two camps" (v. 11).

The covert etymologies of Mahanaim, like those of Penuel, no longer refer to any cultic or sanctified context, nor do they relate to either God or angels—in stark contrast to the overt etymologies. What's more, the covert derivations no longer characterize Jacob as the figure who fought with God but as the fearful Patriarch who trembles before an expected confrontation with his brother.

Alongside traditions about Jacob's wrestling with a divine being at the Jabbok crossing and in the nearby settlements of Penuel and Mahanaim, the Bible has preserved one more tradition, this time locating the confrontation and Jacob's name change at Bethel. This tradition appears in Hosea 12, a chapter that has preserved a number of ancient traditions about Jacob (see also chapter 16). There, in verses 4–5, we read: "In his vigor, he strove [*sarah*] with God. He dominated over an angel and prevailed. He wept and implored him. At Bethel he met him and there he spoke with us [the Septuagint preserves the correct reading, "with him"]." The account strongly resembles the Jabbok story that linked Jacob's name change directly to the confrontation there and used the same words: "For you have striven [*sarita*] with God . . . and have prevailed" (Genesis 32:29); "He strove with God . . . and prevailed" (Hosea 12:4–5). The similarity between these two accounts extends to their content. During the struggle, the divine entity turns to Jacob with a request: "Let me go, for dawn is breaking" (Genesis 32:27), or, as Hosea phrases it, he "wept and implored him."

Hosea's words contain interpretations not only of the name Israel (which is twice interpreted: "he strove [*sarah*] with God"; "he dominated [*va-yasar*] over an angel") but also of two other names for Bethel, the cultic site where, according to this tradition, Jacob meets a divine being: Beth-on ("In his vigor [*ve-'ono*] he strove with God") and Bokhim ("he wept [*bakhah*] and implored him"). The third name of the place, Bethel, receives explicit mention. This is a common method of the biblical writer: to overtly mention one name of a place or person while covertly interpreting its other name(s).

The name Beth-on, "House of Vigor," is alluded to only here in the Masoretic Text, in this allusion in Hosea, and appears in the name's transcription in the Septuagint to Joshua 18:12, 1 Samuel 13:5, and 14:23—verses where the Masoretic Text has recorded the name as Beth-aven (the same consonants but with different vocalization), "House of Iniquity." The pronunciation Beth-aven ridicules and dishonors Beth-on, which apparently was the cultic area of Bethel or one of the cultic sites of that settlement, as we surmise from a comparison of Joshua 7:2 ("Joshua sent men from Jericho to Ai, which lies close to Beth-aven, east of Bethel") with Genesis 12:8 ("From there he moved on to the hill country east of Bethel . . . and he built there an altar to the LORD"). The denigration of Beth-on by pronouncing the second part *aven* is found already in the words of Amos 5:5: "Do not seek Bethel, nor go to Gilgal, nor cross over to Beer-sheba; For Gilgal shall go into exile, and Bethel shall become an iniquity [*le-'aven*]." Hosea's use of *ve-'ono*, "in his vigor," is thus a covert name derivation that alludes to Beth-on.

Hosea's phrase "he wept [*bakhah*]" is an interpretation of the other name for the cultic site in Bethel, Bokhim. The Bible interprets this name several times. It is alluded to twice in connection with Jacob—in Hosea and in Genesis 35:8: "Deborah, Rebekah's wet-nurse, died, and was buried under the oak below Bethel; so it was named *Alon-bakhuth* [Oak of the Weeping]" (we'll discuss this passage below). The decision to identify the weeping at Bokhim with the mourning of Jacob's family over the death of their beloved wet nurse would seem to have sprung from a desire to uproot the more ancient tradition that depicted a divine being's tearful entreaties to Jacob to allow him to retreat, following their struggle there.

The effort to eliminate that widespread tradition is felt even more keenly in the etymology for Bokhim that is found in Judges 2:1–5. Also here God is replaced with an angel, though this angel, rather than beg Jacob-Israel, reproves the Israelites for their continued worship of idols, and it is the people who begin to wail: "As the angel of the LORD spoke these words to all the Israelites, the people broke into weeping. So they named that place Bokhim, and they offered sacrifices there to the LORD" (vv. 4–5).

Another explanation for the name Bokhim is found in Judges 19–21, in the story of the concubine of Gibeah. That story attempts to erase entirely any connection between the appearance of a divine being and a place-name that contains the root *b-kh-h*, "weep." The story describes the tribes of Israel who are at war with the Benjaminites and who occasionally go to Bethel, lamenting before God about the losses they continue to suffer: "For the Israelites had gone up [to Bethel—so in the Septuagint] and wept before the LORD until the evening" (Judges 20:23); "Then all the Israelites, all the army, went up and came to Bethel and they sat there, weeping before the LORD" (v. 26); "The people came to Bethel and sat there before God until evening. They wailed and wept bitterly" (21:2). These verses, which repeatedly emphasize the people's weeping at Bethel over their trials with the Benjaminites, apparently represent a pointed attempt to change the ancient and accepted meaning of the name Bokhim as referring to the weeping of an angel. It was this desire that seems to have prompted the addition of the story of the concubine of Gibeah.

We return now to the words of Hosea: "In his vigor, he strove with God. He dominated over an angel and prevailed. He wept and implored him, at Bethel he met him and there he spoke with us [him]" (12:4–5). In these verses, which mention or allude to all three of the names for the cultic site at Bethel, the words "he dominated over an angel" appear to have been added secondarily. This was done in order to blunt the controversial element at the story's crux, according to which a struggle with God occurred, a struggle that ended with a human victor. It appears that, originally, the verses read: "In his vigor he strove with God and prevailed, He [God!] wept and implored him." The words "He dominated over [*va-yasar 'el*] an angel" were inserted in order to depict a match involving only an angel and to exchange God's tears with those of the angel's. The precise wording of the addition is significant: the writer used the preposition *'el*, "over," a homophone of *'el*, "God," creating an uncommon expression ("dominated over") while replacing the element of "God" in Jacob's new name, *yisra'el*, with a simple preposition.

Apart from the verses in Hosea that locate the confrontation in Bethel, we find echoes of the tradition also in Genesis 35:9–15. This story knows the tradition about the struggle in Bethel and the subsequent Jacob-Israel name change, but it seeks to eliminate it and replace it with a meeting involving only meeting and blessing (like the similar meeting that is depicted in the overt etymologies of Mahanaim and Penuel): "God appeared again to Jacob on his arrival from Paddan-aram, and He blessed him" (v. 9). The name change is no longer explained by a physical struggle—"for you *have striven*," "in his vigor *he strove*"—but is given an entirely different explanation: "God said to him, 'You whose name is Jacob, your name shall no longer be called Jacob, but Israel shall be your name. . . . A nation, yea an assembly of nations shall descend from you. Kings shall issue from your loins" (vv. 10–11). This etymology involves a typical biblical wordplay between *yisra'el* and *melakhim*, the "kings" who will be Jacob's descendants: though the word *melakhim* is used, we are meant to think of its synonym, *sarim*.

In order to uproot all traces of a struggle between Jacob and God, the passage in Genesis 35 insists that the meeting involved only God speaking to Jacob. The point is made three times, compelling the reader to take note of this controversial contention: "God parted from him at the spot where *He had spoken to him*" (v. 13); "and Jacob set up a pillar at the site where *He had spoken to him*" (v. 14); "Jacob gave the site, where *God had spoken to him*, the name Bethel" (v. 15). It is particularly interesting that Genesis 35's polemic against the tradition reflected in Hosea ultimately made its way back to the prophecy itself, at a secondary stage, when the words "there he spoke with him [*'imo*]" were inserted into verse 5. These words sought—in the spirit of Genesis 35—to transform the physical confrontation into an exchange of words only. (One additional complication is that the Masoretic Text of Hosea 12:5, "There he spoke *with us* [*'imanu*]," reflects a textual corruption that originated in a misunderstanding of the pronominal suffix of the previous word, *yimtza'enu*, as "he met *us*" instead of "he met *him*." This, in turn, triggered the change from "with him" to "with us.") The original text of Hosea, therefore, before the additions and changes, was: "In his vigor he strove with God and prevailed, He wept and implored. At Bethel He met him."

Immediately after the story in Genesis, which tried to prevent any impression of a struggle taking place at Bethel, we find the story of Rachel's death on the journey with Jacob and his household from Bethel to Ephrat, just following the birth of her second son (35:16–20). Rachel calls her newborn son Ben-oni, "son of my affliction" or "son of my mourning." (Compare, for example, Deuteronomy 26:14: "I have not eaten of it in my mourning [*be-'oni*]; I have not cleared out any of it while I was unclean, and I have not deposited any of it with the dead.") But the boy's father interprets differently the second part of the name, *'oni*, as "vigor," "strength," and so he gives his son the name Benjamin, *binyamin*, which can be construed as "son of my right [hand]," that is, the son of his power, as in Exodus 15:6: "Your right [hand], O LORD, glorious in power, Your right [hand], O LORD, shatters the foe!"

Either way, Benjamin's names are further interpretations of the name Beth-on, in addition to those we've already seen, alluding to the mourning and weeping that characterize the site. The story of Benjamin's birth therefore links together these two names of the site: Bokhim and Beth-on. Admittedly, the story of Rachel's death does not mention the word "weep," but the portrayal of Rachel's death that appears later, in the book of Jeremiah, revolves entirely around the matriarch's tears: "Thus said the LORD: A cry is heard on high, wailing, bitter weeping, Rachel weeping for her children. She refuses to be comforted for her children, who are gone. Thus said the LORD: Restrain your voice from weeping, your eyes from shedding tears; for there is reward for your labor, declares the LORD: They shall return from the enemy's land" (Jeremiah 31:15–16).

The tradition of Rachel's death, like the tradition we've already discussed about the burial of Rebekah's wet nurse under the Oak of Weeping, was meant to teach how it was not the tears of an angel that were shed in that place (and certainly not the tears of God) but the mournful weeping of members of Jacob's household.

In surveying these overt and covert name etymologies for Jabbok, Penuel, Mahanaim, and Bethel (Beth-on and Bokhim), we have witnessed how these cities, all in the Kingdom of Israel, attracted traditions involving the Patriarch Jacob and his contentious meeting with a divine being. Although Bethel is associated with many events in Jacob's life (Genesis 28:19, 31:13, and so on), Jabbok and its neighboring cities attracted the traditions about this one exploit of the Patriarch. It seems that these traditions that were linked to peripheral cities were the ones in the book of Genesis that ultimately succeeded in preserving elements from the ancient story about Jacob's battle with a heavenly figure.

As we've observed, each tradition deprived the ancient tale of certain elements while preserving others. In presenting all these tales, the book of Genesis was not wanting to tell them for their own sakes. Rather, the Bible sought to remove certain traditions from the nation's identity-building reservoir of stories, traditions that were incompatible with its theological message, and to remake them so that they would be admissible. The impossibility of completely erasing traditions that had been passed orally from generation to generation meant that the Bible had to take a different approach: to allow a bit of the stories and use some of their details while simultaneously revising them, possibly changing most of the original elements.

8

Where Were Rachel and Jacob Buried?

Jacob and his beloved Rachel died separately and were buried apart. Though the book of Genesis tries to present clear details concerning the burial sites of both, we find that a more complicated story awaits, since different cities (and different tribes) claimed the distinction as the final resting place of the third Patriarch and his adored wife.

We'll begin with the tale of Rachel's burial. The book of Genesis tells us that Rachel died in childbirth with her second son, Benjamin, at the end of the family's journey from Haran to the Land of Canaan: "They set out from Bethel; but when they were still some distance short of Ephrath, Rachel was in childbirth, and she had hard labor. . . . Thus Rachel died. She was buried on the road to Ephrath—now Bethlehem. Over her grave Jacob set up a pillar; it is the pillar at Rachel's grave to this day" (35:16–20). Jacob's last words to Joseph, Rachel's firstborn, agree with this version of Rachel's death and burial: "When I was returning from Paddan, Rachel died, to my sorrow, while I was journeying in the land of Canaan, when still some distance short of Ephrath; and I buried her there on the road to Ephrath now Bethlehem" (48:7).

The tradition about Rachel's burial in the territory of Judah near Bethlehem, the city of David's birth, however, is not the only account of her burial. A very different tale is told in the book of Samuel, where we find an alternative account that locates Rachel's burial in the territory of her second son, Benjamin. When the prophet Samuel anoints Saul (who was from the tribe of Benjamin) as the first king of Israel, he informs Saul of a series of signs that will occur on Saul's return, signs that will signify that Saul is God's chosen one. The first of these is that "when you leave me today, you will meet two men near the tomb of Rachel in the territory of Benjamin, at Tzelzah, and they will tell you that the asses you set out to look for have been found" (1 Samuel 10:2).

Tselzah is mentioned nowhere else in the Bible, but the verse is clear in specifying that it is in the territory of Benjamin and nowhere near Bethlehem. The Rabbis noticed the contradiction and solved it in their particular way: "How is it that we find that Rachel is buried in the territory of Benjamin, at Tselzah? And yet she was buried in Bethlehem, in the territory of Judah! . . . but [Samuel] told [Saul]: Now that I speak with you they are at Rachel's tomb. You will go and they are coming, and will find you in the territory of Benjamin, at Tselzah" (Tosefta, *Sota* 11.13). According to the hermeneutic gymnastics of the Rabbis, the two men are, as Samuel speaks to Saul, at Rachel's tomb in Bethlehem (in the territory of Judah) and will meet Saul later, in the territory of Benjamin. Another solution offered by the midrash reverses the order of the words, so that now Samuel directs Saul: "When you leave me today near the tomb of Rachel [i.e., from Bethlehem], you will meet two men in the territory of Benjamin at Tzelzah" (*Genesis Rabbah* 82:9).

It is worth remembering what the Bible says about the burial of Saul: "And they buried the bones of Saul and of his son Jonathan in Tzela [*tzela'*] in the territory of Benjamin, in the tomb of his father Kish" (2 Samuel 21:14). The verse appears to refer to a family grave. Is it possible that these two places, Tzelzah and Tzela, whose names have both a graphic and aural resemblance, are in fact one and the same? If so, then the grave of the tribe of Benjamin's matriarch, Rachel, is also the grave of her renowned descendants, the family of Saul.

The tradition that Rachel is buried in the territory of Benjamin finds support in a prophecy of Jeremiah about the future return of the exiles: "Thus said the LORD: A cry is heard on high [*be-ramah*], wailing, bitter weeping, Rachel weeping for her children. She refuses to be comforted for her children, who are gone. Thus said the LORD: Restrain your voice from weeping, your eyes from shedding tears; for there is reward for your labor, declares the LORD: They shall return from the enemy's land. And there is hope for your future, declares the LORD: Your children shall return to their country" (31:15–17).

The word *be-ramah*, here translated as "on high," was construed in the Septuagint and Peshitta as the prefixed preposition *be*, "in," and "Ramah," a city in the territory of Benjamin (see Joshua 18:25; Nehemiah 11:33). The view that Rachel was buried in Benjamin—despite the well-known tradition in Genesis—was shared also by one of the sages, Rabbi Meir, who determined that "she died [and was buried] in the portion of her son Benjamin" (*Sifre Deuteronomy*, paragraph 352). In point of fact, the tradition that Rachel was buried in the territory of Benjamin fits with the belief that she died while giving birth to that son, particularly in light of the fact that people of note were often buried in their own tribe's territory—so we find in the cases of Jair the Gileadite (Judges 10:5), Jephthah the Gileadite (12:7), Ibzan of Bethlehem (12:10), Elon the Zebulunite (12:12), and Abdon son of Hillel the Pirathonite (12:15).

Interestingly, the New Testament quotes the verses in Jeremiah specifically in order to strengthen a tradition about Bethlehem. The Gospel of Matthew tells of the killing of the boys of Bethlehem, part of Herod's effort to kill the "king of the Jews" whose birth in Bethlehem had been foretold: "Then Herod . . . was in a furious rage, and he sent and killed all the male children in Bethlehem and in all that region who were two years old or under. . . . Then was fulfilled what was spoken by the prophet Jeremiah: 'A voice was heard in Ramah, wailing and loud lamentation, Rachel weeping for her children; she refused to be comforted, for they were no more'" (2:16–18).

What becomes clear is that the dispute over the whereabouts of Rachel's gravesite was political in nature: the tribe of Benjamin claimed their matriarch exclusively, while the tribe of Judah, and particularly the House of David within it, claimed her for itself. It may well be that the historical bonds between these two tribes—both lived under the rule of the House of David in the Kingdom of Judah—stimulated the development of a new tradition that opposed the previous one, which had related Rachel's death and burial in the territory of Benjamin. The new tradition transferred her burial to Bethlehem, the city of David's birth, in order to reinforce the ties between the two tribes and even to create a dependence of the tribe of Benjamin on Judah, in order to transform their association into an unbreakable bond.

Let's move to Jacob. According to Genesis, Jacob, on his deathbed in Egypt, commands his sons to bring his body for burial to the Land of Israel, to the cave of Machpelah in Hebron: "Bury me with my fathers in the cave which is in the field of Ephron the Hittite, the cave which is in the field of Machpelah, facing Mamre, in the land of Canaan, the field that Abraham bought from Ephron the Hittite for a burial site—there Abraham and his wife Sarah were buried; there Isaac and his wife Rebekah were buried; and there I buried Leah—the field and the cave in it, bought from the Hittites" (Genesis 49:29–32). Jacob's sons fulfill their father's wish and carry his body from Egypt in order to bury it in the cave of Machpelah: "His sons carried him to the land of Canaan, and buried him in the field of Machpelah, the field near Mamre, which Abraham had bought for a burial site from Ephron the Hittite" (50:13).

Alongside this tradition, which tells how all of Jacob's sons buried their father, we find a very different one that relates how one son, Joseph, played a greater role. In this tradition Jacob commands only Joseph to bring his body to the Land of Canaan for burial (Genesis 47:29–31), and Joseph brings his father's request before Pharaoh: "My father made me swear, saying, 'I am about to die. Be sure to bury me in the grave which I dug [*kariti*] for myself in the land of Canaan'" (50:5). The root *k-r-h* can be construed either as "dig," as we've translated it here (and see also in Psalm 7:16: "He has dug [*karah*] a pit and deepened it, and will fall into the trap he made"), or as "purchase," as in Hosea 3:2: "I bought her [*va-'ekhreha*] for fifteen [shekels of] silver." Either way, the verse cannot be read as referring to burial in the cave of Machpelah—Jacob did not dig the cave where his ancestors were already buried, and he certainly did not purchase it, since, again, it had already been purchased by Abraham. Is it possible that we have here a remnant of a different tradition concerning the burial of Jacob?

A parallel story to that of the purchase of the cave of Machpelah, albeit brief, is found in an account of Jacob's acquiring property in the Land of Israel on his return to Canaan from exile in Haran: "Jacob arrived safe in the city of Shechem which is in the land of Canaan—having come thus from Paddan-aram—and he encamped before the city. The parcel of land where he pitched his tent he purchased from the children of Hamor, Shechem's father, for a hundred kesitahs. He set up an altar there, and called it El-elohe-yisrael" (Genesis 33:18–20). It is in this piece of land that Jacob buys from the sons of Hamor that Jacob's son Joseph will be buried. When the Israelites return from Egypt, they bring Joseph's bones with them: "The bones of Joseph, which the Israelites had brought up from Egypt, were buried at Shechem, in the piece of ground which Jacob had bought for a hundred kesitahs from the children of Hamor, Shechem's father, and which had become a heritage of the Josephites" (Joshua 24:32).

This tradition, we begin to realize, shares the view that Joseph was buried in the grave of his father, in Shechem, in the piece of land that Jacob had bought there. Except for mentioning that Joseph's burial site was purchased by his father, it is worth noting that the custom of burying a son in the grave of his ancestors is familiar to us (e.g., Samson in Judges 16:31; the kings of the House of David in 1 Kings 14:31). Also relevant to our discussion are Jacob's final words to Joseph before blessing all his sons. After again mentioning his approaching death and his sons' return to Canaan, Jacob adds: "And now, I assign to you one portion more than to your brothers, which I wrested from the Amorites with my sword and bow" (Genesis 48:22). The term used here for "portion" is *shkhem*, the identical spelling and vocalization of the city-name, Shechem, in which Jacob purchased the burial site, and it alludes to the location of the land Jacob gives Joseph. Though it knows a different tradition about how Shechem came to be part of Jacob's property, this verse nevertheless hints, perhaps, at Jacob's desire to be buried in that city.

An echo of the tradition that Jacob was buried in Shechem is heard in the New Testament, in the account of Israel's history that is told by

Stephen to the high priest: "And Jacob went down into Egypt. And he died, himself and our fathers, and they were carried back to Shechem and laid in the tomb that Abraham had bought for a sum of silver from the sons of Hamor [son of] Shechem" (Acts 7:15–16).

The confusion in Acts, in which Abraham (and not Jacob) is identified as the buyer of the tomb in Shechem, mustn't lead us to dismiss outright the tradition it preserves about the burial of one of the Patriarchs in Shechem. Jacob's burial there perfectly concludes the depiction of that Patriarch whose main activities are identified with the Kingdom of Israel (which included the cities of Shechem, Beth El [see chapter 6], and Penuel [see chapter 7]). Just as Abraham's stories are located within the borders of the future Kingdom of Judah and it is there, in Hebron, that he purchases a tomb and is buried, so does his northern descendant Jacob purchase a tomb in Shechem, a city in the future Kingdom of Israel, and it is there—according to one tradition—that he is buried.

As we found with Rachel, so we find here that the divergent traditions about Jacob's burial testify to political wrangling. The Kingdom of Israel claimed Jacob as its own and located his burial in Shechem, the city that housed a major cultic center and was the first capital of the kingdom during the reign of Jeroboam son of Nebat (1 Kings 12:25), in the tomb that Jacob had purchased there. The Kingdom of Judah also staked its claim as the final resting place of the important Patriarch, and so was formed the account according to which Jacob was buried with the rest of the nation's Patriarchs in Judah, in Hebron, David's first capital city when he ruled over the tribe of Judah (1 Kings 2:11). As we saw in the case of Rachel, also here the Judahite tradition prevailed over the Israelite one, which was pushed out of "official" accounts and into the periphery.

What happens to Jacob in Genesis happens to his son Joseph in the Pseudepigraphic book *Testaments of the Twelve Patriarchs*. That work takes what is told about Joseph being brought up from Egypt for burial in Israel and extends it to all of his brothers. Each brother, in his dying testament, commands that his bones be brought out of

Egypt for burial in the Land of Canaan when the nation will return from its Egyptian exile. (This tradition is found also in Rabbinic literature: "[The Israelites] also carried up with them the bones of all the other founders of the tribes" [*Mekhilta de-Rabbi Ishmael, Beshalaḥ*].) This tradition, at odds with what we found in the Pentateuch, relates how Jacob and his sons, including Joseph, were buried together with the Patriarchs in the cave of Machpelah: "And when the children of Israel went out of Egypt they took with them the bones of Joseph and they buried them in Hebron with his fathers, and the years of his life were 110" (*Testament of Joseph* 20:6). Like both his parents, Joseph, too, claims two sacred cities as his final resting place: Shechem, according to the Bible, and Hebron, according to the *Testaments of the Twelve Patriarchs*.

The great extent to which the graves of important figures were used for political purposes has become apparent in these accounts. We are hardly surprised, therefore, when certain figures receive more than one burial, with different groups claiming the deceased as their own. To "divide and share" would, obviously, be impossible.

These two controversies, one concerning the burial site of Rachel and the other of Jacob, are found within the Bible itself, but they are part of a much broader phenomenon that we find also outside the Bible's pages, in which competing sites claim to house the graves of Israel's heroes. For example, the Bible records that Moses was buried at an unknown location on the other side of the Jordan, close to Mount Nebo (Deuteronomy 32:49). Maimonides's grandson, Rabbi David Ha-Nagid, however, in his commentary on the Pentateuch (to Genesis 23:13), relates that Moses was buried in the cave of Machpelah, while Muslim tradition locates the grave in Nebi Musa, between Jerusalem and Jericho. Though we speak of one person, there may be many graves. Sacred geography, it seems, is flexible.

9

Where in the Wilderness Did Israel
Receive the Torah?

The giving of the Torah at Sinai was an event of tremendous magnitude. With "thunder and lightning . . . and a very loud blast of the horn" (Exodus 19:16), the Sinai tradition silenced competing traditions concerning the location of the giving of the Torah—the Law—to Israel. Indeed, more than one site claimed to be the place where Israel received its Torah during the people's wandering in the wilderness.

The story of the Israelites' first stop in the wilderness after crossing the Sea of Reeds contains a mini-giving of the Torah, though we tend to ignore this story in favor of its much more impressive Sinai parallel. For three days the people of Israel wandered in the wilderness without finding water, and with their arrival at Marah (identified as Ein Hawarah, a pool of salty water east of Suez), they were disappointed to discover that the waters were bitter, and so is the place given its name: "They came to Marah, but they could not drink the water of Marah because it was bitter [marim]; that is why it was named Marah" (Exodus 15:23).

The people of Israel are quick to protest. It is the first of numerous complaints that they will voice and that will characterize their stay in the wilderness: "And the people grumbled against Moses, saying 'What shall we drink?'" (Exodus 15:24). Moses cries out to the Lord, who grants a miraculous solution to the Israelites' suffering: "And the LORD showed [Moses] a piece of wood; he threw it into the water and the water became sweet" (v. 25). At Marah we witness the first of the miracles that will punctuate the Israelites' wanderings in the desert: the first of God's many expressions of mercy toward the discontented and ungrateful people.

This gracious act of God, the sweetening of the water, is followed by the giving of a law, a sort of minor giving of the Torah: "There He made for them a fixed rule, and there He put them to the test" (Exodus 15:25). In this verse are mentioned two acts—a giving of the Torah ("He made for them a fixed rule") and a test ("He put them to the test"). They are mentioned in the reverse order in which they occurred, since God first tried Israel with thirst to see whether they would have faith in Him, and when they failed the test and complained, they received a "fixed rule." Proof that the Israelites' thirst indeed represented a test—and was not the result of some glitch or navigational mistake—becomes apparent from the immediate continuation of the narrative. After the miracle at Marah God brings the people to Elim: "And they came to Elim, where there were twelve springs of water and seventy palm trees; and they encamped there beside the water" (v. 27). Had God wanted from the start to prevent any shortage of water He would have brought His people directly to the oasis: God's choice reflects a desire to use the people's thirst in order to test their faith.

As we've said, following the test and the sweetening of the water, God gives a law to Israel. He expects the miracle He has just performed to awaken the people's trust, recognition, and readiness to keep the laws and commandments. The brief, didactic speech that accompanies the giving of the fixed rule contains an overt promise along with a covert threat: "He said, 'If you truly heed the LORD your God diligently, doing what is upright in His sight, giving ear to His commandments and keeping all His laws, then I will not bring upon you any of the diseases that I brought upon the Egyptians, for I the LORD am your healer" (Exodus 15:26). These words resemble the reproachful speeches that we find elsewhere in the Pentateuch and that appear at the end of law collections (Exodus 23:25; Leviticus 26:14–45; Deuteronomy 28:21–68).

The promise of good health and the distinction between the good fortune of Israel and the diseased and plague-ridden fate of the Egyptians are tied to the people's suffering at the beginning of the episode, "but they could not drink the water of Marah" (Exodus 15:23), which is reminiscent of the first of God's plagues against the Egyptians, blood, which prompted a water shortage: "And all the Egyptians had to dig round about the Nile for drinking water, because they could not drink the water of the Nile" (7:24). This is God's way of teaching the Israelites that it is their keeping of His laws and commandments that will distinguish them from the Egyptians and their fate.

A similar idea emerges in Deuteronomy: "And if you do heed these rules and observe them carefully . . . the LORD will ward off from you all sickness; He will not bring upon you any of the dreadful diseases of Egypt, about which you know, but will inflict them upon all your enemies" (7:12–15). We can say more: God, who sweetened the water—or, in the language used in a similar story about the sweetening of the waters of Jericho by Elisha, He "healed" them (see 2 Kings 2:21–22)—will heal the Israelites forevermore—"for I the LORD am your healer"—if they do what is right in His eyes.

The sturdy connection between the miracle and the lesson that follows is expressed also in the verb *yorehu*, from the root *y-r-h*, which plays on the name Marah, "and [the LORD] *instructed him* [*va-yorehu*] a piece of wood" (v. 25). We would have expected to read the verb as derived from *r-'-h*, producing *va-yar'ehu*, "and He showed him," as the Samaritan version of the Torah and the ancient translations understood it. The Rabbis were aware of both possible readings and combined them: "He *showed him* [from the root *r-'-h*] words of the *Torah* [from the root *y-r-h*] which is likened to a tree, as it is said, 'She is a tree of life to those who grasp her' (Prov. 3:18)" (*Mekhilta de-Rabbi Ishmael, Beshalah* 1).

It is interesting to note that the *Mekhilta* cites a verse from Proverbs that likens wisdom to the Tree of Life and assumes that no wisdom exists apart from the Torah. Is it possible that the foundations of the *Mekhilta* tradition rest on the conviction that the tree God showed to Moses was the Tree of Life and that it was a branch from that tree that Moses threw into the water in order to sweeten it? That, at least, is what the writer of *Biblical Antiquities* tells us: "And He showed him the Tree of Life, from which he cut off and took and threw into Marah, and the water of Marah became sweet" (11:15). This tradition was known much later to the writer of the Zohar (*Tikunim*, 88).

The miracle of the sweetening of the water at Marah, the giving of the "fixed rule," and the speech that follows are therefore a foreshadowing and synopsis of what is to come: God acts with gracious favor toward His people and expects that they, in turn, will believe in him, recognize his greatness, and obey his laws. The keeping of God's laws holds the promise of a life without harm, but along with the blessing we hear also a covert threat, since a rejection of these rules and laws will bring disaster onto Israel. In short, the few verses that relate the incident at Marah comprise a parallel story to the giving of the Torah in the wilderness at Mount Sinai.

The placement of our story before that of the gathering at Mount Sinai enables the Pentateuch to reconcile these two competing traditions about the giving of the Torah in the wilderness by presenting the story of Marah as the beginning of a process that was established in order to prepare and instruct the people of Israel about the forthcoming giving of the Torah. That process ends with the dramatic events at the base of Mount Sinai and with the receiving of the Torah there. The Rabbis, who felt this connection between the beginning of the giving of the Law at Marah and the giving of the Law at Sinai, attempted to identify and count the specific laws that were given at Marah:

"There he made for them a fixed rule." There ten laws were given to Israel, seven of which had been commanded to the sons of Noah [these are the seven laws that are binding on all humankind: the prohibitions of idolatry, blasphemy, bloodshed, sexual sins, theft, and eating meat taken from a living animal, as well as the injunction to establish a legal system]. At this time Israel added [the commandment to observe the] Shabbat, [to establish] tribunals, and honoring father and mother. (*Seder 'Olam Rabbah* 5; cf. B. *Sanhedrin* 46b)

Identifying the number of laws given at Marah as ten strengthens even further the connection between the traditions of Marah and Sinai.

The relationship between these two traditions of the giving of the Torah is further buttressed by a tradition found in *Mekhilta de-Rabbi Ishmael* (*Vayassa'* 1), which interprets the words "they traveled three days in the wilderness and found no water" (Exodus 15:22) as speaking about "the words of Torah." This follows the ancient comparison of the Torah to water, such as we find in Isaiah 55:1: "Ho, all who are thirsty come for water." According to the *Mekhilta*, the people of Israel wandered in the wilderness for three days without studying the Torah, and this was what instigated their rebellion against God and why Moses decided that "they would read from the Torah on the Sabbath and on Mondays and Thursdays," frequently enough, in other words, that three days would not pass without Torah reading.

According to this tradition, it was at Marah that Israel received the Law, the Torah, along with the obligation to read from it with fixed regularity. Even more, the *Mekhilta de-Rabbi Ishmael* connects God's rule, "If you truly heed the LORD your God diligently" (Exodus 15:26), which is said in the story of Marah, with the "ten commandments" and so reinforces even further the connection between the events at Mount Sinai and Marah. This tightening of the relationship served to further subdue any tension between the two traditions, which were originally in conflict but which now reach us one alongside the other in a seemingly graceful and easy harmony.

10

Some More Reasons for Eating Matzah

Why do Jews eat matzah—unleavened bread—during Passover? The Passover haggadah both poses and answers that question: "This unleavened bread that we eat—what is its reason? Because the dough of our ancestors had not time to become leavened before the King of Kings, the Holy One, Blessed be He, revealed Himself to them and redeemed them as it is said: And they baked unleavened cakes of the dough that they had taken out of Egypt, for it was not leavened, since they had been driven out of Egypt and could not delay, nor had they prepared any provisions for themselves" (Exodus 12:39). A previous verse in the story of the Exodus has already prepared us for this explanation, which revolves around the limited time the Israelites had for their bread to rise: "So the people took their dough before it was leavened, their kneading bowls wrapped in their cloaks upon their shoulders" (12:34).

The book of Deuteronomy treads the same path left by the writers of the book of Exodus when it proposes an identical explanation for eating matzah: "You shall slaughter the passover sacrifice for the LORD your God. . . . You shall not eat anything leavened with it; for seven days thereafter you shall eat unleavened bread. . . . for you departed from the land of Egypt hurriedly so that you may remember the day of your departure from the land of Egypt as long as you live. For seven days no leaven shall be found with you in all your territory" (16:2–4; see also the sources for Deuteronomy in Exodus 12:15, 13:3, 6, 7). Deuteronomy, which firmly establishes the connection between the passover sacrifice and the holiday of unleavened bread, uses the word "hurriedly" in its explanation for eating the unleavened bread, a word it borrows from God's command for eating the Passover sacrifice in Egypt: "This is how you shall eat it: your loins girded, your sandals on your feet, and your staff in your hand; and you shall eat it *hurriedly*: it is a passover offering to the LORD" (Exodus 12:11).

In our reference to Deuteronomy 16 just now we purposefully omitted two words, since they interrupt the narrative's natural flow. The complete verse reads: "You shall not eat anything leavened with it; for seven days thereafter you shall eat unleavened bread, *bread of affliction* [*leḥem 'oni*], for you departed from the land of Egypt hurriedly" (16:3). The two words *leḥem 'oni* represent the Bible's only admission of an entirely different explanation for the eating of matzah, that it was "bread of affliction." Its inclusion here was an attempt to preserve this other tradition in the nation's consciousness.

What is the meaning of the expression? We met the word *'oni* already in chapter 7, when we discussed the name Rachel gave to her newborn son, Ben-oni, "son of my affliction" or "son of my mourning." It was used often for describing the Israelites' suffering in Egypt: "And the LORD continued, 'I have marked well the affliction of My people in Egypt and have heeded their outcry because of their taskmasters'" (Exodus 3:7); "and the people believed. When they heard that the LORD had taken note of the Israelites and that He had seen their affliction" (4:31); "See, I refine you but not as silver, I test you in the furnace of affliction" (Isaiah 48:10); "You took note of our fathers' affliction in Egypt" (Nehemiah 9:9). Similarly, the verb formed from the same root is commonly found in connection with the slavery in Egypt, such as in Exodus 1:10–11: "So they set taskmasters over them to afflict them with forced labor. . . . But the more they were afflicted the more they increased and spread out"; Genesis 15:13: "And He said to Abram, 'Know well that your offspring shall be strangers in a land not theirs, and they shall be enslaved and afflicted four hundred years'"; and Deuteronomy 26:6: "The Egyptians dealt harshly with us and afflicted us, they imposed heavy labor upon us."

The abstract noun "affliction" appears often paired with the synonymous "oppression" (*laḥatz*), as in Deuteronomy 26:7, "and the Lord heard our plea and saw our affliction, our misery, and our oppression," and Psalm 44:25, "Why do You hide Your face, ignoring our affliction and oppression." Indeed, a synonymous designation for "bread of affliction" is "bread of oppression," the bread of prisoners, usually understood in the sense of scarcity. We see this in the story about the prophet Micaiah, son of Imlah. King Ahab, who hopes that Micaiah's prophecy about the king's death during the war will not be fulfilled and that he will return safely from the battlefield, commands: "Put this fellow in prison, and let his fare be bread of oppression and water of oppression until I come home safe" (1 Kings 22:27 = 2 Chronicles 18:26). It appears also in Isaiah 30:20: "My Lord will provide for you meager bread and water of oppression." Verbs and nouns derived from the root '-*n*-*h* are also associated with imprisonment, as we find in Psalm 105, which tells of Joseph's experiences in Egypt: "They afflicted his feet in fetters, his neck in iron"; and see also Psalm 107:10: "Some lived in deepest darkness, prisoners of affliction and iron."

The term "bread of affliction" suits, therefore, the fare of prisoners, since prisoners are starved, fed insufficiently in order to increase their suffering while nonetheless keeping them alive. And indeed, the root '-*n*-*h* can also connote starvation, as with the test with which God tried the people of Israel in the wilderness: "He afflicted you and starved you" (Deuteronomy 8:3), or in the words of Ezra: "I proclaimed a fast there by the Ahava River to afflict ourselves before our God" (8:21). The words "you shall afflict your souls" in Leviticus 16:31 were interpreted in Jewish law as referring to fasting.

The texts we have brought seem to suggest that a tradition in the ancient past explained the eating of matzah during Passover as deriving from a desire to remember the affliction of the Israelites in Egypt and to remember the food the Israelites were given by their captors. In the words of Rabbi Shimon (*Sifre Deuteronomy*, paragraph 130): "Why is it called the bread of affliction? Because of the affliction they were afflicted in Egypt." Rashi, following this interpretation, wrote in his commentary on Deuteronomy 16, "bread of affliction—which reminds [us] of the affliction they were afflicted in Egypt." The tradition, which was rejected by the Bible and survived in two solitary words in Deuteronomy, found its way to the Passover haggadah, where it was preserved in the only Aramaic passage there, *Ha' laḥma' 'ania'*: "This is the bread of affliction that our forefathers ate in the land of Egypt."

It becomes clear that this tradition, pushed off into the margins during the biblical period and mentioned in the Bible only in the words "bread of affliction," nonetheless continued its life orally until it emerged in the Rabbinic text *Sifre Deuteronomy* and in the Passover haggadah. It is most remarkable that in the haggadah it reaches us in Aramaic, the vernacular of the Jews during the late Second Temple period, as though it was among the common people that the tradition was preserved, despite efforts of the official and institutionalized religion to eliminate (or at least ignore) it. (We'll soon see why.)

Many readers have sensed the conflict between the two traditions: one that relates eating matzah to the Israelites' hurried departure from Egypt, and thus highlights the brief flight from Egypt, and one that viewed it as the "bread of affliction," highlighting the Israelites' experience during their long period of enslavement. One haggadah manuscript has preserved an attempt to harmonize the two explanations: "This is the bread of affliction that our forefathers ate when they left the land of Egypt"—that is to say, the "bread of affliction" was not eaten during the years of enslavement but during the Israelites' departure from Egypt. Another tradition, this one attributed to Rabbi Samuel, construed the word *'oni* differently, effectively disengaging the tradition of eating matzah from the years of Egyptian slavery. According to this interpretation, "bread of affliction" is "bread that you talk [*'onin*] about" (B. *Pesahim* 115b), that is, bread that we speak about during the Passover seder.

If we are correct in supposing that the tradition about "bread of affliction" was rejected in favor of one that associated matzah with the hurried flight from Egypt, what could the explanation have been for such a rejection? The passover sacrifice, we recall, memorializes the redemption from Egypt: "And when your children ask you, 'What do you mean by this rite?' you shall say, 'It is the passover sacrifice to the LORD, because He passed over the houses of the Israelites in Egypt when He smote the Egyptians, but saved our houses'" (Exodus 12:26–27). The Pentateuch, it becomes clear, sought to make similar the two acts of eating: just as eating the passover sacrifice reminds us of the moment of our redemption, so should our eating the unleavened bread remind us of that same event. Instead of eating matzah to remember the years of Egyptian affliction, the Pentateuch preferred to attribute to it a happy explanation, turning it into a reminder of the moment of redemption: the Israelites' passage from slavery to freedom.

Evidence for this effort to liken the eating of matzah to the hurried eating of the Passover sacrifice on the eve of the Exodus can be found in Deuteronomy 16:3, which, referring to the eating of matzah, explains, "for you departed hurriedly." As we've already remarked, the source for the association of "hurriedly" with "unleavened bread" was the tradition in Exodus 12:11, where the word "hurried" refers to the eating of the Passover sacrifice in Egypt, "and you shall eat it hurriedly." It becomes clear that this tendency to connect the eating of matzah with the moment of redemption and not the lengthy period of Egyptian enslavement matches the picture described generally by the book of Exodus, which gives little attention to that period, even though, according to the Pentateuch, it lasted for hundreds of years. Instead, most of the book of Exodus focuses on the Israelites' redemption and the story of their flight from Egypt.

And, truly, it seems more reasonable that eating matzah for seven full days would memorialize a long-lasting plight and not a brief and one-time event—important as that event may have been. It is interesting that, when interpreting biblical verses, Jewish law restricts the obligation to eat matzah to one day only: "'Seven days shall you eat unleavened bread.' That is, it is obligatory to eat unleavened bread the first day only, but the remaining days it is optional" (*Mekhilta de-Rabbi Ishmael*, Bo 8). This interpretation makes the eating of unleavened bread even more analogous to the eating of the passover sacrifice, eaten in memory of the redemption, and so continues the Bible's effort to link the eating of matzah to the eve of the departure and not to the entire period of slavery.

11

Was Worshiping the Golden Calf a Sin?

The Israelites, recent refugees from Egypt now wandering in the wilderness, had trouble exchanging the authority of their Egyptian oppressor with that of an unseen God. They fail the tests that God sets for them and in their audacity even try God with their own test. Meanwhile, their time in the wilderness stretches longer and longer, filling itself with their stubborn ungratefulness.

The worst of all the sins that the Israelites commit in the wilderness is that of the golden calf, an event recounted in Exodus 32. When Moses ascends Mount Sinai to receive the Law and is late to return, the anxious people turn to Aaron and request that he make for them a god that will lead them in the wilderness in place of Moses (v. 1). Aaron molds a golden calf, a molten calf, and the people call out, "This is your god, O Israel, who brought you out of the land of Egypt" (v. 4). When the calf is erected, the people celebrate unrestrainedly, "and they rose to copulate" (v. 6; for this meaning of *letzaḥeq*, "to copulate," see Genesis 26:8).

Meanwhile, at the summit God informs Moses of the sin of the Israelites below and of His decision to destroy them (Exodus 32:7–10), but Moses succeeds in calming God's anger (vv. 11–14). When Israel's leader descends the mountain and witnesses the people in their revelry before the calf, he shatters the two tablets he has brought with him, tablets of the Law that were inscribed by God Himself (vv. 15–19). Moses burns the calf and grinds it to a fine powder, which he mixes with water and forces the Israelites to drink (v. 20). Drinking this water is an ordeal, a trial to prove God's judgment and distinguish the guilty from the not guilty. The Rabbis sensed the correspondence between this ordeal and the "water of bitterness" that suspected adulteresses are forced to drink (Numbers 5:11–31): "This teaches that they tested them in the way that adulteresses were tested" (Tosefta, *Avodah Zara* 4:3; cf. B. *Avodah Zara*, 44a).

The story of the golden calf ends with a massacre carried out by the Levites, who answer Moses's call, "Whoever is for the LORD, come here!" (v. 26), and sweep through the tumultuous crowd, slaughtering three thousand people, and who are then appointed as God's servants (Exodus 32:25–29). Moses will still need to atone for the people's behavior, return to the mountain summit, and receive the tablets for the second time.

Exodus 32 attributes partial responsibility for the sin to Aaron, since he answered the people's request and made the statue. Deuteronomy 9, when it retells the story through the eyes of Moses, places the full weight of guilt with the people. One verse in that chapter, in an attempt to make the story compatible with its counterpart in Exodus, inserted Aaron into the plot: "Moreover the LORD was angry enough with Aaron to have destroyed him; so I also interceded for Aaron at that time" (v. 20).

The trauma of the sin of idolatry along with the Israelites' mistaken attribution of the redemption from Egypt to the golden calf are given poetic expression in Psalm 106, a historical psalm that recounts the Israelites' repeated expressions of ingratitude toward God throughout history: "They made a calf at Horeb and bowed down to a molten image. They exchanged their glory of the image of a bull that feeds on grass. They forgot God who saved them, who performed great deeds in Egypt, wondrous deeds in the land of Ham, awesome deeds at the Sea of Reeds. He would have destroyed them had not Moses His chosen one confronted Him in the breach to avert His destructive wrath" (vv. 19–23). Note the psalmist's ironic comparison between the God of Israel, infinite in power, and the calf, who "feeds on grass," in whose body there is no life, and who is but an "image of a bull" and no more.

But the Pentateuch's story is not the only narrative that tells about a golden calf and the people's worship of it. Indeed, it is with a sense of déjà vu that readers later come upon the story of the division of the united monarchy under the House of David, when Jeroboam (who revolted against Solomon and his son Rehoboam) attempted to draw his people away from Jerusalem's king and Temple and return them to the traditional cult cities of Bethel and Dan, where he erects golden calves (1 Kings 12:26–30). For the writer of Kings, Jeroboam's making of the calves and their placement in the temples is a grave transgression that "proved to be a cause of guilt" (v. 30).

Theirs was the sin of idolatry, as becomes clear in the conclusion to the book of Kings' history of the Kingdom of Israel, with that kingdom's destruction: "They rejected all the commandments of the LORD their God; they made molten idols for themselves—two calves—and they made a sacred post and they bowed down to all the host of heaven, and they worshiped Baal" (2 Kings 17:16). The writer of Chronicles, in his rendition of the monarchic period, places into the mouth of King Abijah, son of Rehoboam from Judah, words directed against Jeroboam, the enemy, and Jeroboam's army "because you are a great multitude and possess the golden calves that Jeroboam made for you as gods. Did you not banish the priests of the LORD, the sons of Aaron and the Levites, and, like the peoples of the land, appoint your own priests . . . a priest of no-gods" (2 Chronicles 13:8–9).

Yet it seems that these biblical historiographers, the writers of Kings and Chronicles who accuse King Jeroboam of idolatry, do not reflect the viewpoint of that monarch or his people with regard to the golden calves that stood in their temples in Bethel and Dan. It would be absurd to think that during a time of crisis—the break from the House of David—Jeroboam would stir up more change and introduce calves for worship were they not already familiar to the Israelites and their ancestors. Indeed, it seems more likely that Jeroboam, in urging the people to return to their traditional places of worship, did so because he believed that the calves were pleasing to God and that erecting them there represented a welcome return to ancestral practice. The notion that Jeroboam's calves were illegitimate was born in the rival kingdom, the Kingdom of Judah, where worship in the Jerusalem Temple was considered the single means of worshiping God.

Many details in the account of the making of Jeroboam's calves remind us of the making of the golden calf in the wilderness:

- Both stories refer to the calf as the "molten calf" (Exodus 32:4, 8; Deuteronomy 9:12, 16; 1 Kings 14:9; 2 Kings 17:16).
- Declarations following the making of the calves use almost identical language. The Israelites in the wilderness call out, "This is your god, O Israel, who brought you out of the land of Egypt" (Exodus 32:8); Jeroboam tells the people, "Here is your god, O Israel, who brought you up from the land of Egypt" (1 Kings 12:28; note the striking resemblance to the first commandment: "I the LORD am your God who brought you out of the land of Egypt" [Exodus 20:2; Deuteronomy 5:6]).
- An altar was built near the calf (Exodus 32:5; 1 Kings 12:32), and sacrifices are offered on it in the ensuing celebrations (Exodus 32:6; 1 Kings 12:32).
- Like Aaron, Jeroboam also serves as priest (Exodus 32:2–6; 1 Kings 12:33, 13:1).
- The names of Jeroboam's two sons—Nadab, who ruled after his father, and Abijah, who died in childhood (1 Kings 14:1, 20, 15:25)—remind us of Aaron's two elder sons, Nadab and Abihu, who died because of their sin (Abihu and Abijah are spelled identically except for an added *vav* and *he*; Leviticus 10:1–2).

The correlation between these two calf narratives was obvious already to the Rabbis: "R. Oshaia said: Until the time of Jeroboam, Israel had suckled from one calf; but from then on, from two or three calves" (B. *Sanhedrin* 102a).

It seems to us that the inhabitants of the Kingdom of Israel understood Jeroboam's real intent and knew that making the calves was an act not of innovation but of restoration. It represented a reembracing of the old ways—a return to the tradition according to which the calf had been made in the wilderness. That, we suggest, had been an act not of revolt or sinfulness but of the founding of Israelite religion—according to a parallel tradition to the one about the construction of the tabernacle and its accoutrements, which also took place in the wilderness. It is evident, too, that the prophets who prophesied in the Kingdom of Israel saw nothing amiss with the inclusion of calves in their cultic rituals: neither Elijah, the great enemy of Baal, Elisha, his disciple, nor the majority of Israel's prophets raised their voices against the calves.

The exception is the prophet Hosea, who criticizes his people: "They have made kings, but not with My sanction; they have made officers, but not of My choice [this alludes to the rule of Jeroboam], Of their silver and gold they have made themselves images. . . . I reject your calf, Samaria! I am furious with them! Will they never be capable of purity? . . . It was only made by a joiner, It is not a god. No, the calf of Samaria shall be reduced to splinters" (8:4–6). And more: "And now they go on sinning; They have made them molten images, idols, by their skill, from their silver, wholly the work of craftsmen. Yet for these they appoint me to sacrifice; they are wont to kiss calves" (13:2).

The continuation of the prophecy compares the sin of the calf and the declaration that precedes it—"This is your god, O Israel, who brought you out of the land of Egypt"—with the first two of the Ten Commandments: "Only I the LORD have been your God ever since the land of Egypt; You have never known a God but Me, you have never had a helper other than Me" (Hosea 13:4; cf. Exodus 20:2–3: "I the LORD am your God who brought you out of the land of Egypt. . . . You shall have no other gods besides Me").

Jeroboam and his subjects, it seems, did not consider themselves as committing a sin against the God of Israel, neither in the making of the calves nor in the declaration that "here is your god, O Israel." One senses that they viewed the calves only as symbolic of the presence of Israel's God in that place, perhaps even as the pedestal on which the invisible God might rest. In that case, there is no significant difference between the calves that stood in the temples in the Northern Kingdom and the cherubs, those winged creatures that served as God's chariot, that stood in the Temple in Jerusalem (1 Kings 6:23–28).

This suggests that Jeroboam was reinstating an ancient tradition when he erected the calves. Wanting to defame the northern king, however, the Pentateuch fashioned the tale of the calf in Exodus 32 as a story about the sin of idolatry. Whoever reads about Jeroboam in the biblical historiography, a corpus hostile to that king who revolted against the House of David, arrives at it only after reading Exodus 32 and, influenced by that story, concludes that Jeroboam spitefully persisted in the same sinful pursuit, the pinnacle of all the transgressions committed in the wilderness. In a similar way, it is quite plausible that the inhabitants of the Israelite kingdom, where Jeroboam was viewed as a "Second Moses" (see chapter 24), also pointed to the correlation between the golden calf of the wilderness and that of their king but viewed in an entirely positive light the making of the first calf, which served as the underpinning and motive for Jeroboam's subsequent act.

We have already mentioned how Exodus 32 portrays Aaron as the transgressor and Moses as the righteous one who atones for the sin. We cannot exclude the possibility, however, that in the tradition that was told in the Kingdom of Israel, which, as we've indicated, portrayed Jeroboam as a second Moses, it was Moses—and not Aaron—who made the calf, and Moses did what he did in order to honor God and not detract from Him. Judges 18:30 alludes to a tradition according to which Moses's grandson was the chief priest in Dan, one of the temples in which were erected a molten calf (see chapter 13). The Judahite view, which detached Moses, the archetype of the prophets, from the priesthood and the House of Aaron, preferred to attribute the making of the calf—deemed a sin—to Aaron in order to eliminate any association between Moses and the priesthood and priestly family that descended from him.

To end this chapter, let's turn our attention to a few verses in Jeremiah (34:18–20) about the covenant broken by the people of Judah when they refused to release their slaves, thus disobeying the laws set out in the Pentateuch. We'll see how, in these verses, an echo—albeit dim—is heard of the legitimacy granted long, long ago to the making of the calf.

Here are two versions of the verses: the longer version from Jeremiah (from the original Hebrew, the Masoretic Text) and a shorter version from the Septuagint. Alongside these two, we present a reconstructed version that reflects, we believe, the source that was used for the other two versions.

Long version (Jeremiah 34:18–20)	Short version (reflected in the Septuagint)	Reconstructed source
¹⁸I will make the men who violated My covenant, who did not fulfill the terms of the covenant which they made before Me, the calf **which they cut in two so as to pass between the halves.**	I will make the men who violated My covenant, who did not fulfill the terms of the covenant which they made before the calf **which they made to worship it.**	I will make the men who violated My covenant, who did not fulfill the terms of the covenant which they made before the calf.
¹⁹The officers of Judah and Jerusalem, the officials, the priests, and all the people of the land **who passed between the halves of the calf . . .**	The officers of Judah, the officials, the priests, and all the people	The officers of Judah, the officials, the priests, and all the people
²⁰I will deliver them to their enemies		

The reconstructed source reflects the view that the calf (connected with the Sinai tradition) was indeed a legitimate part of the worship of God, a symbol of His presence. In the short version we find an exegetical addition that correctly understood the "calf" being referred to as the golden calf, though it denounces it in the spirit of the story in Exodus, "the calf which they made to worship it." Making the calf in order to worship it would mean recognition of its divinity.

The writer of the longer version handled the difficulty in granting legitimacy to the calf differently. According to this writer, the verse refers not to a golden calf but to a real calf, part of a covenant-sealing ceremony in which the calf is divided and then passed through, similar to what is described in Genesis 15: "He brought Him all these and cut them in two" (v. 10); "there appeared a smoking oven, and a flaming torch which passed between those pieces" (v. 17). This interpretation is twice expressed in the course of verses 18–19 in Jeremiah: "the calf which they cut in two so as to pass between the halves," "who passed between the halves." The addition in the long version caused a linguistic problem in verse 18, but it succeeded in expelling any remnant of the tradition of the calf in the wilderness and its legitimacy, a tradition that, despite everything, wondrously managed to survive and be recorded in Jeremiah's prophecy, at the end of the First Temple period.

We've managed to trace a tradition that originated in the Northern Kingdom and that told of a golden calf that was erected at Sinai as a legitimate symbol of the presence of the God of Israel. It was this tradition that Jeroboam heeded when he erected the golden calves at Bethel and Dan. The story in Exodus 32 (as we know it) was written as part of the campaign against Jeroboam and his actions: it is a story of sin and idol worship. But echoes of the ancient story can be heard in the original version of the book of Jeremiah, as we've reconstructed it here. In the end, the story of the calf and its versions and echoes bear witness to the adversarial tension that existed between these two sister kingdoms and between the various manners in which the God of Israel was worshiped in them.

12

Where Was the Law Given?

In the Wilderness or in the Land of Israel?

According to tradition, the Law was given to Israel in the wilderness on Mount Sinai after God had redeemed the Israelites from Egyptian bondage and after Israel's first prophet, Moses, ascended the heights of Mount Sinai, where he received the tablets of the Law from God. This is why the Torah, the Law, is called also "the Torah of Moses," as we find, for example, in the verses that seal the prophetic corpus as a whole: "Be mindful of the Teaching [the Torah] of My servant Moses, whom I charged at Horeb with laws and rules for all Israel" (Malachi 3:22). In chapter 9 we saw how another tradition beside the one of the giving of the Law at Mount Sinai existed, though it was pushed off to the margins and even silenced: the tradition about receiving the Law at Marah, a site also located in the wilderness.

The notion of the Law being given in the wilderness following the Exodus from Egypt served two aims. First, it set up an equation whereby the miracles that God performed in order to redeem the Israelites from Egyptian slavery obligated their subsequent obedience to His laws. It is no surprise that the first of the Ten Commandments states: "I the LORD am your God who brought you out of the land of Egypt, the house of bondage" (Exodus 20:2 = Deuteronomy 5:6). Following this declaration comes the rest of the commandments, beginning with the charge to recognize only the God of Israel, "You shall have no other gods besides Me" (Exodus 20:3 = Deuteronomy 5:7), and to uphold all of His commands.

The second aim served by the giving of the Law in the wilderness was that it promoted an isolationist ideology: the Israelites receive their Law in the wilderness, a no-man's-land, in a cultural vacuum. Those who subscribed to this view claimed that also in the past, during the period of the Patriarchs as well as in Egypt, no substantial contact existed between the Israelites and their surroundings, so that the nation arrived to the wilderness and to the giving of the Law as a tabula rasa, free of foreign influence. This was necessary—the isolationist ideology proposes—because the Law of Israel is a divine law and shares nothing with the beliefs, practices, or laws of the nations that surrounded Israel or in which Israel dwelled. According to this view, once the Israelites enter the Land of Israel no new laws will be given; the Law that was received in the wilderness, in splendid isolation, will comprise the Israelites' law code for all generations, and they will require no further law-giving during all the years that they will live in Israel.

Most of the Bible shares this mainstream view, which explains why there are no leaders, judges, or kings who fix rules or establish laws in Israel (except for the chapter in Joshua that we will discuss now and one other verse—apparently an addition—in 1 Samuel that relates how David established one rule [30:25]). All the law codes are presented in the Pentateuch, and all were given to Israel between Mount Sinai and the plains of Moab, before the Israelites crossed the Jordan and reached the Promised Land.

And yet one chapter in the Bible—the last in the book of Joshua—does not share this view, neither with regard to the isolationism that characterizes the nation's history nor with regard to the giving of the Law at Mount Sinai. And though this chapter stands in complete disagreement with the Bible's dominant tradition, it was preserved due to the Bible's practice of incorporating divergent traditions by altering them or interpreting them and not simply omitting them as having no value.

Joshua 24 recounts Joshua's leave-taking of his people, in Shechem. Joshua delivers a speech at the gathering, in which he lays out a very different version of Israelite history, from its beginnings until the conquest of the land and settlement there (vv. 1–15). Following this historical survey, which emphasizes God's redeeming acts for His people, Joshua makes a covenant for the people, binding them to worship God alone, and also makes a "fixed rule," that is, he gives to them the Law (vv. 16–28).

Joshua 24 grants priority to the temple in Shechem, something that does not shock us when we recall Shechem's centrality in Pentateuchal traditions: it was in Shechem that Abraham built the first altar to God immediately on his entrance into the land (Genesis 12:6–7); Jacob bought a parcel of land in Shechem when he returned from Haran and built there an altar to God (33:18–20); Moses had commanded that an altar be built close to Shechem when the Israelites entered the land (Deuteronomy 27:1–8), a command that Joshua fulfilled (Joshua 8:30–35). This succession of episodes creates the impression that one could not enter the Land of Israel without first building an altar to God in Shechem. If we add to this string of traditions the tradition of a family grave existing in Shechem—that of Joseph and even Jacob (see chapter 8)—we come to realize the centrality of Shechem and its temple for the Northern Kingdom, that is, the Kingdom of Israel.

The Samaritan community, for whom the Pentateuch alone comprises its Holy Scripture, continued this belief in the centrality of Shechem. It recognized Shechem as the chosen place that houses the one and only temple—Shechem and not Jerusalem—where Israel must worship its God from the moment it entered the Land of Israel. The Samaritan version of the Pentateuch even contracts the Ten Commandments that we know from the Masoretic Text into nine and adds a different tenth commandment, which addresses the sanctity of Shechem. This commandment is composed using verses in Deuteronomy 27:

> As soon as you have crossed the Jordan into the land of the Canaanites that you are about to enter and possess you shall set up large stones. Coat them with plaster and inscribe upon them all the words of the Teaching. Upon crossing the Jordan, you shall

set up these stones, about which I charge you this day, on Mount Grizim [and not Mount Ebal, the Mount of the Curse, as written in the masoretic version of Deuteronomy 27:4]. There you shall build an altar to the LORD your God, an altar of stones. Do not wield an iron tool over them; you must build the altar of the LORD your God of unhewn stones. You shall offer on it burnt offerings to the LORD your God, and you shall sacrifice there offerings of well-being and eat them rejoicing before the LORD your God on that mountain beyond the west road, that is in the land of the Canaanites who dwell in the Arabah—near Gilgal, by the terebinth of Moreh. (Samaritan Pentateuch to Exodus 20:14b)

When we read Joshua's farewell speech at Shechem, we find a very different version of Israelite history from that in the Bible's main narrative. According to this history, the people of Israel always worshiped idols: "In olden times, your forefathers—Terah, father of Abraham and father of Nahor—lived beyond the Euphrates and worshiped other gods" (Joshua 24:2). The Israelites' worship of idols continued, according to this chapter, when they lived in Egypt, as we learn from Joshua's words: "Now, therefore, revere the LORD and serve Him with undivided loyalty; put away the gods that your forefathers served beyond the Euphrates and in Egypt, and serve the LORD" (v. 14). The notion that the Israelites worshiped idols in Egypt is shared by only one other chapter in the Bible, in Ezekiel: "I said to them: Cast away, every one of you, the detestable things that you are drawn to, and do not defile yourselves with the fetishes of Egypt—I the LORD am your God. But they defied Me and refused to listen to Me. They did not cast away the detestable things they were drawn to, nor did they give up the fetishes of Egypt. Then I resolved to pour out My fury upon them, to vent all My anger upon them there, in the land of Egypt" (20:7–8).

The view that the Israelites did not stop worshiping idols when they became a nation and that their idol worship persisted up until Joshua's parting words is consistent with what Joshua relates about the Israelites' passage from Egypt to Israel. After mentioning the Exodus and the crossing of the Sea of Reeds (Joshua 24:5–7), Joshua quickly sums up the wilderness years with the words "You had lived a long time in the wilderness" (v. 7), making no mention of any of the events that occurred there according to the account in the Pentateuch, the most important among them being the giving of the Torah. The reason seems obvious: the giving of the Law was impossible so long as the Israelites continued to worship idols, seeing that the first condition for receiving the Law was accepting the one God: "You shall have no other gods besides Me" (Exodus 20:3 = Deuteronomy 5:7).

The internal logic of the tradition that we find in Joshua 24 permits the giving of the Torah to the Israelites only now, in Shechem, after they have committed themselves to worshiping God alone and are ready to accept the yoke of the covenant that will be established with Him:

In reply, the people declared, "Far be it from us to forsake the LORD and serve other gods! For it was the LORD our God who brought us and our fathers up from the land of Egypt, the house of Bondage, and who wrought those wondrous signs before our very eyes, and guarded us all along the way that we traveled and among all the peoples through whose midst we passed. And then the LORD drove out before us all the peoples—the Amorites—that inhabited the country. We too will serve the LORD, for He is our God." (vv. 16–18)

Once the people have firmly committed to serve God, Joshua directs them to cast off the foreign gods in their possession ("Then put away the alien gods that you have among you and direct your hearts to the LORD, the God of Israel" [24:23]), at which point the people reaffirm their willingness to receive the burden of worshiping God: "We will serve the LORD our God, and we will obey him" (v. 24). The people's removal of the idols, their acknowledgment of God, and their willingness to serve Him open the way for Joshua to finally give the Torah to Israel: "Joshua made a covenant for the people on that day and he made a fixed rule for them in Shechem. Joshua recorded all this in a book of divine Torah. He took a great stone and set it up under the *'alah* [this is a deliberate alteration of the word *'elah*, "terebinth"; see below] in the sacred precinct of the LORD" (vv. 25–26).

These verses—few as they are—represent an alternative tradition to that of Moses giving the Torah to Israel in the wilderness. According to Joshua 24, Joshua gave the Torah to Israel in the temple in Shechem. The polemic between this and the dominant Sinai tradition is noticeable when we compare our verses with those from the Pentateuch. The people's words in Joshua 24:24, "We will serve the LORD our God, and we will obey him," are an interpretation and expansion of the people's words at Sinai: "All that the LORD has spoken we will do and obey" (Exodus 24:7). The statement "he made a fixed rule for them in Shechem" (Joshua 24:25) is a clear parallel to what is said about the giving of the Law at Marah before the events of Sinai: "There He made for them a fixed rule, and there He put them to the test" (Exodus 15:25; see chapter 9). The relationship between these verses was felt by the writer of the *Tanḥuma* when he concluded, "Moses wrote the Torah, as it is said, 'Moses wrote down this Torah' (Deut. 31:9), and Joshua, too, 'Joshua recorded all this in a book of divine Torah' (Josh. 24:26). In all [they are equal]" (*Tanḥuma, Tetzaveh* 9).

That Joshua assumes Moses's place as Israel's giver of the Law should not surprise us, since more than once he is portrayed as a "second Moses." We'll illustrate this with two of the many available examples, the first having to do with crossing water.

The miracle of splitting the Jordan by Joshua seals the Exodus experience and marks the Israelites' entrance into the Land of Israel. In the story we hear echoes of the story of Moses splitting the Sea of Reeds, which began the story of the redemption of Israel from Egypt. At the end of the account of the parting of the Jordan, it is said: "On that day the LORD exalted Joshua in the sight of all Israel, so that they feared him all his days as they had feared Moses" (Joshua 4:14; cf. 3:7: "The LORD said to Joshua, 'This day, for the first time, I will exalt you in the sight of all Israel, so that they shall know that I will be with you as I was with Moses'"). These words recall what is said in the Pentateuch following the splitting of the Sea of Reeds: "The people feared the LORD, they had faith in the LORD and His servant Moses" (Exodus 14:31).

The description of the stopping of the Jordan, too, in which "the waters of the Jordan . . . [stood] in a single heap" (Joshua 3:13), contains an echo from the Song of the Sea, where the Sea of Reeds is said to have "stood straight like a heap" (Exodus 15:8).

Another way in which Joshua is depicted as a second Moses concerns the tradition of the burning bush, where an angel of the Lord appears to Moses, who, turning to see it, hears a call to "remove your sandals from your feet, for the place on which you stand is holy ground" (Exodus 3:5). Similar words are spoken by the "captain of the LORD's host," who reveals himself to Joshua on the eve of the battle of Jericho: "Remove your sandal from your foot, for the place where you stand is holy" (Joshua 5:15). It is an interesting fact that many Hebrew manuscripts of the Bible, along with some of the ancient versions, formulate the verse in Joshua in the plural ("sandals," "feet"), as it appears in Exodus. In this way they continue to strengthen the explicit similarity between the verses, whose aim, as we said, was to direct our attention to the likeness between Joshua and his mentor, Moses. (On the flow of traditions in the opposite direction, from Joshua to Moses, see chapter 5.)

A glance at Joshua 24 reveals, therefore, a remarkable tradition. It was told, no doubt, by pilgrims on their journey to the temple in Shechem, worshipers confident that Israel had received its Torah in Shechem at the site where the temple now stood. These worshipers knew of the sacred terebinth tree that grew there, under which Joshua had placed a stone as an eternal reminder of the giving of the Law at that place.

The tradition of the giving of the Law in Shechem, integral to the worldview of the Northern Kingdom's inhabitants, must have awakened significant opposition among those who held to the wilderness tradition, particularly among the supporters of the Jerusalem Temple. Evidence for the polemic waged by these opponents against the sanctity of Shechem and the giving of the Torah there awaits us in a most surprising place: Genesis 35, the story of Jacob's journey to Bethel in order to build an altar to the Lord on his return from exile in Haran (vv. 1–7). To this story, a tradition seems to have been appended that told of the removal of alien idols and their subsequent burial beneath the terebinth in Shechem. The tradition begins with Jacob's command, "Put away the alien gods in your midst" (v. 2), and continues with a description of the people's compliance: "They gave to Jacob all the alien gods that they had, and the rings that were in their ears, and Jacob buried them under the terebinth that was near Shechem" (v. 4).

One should notice that Jacob was not commanded by God to remove these alien gods but only to proceed from Shechem to Bethel and to erect there an altar: "God said to Jacob, 'Arise, go up to Bethel . . . and build an altar there'" (Genesis 35:1). The act of removing the idols and burying them is depicted, therefore, as the fruit of Jacob's own initiative, and the members of Jacob's household indeed fulfill his instruction before they turn to God's command. On the other hand, another of Jacob's instructions (about whose execution, however, we don't hear) deals, as we would expect, with preparations for the anticipated meeting with God, "purify yourselves and change your clothes" (v. 2). We can compare the instructions given to the Israelites at Mount Sinai: "Moses came down from the mountain to the people and warned the people to stay pure and they washed their clothes" (Exodus 19:14).

The tradition about casting off idols in Genesis 35 calls to mind the assembly in Shechem that is described in Joshua 24: Jacob's command to the people to rid themselves of idolatry, "Put away the alien gods in your midst" (Genesis 35:2), reminds us of Joshua's words to "put away the alien gods that you have among you" (Joshua 24:23). Both traditions describe an object's burial under the terebinth tree in Shechem: "And Jacob buried them under the terebinth that was near Shechem" (Genesis 35:4), and "[Joshua] took a great stone and set it up under the terebinth in the sacred precinct of the LORD" (Joshua 24:26).

We begin to comprehend the relationship between the two episodes when we realize how the primary components of the tradition in Genesis 35—the Shechem terebinth and what is buried beneath it—are both found in Joshua 24; indeed, they are both taken from it. It is as though the Pentateuch tells readers of Genesis 35 that the place that some consider to be sacred, the temple in Shechem, is actually not holy at all but impure. Moreover, what is actually buried under the terebinth are alien gods that were buried there by Jacob. It would be inconceivable for a place concealing the remnants of idol worship to be sacred.

The polemical story in Genesis 35 thus strikes out against the belief in Shechem's sanctity. Even more, the story stresses the impurity that saturates the earth under the holy tree in that city, the "terebinth that was near Shechem." The story's polemical character was felt by the Greek translator of the Septuagint (or by the scribe who wrote the Hebrew manuscript from which that translator worked), who added: "until this very day." The appended words take the story out of its immediate, onetime context, which describes an event that occurred in the distant past, and grant it continuing relevance: the site remains contaminated until this very day. In order to strengthen the argument and emphasize Shechem's defilement, the story depicts Jacob burying the idols—not burning them and tossing the ashes into the wind, as we would expect from the laws in the Pentateuch (see Deuteronomy 7:5, 25, 12:3) or from Moses's actions with the molten calf (Exodus 32:20), or even what the kings of Judah did when they cleansed the temple and Jerusalem (1 Kings 15:13; 2 Kings 23:6).

One quick remark regarding the vocalization *'alah* instead of *'elah*, "terebinth," that we find in the Masoretic Text of Joshua 24:26. It is worth noting that the Septuagint preserves the original reading of *'elah*, "terebinth." The change in the vowels (which involved replacing the *tsere* under the letter *'alep* with *patah*), producing a word with no meaning, *'alah*, stems from the work of the Masoretes (ninth-century scribes who inserted the vowel signs into the text), who didn't care about the polemical strategy of the addition in Genesis 35. Instead, they were concerned with avoiding a contradiction between Genesis 35 and Joshua 24: under the terebinth (*'elah*) were buried the idols in the days of Jacob, while under the *'alah* (whatever that may be) Joshua placed a stone. The word *'alah*, with this specific vocalization, appears only here in the entire Bible. Also, manuscripts of *Targum Jonathan ben Uzziel* to the Prophets reflect the original reading of the word, *'elah*, "terebinth."

In Shechem, therefore, there was a tree to which the inhabitants of the North attributed great sanctity, a situation expressed also in the many names that we find for it. One is found in Genesis 12:6, where the tree is called Elon Moreh, "Oak of the Oracle," and its location identified as the spot where Abraham erected an altar. A similar name, Elo-nei Moreh, appears in the description of the ceremony of blessing and curse that takes place in Shechem immediately following the Israelites' entrance to the Land of Israel (Deuteronomy 11:30). In Judges 9:37 we find Elon-meonenim, which carries the same meaning as Elon Moreh (compare Habakkuk 2:18, "For an image and a false oracle [*moreh*]," with Deuteronomy 18:10–11, "Let no one be found among you who . . . is an augur, a soothsayer [*me'onen*], a diviner, a sorcerer . . . who casts spells or one who consults ghosts or familiar spirits"). The tree is known also as Elon Mutzav (Judges 9:6; *matzevah* signifies a pillar, a sacred stone that was set up for cultic purposes). *Targum Jonathan ben Uzziel* translates this name as *meishar qamta'*, which Rashi explains as "a valley in which were placed pillars"; the Septuagint records the name as *Alon Ha-Mutzav* (or *ha-matzevah*).

This verse perhaps indicates that the stone that stood under the holy tree in Shechem served as a cultic pillar. It is indeed interesting to observe the discomfort of the Aramaic translators with the existence of such holy trees, especially in and around Shechem, which led them to prefer to construe *'elon* not as a type of tree but as *mishor*, "valley." We've already mentioned *Targum Jonathan ben Uzziel* to Judges 9:6 (*meishar qamta'*), but here we will mention also his translation of Judges 9:37, where *'elon me'onenim*, "Oak of the Soothsayers," is translated as "Valley of the Soothsayers," and so also *Targum Onqelos* to Genesis 12:6, which translated Elon Moreh with *meishar moreh*, "Valley of the Oracle."

Where Was the Law Given?

The polemical verses in Genesis 35 returned to play a similar role in the anti-Samaritan polemic during the Rabbinic period.

> R. Ishmael son of R. Yossi went up to pray in Jerusalem. He passed a terebinth grove and was seen by a Samaritan who asked him, "Where are you going?" He said: "To go up to worship in Jerusalem." He said: "Would it not be better to pray at this blessed mountain than at that dunghill?" He said: "I will tell you what you resemble, a dog eager for carrion. Because you know that idols are hidden beneath it, for it is written, 'And Jacob hid them,' therefore you are eager for it." (*Genesis Rabbah* 81:3)

The recurrence of the controversy during the Rabbinic period is evidence that the battle for prestige between Shechem and Jerusalem was not concluded during the biblical period; indeed, its fire continued to blaze as the chasm between Jews and Samaritans deepened. We have seen how, to the Sinai-Shechem conflict, another front was added: Jerusalem, the city that had come to lead the attack against Shechem's sanctity. In Jerusalem, which claimed primacy, there even developed a tradition that told how, within its walls, the Torah would again be given in the Days to Come, this time to the nations of the world:

> In the days to come the Mount of the LORD's House shall stand firm above the mountains and tower above the hills; and all the nations shall gaze on it with joy. And the many peoples shall go and say: "Come, let us go up to the Mount of the LORD, to the House of the God of Jacob; that he may instruct us in His ways, and that we may walk in His paths." For Torah shall come forth from Zion, the word of the LORD from Jerusalem. (Isaiah 2:2–3)

13

When and How Was the
City of Dan Sanctified?

After leading his revolt, establishing the Kingdom of Israel, and splitting the tribes of Israel from the tribe of Judah—thus disassociating his
new kingdom from the Davidic dynasty and its capital, Jerusalem—
Jeroboam son of Nebat was in need of an alternative capital. Jerusalem
was not only the administrative seat of the Kingdom of Judah but its
religious heart, in which was kept the Ark of the Lord, the Ark that had
accompanied Israel since the days in the wilderness and signified the
presence of God and His approval of the Temple, His dwelling place.
The book of Kings reports King Jeroboam's fear that the people will
continue to cling to Jerusalem: "Jeroboam said to himself, 'Now the
kingdom may well return to the House of David. If these people still
go up to offer sacrifices at the House of the LORD in Jerusalem, the
heart of these people will turn back to their master, King Rehoboam
of Judah; they will kill me and go back to King Rehoboam of Judah'" (1
Kings 12:26–27). The king thus resolved to fashion two golden calves
in commemoration of the wilderness tradition and as a substitute for
the Ark, which was in Jerusalem (see chapters 11 and 24). He placed
the calves in the Kingdom of Israel's temples, considered sacred for
generations: "He set one in Bethel and placed the other in Dan" (v. 29).

The tradition of Bethel's sanctity roots itself in the Patriarchal stories, particularly the story of Jacob's dream, where Jacob sees that "a
stairway was set on the ground and its head reached to the heavens,
and angels of God were going up and down on it" (Genesis 28:12), after

which he declares, "How awesome is this place! This is none other than the house of God [*beit 'elohim*], and this is the gate to heaven" (v. 17). The story ends with Jacob's vow and pronouncement: "The LORD will be my God. And this stone, which I have set up as a pillar, will be the house of God [*beit 'elohim*]" (vv. 21–22). The sanctity of Bethel—*beit 'el*—was well secured.

But what of the sanctity of Dan? That Israelite city and its cult were founded when the Danites settled in Laish, in the North (Judges 18). True, that story—along with the next (about the concubine of Gibeah, in Judges 19–21)—is framed by the repeating formula, "In those days there was no king in Israel; every man did as he pleased" (Judges 17:6, 21:25, the first part of the formula appears in 18:1, 19:1). The repetitions emphasize the anarchy that reigned then in Israel and justify the approaching transition from the weak and unstable rule of the judges to the establishment of the monarchy. Even so, the original meaning of the story about the Danites was quite different: it aimed to mock and ridicule the worship of God in Dan and to recount the sins of its founders.

The incident with which the story begins concerns Micah, a man from the hill country of Ephraim. Micah steals silver from his mother, but when he learns that she has uttered a curse on the unknown thief, he quickly and fearfully returns the stolen property. Upon discovering his identity, Micah's mother hurriedly lifts the threat of her curse and even vows to consecrate the returned silver and make from it a "sculptured image and a molten image" (Judges 17:1–4) or even "an ephod and teraphim" (v. 5; all these terms appear also in the story's continuation, in Judges 18:14, 17–18, and 20). With the stolen silver now safe, Micah's mother upholds her promise, although she dedicates only a small portion of the silver to the making of the sculptured and molten image. Once these cultic implements have been made, Micah is in need of religious officiators. Initially, he nominates one of his sons to serve as priest (Judges 17:5) but soon decides to hire the services of a Levite, who arrives from Bethlehem (vv. 7–13).

The tale's continuation redirects the spotlight to another arena, to the Danites, who now search for new territory, their original land between Tzora and Eshtaol having proved insufficient. The Danites dispatch spies, who pass Micah's house and see his house-shrine. When they later migrate northward to the territory their spies find for them, they, too, stop at Micah's house in the hill country of Ephraim and persuade the shrine's priest to join them. Well armed, they remove the cultic implements by force and threats. When the Danites arrive in their new territory, to the city Laish (whose name they change to Dan), they establish a temple there and erect in it the pilfered images. In this way we learn that the Danite cult was founded on twofold thievery: Micah robbing his mother and the Danites robbing Micah.

When we examine the terms that characterize the cultic articles Micah made, we find that they also reflect poorly on the Danites and their temple. To understand that the Danites' installation of these articles signals their practice of idolatry, we need only remember Deuteronomy 27:15: "Cursed be anyone who makes a sculptured or molten image, abhorred by the LORD a craftsman's handiwork." The word *masekha*, "molten image," of course reminds us of the calf that the Israelites made in the wilderness (see, e.g., Exodus 32:4; Deuteronomy 9:17). The names of the other objects, the ephod and teraphim, conjure up memories of idolatry. Though the ephod is the name of an article of the priests' clothing and though it was made in the wilderness according to a divine command (e.g., Exodus 28:6), it is also the name of a pagan object, as we see when the judge Gideon erects an ephod in Ophrah: "There all Israel went astray after [the ephod] and it became a snare to Gideon and his household" (Judges 8:27). Likewise do the teraphim in our story bring to mind the teraphim Rachel stole from her father when she set out with Jacob and his household for Canaan (a story that begins in Genesis 31:19), the same teraphim that Laban referred to as "my gods" (v. 30).

Incidentally, it is worth taking a moment to consider the deliberate use our tale makes of the story of Rachel and the teraphim.

- About Rachel it is said, "Rachel stole her father's household idols [*teraphim*]" (Genesis 31:19), while about the Danites we read, "[They] took the sculptured image . . . and the household idols [*teraphim*]" (Judges 18:17).
- In both stories the robbed individuals set out in pursuit of the thieves: "[Laban] caught up to him in the hill country of Gilead" (Genesis 31:23); "[Micah's men] caught up to the Danites" (Judges 18:22); both verses include the rarely used root *d-b-q*, "catch up."
- The victims complain to the robbers: Laban asks, "But why did you steal my gods?" (Genesis 31:30), and Micah complains: "The gods that I made, you have taken" (Judges 18:24).
- The claimant fails to retrieve his stolen property, and both he and the accused go on their way: "Then Laban left on his journey homeward. Jacob went on his way" (Genesis 32:1–2); "the Danites went on their way and Micah, realizing that they were stronger than he, turned back and went home" (Judges 18:26).

The comparison presents the Danites in a harsher light than Rachel. While the matriarch did what she did in secret, after Laban left to shear his sheep, the Danites steal in broad daylight, for all to see. While Jacob, ignorant of the theft, denies it, the Danites deny nothing and even threaten to kill Micah and his men, who seek the return of their property: "Don't do any shouting at us, or some desperate men might attack you, and you and your family would lose your lives" (Judges 18:25).

The plainly mocking tone of the story of Micah's sculptured image and of the foundation of the cult in Dan reflects the story's having been written in the Kingdom of Judah, where it effectively reputed the legitimacy of the Danite cult. Behind the story's hostile, polemical character, however, is it at all possible to detect anything of the narrative that the Danites themselves told about the beginnings of their worship of God in their city? It is hard to believe that the Danites, like inhabitants of other sacred cities, did not tell stories about their city's founding and the beginnings of its cult. One can be sure that the story in Judges was not the story told in Dan itself.

In fact, the Danites' own tale seems to float just below the surface of the story in Judges. Just as the tale of Rachel and the teraphim was used by the Judahite writers to mock Dan's sanctity, so did another biblical story, that of the Exodus and the conquering of the land—the most important and formative event in the collective memory of the Israelites during the biblical period—also leave its mark on our story. In this case, however, the work was that of the writers from Dan and the Kingdom of Israel. Echoes from the stories of the Exodus and the conquering of the Land of Israel can still be heard in this story, even in its present, antagonistic version. Here are its details, revealed through a comparison with the Pentateuch's story of the Exodus.

- Spies are dispatched by the community leaders in order to explore the territory to be conquered (Numbers 13:1–10; Judges 18:2).
- The spies return with a detailed report of what they have seen (Numbers 13:26–33; Judges 18:8–10), and the phrasing is similar: "The land that we traversed and scouted is a very, very good land" (Numbers 14:7); "For we found that the land was very good" (Judges 18:9).
- The people who hear the spies' reports respond inappropriately. In the Pentateuch, the Israelites become frightened, falling into a disarray of helplessness (Numbers 14:1–4), whereas in our story it becomes apparent from the reprimand of the spies—"and you are sitting idle! Don't delay; go and invade the land and take possession of it" (Judges 18:9)—that the people balked at entering and taking possession of the land that they were promised.
- When they set out, it is not only the warriors who are mentioned but also the rest of the people along with their cattle and herds (Exodus 12:37–38; Judges 18:21).
- From Egypt, "about six hundred thousand" fighters left (Exodus 12:37), and in the tribe of Dan they were "six hundred strong, girt with weapons of war" (Judges 18:11).
- In the course of their wanderings and on the way to the designated territory, the journeyers acquire cultic articles, which they will erect afterward in the temple that they build at their destination. Just as

in Solomon's temple is placed the Ark of God, which was formed at the base of Mount Sinai (1 Kings 8:9), so the Danites set up Micah's sculptured image in their city (Judges 18:30).

- The change of the city's name from Laish to Dan—"and they named the town Dan, after their ancestor Dan who was Israel's son. Originally, however, the name of the town was Laish" (Judges 18:29)—harks back to the similar changes in the names of cities settled by the Israelites in their land. (See, e.g., 1:17: "And Judah with its brother-tribe Simeon went on and defeated the Canaanites who dwelt in Zephath. They proscribed it, and so the town was named Hormah." See also vv. 10–11, 23.)

The desire to shape the beginning of life at Dan and the cult there as a sort of mini-Exodus, an Exodus experienced solely by the tribe of Dan, is noticeable in another detail. At the close of the story in Judges 18, the reader notices a certain duplication between verses 30 and 31: according to verse 31, the sculptured image stood "throughout the time that the House of God stood at Shiloh," and verse 30, speaking also about the sculptured image, states: "The Danites set up the sculptured image for themselves and Jonathan son of Gershom son of Manasseh, and his descendants, served as priests to the Danite tribe until the land went into exile." But the verses also contain a contradiction: Did worship in Dan continue until the destruction of Shiloh in the days of Samuel at the end of the period of the judges, or did it continue until the destruction of the Kingdom of Israel? Verse 31 also reveals the identity of the priesthood that served in Dan, but the name Manasseh—*menasheh*—is written strangely in the verse, with the letter *nun* raised, floating above the other letters. This odd phenomenon has a curious explanation: originally, the name was not *menasheh*, but *mosheh*—Moses, the leader of the Israelites at the time of the Exodus. Moses's genealogical details—that he was from the tribe of Levi (Exodus 2:1) and that one of his sons was named Gershom (2:22, 18:3)—correspond with those in our story.

At a secondary stage, however, someone wanted to prevent any association between the cult at Dan and Moses and his descendants and decided to transform the name *mosheh* into *menasheh*, but finding no room for the necessary *nun*, he hung the letter above the already written name. Scribes who subsequently copied the manuscript faithfully represented the graphic peculiarity and left the *nun* hanging above the word (this is not the only case where we have hanging letters; see, e.g., Psalm 80:14; Job 38:13). Some manuscripts of the Septuagint indeed preserve the reading "Moses," and even the Rabbis sensed that the verse referred not to Manasseh but to Moses: "Was he the son of Manasseh? Surely he was the son of Moses, for it is written, 'the sons of Moses: Gershom, and Eliezer' (1 Chron. 23:15), but [you must say that] because he acted [wickedly] as Manasseh, the Scriptural text ascribed his descent to Manasseh" (B. *Bava Batra* 109b). Rashi explains: "In regard for Moses's honor is the *nun* written, in order to change the name, and it is written hanging, to say that it was not Manasseh but Moses" (Rashi to Judges 18:31). Manasseh, of course, was one of the worst transgressors amongst the kings of Israel (2 Kings 21:1–18).

Parenthetically, we will add that it is no wonder that Jeroboam, who is portrayed in traditions from the Kingdom of Israel as a "second Moses" (see chapter 24), decided to renew the cult of the golden calf (which was also connected with the Exodus story) specifically in the city of Dan, whose sanctification, as we have seen, was apparently established on the foundations of the Exodus tradition.

We return now to the duplication that we found in the closing verses of the story of the founding of the temple in Dan. It seems that, in the story that was hostile to Dan, there originally appeared only verse 31: "They maintained the sculptured image that Micah had made throughout the time that the House of God stood at Shiloh." The people of Dan, or writers from the Kingdom of Israel, who wanted to defend the honor of their temple and challenge their opponents, introduced verse 30 into the story at a secondary stage. From it we learn that the temple in Dan remained functioning for a long period and that, in the Kingdom of Israel, Moses (as the name originally appeared) was considered the founder of the priesthood that served there. It is interesting that, according to this tradition, there did not exist the separation of authority that was the norm in the Kingdom of Judah between prophet (Moses) and priest (Aaron and his brothers) and that in the Kingdom of Israel Moses was the archetype also for the priesthood. The battle between the different views continued to rage, therefore, even after the addition of verse 30, which mentions Moses, as evidenced by the unsuccessful attempt to obscure his identity by changing the name to Manasseh.

The ancient story about the founding of the cult in Dan was, as we said, a tale of a mini-Exodus, and its protagonist was a priest, a descendant of Moses, the hero of the Exodus from Egypt. In a tale that tells of a cult's origins, however, a reader also expects some sign that God chose that particular spot and that the worship of God in that place corresponded with the Deity's desire. This is what we find in many stories about the origins of cultic sites. We've already mentioned the story of Jacob's vision in Bethel, his dream of the stairway, and we also recall how Jacob was again granted a vision in Bethel when he returned from exile in Haran (Genesis 35:9–15). The location of the cult in Jerusalem was determined only when the plague, that struck all of Israel (as a punishment for the census David ordered), was halted exactly there: "But when the angel extended his hand against Jerusalem to destroy it, the LORD renounced further punishment and said to the angel who was destroying the people, 'Enough! Stay your hand!' The angel of the LORD was then by the threshing floor of Araunah the Jebusite" (2 Samuel 24:16); this is the place where David will be commanded to build the altar to the Lord (v. 18).

The writer of the book of 1 Chronicles even adds a further miraculous element. In his retelling of the tale, he recounts how fire descended from heaven to the chosen altar: "And David built there an altar to the LORD and sacrificed burnt offerings and offerings of well-being. He invoked the LORD, who answered him with fire from heaven on the altar of burnt-offerings" (21:26). A similar miracle takes place, according to the Chronicler, when Solomon's temple in Jerusalem is consecrated, the final act in the establishment of the cult in that city whose beginnings were in the story of the threshing floor of Araunah:

When Solomon finished praying, fire descended from heaven and consumed the burnt offering and the sacrifices, and the glory of the Lord filled the House. The priests could not enter the House of the Lord, for the glory of the Lord filled the House of the Lord. All the Israelites witnessed the descent of the fire and the glory of the Lord on the House; they knelt with their faces to the ground and prostrated themselves, praising the Lord, "For He is good, for His steadfast love is eternal." (2 Chronicles 7:1–3)

In this description we see the clear stamp of the story of the consecration of the altar at the base of Mount Sinai: "Moses and Aaron then went inside the Tent of Meeting. When they came out, they blessed the people; and the Presence of the Lord appeared to all the people. Fire came forth from before the Lord and consumed the burnt offering and the fat parts on the altar. And all the people saw and shouted and fell on their faces" (Leviticus 9:23–24).

Miracles like these—fire descending from the heavens or a vision of God testifying to His wanting the cult in that place—have been erased entirely from the story of Dan. The explanation of God's attachment to the site seems to have been lost entirely with the tale's transformation from one of praise to one of derision: the story we now have has been presented to us in order to disgrace that city and its cult. Only a bit of the tradition that exalted the temple in Dan has reached us, and that only by way of our reconstructing its shadow, using the tools of literary archaeology.

3

Biblical Heroes and Their Biographies

14

What Did Ham Do to His Father?

When the waters of the Flood subsided and Noah and his sons finally stepped off the ark, Noah plants a vineyard. (He is the first to do so: he is the first vintner according to the book of Genesis.) Noah drinks, and his son Ham sees his drunken father naked and tells his brothers, Shem and Japhet. Concerned for their father's honor, Shem and Japhet cover him, taking care not to look. When Noah awakens from his stupor, he curses Canaan, Ham's son, and blesses Shem and Japhet (Genesis 9:20–27).

While the particular sin of Ham is not stated explicitly, it is clear that it was sexual. Evidently, the Flood was inadequate to effect real change: the Flood came after the sons of god had relations with the daughters of men (Genesis 6:1–4; see chapter 2), intimate relations incongruous with the laws of Creation, and then, immediately following the Flood, we find another sexual sin, in this case involving a son and his father. We see here a pessimistic view of human nature: left to their own devices, humankind quickly returns to its sinful ways.

But what was Ham's sin? The drunken Noah lies in his tent, and his nakedness is seen by his son. On the surface of it, Ham's involvement would appear to be limited to the act of seeing: "Ham the father of Canaan saw his father's nakedness" (Genesis 9:22). It expresses more than a simple lack of respect for his father, though, since Ham doesn't hurry to cover his father's nakedness but rushes, instead, to share his impressions with his brothers: "And [he] told his two brothers outside." Strengthening the impression that we deal only with Ham's disrespect toward his father, his witnessing something and no more, is the response of his brothers. Shem and Japhet, unlike Ham, act quickly to cover their father, taking care not to glimpse Noah's naked body: "But Shem and Japhet took a cloth, placed it against both their backs and, walking backward, they covered their father's nakedness; their faces were turned the other way, so that they did not see their father's nakedness" (v. 23).

And still, we cannot help but suspect that the story intimates that a transgression more serious than merely "peeping" took place. In Biblical Hebrew, "see nakedness" carries also sexual meaning, as, for instance, in Leviticus 20:17: "If a man marries his sister, the daughter of either his father or his mother, so that he *sees her nakedness and she sees his nakedness* ... they shall be cut off in the sight of their kinsfolk. He has uncovered the nakedness of his sister, he shall bear his guilt." Our suspicions are strengthened by Noah's reaction: "Noah woke up from his wine and knew what his youngest son had done to him" (Genesis 9:24). The words "done to him" are a bit strong for referring to the consequence of merely being "seen"—which leaves no physical trace—whereas upon waking, Noah is immediately aware that something has been done to him.

The curse and punishment are directed at Canaan, Ham's son. This accords with the "measure for measure" principle: the son's violation of his father causes his own son to be harmed. The Bible defames both Canaanites and Egyptians, who were also Ham's descendants (see Genesis 10:6), and associates each with some sort of unsanctioned sexual activity. Leviticus 18, which addresses incest, begins: "You shall not copy the practices of the land of Egypt where you dwelt or of the land of Canaan to which I am taking you; nor shall you follow their laws" (v. 3), and see the fears voiced by Abraham in Genesis 12 regarding his wife's fate in the hands of the Egyptians, particularly vv. 11–12: "I know what a beautiful woman you are. If the Egyptians see you ..." The idea is found also in Ezekiel 23:8: "She did not give up the whoring she had begun with the Egyptians," and verse 20, in which the Egyptians are described as those whose "members were like those of asses and whose organs were like those of stallions." This sexual vilification of Egypt and Canaan is rooted in the story of Ham and his father and is evidence that the kernel of that story indeed alludes to a sexual act.

Thus far we have taken into consideration the sexual transgressions that occurred both immediately before the Flood (the story of miscegenation between sons of god and daughters of men) and after it (the story of Ham). A broader view brings us to consider also the story of Sodom and Gomorrah, in Genesis 19. The symmetry between the beginning and end of the Flood story and the beginning and end of the story of Sodom and Gomorrah, we suggest, will help illuminate the nature of Ham's act.

The beginning and end of these stories display perfectly oppositional symmetry. Like the Deluge story, the tale of Sodom and Gomorrah is caught between two pictures of sexual depravity. The behavior of the Sodomites, who threaten Lot's guests and demand to "know" them (Genesis 19:5), is evidence of the city's perversion that justifies its destruction. Following the city's devastation, Lot's daughters force their father to have relations with them (vv. 30–38). We can best see the symmetry with the help of this table.

	Flood	Sodom
Before	sons of god → daughters of men (males → females)	humans → angels (males → males)
After	father → son (male → male)	daughters → father (females → male)

The scene that opens the Flood story is one in which males (sons of god) initiate relations with females (daughters of men). In the scene that closes the story of Sodom, females (Lot's daughters) initiate relations with their father. In both stories, the unions result in progeny. In the scene that opens the story of Sodom, the Sodomites pursue relations with male angels (Genesis 19:5), corresponding to the closing picture of the Flood story, which, as we'll soon see, speaks of sexual relations between men.

The oppositional relationship between the stories is not only of a chiastic nature—that is, between the scene that opens one story and the scene that closes the other—but also horizontal—between the opening and the closing scenes. Regarding the opening scenes, in the Flood story we find that the divine beings pursue relations with the daughters of men (Genesis 6:2), whereas in Sodom and Gomorrah it is the humans who desire relations with the angels (19:5), with relations being consummated in the former but not the latter.

The story of the Flood ends with Noah freely drinking himself into a stupor (Genesis 9:21), whereas the story of Sodom ends with Lot's daughters compelling their father to drink till drunkenness (19:33–35). Noah realizes what has occurred, "Noah woke up from his wine and knew what his youngest son had done to him" (9:24), whereas Lot has no idea, "He did not know when she lay down or when she rose" (19:33, 35). Noah, who knows what his son has done, curses the son of his son, Canaan (9:25), while Lot, who remains ignorant, does not curse his daughters' offspring (though they, too, will be included among the cursed and will be forbidden admission into the congregation of the Lord; see Deuteronomy 23:4).

Midrash *Genesis Rabbah* 51:8, we should mention, sensed the connection between the two stories and concluded that Lot was aware of his eldest daughter's rising to leave: "'He did not know when she lay down or when she rose,' [there is] a dot above [the word *u-ve-qumah*, "when she rose," meaning]: her laying down he did not know but her rising up he did." The tradition refers to a dot that appears above the word *u-ve-qumah* in Hebrew manuscripts of the Bible; it was this solitary mark that caused the writers of the midrash to conclude—as was their way with other words where similar marks appear—that the word should not be understood literally. According to this midrash, Lot, upon waking, knew very well what had taken place (just as Noah "knew what his youngest son had done to him"), and yet he failed to prevent the same event from occurring the following night, with his younger daughter. We see here how the story about Noah colored the sages' reading of the Lot story and led them to tighten the connection between the stories even more.

All this suggests an ancient tradition that recounted how Ham had relations with his father, a tradition that the Bible sought to conceal or, at the least, make do with an oblique allusion using vague language. In Rabbinic literature, however, the original tradition in all its strength swims just under the surface: "'And he knew what his youngest son had done to him.' Rav and Samuel [differ.] One says that he castrated him, the other says that he sexually abused him" (B. *Sanhedrin* 70a). While the notion that Ham castrates his father is found nowhere in the biblical story, it has not been plucked from nowhere. Philo of Byblos attests to a Phoenician tradition about the god Kronos, founder of the city Byblos, who castrates his father, Uranus, with Uranus's own knife. A Hurrite tradition tells how the god Kumarbi rebelled against the ruler of heaven, the god Anu, causing Anu to flee and allowing Kumarbi to reign in his stead. Kumarbi goes so far as to bite Anu's knee and swallow his genitals, for which he is cursed.

These traditions parallel the Greek myth about Kronos, who castrated his father, Uranus (the sky), and ruled in his stead. Each of these traditions speaks about a mythological, intergenerational conflict, but what was told in the polytheistic nations surrounding Israel about the battles of gods was transferred, in the monotheism of the Bible, to the human realm.

It becomes apparent, therefore, that the story about Noah and Ham developed through three stages. The first corresponds to the mythic tradition about a son injuring his father in order to prevent the father from producing more sons and dilute the older son's inheritance. The midrash states this explicitly in the case of Ham: "The Holy One, blessed be He, meant to issue four sons from Noah who would inherit the four winds of the earth. Ham said: I will castrate my father so that he will not produce a fourth son, in order that [this fourth son] will not share the world with us" (*Midrash ha-Gadol* to Genesis 9:25). Rashi, in his commentary on Genesis 9:25, writes that the castration was performed "for inheriting the world." Indeed, an act of castration would leave unquestionable evidence of the crime: "And [Noah] knew what his youngest son had done to him" (v. 24), and would also be grounds for the curse directed at the perpetrator's son: the one who was prevented from producing more sons utters a curse on the son of the one who castrated him. Also this idea is stated explicitly in Rabbinic literature: "You prevented me from producing a youngest son who would serve me; consequently, the same man [you] will be his brother's slave. . . . You prevented me from producing a fourth son, consequently I curse your fourth son" (*Genesis Rabbah* 36:7).

The Pentateuch retreated from the idea of the castration: Noah, "a righteous man" (Genesis 6:9), did not deserve such a fate. And so, in the second stage of the story's transformation, Noah's emasculation was replaced with sexual relations with his son. This stage is alluded to in the biblical story by the use of the expression "see nakedness" and is suggested also by the story's correlation with the Sodom and Gomorrah story, as we saw above. The third stage in the story's development involved the notion that Ham sinned only by "seeing" his father's nakedness and then running to tell his brothers.

The Bible struggles between these two last concepts and leaves readers in an interpretative fog, allowing them to decide. This choice demonstrates one of the Bible's fundamental principles of not always limiting readers to one interpretative channel. On the contrary, in certain cases the Bible encourages readers to consider a variety of options and assumes responsibility for the possibility that not everyone will reach identical conclusions.

Why, one may ask, was such an ugly tale about the righteous Noah not removed entirely from the Pentateuch? To this question we will say—apart from our general answer to such questions, which we offered in the introduction—that the story disparages two nations with whom ancient Israel was in contact, Egypt and Canaan, and calls for Israel's utter separation from them. It is also possible that the story was also used to justify the Israelites' conquest of the Land of Canaan. At least that is what is stated overtly in the Talmud: "The Canaanites said, The Land of Canaan belongs to us. . . . Geviha son of Pesisa said to them, . . . But [you are wrong, since] it is written in the Torah, 'Cursed be Canaan a servant of servants shall he be unto his brethren.' [Now:]

if a slave acquires property, to whom does he belong, and whose is the property?" (B. *Sanhedrin* 91a). Perhaps our story also reflects a rejection of excessive drinking that leads to drunkenness and unseemly behavior, a theme found in biblical literature, such as in Proverbs' explicit warnings (23:30–35). See also the conclusion drawn in the midrash, "Wherever you find wine you will find failure" (*Tanḥuma Buber, Noah* 21), to which many examples are brought, the first being the story of Noah. In any event, we can, at the least, say that the obfuscation of the story's objectionable contours was evidently enough to assure its place in the Bible.

15

Out of the Fire

Recovering the Story of Abraham's Origins

The Pentateuch is content with a laconic mention of Abraham's birth: "Now this is the line of Terah: Terah begot Abram, Nahor, and Haran" (Genesis 11:27). We rapidly learn of Abram's marriage to Sarai and of Sarai's barrenness (vv. 29–30), of the journey of Sarah and Abraham (as they will later be called) and Abraham's father "from Ur of the Chaldeans for the land of Canaan," and of their arrival to Haran (vv. 31–32), at which point we are ready to accompany the Patriarch on his journey to Canaan after God commands him to "go forth [*lekh lekha*]" (12:1).

Indeed, we are left to wonder why the Torah dodges this opportunity to tell us about Abraham's birth, seeing that the Bible relates many tales about the miraculous births of its heroes (most of them sons of barren women: Isaac, Jacob, Samson, and Samuel). Why was this part of the biography of the first forefather so diminished? In fact, it is not only Abraham's birth story that is missing from the Torah; his childhood and adolescence are also left unmined. Our first glimpse of Abraham as an active character comes only when he is already in Canaan and a (relatively) old man of seventy-five years (Genesis 12:4).

Before we address these questions directly and try to reconstruct the missing tradition about Abraham's youth, let us consider three distinct explanations that the book of Genesis offers for Abraham's leaving his father's home and journeying to Canaan.

1. Fulfilling His Father's Ambition

According to Genesis 11:27–32, which begins with "This is the line of Terah," it was Terah, Abraham's father, who initiated the departure from Ur of the Chaldeans to Canaan: "Terah took his son Abram, his grandson Lot the son of Haran, and his daughter-in-law Sarai, the wife of his son Abram, and they left with them from Ur of the Chaldeans for the land of Canaan; but when they had come as far as Haran, they settled there. The days of Terah came to 205 years; and Terah died in Haran." The natural continuation of these verses is found in Genesis 12:4–5: "Abram was seventy-five years old when he left Haran. Abram took his wife Sarai and his brother's son Lot, and all the wealth that they had amassed, and the persons that they had acquired in Haran; and they set out for the land of Canaan and they arrived to the land of Canaan." According to these verses, Abraham continues the journey that his father had begun.

Let's look at the chronology of this short episode. First we are told that "when Terah had lived 70 years, he begot Abram, Nahor, and Haran" (Genesis 11:26). Since, as we said, Abraham was 75 years old when he left Haran, we understand that Terah, at that point, was 145 years old. By this calculation, after Abraham left Haran, Terah lived 60 more years until his death at the age of 205 (v. 32). The reason Terah decided to stay in Haran and give up his idea of reaching the Land of Canaan—and why the son fulfills the father's ambition instead—is unknown.

The Samaritan version of the Torah preserves a different calculation of Terah's age at the time of his death: "145 years." According to the Samaritan Pentateuch, Terah died in Haran at roughly the time he arrived there, which would explain why he didn't continue the journey and why Abraham is presented as carrying out his father's wish. The chronology of the Samaritan Pentateuch is found also in the New Testament: "Then [Abraham] departed from the land of the Chaldeans, and lived in Haran. And after his father died, [God] removed him from there into this land in which you are now living" (Acts 7:4). It seems to us that this chronology, reflected in the Samaritan Pentateuch and the New Testament, is the original. (We will discuss the rationale of the masoretic version below.)

2. Obeying God

A different notion is found in Genesis 12:1–4, which depicts Abraham's journey to Canaan as the Patriarch's response to a divine command: "The LORD said to Abram, 'Go forth from your land and from your birthplace and from your father's house to the land that I will show you.'" One notes how, from this standpoint, Abraham leaves his home and birthplace, which is not named (though it is certainly not Haran), without being told the name of the land to which he is being directed. His ready response to the divine command elevates him significantly in our estimation, in comparison with the previous version. This time, Abraham's departure represents his fulfilling a test set by God, a trial the midrash viewed as one of "the ten tests [that] our father Abraham . . . was tested [with] and he stood steadfast in them all" (Mishnah *Avot* 5:3). A number of ancient Jewish sources have preserved a list of these tests, and all of them include the command to "go forth from your land" (e.g., *Avot de-Rabbi Natan*, version A, 33; *Pirkei de-Rabbi Eliezer* 26–31; the tradition is found already in *Jubilees* 17:17).[1]

3. An Expression of God's Mercy

The third view, like the first, clearly identifies Abraham's starting point as Ur of the Chaldeans. In the story of the Testament between the Parts (Genesis 15), God says to Abraham: "I am the LORD who brought you out from Ur of the Chaldeans to assign this land to you as a possession" (v. 7; see also Nehemiah 9:7: "You are the LORD God, who chose Abram, who brought him out of Ur of the Chaldeans and changed his name to Abraham"). The wording of the verse bears the stamp of the first commandment: "I the LORD am your God who brought you out of the land of Egypt, the house of bondage" (Exodus 20:2 = Deuteronomy 5:6). In the light of this analogy, we understand

---

1. Quotations from *Jubilees* are taken from *The Old Testament Pseudepigrapha*, vol. 2, trans. O. S. Wintermute, ed. J. H. Charlesworth (New Haven: Yale University Press, 1985).

God's words to Abraham as an expression of divine mercy. This view, therefore, is at odds with the notion that the journey comprised a trial by which Abraham was tested and that it was Abraham's response to the command to "go forth."

The most urgent tension is felt between the two first viewpoints, one depicting the trip as Terah's initiative, the other as a trial by which Abraham is tested. Already within the Bible, changes were inserted into the first tradition in order to blur this tension:

- Terah's death at 145 years, as recorded in both the Samaritan Penta-teuch and the New Testament, reflects, as we have said, the original version. By extending his life, the masoretic version wanted to create the impression that Terah changed his mind about his decision to journey to Canaan, while his son Abraham answered the divine command to "go forth" and to leave his father—still alive—behind.
- The words "and they left with them" in Genesis 11:31 ("Terah took his son Abram, his grandson Lot the son of Haran, and his daughter-in-law Sarai, the wife of his son Abram, *and they left with them* from Ur of the Chaldeans for the land of Canaan") are problematic in their present context. The original version is probably what we find in the Samaritan Pentateuch, Septuagint, and Vulgate: "Terah took his son Abram and Lot the son of Haran and Sarai his daughter-in-law the wife of Abram his son, and *he took them out* from Ur of the Chaldeans." Crediting Terah with initiating the journey was problematic for a tradition that emphasized how Abraham's journey to Canaan was the result of a divine command to "go forth . . ." For this reason, that part of the story line was obscured by changing *va-yotze'*, "and he took them out," into *va-yetz'u*, "and they left," transforming the departure into a collective act, similar to what is told in Genesis 12:5 of Abraham and his household: "And they set out for the land of Canaan."

Bolder attempts to create a compromise between these first two viewpoints were made outside the Hebrew Bible: "The God of glory appeared to our father Abraham, when he was in Mesopotamia, before he lived in Haran, and said to him, 'Go forth from your land and from your birthplace to the land that I will show you.' Then he departed from the land of the Chaldeans, and lived in Haran. And after his father died, God removed him from there into this land in which you are now living" (Acts 7:2–4). This hermeneutical feat manages to place the divine command before the family's departure from Ur of the Chaldeans and is an example of a common midrashic principle, "there is no earlier and later in the Torah"—that is, the biblical chronology is not binding. The New Testament has deleted from its version of the command the words "and from your father's house," since Abraham leaves Ur with his father and his father's household. As we've already written, the writer of Acts assumes the chronology as it is preserved in the Samaritan Pentateuch, according to which Abraham continues to Canaan from Haran after his father dies.

The placement of the command to "go forth" while Abraham still lived in Ur, is found also in the midrash: "While Terah was still in Ur of the Chaldeans the utterance to Abraham was [heard] 'Go forth,' and nevertheless Terah went with him and died in Haran after some time" (*Leqah Tov* to verse 28b).

The Jewish historian Flavius Josephus found his own way to coordinate the two concepts: "Terah [came] to hate Chaldea due to the loss of his lamented Haran, [so that] they all migrated to Haran in Mesopotamia, where Terah also died and was buried, after a life of 205 years. . . . and at the age of seventy-five he [Abraham] left Chaldea, God having bidden him to remove to Canaan, and there he settled" (*Jewish Antiquities* 1.6.5–1.7.1).[2] Josephus has removed any notion that the trip resulted from Terah's initiative, and he provides a different rationality for Abraham's departure from Ur of the Chaldeans, thereby smoothing over the rough spots between these two traditions that sit side by side in Genesis 11–12.

2. Except for the spelling of the names, the translation is that of H. St. J. Thackeray, *Josephus, Jewish Antiquities, Books I–IV* (London: Loeb Classical Library, 1930).

The rationales behind the second and third traditions that we listed above are not difficult to understand. That the second, which involves God's command to "go forth," represents a test is clear. As we've said, these words open a whole series of trials by which Abraham is tested, and the series ends with the same command to "go forth" in Genesis 22:2: "Take your son, your only one whom you love, Isaac, and go forth to the land of Moriah" (this is the opening of the *Aqedah*, the Binding of Isaac). As the midrash phrases it: "The Holy One, blessed be He, said to Abraham: 'The first test and the last test I try you with "go forth": "Go forth from your land," and "Go forth to the land of Moriah"'" (*Tanḥuma Buber, Lekh* 4).

The motive for the third tradition that we presented, the tradition with "I am the LORD who brought you out," is also clear. This tradition highlights God's benevolence in removing Abraham from Ur, despite the fact that no attempt is made to elucidate what necessitated God's compassion. That said, we must admit that the questions raised by the first tradition are puzzling: What caused Terah to decide to leave Ur of the Chaldeans and go to the Land of Canaan? We'll focus, therefore, on that enigmatic tradition, and perhaps our consideration of it will help clarify things also with regard to the other tradition about Ur of the Chaldeans and explain God's compassionate act in delivering Abraham from there.

We'll look first at Genesis 11:27–31, verses that explain why Abraham's nephew Lot left with his grandfather Terah but without his father, Haran, who died in Ur of the Chaldeans. Nothing is said regarding the circumstances of Haran's untimely death during the lifetime of his father. Does a connection exist between Haran's death and Terah's departure from Ur of the Chaldeans, as Josephus indicated in the passage we cited above?

The Bible's brief tradition about the death of Haran becomes a bit clearer in post-biblical literature, where we find an expanded version that tells of Abraham battling idolatry and Haran dying in a fire (this is a clear midrash on the name Ur, which also means "fire"). The story's earliest appearance seems to be in *Jubilees*:

Abram arose in the night and burned the house of idols. And he burned everything in the house. And there was no man who knew. And they rose up in the night and they wanted to save their gods from the midst of the fire. And Haran rushed to save them, and the fire flared up over him. And he was burned in the fire and died in Ur of the Chaldees before Terah, his father. And they buried him in Ur of the Chaldees. And Terah went out of Ur of the Chaldees, he and his sons, so that they might come into the land of Lebanon and into the land of Canaan. (12:12–15)

A more developed tradition about Abraham being rescued from the fire, from the *ur*, is found in *Biblical Antiquities*:

And they took him and built a furnace and lit it. And they threw bricks burned with fire into the furnace.... [A]nd he took Abram and threw him along with the bricks into the fiery furnace. But God caused a great earthquake, and the fire leapt out of the furnace in flames and sparks and it burned all those standing in front of the furnace.... But Abram had not even the slightest injury from the burning of the fire. And Abram came up out of the furnace, and the fiery furnace collapsed and Abram was saved. (6:16–18)

Rabbinic literature has much to say about the death of Haran in the fire and Abraham's escape from it, such as this example from *Genesis Rabbah*:

He said to him [Nimrod to Abraham] ... "I worship nothing but the fire. Behold, I will cast you into it, and let your God whom you worship come and save you from it." Now Haran was there. He stood, undecided, and said [to himself]: "Whatever will be: If Abram is victorious, I will say that I am of Abram's belief, while if Nimrod is victorious, I will say that I am of Nimrod's." When Abram descended into the fiery furnace and was saved, they asked [Haran], "Of whose [belief] are you?" He said to them: "Of

Abram's." They seized him and cast him into the fire; his inwards were scorched and he died in his father's lifetime. Hence it is written, "And Haran died in the lifetime of his father Terah." (38:13)

This tradition of Abraham being thrown into the fire and then rescued from it bears close resemblance to the Bible's story about Daniel's three friends, Hananiah, Mishael, and Azariah, whom Nebuchadnezzar, the king of Babylon, cast into the fire when they refused to prostrate themselves and worship a statue of gold (Daniel 3). The similarity leads us to wonder: Did lacunae in the biblical story about Haran's death and Terah's departure for the city of Haran trigger the development of the traditions we found in post-biblical literature, which were patterned after the Daniel tradition? Or is the reverse true: Did an ancient story about Haran and Abraham (a story that for some reason was omitted by the Pentateuch) leave its imprint in Daniel 3 and then reappear, returning to the surface in apocryphal and Rabbinic literature?

The second possibility seems most likely to us, that the Pentateuch knew the tradition about Haran's death in the fire and Abraham's safe escape and rejected it. It is our task, then, to find evidence for the early existence of that tradition and its rejection and also to explain what caused the biblical writers to refuse that tradition's inclusion in their story.

Regarding Haran, the Bible relates that "Haran died in the lifetime of ['al pnei] his father Terah, in his native land, Ur of the Chaldeans" (Genesis 11:28). In Numbers 3:4 we read about a similar event regarding the sons of Aaron the priest: "And Nadab and Abihu died before [lifnei] the LORD, when they offered alien fire before [lifnei] the LORD in the wilderness of Sinai and they had no sons, so Eleazar and Ithamar served as priests *in the lifetime of* ['al pnei] their father Aaron." In Chronicles' retelling the story of the death of Aaron's sons we find: "Nadab and Abihu died *before* [lifnei; i.e., "during the life of"] their father, and they had no sons, so Eleazar and Ithamar served as priests" (1 Chronicles 24:2). It is quite possible that Chronicles preserves here the original version of the verse in Numbers, which would have read: "And Nadab and Abihu died *in the lifetime of* [*'al pnei*] Aaron their father, when they offered alien fire *before* [*lifnei*] the LORD."

A reference to the death of a son during the lifetime of his father using the term *'al pnei* is found only in these two episodes, both of which involve fire. About Haran we are told that it occurred in "*Ur* of the Chaldeans"; regarding Nadab and Abihu it is told: "And fire came forth from the LORD and consumed them; thus they died before the LORD" (Leviticus 10:2). The Rabbis linked the stories of Haran and Aaron's sons by way of the expression *'al pnei*: "'So it was Eleazar and Ithamar who served as priests in the lifetime of [*'al pnei*] their father Aaron' (Num. 3:4). Rabbi Isaac said: During the life [of Aaron] . . . it is said here [in the story of Nadab and Abihu] *'al pnei* and it is said [there, in the story of Haran] *'al pnei*. . . . Just as *pnei* there [means] in his lifetime, also *pnei* here [means] in his lifetime" (*Tanḥuma Buber, Aḥarei* 9 [33a]).

An echo of the ancient story that we seek to reconstruct can possibly be found in the stories about Haran's son Lot that are found in Genesis. Haran was burned in a fire (because he sinned), but his son Lot, who did not sin, was not burned when "the LORD rained upon Sodom and Gomorrah sulfurous fire from the LORD out of heaven" (Genesis 19:24). Instead, Lot was rescued from the burning city by God's messengers: "And they brought him out [*va-yotzi'uhu*] and left him outside of the city" (v. 16). It seems likely that both the story about the death of Nadab and Abihu by fire and that about the rescue of Lot from the burning city knew the ancient tradition about the death of Haran in a fire and made use of it. The use of the verb "to bring out" for describing Lot's escape from the fire makes us reconsider God's words to Abraham in a verse we've already brought, from the Testament between the Parts: "He said to him, 'I am the LORD who *brought you out* from Ur of the Chaldeans'" (Genesis 15:7). We assume that this tradition refers to the story of the burning of Haran in the fire and Abraham's rescue from it and that its mention of *ur* indeed alludes to the name derivation of Ur in the lost tradition as "fire," "furnace." This name derivation is expressed explicitly in other sources, such as *Targum Pseudo-Jonathan* to this verse or *Genesis Rabbah* 44:13: "'I am the Lord who brought you out from Ur of the Chaldeans,' Rabbi Liezar ben Jacob [said,] Michael descended and saved Abraham from the furnace." If Genesis 15:7 is in fact alluding to the ancient story of Abraham being rescued from a fire, then we do not have three traditions about the reasons for leaving Canaan, since what we previously identified as the third tradition is none other than an explicit expression of the tradition concealed in the first.

The reader who is willing to accept our hypothesis that an ancient story about Haran's death in the *ur* and Abraham's rescue from it was rejected by the Torah will still ask—and with good reason—about the reason the Bible would suppress such a story. While the Bible does allude to the tradition that the ancestors of the Patriarchs lived lives of idolatry on the other side of the river—"In olden times, your forefathers—Terah, father of Abraham and father of Nahor—lived beyond the Euphrates and worshiped other gods" (Joshua 24:2; and see chapter 12)—the Torah tries to minimalize this impression, rejecting even the shadow of idolatry from the nation's Patriarchs. The Torah depicts Abraham as never having known or seen idolatry, and so it chooses to open the story of his life in Canaan and to make do with only minimal details of anything earlier.

Even a story that told of Abraham's heroic battles against idol worship would jeopardize the idea that he lived a life untouched by idolatry. For this reason, it seems, the Torah forfeited the story of Abraham's rescue from the fiery furnace and of the idol worshiper Haran being burned in the flames of the furnace, the *ur*. Forgoing that tradition, moreover, made it possible for the Torah to portray Abraham as one who answered a test posed to him by the God of Israel when he was a childless man at a relatively advanced age (remember, he was seventy-five when he left for Canaan)—a factor that, for the reader, makes his faith in God's promise to give him not only a land but also children even greater.

The story that had been rejected from Genesis continued its life orally. The well-known story in Daniel was formulated in its image: Abraham's descendants, now living in Babylon, behave as did their ancient forefather when he lived in that same land. In post-biblical literature the tradition returned and burgeoned forth, both in the apocryphal and pseudepigraphal corpora, as well as in Rabbinic literature. The story of Abraham being rescued from the flames is familiar to all who read and study Rashi's commentary, and many assume—erroneously—that it is found also in the biblical narrative, a clear confirmation of our sense that we have here not a later creation but an ancient tradition that has finally returned to the surface.

16

....

The Reinterpretation of a Name

Jacob's In Utero Activities

The birth of the twins Jacob and Esau did not progress altogether smoothly. Before proceeding into the world, the twins fought fiercely—"the children struggled in her womb" (Genesis 25:22)—at which point Esau appears first, and "then his brother emerged, holding on to the heel ['*aqev*] of Esau; so they named him Jacob [*ya'aqov*]" (v. 26). Not simple wordplays, biblical name etymologies often shed light on the beliefs and worldviews—sometimes even the ideological conflicts—of the ancients. Moreover, they can enable us to reconstruct traditions that have otherwise disappeared.

The Bible contains more than one explanation for many names, including Jacob. The placement of one of the explanations for Jacob's name in his birth story, "holding on to the *heel* of Esau," does not necessarily mean that it is the only or oldest explanation or even that it was the most well known. Quite the opposite, we propose, is true: this etymology was placed here in order to dispute the prevailing explanation of the name *ya'aqov* and to offer an alternative that would cast a more favorable light on the business of the twins' birth. The popular tradition and the story it conceals are the topic of this chapter.

The root of the Hebrew name Jacob, '-*q*-*v*, sometimes appears with the meaning "deceive," "cheat," such as we find in 2 Kings 10:19: "Jehu was acting *with deceit* [*be-'oqbah*] in order to exterminate the worshipers of Baal." This is the meaning of the root also in the Jacob and Esau story cycle. After Jacob acquires his brother's blessing from their father "with guile" (27:35; when Jacob dresses in his brother's clothes and tricks his near-blind father into thinking that he is Esau), the betrayed Esau explains his brother's name as deriving from the verb "to cheat": "Was he, then, named Jacob that he might cheat me [*va-ya'aqveni*] these two times? First he took away my birthright and now he has taken away my blessing!" (Genesis 27:36).

The derivation of Jacob's name from *'oqbah*, "deceit," is found also in the book of Hosea, when that prophet hurls harsh blame onto the people of Israel and depicts them as the heirs of their ancestor Jacob: "like father, like son." The people, Hosea says, now mimic Jacob, whose life story was riddled with the Patriarch's questionable moral behavior. Among other things, Hosea alludes to the story of Jacob's birth: "In the womb he deceived [*'aqav*] his brother" (12:4). With these words the prophet refers to a birth tradition that is unlike the one we find in Genesis 25: we cannot call Jacob's holding on to the heel of his brother an act of deception, even if it was meant to delay Esau's birth. Hosea, on the other hand, blames Jacob with deceiving his brother already inside their mother's womb.

Hosea knows a different tale about the birth of Jacob and Esau, one that was similar to what is told in Genesis 38 about the birth of another set of twins, the sons of Judah and Tamar, Perez and Zerah (this is the only other birth story of twins in the Bible). According to Genesis 38, Perez, who should be born second, manages to scoot out before his brother, Zerah:

> When the time came for her to give birth, behold, there were twins in her womb! While she was in labor, one of them put out his hand, and the midwife tied a crimson thread to that hand, to signify: This one came out first. But just then he drew back his hand, and out came his brother; and she said, "What a breach you have breached [*paratzta . . . paretz*] for yourself!" So he was named Perez [*peretz*]. Afterward his brother came out, on whose hand was the crimson thread; he was named Zerah. (vv. 27–30)

The striking resemblance between this story and that of Jacob and Esau suggests that the prebirth conflict between Jacob and Esau was like that between Perez and Zerah: it was a fight over the birthright, a fight over which of the twins would succeed in being born first. Such a tale about a struggle that ends with Jacob victoriously cheating his brother out of his firstborn status would have cast a shadow over the Patriarch, and it was consequently rejected by the biblical writers. In its stead a tradition was brought that only hints at a feeble attempt of Jacob's to delay his brother's birth by clinging to the latter's heel, and no more. That this was Jacob's purpose in holding to his brother's heel is not made explicit, but the Bible does not try to deny the tradition entirely; it doesn't claim that no struggle took place between the brothers. Instead, the Bible chose to admit a conflict—but to minimize it as much as possible.

The relationship between the two birth stories is made obvious by the phrase that appears in both, "Behold, there were twins in her womb" (Genesis 25:24, 38:27), a locution unique to these two stories. The sages were aware of this relationship. In *Genesis Rabbah* 85:13, significance is granted to the different spelling of "twins" in the two stories (one letter is missing in Genesis 25:24): "'Behold, there were twins in her womb' (Gen. 38:27): 'twins' is written fully [i.e., with the *'alep*, implying that] both were righteous; later on [in Genesis 25:24, there appears] 'twins' [with no *'alep*, implying that] one was righteous and one was wicked." The sages wanted to teach that the different spelling of the word "twins" alludes to the perfection of one pair, Perez and Zerah, and the imperfection of the other. Another Rabbinic tradition also draws a comparison between the two stories: "There were two that covered themselves with a veil and gave birth to twins, Rebekah and Tamar" (*Genesis Rabbah* 60:15).

The tradition about one twin stealing the birthright at the moment of birth was rejected from the Jacob and Esau cycle. It left its imprint on the other tale, however, which is set two generations later—the story of Jacob's twin grandsons, the sons of Judah and Tamar: Perez and Zerah. That story, it seems, was written in an effort to slander the tribe of Judah and, in particular, Perez's renowned descendant, David, and his line. The story of Judah and Tamar was probably created in the Kingdom of Israel, the chief rival of the Kingdom of Judah. Its writers wanted to show how David, like his ancestor, had stolen what was not his: just as Perez stole the firstborn rights from his brother Zerah, so David took the kingdom from Saul, the first king of Israel, and his line.

Even in this role, however, the Perez and Zerah birth story in Genesis 38 still manages to retain the imprint of its source, the rejected tradition about the birth of Jacob and Esau. The story covertly interprets Zerah's name (the root *z-r-ḥ* means "shine") as being related to the dark red thread that was tied to the newborn's hand. Various commentators have remarked on this explanation of Zerah's name, among them Rashi: "for the shining [*zriḥat*] appearance of the crimson [thread]." But this name derivation suits equally—and, perhaps, even more—Esau's other name, Edom, since Edom (which has the same spelling as *'adom*, "red") and *shani*, "crimson," are synonyms. We see this clearly in the words of the prophet Isaiah: "[If] your sins be like crimson [*ke-shani*], they can turn snow-white; be they red [*ya-'adimu*] as dyed wool, they can become like [white] fleece" (1:18). The crimson thread, then, was originally tied to the hand of the infant Esau (i.e., Edom), who should have been born first had not Jacob slyly managed to push himself out instead—like what is told about Perez pushing his way out into the world before his brother, Zerah.

It is worth noting that Zerah is not exclusively the name of a Judahite clan but also belongs to an Edomite tribe through Esau/Edom's son Reuel (Genesis 36:17; 1 Chronicles 1:37). Indeed, the association between Zerah and Edom is noted in Moses's blessing in Deuteronomy 33, where the root *z-r-ḥ* is associated with still another name for Edom, Seir (see Genesis 36:8): "He said: The LORD came from Sinai; He shone [*zaraḥ*] upon them from Seir" (Deuteronomy 33:2). This blessing overtly mentions one name of Edom's, Seir, while covertly playing with another, Zerah, demonstrating how, even in the original tradition about Esau/Edom, a wordplay punning on "Zerah" might have appeared.

We have reconstructed an ancient tradition about the birth of Jacob and Esau by using a story that was influenced by it and even cast in its mold (with support for the reconstructed story found in an allusion made by the prophet Hosea). The original story can be compared to a distant star whose light reaches us now, though the star itself no longer exists. The pre-biblical story about Jacob and Esau was rejected and disappeared, but in its mold was created the story of Perez and Zerah, which reflects the light of the absent story; with its help we are able to reconstruct the missing tale.

Though the authoritative story no longer blames Jacob with any act of deceit in his mother's womb, the biblical writers did not manage to banish the ancient tradition entirely, and it continued to make its way, being told and retold over time. The tradition surfaced not only in Hosea but also in the words of other prophets who blamed the people of Israel with deceitful behavior that was reminiscent of their forefather Jacob. When the prophet cries out, "Though I know that you are treacherous, that you were called a rebel from the womb" (Isaiah 48:8), he means that Jacob's name and perfidious nature were decided already in his mother's womb by his iniquitous deeds. Jeremiah 9:3–5 also contains echoes of the ancient interpretation of Jacob's name, which based itself directly on the tradition of his in utero deceit:

> ³Beware every man of his friend!
> Trust not even a brother!
> For every brother acts deceitfully [*'aqov ya'aqov*],
> Every friend is base in his dealings.
> ⁴One man cheats the other,
> They will not speak truth;
> They have trained their tongues to speak falsely;
> They wear themselves out working iniquity.
> ⁵You dwell in the midst of treachery.
> In their treachery they refuse to heed Me, declares the LORD.

The prophet Jeremiah, wanting to illustrate the prevalent depravity and deceit among the people, triggers the memory of Jacob and Esau. It is not only friends whom one cannot trust; beware even of your brother! These verses, constructed in a chiastic arrangement (i.e., "friend . . . brother, brother . . . friend"), identify the brother, and not the friend, as the deceiver, like the nation's Patriarch in his dealings with his sibling.

We find an additional verse in Jeremiah that reflects the same tradition about Jacob's cheating, which was known to both the prophet and his audience (Jeremiah would not allude to an event that did not resonate with his listeners): "Most deceitful ['aqov] is the heart, it is perverse—who can fathom it? I the LORD probe the heart, search the mind, to repay every man according to his ways, according to the fruit of his deeds" (17:9–10). Though this verse does not speak about Jacob, the use of the root '-q-v is not coincidental, and it seems most likely that listeners and readers pictured the figure of Jacob, the model deceiver. We surmise this from the last words ("to repay every man according to his ways [drakhav], according to the fruit of his deeds"), which are borrowed from Hosea's words about Jacob ("and punished Jacob for his ways [drakhav], according to his deeds") and are placed right before that prophet's interpretation of Jacob's name: "In the womb he deceived ['aqav] his brother" (12:4).

A different tactic for dealing with the meaning of Jacob's name was in changing it so as to convey the opposite of "deceit" and "cheating." This explains the creation of Jacob's other name, Yeshurun, in which we hear the element yashar, "honest." Its success in entering the canon was limited, appearing only in the poems of Deuteronomy: "So Yeshurun grew fat and kicked" (32:15); "Then He became King in Yeshurun" (33:5); "O Yeshurun, there is none like God" (v. 26). The name appears also in Isaiah 44:2, where it is part of a polemic against the view that Jacob cheated while in his mother's womb: "Thus said the LORD, your Maker, Your Creator who has helped you since the womb, Fear not, My servant Jacob, Yeshurun whom I have chosen." The prophet makes the point that Yeshurun/Jacob was chosen by God—and was even given the name Yeshurun—already in his mother's womb.

Alongside the partial acceptance of the name Yeshurun were attempts to impose the meaning of yashar, an antonym of 'aqav, to another of Jacob's names, Israel (*yisra'el*), in which the consonants *y-s-r* also appear (in Hebrew, the phonemes *sh* and *s* are both produced by the same letter). So we see in the words of Balaam: "Who can count the dust of Jacob, number the dust-cloud of Israel? May I die the death of the righteous [*yesharim*], may my fate be like theirs!" (Numbers 23:10). The prophet Micah knew well that this meaning was related to the name Israel, and he drew upon it to lay blame on the people: "The one who is dubbed House of Jacob—Is the LORD's patience short? Is such His practice? To be sure, My words are friendly to those who walk righteously [*ha-yashar*]" (2:7). When Micah says, "The one who is dubbed House of Jacob," he alludes to the story in which Jacob's name was changed to Israel in Genesis 32:29: "'Your name shall no longer be dubbed Jacob but Israel.'" The prophet disagrees with the version in Genesis and insists that his name has remained Jacob, since he is not righteous and does not deserve the name Israel, a name only belonging to one who "walks righteously."

Isaiah 48:1 also makes use of the Jacob-Israel name change: "Listen to this, O House of Jacob, Who are called Israel . . . who swear by the name of the LORD and invoke the God of Israel not in truth and sincerity." But this prophet makes use of the other tradition about Jacob's name change that is in Genesis: "No longer Jacob shall your name be said, but Israel" (35:10). The prophet turns to the people with the name House of Jacob, the label that still fits despite their name change, since the nation has sworn falsely, deceitfully. Another wordplay between the roots '*-q-v*, here meaning "crooked," and *y-sh-r*, "straight, level," is found in the words of the same prophet: "Let the *crooked* ground become *level*" (Isaiah 40:4).

Once more Micah plays between these two names so laden with significance: "Hear this, you rulers of the House of Jacob, you chiefs of the House of Israel, who detest justice and *make crooked* [*me'akshim*] all that is straight/righteous [*ha-yeshara*]" (3:9). The nation's primary label, which attests to its fundamental nature, is House of Jacob, and so the prophet calls it in the verse's first stich. He then explains why the people are undeserving of their second name, Israel: they pervert all that is straight and just. The root that is used here, *'-q-sh*, "make crooked, pervert," is related to and close in meaning to *'-q-v*, with which it shares the same first two letters.

We leave the prophets now and return to Genesis, where the tradition about an act of treachery during the twins' birth was transformed into a milder story about a struggle in which Jacob was at a disadvantage and his brother, Esau, emerged as Isaac and Rebekah's firstborn. The acceptance of this tamed version effectively delayed the transference of the firstborn rights from Esau to Jacob until their adulthood, to the episode of the lentil porridge (Genesis 25:27–34). Admittedly, in that story Jacob takes advantage of Esau's weakness, his hunger and great thirst on returning from the field, but Esau is fully aware of what is happening and knowingly gives away his birthright. Even after eating and drinking he shows no sign of regretting relinquishing the birthright to Jacob, and the episode concludes: "Thus did Esau despise the birthright" (v. 34).

It is to this episode that Esau refers when he interprets Jacob's name: "And he said, 'Was he, then, named Jacob that he might deceive me [*va-ya'qveni*] these two times? First he took away my birthright and now he has taken away my blessing'" (27:36). On the one hand, the writer of Genesis has retained the interpretation of Jacob's name from *'oqbah* and relates it to Jacob's taking the firstborn status; on the other hand, he attributes the explanation to Esau, who "despised" his birthright and so (we are led to believe) has no right to complain about his fate. Readers, in any case, will not blame Jacob in the matter.

As we've seen, name etymologies are no trivial matter. Whether overt or covert, these traditions are not simple wordplays or decorative literary elements. Indeed, they often preserve residue from ancient ideological debates and offer evaluations and judgments of character. Sometimes, as we've just seen, they preserve ancient traditions that were otherwise lost.

17

Were the Israelites Never in Egypt?

A Peculiar Tradition about Ephraim

Novice readers have given a bad name to Chronicles' genealogical lists of the tribes of Israel, which take up that book's first nine chapters, as though the lists comprise merely random compilations of names. With proper deciphering tools, however, one discovers fascinating concepts and invaluable information there about the history of Israel, its tribes and settlements, throughout the biblical period. In the middle of the vast profusion of names are embedded short anecdotes that are otherwise unfamiliar to us, like that involving Jabez (*yabetz*) the Judahite, whose mother gave him his name "because I bore him in pain [*be-'otzev*]" (1 Chronicles 4:9). (Compare the curse in Genesis 3:16: "In pain [*be-'etzev*] will you bear children.") Jabez prays to God to remove the menace summoned by his name—"'Oh bless me . . . and make me not suffer pain from misfortune!' And God granted what he asked for" (1 Chronicles 4:10). Some of the anecdotes are enigmatic, like one that tells about another Judahite family: "And Jokim, and the men of Cozeba and Joash, and Saraph, who married into Moab and Jashub Lehem, the records are ancient" (v. 22). Indeed, this verse is hopeless.

We'll discuss now one anecdote that was placed into the genealogies of Ephraim son of Jacob. We'll try to uncover its particular concept of history and compare it with the more common biblical view.

The sons of Ephraim: Shutehelah his son Bered his son Tahath his son Eleadah his son Tahath his son Zabad his son Shuthelah also

Ezer and Elead. The men of Gath, born in the land, killed them because they had gone down to take their cattle. And Ephraim their father mourned many days, and his brothers came to comfort him. He cohabited with his wife, who conceived and bore a son; and she named him Beri'ah, because misfortune was in his house. His daughter was She'erah, who built both Lower and Upper Beth-horon, and Uzzen-she'erah. (1 Chronicles 7:20–24)

The relationships between the names at the beginning of the anecdote can be understood in two ways: first, by understanding the repeating term *beno*, "his son," as signifying the son of the previous name, thus giving us a genealogical list of a number of generations (Bered is the son of Shuthelah, Tahath is the son of Bered, etc.). Alternatively, one can understand each appearance of *beno* as referring back to Ephraim, so that all the names refer to Ephraim's sons. (Compare the mention of Shuthelah, Becher, and Tahan in the list of Ephraim's descendants in Numbers 26:35–37.) The second option is what is dictated by the context—it would be hard to imagine so many generations of descendants living contemporaneously. Ephraim mourns the deaths of his sons. On the other hand, our supposition that those killed by the men of Gath were all brothers raises an awkward problem: Are we to understand that Ephraim named two of his sons Shuthelah, two sons Tahath, and two more Eleadah and Elead? We must conclude, therefore, that the list has suffered from copying blunders, which created the duplications.

Like the anecdote about Jabez that we related above, which contains an etymology of Jabez's name, this tale also includes name derivations: Beri'ah, born to Ephraim after the death of his other sons, carries a name that memorializes the tragedy: "because misfortune [*be-ra'ah*] was in his house" (1 Chronicles 7:23). The wordplay does not follow regular Hebrew grammar: instead of *ki ra'ah* it has *be-ra'ah* in order to include all the sounds in Beri'ah's name. It is worth noting that, according to the genealogical lists of Benjamin in 1 Chronicles 8, there was a Beri'ah from the descendants of Benjamin who is also mentioned in connection with the people of Gath: "And Beri'ah and Shema—they were chiefs of clans of the inhabitants of Aijalon, who put to flight the inhabitants of Gath" (v. 13). The verse might reflect an interclan status struggle, as though the Benjaminites are gloating: "You Ephraimites were defeated by the people of Gath, but we Benjaminites succeeded—and took revenge for your loss, and drove away the inhabitants of Gath."

Another name etymology (this time covert) in the story of the Ephraimites is a midrash on the name of the city Uzen-she'erah, which, according to the story, was built—together with the cities Lower and Upper Beth-horon—by Ephraim's daughter She'era. The verse means to tell us that She'era was the only one of Ephraim's descendants to survive, the only to "remain" (*she'ar*) after the violent confrontation with the people of Gath. That she was the sole survivor of her father's progeny—until the birth of Beri'ah—explains the fact that she is credited with the building of cities. The Bible has a number of traditions crediting the building of cities to various heroes, for example, Cain, who builds the first city (Genesis 4:17); Asshur, who builds "Nineveh, Rehoboth-ir, Calah, and Resen between Nineveh and Calah, that is the great city" (10:11–12); Joshua, who builds Timnath-serah (i.e., Timnath-heres, in Joshua 19:50; see chapter 5); Hiel the Bethelite, who builds Jericho (1 Kings 16:34). In no tradition will you find a city's establishment being attributed to a woman, however, except in this story about Uzen-She'era, where a woman, in the absence of men, does a man's work.

The story about Ephraim and the deaths of his sons in Chronicles not only is a story of origins, of the origins of cities, but carries with it the distinctive markings of the Patriarchal stories in Genesis generally. The description of Ephraim in mourning—"And Ephraim their father mourned many days, and his brothers came to comfort him" (1 Chronicles 7:22)—resembles closely the disconsolate Jacob, who believed that his son Joseph (Ephraim's father) had died: "Jacob rent his clothes, put sackcloth on his loins, and mourned for his son many days. All his sons and daughters sought to comfort him" (Genesis 37:34–35).

Similar language appears also in Jeremiah's prophecy about Joseph's mother, Rachel: "Rachel weeping for her children, she refuses to be comforted for her children, who are gone" (31:15).

The frame story in the book of Job is also relevant for us here, since it, too, was written in the spirit of the Patriarchal narratives. Following the deaths of Job's sons, "Job's three friends heard about all these calamities that had befallen him, each came from his home. . . . They met together to go and console and comfort him" (2:11). Other motifs from the story in Chronicles also match the atmosphere of the Patriarchal stories: the portrayal of the family as herdsmen (cf., e.g., Genesis 37:2, 12, 46:32–34), a conflict with the other inhabitants of the land (Abraham: Genesis 21:25; Isaac: 26:13–21; Jacob: Genesis 34), the naming of children along with the name etymologies (Isaac: Genesis 21:6; Jacob: 25:26; Jacob's sons: 29:32–30:34, etc.).

When we read the short anecdote in Chronicles, the considerable correspondence between it and the Patriarchal stories causes us to wonder even more since, according to the main current of biblical historiography (including the book of Genesis), Joseph's son Ephraim was born in Egypt after the birth of Joseph's firstborn, Manasseh. Even the etymology of the name Ephraim carries the imprint of Egyptian exile: "Before the years of famine came, Joseph became the father of two sons, whom Asenath daughter of Pot-phera, priest of On, bore to him. Joseph named the first-born Manasseh, meaning 'God has made me completely forget my hardship and my parental home.' And the second he named Ephraim, meaning, 'God has made me fertile [*hifrani*] in the land of my affliction'" (Genesis 41:50–52).

According to the Pentateuch, the tribe of Ephraim left Egypt for Canaan only many years later, along with the other tribes. We read, for example, in Numbers, which lists "the Israelites who came out of the land of Egypt": "These are the descendants of Ephraim by their clans: Of Shuthelah, the clan of the Shuthelahites; of Becher, the clan of the Becherites; of Tahan, the clan of the Tahanites. These are the descendants of Shuthelah: of Eran, the clan of the Eranites. Those are the clans of Ephraim's descendants; persons enrolled: 32,500" (26:4).

We've already pointed to the resemblance between this listing of the

Ephraimites in Numbers and that in 1 Chronicles 7. Despite this resemblance, we find an astonishing yet glaring contradiction: according to the story in Chronicles, Ephraim lived and fathered all his children in the Land of Israel, and his daughter She'erah built cities in Israel, while, according to the entire Pentateuchal tradition, Ephraim and all his children were born, lived, and died in Egypt, never once setting foot in the Land of Israel. Indeed, one wonders whether the words "born in the land" (v. 21) did not originate as the emphatic addition of a reader who knew the Pentateuch's tradition and directed his words at the sons of Ephraim and not the people of Gath—but his comment, like many written intermarginally or interlinearly, was inserted into the wrong place during the course of copying.

The book of Chronicles knows nothing about Ephraim having lived in Egypt, and it locates the births of his sons in Canaan. This short anecdote assumes continuous dwelling in the Land from the period of the Patriarchs on, at least regarding the tribe of Ephraim, and it does not accept, therefore, the burden of the Egyptian enslavement tradition or the Exodus tradition at all. Perhaps it is not even aware of it!

The Exodus is the central event of Israel's history during the biblical period. It establishes the source of the people's loyalty to God, as stated explicitly in the first commandment: "I the LORD am your God who brought you out of the land of Egypt, the house of bondage" (Exodus 20:2 = Deuteronomy 5:6). The editions of the Ten Commandments assign the Exodus commensurate status with the Creation. Whereas the book of Exodus justifies the Sabbath commandment by way of the Creation—"For in six days the LORD made heaven and earth and sea, and all that is in them, and He rested on the seventh day; therefore the LORD blessed the sabbath day and hallowed it" (20:11)—its parallel in Deuteronomy pins the obligation for observing the Sabbath onto God's redemption of Israel from Egyptian bondage: "Remember that you were a slave in the land of Egypt and the LORD your God freed you from there with a mighty hand and an outstretched arm; therefore the LORD your God has commanded you to observe the sabbath day" (5:15).

The Exodus story can be seen as the watershed event of biblical historiography that determined the shape of everything that came before and after, including the future Redemption. (For an example of the former, see chapter 25; regarding its influence on the future, see, e.g., Isaiah 43:18–19: "Do not recall what happened of old, or ponder what happened of yore! I am about to do something new; even now it shall come to pass, suddenly you shall perceive it: I will make a road through the wilderness and rivers in the desert.")

Anecdotes such as this one are proof that readers must listen not only to the forceful, central current of the biblical narrative but also to the smaller rivulets of traditions that ripple more quietly: it is these traditions that preserve divergent and even disparate points of view that escaped the stronger current's sweeping flood. The tradition about the lives of Ephraim and his children in the Land of Israel is one such unusual view and comprises one of the few witnesses to a distinctly alternative tradition about the history of Israel during the biblical age, a tradition unfamiliar with the descent of Jacob's family to Egypt and the departure of all the tribes from Egypt.

The contradiction between our anecdote and the mainstream tradition was noticed already in ancient times, when efforts were made to somehow align it with the Exodus tradition. In the Aramaic translations of the Bible, for instance, we find the idea that the Ephraimites left Egypt and returned to Israel earlier than the other tribes, and it was then that our story occurred. According to these translations, the Ephraimites' departure is attributed to an error they made in calculating the end of Egyptian servitude or even to a rebellion against the divine plan, an interpretation that finds its proof text in an historical psalm: "The Ephraimite bowmen who played false in the day of battle, they did not keep God's covenant, they refused to follow His instruction" (Psalm 78:9–10). As a result, the Ephraimites entered into a conflict with the Philistines (the people of Gath) and were defeated. In order to avoid frightening the rest of the nation, God then prevented the Israelites from crossing through Philistine territory, as we read: "Now when Pharaoh let the people go, God did not lead them by way of the land of the Philistines, although it was nearer; for God said, 'The people may have a change of heart when they see war, and return to Egypt'" (Exodus 13:17). This verse, according to the Targums, teaches us that the bones of the Ephraimites were still lying about on the roads in Philistia. See, for example, *Targum Pseudo-Jonathan* to Exodus 13:17:

Now when Pharaoh let the people go, God did not lead them by way of the land of the Philistines, although it was nearer; for God said, lest the people may have a change of heart when they see their brothers who died in battle, two hundred thousand men, soldiers from the tribe of Ephraim clutching their shields and spears and weapons, who had gone down to Gath to plunder the cattle of the Philistines, and because they had disobeyed God's prohibition and had left Egypt thirty years before the end they were delivered into the hands of the Philistines and killed. . . . And if they will see this they will be afraid and return to Egypt.

See also the *Mekhilta de-Rabbi Ishmael*:

"For God said, The people may have a change of heart when they see war." . . . This refers to the war of the sons of Ephraim . . . as it is said, "the Ephraimite bowmen who played false in the day of battle [Ps 78:9]." Why? Because "they did not keep God's covenant, they refused to follow His instruction" (v. 10). That is, because they ignored the stipulated term, because they violated the oath. Another interpretation: So that they should not see the bones of their brethren lying around in Philistia and turn back. (*Beshalaḥ* 43–53)

These efforts of early interpreters cannot bridge the chasm between the two traditions: between the Pentateuch, which relates that Ephraim was born and lived in Egypt and that his descendants, along with the rest of the Israelites, left Egypt only later; and the tradition in Chronicles, according to which Ephraim never set foot in Egypt but lived his life in the Land of Israel, where his children were born and were killed. Were the book of Chronicles to have been written solely in order to bring us this one tradition, it would have been enough.

18

Moses's Most Miraculous Birth

The birth story of Moses, the chief human hero of the books of Exodus through Deuteronomy, is brief, almost stingy in its details. When Pharaoh's efforts to diminish the Israelite population—by enforcing harsh labor and by issuing an edict ordering the midwives to kill all newborn sons—fails, he instructs "all his people, saying, 'Every boy that is born you shall throw into the Nile, but let every girl live'" (Exodus 1:22). (Interestingly, the Pentateuch does not explain this decision to harm only boys.)

In the barest of language, the narrative then proceeds to relate an event the likes of which have occurred countless times in human history: "A man of the house of Levi went and married a Levite woman. The woman conceived and bore a son" (Exodus 2:1–2). A nameless man and woman—only their tribal affiliation is mentioned—are married, and the woman becomes pregnant and gives birth to a son. (We do notice a strange detail in the verse's continuation: "And she saw how he was good, and she hid him for three months" [v. 2]. Has there yet been a mother who didn't think her child "good"?) For three months the mother was able to protect her son from Pharaoh's edict, and only "when she could hide him no longer" (v. 3)—a determination about which we have no explanation—does the woman place the boy inside a reed basket and set the basket onto the Nile.

At this point the story turns to a description of the infant's wondrous rescue by Pharaoh's daughter and his subsequent arrival to the palace. While one might call Moses's being pulled from the Nile (where he had floated in a womblike ark in watery surroundings) by the woman who will be his mother/adopter a type of metaphoric birth story that overshadows the story of his biological birth, our interest is in the latter, the tale of Moses's actual birth, the reasons for the scant mention it receives in Exodus, and the cloud that has been allowed to obscure it from us.

It is a remarkable fact that Moses—the first prophet, the one who delivers the Israelites from Egypt, gives them the Law, and leads them through forty years of wandering in the wilderness—did not warrant an elaborate birth story. Measured against the elaborate tale told about Isaac's birth (Genesis 18 and 21) and the detailed treatments of the births of Jacob and Esau (see chapter 16), Samson (see chapter 21), and Samuel (1 Samuel 1–2), the leanness of our verse—"A man . . . went and married a . . . woman. The woman conceived and bore a son"—is extraordinary and leads us to suspect that the Pentateuch's account was meant to contend with another: one that brimmed with wonders and miracles but that offended the Bible's sensibilities—in fact, one that the Pentateuch's writers wished to quell.

In the ancient world generally and in Israel in particular, birth stories comprised a number of relatively uniform motifs:

- A couple, sometimes elderly, is childless (Abraham and Sarah, Isaac and Rebecca, Manoah and his wife, Elkanah and Hannah, the Shunammite woman and her husband), usually because of the woman's barrenness.
- A divine messenger announces the imminent birth (Abraham's three visitors; God's words to Rebecca, "two nations are in your womb" [Genesis 25:23]; the angel who meets Manoah's wife in the fields; Elisha, who tells the news to the Shunammite woman; the Delphic Oracle, which announces the birth of Oedipus).
- The child's enemies attempt to prevent his birth (Oedipus's father seeks to kill him; Herod tries to harm Jesus).
- A series of wondrous events are connected to inception, pregnancy, and birth (impregnation by a god in the guise of a snake, as told about the birth of Alexander the Great).

- The pregnancy is particularly short or long (Isaac, Moses, Samuel in post-biblical literature).
- The birth is miraculous (the birth of Athena from Zeus's forehead).

Against all this narrative wealth, the Pentateuch's account of Moses's birth is indeed humble. When we turn to post-biblical sources from the Apocrypha onward, however, we find preserved a different version of Moses's birth, one that corresponds nicely with the prevailing pattern of birth stories described here. We propose that such an account, which we will present in a moment, was not a belated attempt to supply Moses with what the Pentateuch hadn't in order to set him on equal footing with other biblical figures; instead, it represented the reinstatement of ancient traditions that the Pentateuch had sought to blur and suppress, traditions that continued to be told orally for generations until they returned, in all their strength and splendor, to written literature. This conjectured story about Moses's birth includes a miraculous announcement of the impending birth, an exceptional pregnancy, and an unusual birth. Through the reconstruction of this story, we suggest, we may find answers to the questions we posed earlier, about the present form of the biblical narrative.

It was impossible to relate how Moses's parents had been childless before his birth, since the Pentateuch assumes that Moses was the youngest among other children: Aaron, we remember, was three years his senior (Exodus 7:7), and his sister Miriam must have been even older, since she kept watch over him when he floated in the Nile and intermediated between Pharaoh's daughter and the children's mother (2:4–8)—the midrash *Exodus Rabbah* (1:13) specifies that she was six years older than Moses. Apart from this motif, however, all the other birth-story motifs that we have mentioned can be found in relation to Moses in Jewish (post-biblical) sources.

In the ancient sources, the announcement of Moses's birth takes a number of different forms, but the underlying assumption is the same: the inconceivability that a figure of such importance would have arrived without the world's waiting for him with bated breath. His expected arrival was known, according to various sources, to Pharaoh and his magicians as well as to Amram and Miriam. The Egyptian magicians were alerted to the birth by their astrological powers: "[Pharaoh's] astrologers told him: Israel's redeemer has been conceived in his mother" (*Exodus Rabbah* 1:18). Pharaoh was informed either by his magicians or by a dream, as here, in *Targum Pseudo-Jonathan* to Exodus 1:22: "Pharaoh was sleeping and he saw in a dream, and behold, all of the land of Egypt was resting on one side of the scales, and a young lamb on the other," a dream the magicians interpret as referring to Moses. Pharaoh's daughter also had a dream that sent her to the Nile, where she saved ("gave birth" to) Moses (*Biblical Antiquities* 9:15). God spoke of the matter to Amran when He appeared to him in a dream: "And God . . . appeared to him in his sleep . . . [and told him how] this child, whose birth has filled the Egyptians with such dread that they have condemned to destruction all the offspring of the Israelites, shall indeed be thine. . . . These things revealed to him in a dream, Amram on awakening disclosed [it] to Jochabed his wife; and their fears were only the more intensified by the prediction in the dream" (Josephus, *Jewish Antiquities* 2.9.3). Miriam knew of her brother's birth from her own prophecy: "And the spirit of God came to Miriam in the night and she saw a dream and told her parents, saying . . . the one who will be born from you will be thrown to the water because by his hand the waters will be dried and I will make through him signs and save my people" (*Biblical Antiquities* 9:10). The midrash also states that "Miriam prophesied and said, 'my mother is destined to give birth to a son who will deliver Israel'" (*Exodus Rabbah* 1:22). Indeed, according to this midrash, it was their knowledge of the danger awaiting Egypt that propelled Pharaoh and his magicians to try to kill the boy before—or soon after—his birth.

Our hypothesis that the midrash returns here to a pre-biblical story, to a story that the Bible rejected, makes sense of Pharaoh's determination to kill the males, which, as it appears in the Bible, runs counter to logic. Men provided the Egyptians with a workforce, making it hard to explain the decision to eliminate such a cheap source of labor. Moreover, if one wants to prevent a nation from increasing its population, one needs to disable the women, not the men: one surviving male can father hundreds of children each year, whereas a woman who manages to survive can give birth only once a year. This problem is noted in the midrash: "The Holy One, blessed be He, said to Pharaoh: whoever advised you thus is foolish, you should have killed all of the females. If there are no females, how will the men marry women? One woman cannot marry two men, [but] one man can marry ten or a hundred women" (*Exodus Rabbah* 1:14). Exodus's account of Pharaoh's ordering the midwives to kill the sons and the command that he gives his people to throw the newborn sons into the Nile thus appear to be a remnant from the more ancient tradition, which told how Pharaoh's fears drove him (like Oedipus's father in the Greek tradition) to attempt to kill the child before his birth or soon thereafter.

Regarding Jochabed's pregnancy we find that ancient sources knew a handful of wondrous motifs. At first the midrash emphasizes how Jochabed was an old woman, 130 years old (*Exodus Rabbah* 1:19). (The tradition arrives at that number because it assumes the period of the Israelites' enslavement in Egypt to have been 210 years [an interesting story in itself that we cannot address here] and that Jochabed was born on the day of their arrival in Egypt. Since Moses was 80 years old when Israel left Egypt, his mother had to have been 130 years old at his birth.) The midrash relates how the "signs of youth" returned to Jochabed and how, in her old age, she had already experienced   as had Sarah, too (see Genesis 18:11) — a cessation of "the way of women" (*Exodus Rabbah* 1:19).

But that's not all. We also find sources that tell how Jochabed's pregnancy was unusually brief. According to *Targum Pseudo-Jonathan*, Moses was born after only a six-month pregnancy, a notion thought to be miraculous in the ancient world. (*Midrash ha-Gadol* to the verse relates how the pregnancy lasted precisely six months and two days.) What's more, the birth itself was exceptionally easy, the contractions being so light that Jochabed felt no pain, and the Egyptian guards were oblivious to the birth. This is told by Josephus (*Jewish Antiquities* 2.9.4) and *Exodus Rabbah* (1:20).

The midrash even adds that Jochabed's painless and trouble-free delivery was evidence of her righteousness, since righteous women "do not share the fate of Eve"; that is, they are excluded from the curse according to which "in pain you will bear children" (Genesis 3:16). Moreover, Moses "was born circumcised" (*Exodus Rabbah* 1:20; see also *Biblical Antiquities* 9:13), his flesh already reflecting God's covenant, evidence that the baby Moses's relationship with God was established already in his mother's womb, an expression, of sorts, of "before I created you in the womb, I selected you, before you were born, I consecrated you" (Jeremiah 1:5). And finally, when Moses was born, "the house filled with light" (*Exodus Rabbah* 1:20), as was also told, for instance, regarding the birth of Noah (1 Enoch 106:2; *Genesis Apocryphon* col. 5, lines 11–13). Might the words "and she saw how he was good" in Exodus 2:2 allude to a tradition about the appearance of light or of a shining star at the moment of Moses's birth? In the opinion of the same midrash, the proof text for the appearance of light at Moses's birth was through the linguistic connection between "and she saw how he was good" in our story with "God saw that the light was good" in the story of the Creation in Genesis 1:4. In this way, post-biblical literature restored to Moses what the Bible had taken from him: a spectacular and vivid birth.

Before explaining why, in our opinion, the Pentateuch tried to repudiate the previously wonder-filled story of Moses's birth, it is important to acknowledge the tradition's unambiguous manifestation in stories about the birth of Christianity's founder, Jesus. We refer primarily to Jesus's birth story as shaped in the Gospel of Matthew, the first book in the New Testament. The writer of that Gospel tried to depict Jesus as a sort of "second Moses," to present the figure who brings the "New Testament" as corresponding to the one who had previously brought the "Old Testament." It was in this context that he shaped his story about Jesus's birth by using motifs known to readers from the ancient Jewish traditions about the birth of Moses.

The Gospel of Matthew tells of an angel who gives news to Joseph, the husband of Jesus's mother, Mary, about the approaching birth of

Jesus and makes known the baby's destiny as Israel's Redeemer (1:20–21). Matthew tells of the wise men from the East who saw a star heralding the birth of the "king of the Jews" in Bethlehem (2:1–2) and of King Herod's terror, when he learns of it, lest the star's appearance heralds the truth of an ancient prophecy about the birth of Israel's messiah in that city (Micah 5:1), an event that would mark the end of Herod's rule. In order to prevent such a circumstance, Herod commands that "all children in Bethlehem and its borders two years and younger" be killed (Matthew 2:16). Jesus is saved when his father flees with him to Egypt, following an angel's directive, and he stays there until Herod's death, when an angel tells Joseph: "Rise and take your son . . . and return to the Land of Israel because those who sought the death of the boy have died" (v. 20).

It is not difficult to see how, behind these events, stand biblical—and even pre-biblical—traditions about Moses: the announcement to the father about the birth of his son; the light or star signaling the birth of the boy; wise men or magicians who, after the sign, learn of the birth; the evil king who fears the boy; and the king's attempts to kill him by massacring all the children among whom he might be found. The story of Joseph and Jesus fleeing to Egypt and their return from there after Herod's death is built upon a biblical motif, too: Moses's flight from Pharaoh to Midian (Exodus 2:9) and his return to Egypt after being told that "all the men who sought to kill you are dead" (4:19). We also recall how, according to several Christian traditions, Jesus was born after only six months of his mother's pregnancy, just as we found told in midrashic traditions relating to Moses.

Jesus's birth story in the Gospel of Matthew is thus a prism in which are reflected traditions about Moses that were known to Matthew and that Matthew used in order to construct his story. Matthew, who lived in the Land of Israel during the first century and who was perhaps a Jew, mined traditions from the biblical story and, primarily, from oral traditions that were known also to Flavius Josephus and the Rabbis. This fantastic story, as we said, did not win a place in the Pentateuch, where it left only vague imprints.

Why did the writers of the Hebrew Bible suppress the wondrous motifs in their telling of the birth of Moses? The answer stems apparently from the way in which the Pentateuch grappled with the tremendous stature of Moses (a subject we discussed in connection with the splitting of the sea in chapter 3 and to which we'll return in our discussion of Moses's death in chapter 20). The biography of Moses, which stretches over four of the Pentateuch's five books and whose hero is referred to throughout the entire Bible (e.g., Joshua 4:14, Judges 3:4, 1 Kings 8:53, Isaiah 63:12, Psalm 103:7, Nehemiah 9:14, and many more), could easily have kindled a personality cult. The many instances in which he appears before the Israelites as a messenger of God, as a leader, lawgiver, prophet, general, and poet, were liable to blur the distinction between the message bearer and the message Sender and to confer on the servant the glory and honor that belong to the Lord.

An exceptional birth story (like the story of someone leaving this world in an extraordinary way) is one ingredient for conjuring a larger-than-life, mythical figure. Barring it from Scripture helped to portray a mortal figure that lacked any divine dimension. Depicting the infant Moses as being sent off into the Nile, where he was vulnerable to the whims of the current and the crocodiles, dependent entirely on God—the story's true hero—to rescue him from his predicament, helped, too. The birth of Moses in the Pentateuch is thus like that of any other person; in this way, he deserves recognition as a great man, but nothing more.

What's more, extraordinary birth stories indicate, ultimately, the selection of an individual as part of a preordained divine plan: already in his mother's womb the child's lofty destiny was set. Instead, in everything concerning Moses, the Pentateuch prefers to tell a slightly different story in which a human being slowly proves himself worthy of his mission through his actions and confrontations in which he fights for justice: the story of Moses killing the Egyptian, the episode about the two Hebrews fighting with one another, and the story of the Midianite shepherds and the daughters of Jethro (Exodus 2:11–17). The miraculous rescue from the waters of the Nile might already indicate the infant Moses's having been chosen by God, but the three tales in which he later fights for justice represent the stages in which we discover the rightness of that choice. An extensive and miraculous birth story would diminish the power of those three stories and undermine the educational goal of the Pentateuch to draw a relationship between the deeds of the young Moses and the characteristics that are later revealed in him.

Finally, it is important to note that the Pentateuch's intentional obfuscation of the ancient story about Moses's birth and the way in which it treats his death and minimizes his role in the splitting of the sea correspond with similar tendencies that emerged in post-biblical literature, where we find a similar discomfort when it comes to differentiating the roles between the Sender and the one sent. We see this particularly in the Passover haggadah that is traditionally read on Passover eve. Moses is absent from the haggadah, and except for the citation of one fragmentary verse mentioned only incidentally ("they had faith in the LORD and His servant Moses" [Exodus 14:31]), his role seems to have been forgotten. More accurately, the haggadah tells us unambiguously that the redemption from Egypt was the work of God alone, who proclaims, "I and not an angel, I and not a seraph, I and not a messenger." There is no doubt that the "messenger" (*shaliah*) referred to is Moses (in addressing him at the burning bush, God says, "Come, therefore, I will send ['*eshlahakha*] you to Pharaoh and you shall free My people, the Israelites, from Egypt" [Exodus 3:10]) and that his banishment from the story told at the seder table was aimed at preventing him from filling too sublime a role in the tale, like the Pentateuch's aim in its telling of his birth story.

19

Moses's African Romance

When Pharaoh learned that Moses had struck an Egyptian, he sought to kill Moses and, according to the Pentateuch, "Moses fled from Pharaoh. He arrived in the land of Midian, and sat down beside a well" (Exodus 2:15). There Moses meets the daughters of Jethro, including Zipporah, whom he marries and who gives birth to his two sons. The words "he arrived in the land of Midian" come immediately after we read "[Pharaoh] sought to kill Moses, but Moses fled from Pharaoh," in order to show us that the events followed swiftly. Moreover, what happens to Moses in Egypt and Midian forms two parts of a single image: in Egypt Moses interfered in order to defend a Hebrew man from an Egyptian who sought to injure him (vv. 11–12) and also to separate two Hebrew adversaries (vv. 13–14), and in Midian he intervenes in order to rescue Jethro's daughters from the shepherds (vv. 15–17). These three short stories reveal Moses's sense of fairness: his unwillingness to stand idle when witnessing injustice between Egyptian and Hebrew, Hebrew and Hebrew, and even two foreigners reflects a swift escalation in Moses's resolve to promote justice.

To our surprise, several other sources relate an important and lengthy episode that occurred at some point between Moses's flight from Egypt and his arrival in Midian: a prolonged stay in Ethiopia (Cush) during which he marries an Ethiopian woman. The earliest post-biblical witness that ties Moses to Ethiopia and Ethiopians is the treatise written by the Jewish-Hellenistic writer Artapanus, *Concerning the Jews*. In the work, which is a sort of biography of Moses, Artapanus tells about Moses, the adopted son of the Egyptian Chenephres, ruler of Memphis, a man who "was loved by the multitudes" and who set out to fight the Ethiopians, the Egyptians' neighbors on their southern border.

Chenephres envied Moses and assigned to him an Egyptian army of untrained farmers, which, he assumed, would lead to Moses's defeat and death on the battlefield. (This is similar to Saul's attempts to kill David by sending him to fight the Philistines and demanding that he bring a dowry of one hundred Philistine foreskins [1 Samuel 18:25].) To Chenephres's dismay, Moses defeats the Ethiopian enemy after ten years of fighting and achieves their surrender. Artapanus also relates how the Ethiopians, "even though they were enemies, loved Moses" and how they and their priests even learned from him to circumcise their sons.

Flavius Josephus followed Artapanus with an impressive, expanded version of the story of Moses's war against the Ethiopians. He relates that after Moses, head of the Egyptian army, had pushed the Ethiopians back to their walled capital, Sheba, the Egyptians began an unsuccessful siege on the city that lasted many days. Josephus continues:

> Moses, then, was chafing at the inaction of his army . . . when he met with the following adventure. Tharbis, the daughter of the king of the Ethiopians, watching Moses bringing his troops close beneath the ramparts and fighting valiantly, marveled at the ingenuity of his maneuvers and, understanding that it was to him that the Egyptians . . . owed all their success, . . . fell madly in love with him; and under the mastery of this passion she sent to him the most trusty of her servants to make him an offer of marriage. He accepted the proposal on condition that she would surrender the town, and took an oath to take her to wife and not violate the pact once he would be master of the town, whereupon action outstripped words. After chastisement of the Ethiopians, Moses rendered thanks to God, celebrated the marriage, and led the Egyptians back to their own land. (*Jewish Antiquities* 2.10.2)

The tradition that ties Moses to an Ethiopian wife returns, with several alterations, in *Targum Pseudo-Jonathan* to Numbers 12:1 ("Miriam and Aaron spoke against Moses because of the Cushite woman he had married," a verse to which we'll soon turn) and in late midrashic literature, in a work that has been called "The Chronicles of Moses Our Teacher." Both sources admit that Moses indeed reached Ethiopia, though they claim that he arrived there as a refugee fleeing Pharaoh. Moses, according to "The Chronicles of Moses Our Teacher," rose to greatness in the Cushite monarchy as an advisor to King Kinknos and, following that king's death, succeeded him. Moses was then married—according to Cushite custom but against Moses's wishes—to the king's widow, though he avoided relations with her because he remembered the prohibition against marrying non-Israelites (see, e.g., Abraham's words to the slave in Genesis 24:3: "You will not take a wife for my son from the daughters of the Canaanites"), so that, when Kinknos's son reached adulthood, the Cushites sent Moses away, and he left for Midian.

The discrepancy between the ancient tradition, according to which Moses himself chose to marry the Cushite princess in exchange for the city's surrender, and the later one, which relates how the Cushites insisted on Moses's marrying their widowed queen, reflects a change made when the tradition became assimilated into Rabbinic literature—due, among other reasons, to the difficulty in accepting the notion that Moses married a Hammite (Cush was one of the sons of Ham [Genesis 10:6]). Even that emendation, however, does not erase the fundamental tradition about a marital connection, whether or not it was consummated, between Moses and a Cushite woman.

How did Flavius Josephus (and others who followed him) know the story of Moses's African marriage? Some scholars presume that the tradition of marriage between Moses and the Cushite woman was known to Artapanus or another Jewish-Hellenistic writer with whom Flavius Josephus was familiar. This is impossible to prove, but even if correct, we are still left wondering how the story began and where it first appeared.

As far as we can tell, the story must be related to the verse that we cited above from Numbers, which appears in the course of the story about the Israelites wandering in the wilderness: "And Miriam and Aaron spoke against Moses because of the Cushite woman he had married, because he married a Cushite woman" (12:1). Miriam and Aaron's words provoke a rebuke by God, and Miriam is even punished with leprosy: having spoken about the Cushite (*kushit* means also "black woman"), she now becomes stricken with "snow-white scales" (v. 10). The tone of Numbers 12 makes it clear that Miriam and Aaron fault Moses for committing an act that was forbidden by God, but God chastises them for comparing themselves with Moses, since Moses's prophetic status was far superior to theirs: "How then did you not shrink from speaking against My servant Moses" (v. 8).

Who is the "Cushite woman" against whom Miriam speaks as she casts aspersions on her brother? According to Rabbinic literature (e.g., *Sifre Numbers* 99), Miriam is speaking about Zipporah, Jethro's daughter and Moses's wife, and her rebuke, moreover, doesn't refer to Zipporah's marriage to Moses but, conversely, to Moses's abstinence from intimate relations with his wife once he had been granted a prophecy. The Rabbinic traditions, therefore, do not speak of marriage but of celibacy in marriage, an interpretation that, though in complete contradiction to the verse itself, was probably an attempt to combat a different interpretation, such as the one we have found, according to which the verse refers to Moses's marriage to an African woman.

The identification of the Cushite woman with Zipporah was accepted also by Rashi and some modern-day researchers, though without the story of separation from her. Among other things, these commentators cite Habakkuk 3:7, which places "the tents of Cushan" and "the pavilions of the land of Midian"—Zipporah being a Midianite—as partners in the verse's semantic parallelism (and therefore as synonyms). According to these researchers, Zipporah is indeed the referent in Numbers 12:1, though they have no explanation for Miriam's anger, since Moses had married Zipporah already many years earlier.

Other scholars have understood the verse in Numbers as referring to an unknown African woman whom Moses married during Israel's wanderings in the wilderness or to an African woman who was among the multitudes that left Egypt with the Israelites (Exodus 12:38). Still others believe that the verse alludes to some tradition about a marriage between Moses and a Cushite woman that took place in the years between his flight from Egypt and his arrival to the well in Midian. Thus, for example, Rashbam comments: "[Moses] ruled over the land of Cush forty years and he took one queen but did not have relations with her . . . and they [Miriam and Aaron] did not know when they spoke of him that he had not had relations with her." Moses Mendelssohn, in his commentary on the Torah, gave a similar reading of the verse: "There is no doubt that many things happened to Moses between his escape from Pharaoh until he was eighty years old . . . and they were not written about in the Torah because there was no need."

While one may claim that the tradition about Moses and his marriage in Cush was born out of a need to explain the appearance of the Cushite woman in Numbers 12, it is difficult to imagine how such a long and developed story would emerge out of one odd and abstruse verse—the more so when we consider that the verse appears in Numbers, far from the description of the young Moses's life. What's more, the parallelism in the verse from Habakkuk between Midian and Cush makes possible a much simpler interpretation of the verse by identifying the Cushite woman with Zipporah. It is therefore more probable that Artapanus—an Egyptian living toward the end of the biblical period during the second century BCE—and Flavius Josephus after him reflect in their words an older tradition that was known by the ancient Israelites but that was rejected. This tradition was not accepted into the biography of the young Moses but was alluded to in the periphery, in the story of Miriam's leprosy.

We can assume that ancient traditions that were told among the Israelites included wondrous tales about Moses, the ancient hero who stood at the head of an untrained army, proved his military greatness, and won not only an impressive victory but also the heart of the princess, the daughter of his opponent. Ancient Egyptian legends tell of a war between Egypt and Cush, an event that occurred many times in history, and wondrous campaigns are memorialized in ancient Egyptian epics. It is perhaps relevant here to mention the Egyptian tale about Sanhath, an official in the Egyptian king's court who fled because of a rebellion, arrived in Canaan, married the daughter of one of the rulers there, and became the ruler himself.

We'll never know what exactly was told among the ancient Israelites about the sublime figure of Moses, but his having been an Egyptian prince for a certain period and his subsequent heroic actions as the commander at the head of the Israelites (Numbers 21:32–35, Deuteronomy 1;4, etc.) would certainly have provided a starting point for the development of traditions about his military courage while still in Pharaoh's palace and also romantic episodes in which he played a starring role. The Pentateuch tried to destroy such traditions, since they presented the young Moses as collaborating with the Egyptians, on the one hand, and as marrying a Cushite woman, the daughter of the cursed Ham, on the other (see chapter 14). But what the Pentateuch was unable to suppress continued to be passed on orally until the traditions rose to the surface in the periphery, in the story of Miriam's leprosy and with even greater force in post-biblical literature, beginning with a writer living in Hellenistic Egypt, the land in which Moses's heroic acts were set.

20

Moses's Necessary Death

It was crucial that the Pentateuch include a report of Moses's death, by which it sought to instill firmly and deeply in readers' minds two related concepts: its war against a personality cult (we've already found clear expressions of this in the shaping of Moses's birth story [chapter 18] and in the story of his splitting the Sea of Reeds [chapter 3]) and its determination to prevent a depiction of Moses that was of mythological proportions. Any image of a transition from life on earth to eternal life—such as of a heavenly ascension to join God—would have had the potential to transform Moses into a God-like figure and endanger the fledgling monotheistic religion that was defending itself against a pagan environment.

This is also the reason that the Pentateuch tried to muffle stories about the immortality of Enoch son of Jared, who, of all the figures in the line between Adam and Noah, is conspicuous not only because he represents the seventh generation of humanity but because he lived for 365 years, like the days of the solar year. (Is this perhaps an allusion to a mythological tradition that connects him with a solar deity?) Instead of reading "After the birth of Methuselah, Enoch lived [*x* amount of years]," as we find regarding all other figures in this "record of Adam's line" in Genesis 5, the verse regarding Enoch differs: "Enoch walked with God after he begot Methuselah 300 years," and instead of the usual "then he died," we find: "Enoch walked with God; then he was no more, for God took him" (vv. 22, 24).

It appears that the Pentateuch responds here, with an ambiguous, partial concession, to a tradition that told of Enoch's immortality. The reader can understand Enoch's "walking with God" as referring to his righteous behavior, similar to what will be told about Noah in the next chapter: "Noah was a righteous man; he was blameless in his age; Noah walked with God" (Genesis 6:9). On the other hand, since the expression "Enoch walked with God" appears twice, the reader can also understand that Enoch walked with God both during his earthly lifetime and after God had "taken" him up to the heavenly abode.

The expression "he was no more" is likewise equivocal: on the one hand, it can indicate Enoch's death, as in Psalm 39:14: "Look away from me that I may recover, before I pass away and am no more," but it might refer to a passing from life on this earth to another existence. The same can be said about the expression that God "took him." Being "taken" can refer to death (as in Ezekiel 24:16: "O mortal, I am about to take the delight of your eyes from you through pestilence; but you shall not lament or weep or let your tears flow"), or, alternatively, to a person's being taken alive to heaven, as we hear the disciples tell Elisha before Elijah's ascendance to heaven (a story we'll return to shortly): "Do you know that today the LORD will take your master from you" (2 Kings 2:3).

The avoidance of any explicit and unambiguous statement in Enoch's story, this hesitancy, bears witness to the Pentateuch's effort to silence the tradition of Enoch's ascendance to heaven. But it did not eradicate it—it could not, due to the tradition's widespread popularity. Instead, it enshrouds the tradition in ambiguity, leaving exposed only brief and equivocal references. Despite these efforts, the tradition that Enoch didn't die continued to be told, and it found its way to the rich literature about Enoch that emerged during the Second Temple period and even to the New Testament ("By faith Enoch was taken up so that he should not see death" [Hebrews 11:5]).

However, where Second Temple period literature speaks openly about Enoch's righteousness, his ascendance, his heavenly journeys, and his being seated to the right of God, Rabbinic literature tells very little and instead emphasizes the opposite: not only did Enoch die like all humans, but his death came prematurely due to his wickedness. "A matron asked Rabbi Yossi: We don't find Enoch's death [mentioned in the Bible]! He said to her ... when it says, 'he was no more because He took him,' etc.—[this means that] he is no more of this world [having died], because God took him." And also: "Rabbi Hama Bar Hoshaya said: [Enoch] is not inscribed in the tomes of the righteous but in the tomes of the wicked. Rabbi Aibu said: Enoch was a hypocrite, sometimes righteous sometimes wicked. The Holy One blessed be He said: While he is righteous I will remove him" (*Genesis Rabbah* 25:1). *Targum Onqelos* translated "for God took him" as "because God killed him," asserting Enoch's indisputable death. On the other hand, the translation in *Targum Pseudo-Jonathan* reflects the tradition that the Pentateuch rejected, "for he was no more with the inhabitants of the land because he was taken and rose to heaven," demonstrating that the tradition found its way also to the Rabbinic world.

Let's move now from Enoch to Moses. Though the Pentateuch dedicates significant space to the story of Moses's death in Deuteronomy 34, one senses a veil of wonderment and mystery spread over the story, while below the surface we notice signs of a polemic against the belief in Moses's immortality. God explicitly assigns the time and place of Moses's death at the threshold of the Promised Land, to which Moses had led the people. After viewing the whole land from Mount Nebo's summit, it's clearly stated that Moses dies: "So Moses the servant of the LORD died there, in the land of Moab, at the command of the LORD" (v. 5).

Moreover, Moses is buried not at the mountain's summit, close to God, but in a valley, far from God's abode, thus preventing even the slightest suspicion that Moses might nonetheless be present among God's assembled council. Although Moses's burial is unlike that of any ordinary human, since God Himself tends to it, he is buried nonetheless: "He [the subject is God, who is mentioned at the very end of the previous verse] buried him in the valley in the land of Moab, near Beth-peor." The place of Moses's grave remains unknown: "And no one knows his burial place to this day" (Deuteronomy 34:5–6). One can interpret this as an attempt to prevent the gravesite from becoming a pilgrimage destination, part of a cult of gravesites and holy relics the likes of which the Bible despises. But if one chooses, one may read into the undisclosed location an intimation that Moses, in fact, was never buried because he never died.

Unlike other humans, Moses reaches his final day with no signs of aging: "Moses was a hundred and twenty years old when he died; his eyes were undimmed and his vigor unabated" (Deuteronomy 34:7). His age deserves our special attention. At the very beginning of the Pentateuch, in the story that sets the limit to human life span—the story of the sons of god having relations with the daughters of men (Genesis 6:1–2; see chapter 2)—God states: "My breath shall not abide in man forever, since also he is flesh; let the days allowed him be one hundred and twenty years" (v. 3). God, who set the boundary to human life span in order to exclude human beings from the immortality that is the province of God alone, now enforces this boundary at the very end of the Pentateuch, with the death of Moses, thereby signaling to readers that, to be sure, Moses came closer than any other to crossing the border into immortality, but God stopped him and put an end to his life.

It is interesting that the midrash linked Genesis 6:3 with the story of Moses's death with the question, "Where is Moses mentioned in the Torah? 'Since also he is flesh' (Genesis 6:3)" (B. *Hullin* 139b). This interpretation is based on gematria (the ancient practice of assigning a numerical value to letters and thus find meaning in the corresponding values of different words and phrases) in that "Moses" and "since also" share the same numerical value of 345. This is asserted explicitly by Rabbi Hanina bar Papa: "*be-shagam* ["since also"] and *mosheh* ["Moses"]: their numerical value is the same" (*Genesis Rabbah* 26:6).

To this internal evidence of the polemical nature of the story of Moses's death, that it opposed the tradition of his immortality, we may add an indirect, external piece of evidence: the story of Elijah's ascendance heavenward in a storm (2 Kings 2:1–18). It is well known that the story of the prophet Elijah's life follows the contours of Moses's life. One obvious example of this is the story of Elijah at Horeb in 1 Kings 19: Elijah, exasperated with the Israelites' destruction of God's altars and killing of prophets, reaches the mountain of God at Horeb, where, after fasting for forty days and forty nights, he receives a vision of God at the entrance to "the cave." This refers to the same "cleft in the rock" where Moses (who also fasted for forty days and forty nights [Deuteronomy 9:9]) was granted a similar vision (Exodus 33:17–23).

The corresponding motifs between the stories of Moses and Elijah continue until the end of their earthly lives. In the story of Elijah's departure from this world, he first crosses the Jordan on dry land (2 Kings 2:8) like Moses, who divided the Sea of Reeds for the Israelites. The reader of the tale of Elijah's ascendance may wonder why the prophet divides the Jordan and passes from Jericho to the eastern bank in order to be taken from there. It is clear that, also in this detail, we have an allusion to Moses's story. The spot where Elijah ascends heavenward, on the far bank of the Jordan, facing Jericho, is the site reached by Moses before his death: "from the steppes of Moab to Mount Nebo, to the summit of Pisgah, opposite Jericho" (Deuteronomy 34:1).

It is reasonable to say, therefore, that Elijah's biography also took its final chapter from Moses's life story—only that chapter in Moses's life, his heavenly ascent, was suppressed and has disappeared; only its echo, Elijah's ascent, remains. We have already mentioned the similarity of this phenomenon to the light of a distant star that we continue to see even after that star has died.

One may ask, why did the biblical narrators of Elijah's life story decide to preserve the element of his ascent heavenward in a whirlwind? Did they not fear that Elijah, too, might reach mythic, superhuman proportions? The answer rests in the fact that the story of Elijah's ascent did not reach us in its fullest glory. The storyteller refers to Elijah's ascent as an already known datum in a subordinate clause that pinpoints the time of the prophets' departure for Gilgal: "When the LORD was about to take Elijah up to heaven in a whirlwind, Elijah and Elisha had set out from Gilgal" (2 Kings 2:1).

When the narrator reaches the exact moment of the prophet's ascent, he grants the event little space, one verse only: "As they [Elijah and Elisha] kept on walking and talking, a fiery chariot with fiery horses suddenly appeared and separated one from the other; and Elijah went up to heaven in a whirlwind" (2 Kings 2:11). The next verse has already left Elijah and turns to Elisha and his response: "Elisha saw it, and he cried out, 'Oh father, father! Israel's chariots and horsemen!' When he could no longer see him, he grasped his garments and rent them in two" (v. 12).

The cause for this curtailment of Elijah's ascent tale is the function of 2 Kings 12 as the introduction to the stories about Elijah's heir, Elisha, and not as the closing story of Elijah's life. The entire chapter leads to the recognition that "the spirit of Elijah has settled on Elisha" (v. 15). Elisha is the hero of this story, which describes his determination, devotion to his master, and desire to be Elijah's heir. Elisha is the one who appears in every one of the story's scenes, and he is a partner in every interaction, whether it is with other prophets or with Elijah, his teacher. The miracle of Elijah's immortality reaches us, therefore, only through a back door and not by the main entrance as an official story about the end of Elijah's life on this earth.

Nevertheless, and notwithstanding the Bible's minimizing the story out of its reluctance to deal with the delicate subject of immortality, Elijah's character subsequently experienced an impressive metamorphosis due to the reference to his not having died. Elijah, whom the Bible portrays as an angry, jealous prophet who fights without mercy and without compromise against the worship of Baal, which had spread in Israel, is transformed in post-biblical Jewish literature into a man of infinite kindness and grace, the benevolent prophet who helps people in need. He appears in Rabbinic academies, reveals hidden mysteries, rescues victims of blood libel, arrives to every Passover seder, is present at every circumcision ceremony, and more.

The beginnings of this metamorphosis are recognizable already in the sealing words of prophetic literature, in the verses that close the book of Malachi and that present Moses and Elijah, the two prophets of Horeb, side by side: "Be mindful of the Teaching of My servant Moses, whom I charged at Horeb with laws and rules for all Israel. Lo, I will send the prophet Elijah to you before the coming of the awesome, fearful day of the LORD. He shall cause fathers and sons, and sons and fathers to repent, so that when I come I do not strike the whole land with utter destruction" (3:22–24). Elijah, the single prophet who never died, will return to lead the people to repentance and thereby save them from the horrors of the "day of the Lord." If Elijah's character could be so transformed due to his never having died, the reader can only imagine to what dimensions the figure of Moses would have reached had he, too, been spared death in the pages of the Pentateuch.

In passing, we will mention that the place of Moses's death and burial and of Elijah's ascension in a whirlwind, across the Jordan and opposite Jericho, marks also the spot where Elisha dies and is buried, verifying that these were identical phenomena. Proof that it is indeed the same region is found in the reference to the "bands of Moabites" in the story of Elisha's death (Moses, as will be remembered, ascended to his death "from the steppes of Moab"): "Elisha died and he was buried. Now bands of Moabites used to invade the land at the coming of every year. Once a man was being buried, when the people caught sight of such a band; so they threw the corpse into Elisha's grave and made off. When the [dead] man came in contact with Elisha's bones, he came to life and stood up" (1 Kings 13:20–21).

This story of Elisha's death and burial and of the miracle that occurs at his grave is exceptional indeed: the burial of Elisha, who, unlike Moses and Elijah, became ill and died like any human ("Elisha had been stricken with the illness of which he was to die" [1 Kings 13:14]), is unremarkable and unaccompanied by any expressions of mourning by his admirers. Moreover, there are no witnesses to the miracle that takes place, and the miracle itself seems unnecessary: the one restored to life remains anonymous. (Rabbinic literature identified him with the son of the Shunammite woman [*Shoher Tov* 26:7] or with Shalum ben Tikvah, the husband of Huldah the prophetess [*Pirkei de-Rabbi Eliezer* 33].) Following the resurrection, nothing is mentioned of anyone who ever needed him, who was happy with his return to life, or who thanked the prophet Elisha for continuing to return the dead to life even from his own grave. (He first brought back to life the son of the Shunammite woman in 2 Kings 4:8–37.)

A different reading of this short story, however, makes us question anew whether the dead body that was cast into Elisha's grave was indeed the one returned to life. Is it possible that the words "he came to life and stood up" refer to Elisha, who was mentioned at the end of the previous sentence: "When the man came in contact with the bones of Elisha"? The storyteller, it seems, casts a veil of obscurity over the image. The reader who wants to believe that Elisha returned to life from his grave (whose location is unknown)—even though no continuation of the story follows and the prophet is never seen or heard from again—can believe so. A reader who wishes to believe that a different body returned to life after touching the prophet's bones can believe that. In either case, doubt will have been awakened: Why didn't this prophet, the great resurrector, prevent his own illness and death, or, instead, resurrect himself from the dead? This brief story with its two possible interpretations was meant to cast doubt on the powers of this holy man's grave and also to obscure its location, as in the case of Moses.

The possibility that the story about Elisha's grave speaks about the prophet himself returning to life is found in Ben Sira: "No word could overcome him, and from under him his flesh was created. In his life he did great wonders, and in death he wrought miracles" (48:14–15). "His flesh was created" seems a poetic expression of the prophet's physical resurrection. The Septuagint's translation of Ben Sira reflects "his flesh prophesied" instead of "was created"—a difference in Hebrew of only one letter in what seems not to have been an accidental corruption of the text but an intentional emendation meant to diminish the prophet's stature. Incidentally, the Rabbinic sages did not entertain the possibility that Elisha was the one resurrected, and who can say whether they avoided the subject in order to refrain from spreading a tradition that so resembled the story of the resurrection of Jesus after his burial. The many similarities that early Christians drew between Elisha and their messiah are well known.

Let us return to Moses. The ancient story about Moses's end found further indirect expression in ancient Christian literature in the New Testament. To a great extent Christianity fashioned the image of Jesus following patterns cut by Moses (see chapter 18) and Elijah. An obvious expression of this tendency is noticeable in the story of the transfiguration, where Jesus ascends a high mountain with Peter, Jacob, and his brother John and is suddenly transformed before their eyes:

> And behold, there appeared unto them Moses and Elijah talking with him. Then answered Peter, and said to Jesus, Lord, it is good for us to be here: if you will, let us make here three tabernacles; one for you, and one for Moses, and one for Elijah. While he was speaking, behold, a bright cloud overshadowed them: and behold a voice out of the cloud, which said, This is my beloved Son, in whom I am well pleased; hear you him. And when the disciples heard it, they fell on their face, and were sore afraid. And Jesus came and touched them, and said, Arise, and be not afraid. And when they had lifted up their eyes, they saw no man, save Jesus only. (Matthew 17:3–8; cf. Mark 9:4–8; Luke 9:30–36)

Elijah was incorporated also into the story of Jesus's death. When Jesus calls out from the cross, "My God, my God, why have you forsaken me?" his listeners assume that "to Elijah he is calling" (Matthew 27:47), since "my God" (*'eli*) sounds like "Elijah" (*'eliyahu*), while others say, "Let us see whether Elijah will come to save him" (v. 49).

Indeed, the story of Jesus's death in the New Testament combines two models that deal with the end of a holy person's life. According to the first, the person rises directly heavenward; according to the second, he dies, is buried, and is resurrected. On the one hand, Jesus dies on the cross and is buried, the location of his grave is known (Matthew 27:45–61; cf. Mark 15:33–47; Luke 23:44–56; John 19:28–42), and his grave is sealed, with a guard posted there (Matthew 27:62–66). On the other hand, Jesus rises from the dead (Matthew 28:1–15; cf. Mark 16:1–8; Luke 24:1–12; John 20:1–18) and even appears to his disciples (Matthew 28:16–20; cf. Mark 15:14–18; Luke 24:36–50; John 20:19–23).

The Gospel of Mark tells of Jesus's heavenly ascent: "So the Lord Jesus, after speaking with his disciples, was taken up to heaven and sat down at the right hand of God" (16:19; cf. Luke 24:51). An expanded version of the description of Jesus's ascent is found in the book of Acts: "And when he had said this, as they were looking on, he was lifted up, and a cloud took him out of their sight. And while they were gazing into heaven as he went, behold, two men stood by them in white robes, and said, 'Men of Galilee, why do you stand looking into heaven? This Jesus, who was taken up from you into heaven, will come in the same way as you saw him go into heaven'" (1:9–11).

Here we see how material that the Bible sought to silence in its version of Moses's death—and, to a certain extent, Elijah's—is fully and openly reinstated in the New Testament's story of Jesus. The creators of the story of Jesus's life knowingly returned not only to the story of Elijah's ascent but also to a tradition that was still known to them about the heavenly ascent of Moses. Evidence of the tradition that Moses did not die emerges also from the words of Josephus: "A cloud suddenly descended upon him and he disappeared in a ravine. But he wrote about himself in the sacred books that he died, for fear lest they should venture to say that by reason of his surpassing virtue he had gone back to God" (*Jewish Antiquities* 4.8.48). Similarly, the Babylonian Talmud preserves the clear opinion that Moses ascended to heaven without dying: "Moses did not die but stands and serves on high" (*Sota* 13b).

According to the Pentateuch, Moses was denied the opportunity to lead the Israelites into the Land of Israel due to his transgression of striking the rock instead of speaking to it, as he had been commanded to, and he died just beyond its borders (Numbers 20:12–13, 27:12–14; Deuteronomy 32:48–52). A different perspective is presented by Psalm 106: "They provoked wrath at the waters of Meribah and Moses suffered on their account" (v. 32). In the opinion of this psalm, it was not Moses who sinned but the people, and he was punished on their account. The sin that is attributed to Moses, however, is just one part of the Pentateuch's broader effort to show us that Moses was not perfect. He, too, was human—flesh and blood—at birth and also at death.

21

Son of God?

The Suspicious Story of Samson's Birth

The story of Samson's birth in Judges 13 opens the Bible's biography of Samson, which moves from his birth to his death, three chapters later, in Judges 16. Samson's birth story represents one in a succession of biblical stories about barren women (Sarah, Rebekah, Rachel, Hannah, the Shunammite woman), all of which end with the birth of a son.

In Judges 13 an angel of God appears to Samson's mother (though she does not recognize him as such) and announces the approaching birth of her son, who will be a Nazirite from birth and who will deliver the Israelites from their Philistine enemies. After the woman's husband, Manoah, asks to meet the messenger—who, the woman claims, is a man of God—the angel again appears to the woman when she is alone. She brings the angel and her husband together, and then she and her husband watch as the angel ascends heavenward amidst flames from the rock. When Manoah realizes that they have seen an angel of God, he fears for their lives, but the woman calms him. With the birth of her son, she gives the boy the name Samson.

A number of details in this story both awaken our wonder and demand our attention. The revelation of the messenger/angel to the woman (and not the man) is described with the words "an angel of the LORD appeared to the woman" (Judges 13:3), typical language for describing revelation (cf., e.g., Genesis 12:7; 1 Kings 9:12). In presenting the woman's report of this meeting to her husband, however, the narrator writes: "The woman *came* and told her husband, 'A man of

God *came* to me'" (v. 6). The root *b-w-'*, "come," is used twice: first by the narrator to describe the woman's approaching her husband, and then in the words the woman uses to describe the angel's appearance. The biblical writer's repetition of the root is his signal to us to draw an analogy from the first to the second. The two "comings," he is suggesting, were but "appearances" and carry no sexual implication, though the sexual meaning of the verb "come" was well known (e.g., "He *came* to Hagar and she conceived" [Genesis 16:4]; see also Genesis 29:21; 2 Samuel 16:21–22).

The woman's husband will also use the root *b-w-'* when he asks that the angel reappear, this time before both him and his wife. Manoah's words, too, foil any possible sexual connotation: "Manoah pleaded with the LORD, 'Oh my LORD!' he said, 'please let the man of God that You sent come to us again'" (Judges 13:8). When the angel again appears to the woman, the narrator marks his visit with the words "God heeded Manoah's plea, and the angel of God came to the woman again" (v. 9), but when Manoah turns to the visitor, he does not ask, "Are you the man who came to my wife?" but "Are you the man who spoke to my wife?" (v. 11): Manoah, we are to understand, is certain that only words were exchanged between his wife and the angel/man.

Both the use of the root *b-w-'* and the simultaneous insistence that nothing sexual occurred between the angel and the woman appear to be directed at combating the view—or, really, the mythical tradition—according to which a creature not of this world, a divine being, had sexual relations with Manoah's wife: he "came" to her, and from this union was Samson born. It is as though the storyteller reassures us: "True, the angel did indeed 'come' to Manoah's wife, but do not make the mistake of thinking that the verse speaks of him coming to a woman in the sexual meaning of the word: it speaks simply of his appearing before her."

And yet we are dubious. Why does the angel appear the second time to the woman when she is alone? Rabbi Isaac Abarbanel, in his commentary on Judges, sensed the difficulty and tried to address it: "And he said that he came to the woman because she was more ready

... and also he came to her now, the second time, because she would recognize him and would know that it was he that came to her the first time, something that wouldn't have been were he to come to Manoah. Because he didn't know whether it was he that came to his wife or not."

Abarbanel's explanation does not completely eliminate the problem. Why doesn't the angel appear to the woman and her husband when they are together, as they had requested: "Let the man of God that You sent come to us again, and instruct us how to act with the child that is to be born" (Judges 13:8)? In that way, too, the woman would be able to confirm that the man was the same who had previously told her of the birth of her son.

The story's intentions begin to emerge when we notice details that are provided at the end of the second meeting between the woman and the angel: "And the angel of God came to the woman again. She was sitting in the field and her husband Manoah was not with her" (Judges 13:9). This time the meeting takes place not only without the husband but also outside the town, that is, with no witnesses, in the field—a place perfect for trouble. Crimes occur in the field: Cain murdered his brother Abel in the field (Genesis 4:8); out in the fields, the son of the wise woman of Tekoa is said to have come to blows with his brother and to have killed him (2 Samuel 14:6); and it is for corpses—unidentified murders—that are found in the fields that the "beheaded heifer" ritual is performed (Deuteronomy 21:1).

Moreover, in the field, where a woman has no ability to protect herself and call for help, rape prevails: "But if the man comes upon the engaged girl in the field, and the man lies with her by force, only the man who lay with her shall die, but you shall do nothing to the girl. The girl did not incur the death penalty, for this case is like that of a man attacking another and murdering him. He came upon her in the field; though the engaged girl cried for help, there was no one to save her" (Deuteronomy 22:25–27; see also chapter 26 on the meeting of Isaac and Rebekah in the field).

The fact that the meeting takes place in the field and the narrative's particular note of the woman being without her husband awaken our suspicion, therefore—if only of the possibility—that something un-seemly occurred between the angel and the woman. The narrator, who leaves us his official version of the events, does not share our doubt. He admits that the circumstances would have allowed the angel to "come" to the woman, but, according to his account, no such violation occurred: the angel coming to her was simply his appearing to her and no more.

As a result of the angel's appearance, the barren woman conceives and gives birth to a son, whom she names Samson (Judges 13:24). The woman gives the newborn his name both because she is the dominant figure in the story and because she was the one to whom was given the news of his expected birth. No etymology is provided when Samson's mother names him, an almost singular phenomenon in the Bible, so that this, too, should catch readers' notice. The storyteller, it seems, wanted to avoid providing any interpretation of the name in order to sidestep the inherent relationship between *shimshon*, "Samson," and *shemesh*, "sun," a relationship that reflects some sort of pagan, mytho-logical belief.

The relationship between the boy's name and the sun was under-stood already by early interpreters, however, who sought to circumvent the problem by offering their own etymologies. According to Jose-phus: "And when the boy was born they called him Samson, meaning 'their might'" (*Jewish Antiquities* 5.8.4), an interpretation that bases itself, apparently, on a verse in the Song of Deborah in Judges 5: "So may all Your enemies perish, O LORD, but may His friends be as the sun rising in might" (v. 31).

The Talmud, too, sought to undermine any notion that Samson was named—heaven forbid—after a foreign deity. There, "sun" becomes a nickname for God, this, too, based on a biblical verse: "Rabbi Jochanan said, Samson is named after the name of the Holy One, blessed be He, as it is said, 'For the Lord God is sun and shield' (Ps. 84:12).... As the Holy One, blessed be He, protects the whole world, so does Samson protect Israel in his generation" (B. *Sota* 10a).

Another example of the removal of the threat inherent in the relationship between *shemesh* and *shimshon* (and note: we are told that Samson lived his life between Tzorah and Eshtaol, an area in which also the town of Beit Shemesh was located, though the name Beit Shemesh, "House of the Sun," is avoided in the stories about Samson) is found in the tale of Samson's wedding feast at Timnah, where he challenges the Philistine townsmen with a riddle (Judges 14:12–20). The townsmen, who wrest the riddle's answer from Samson's wife using threats, tell the solution to Samson at the very last moment, "on the seventh day, before the sun set" (v. 18), where the word used for "sun" is not the usual *shemesh* but *heres*, the same word we saw used in relation to Joshua's sun connection (see chapter 5).

Indeed, we recall how in that story the special relationship between Joshua and the sun became expressed (among other ways) through the name of the city where he was buried, Timnath-heres. In Samson's story, too, the sun element in the name of the city Timnah, Timnath-heres (although it is a different Timnath-heres, this one in Judah and not in Ephraim), is explained in a way that removes any suspicion of a mythological foundation. According to the covert name etymology in Judges 14, the city is called Timnath-heres because it was just before the sun set on the seventh day of the wedding feast that the countrymen discovered the secret of Samson's riddle: in that, and only that, lies the connection between Samson and the sun.

The efforts exerted by the biblical narrator to remove the troublesome notion that Samson was the son of the angel who heralded the news of his birth—or the son of a sun god—were not entirely successful. Josephus describes Manoah as being unable to quiet his suspicions:

[Manoah] was moreover madly enamored of his wife and hence inordinately jealous. Now once when his wife was alone, a specter appeared to her from God, in the likeness of a comely and tall youth, bringing her the good news of the approaching birth of a son through God's good providence—a son goodly and illustrious for strength, by whom, on his reaching man's estate, the Philistines would be afflicted. He further charged her not to cut the lad's locks, and that he was to renounce all other form of drink (so God commanded) and to accustom himself to water only. And having thus spoken the visitor departed, having come but to execute God's will. The woman, when her husband arrived, reported what she had heard from the angel, extolling the young man's comeliness and stature in such wise that he in his jealousy was driven by these praises to distraction and to conceive the suspicions that such passion arouses. But she, wishing to allay her husband's unreasonable distress, entreated God to send the angel again that her husband also might see him. And again by the grace of God the angel came, while they were in the suburb, and appeared to the woman when parted from her husband. She besought him to stay until she could fetch her husband and, obtaining his assent, went in pursuit of Manoah. But the husband, on beholding the angel, even then did not desist from his suspicion. (*Jewish Antiquities* 5.8.2–3)[1]

It becomes clear that the story of Samson's birth, as formulated in the book of Judges, was aimed at uprooting an ancient tradition that told how Samson was the son of a divine being and human woman, a tradition like that of the sons of god and daughters of men with which we dealt in chapter 2. And just as that story ended with the birth of giants, so, too, does the Bible allude to Samson's exceptional physical dimensions in the story about his ripping out the gates of Gaza and carrying them to the top of the mountain that is near Hebron (Judges 16:1–3). Samson's massive size, a detail muffled in the biblical version, is made starkly explicit by the Rabbis: "Rabbi Shimon the pious said: Samson's shoulders measured sixty cubits, as it is said, 'But Samson lay in bed only till midnight. At midnight he got up, grasped the doors of the town gate together with the two gateposts, and pulled them out along with the bar. He placed them on his shoulders,' teaching us that the gates of Gaza were not less than sixty cubits [more than twenty yards]" (B. *Sota* 10a).

1. *Josephus, Jewish Antiquities, Books V–VIII*, trans. H. St. J. Thackeray and R. Marcus (London: Loeb Classical Library, 1934).

194

This reconstructed tradition, according to which Samson was a giant born of a divine father and mortal mother, has parallels in the cultures that surrounded the ancient Israelites. Of particular interest to us is the story of the birth of Heracles. According to Greek myth, Heracles's father was Zeus, the supreme god of the pantheon. Zeus comes to Thebes when Heracles's mother, Alceme, is by the river and, disguised as her husband, Amphitryon (who is away at war), has intercourse with her. A short while later the triumphant Amphitryon returns home, only to wonder at his wife's belief that she has already slept with him that day, and he, too, has relations with her. From these two consecutive couplings Alceme gives birth to twins, who were very different one from the other: the larger Heracles resembled his father, Zeus, in height, appearance, and ability, while his brother, the son of Amphitryon, was of human proportions. At Zeus's bidding, Amphitryon was persuaded to raise Heracles as his son.

Unlike the mythical story of Heracles, the biblical story (like the other birth stories we mentioned above) speaks of a barren woman. It may be that the pattern of the barren woman replaced the mythical motif about gods having relations with women. The expression used in the stories of Leah's and Rachel's pregnancies, "and He opened her womb" (Genesis 29:31, 30:32), where the subject is God, endures as the linguistic remains of that mythic tradition.

Rejected from the Bible, the mythical concept continued its life quietly until it bubbled to the surface in the New Testament in the story of the birth of Jesus, the son of God and the mortal Mary. According to the Gospel of Matthew, Jesus's mother (who is not depicted as barren) conceives Jesus before having relations with her husband, just like what is told about the mother of Heracles: "Now the birth of Jesus Christ took place in this way. When his mother Mary had been betrothed to Joseph, before they came together she was found to be with child of the Holy Spirit" (Matthew 1:18). Like Amphitryon, who agreed, after being urged by Zeus, to remain with his wife, so, too, does Joseph agree to remain with Mary:

Then Joseph her husband, being a just man, and not wanting to make her a public example, was minded to put her away secretly. But while he thought about these things, behold, an angel of the Lord appeared to him in a dream saying, "Joseph, son of David, do not be afraid to take to you Mary your wife, for that which is conceived in her is of the Holy Spirit. And she will bring forth a Son, and you shall call His name Jesus, for He will save His people from their sins." (vv. 19–21)

In this story there is even an announcement of Jesus's destiny, as there was regarding Samson: "He shall be the first to deliver Israel from the Philistines" (Judges 13:5). In the parallel story in the Gospel of Luke (1:26–38), the angel Gabriel tells the betrothed (yet still virgin) Mary the news of Jesus's birth in a private exchange that takes place while they are entirely alone.

In Christian tradition, Jesus is granted ascendance and divinity, as was Heracles, while Samson, like the sons of gods in Genesis 6, finishes his life as a human being, buried under the collapsed ruins of the temple of Dagon in Gaza. Once myth is rejected, death becomes inevitable, and Samson's death, however heroic, is necessarily final; it is a death from which there can be no resurrection. In belief systems that open themselves up to myth, heroes born to divine fathers will ultimately become gods. In Jewish tradition, which replaced the divine father with a human one, a hero's biography concludes with his death.

22

A Cinderella Tale

Clues to David's Lost Birth Story

David is first presented to readers in the book of Samuel after God has become fed up with Israel's first king, Saul, and dispatches the prophet Samuel to anoint the new king: "Fill your horn with oil and set out; I am sending you to Jesse the Bethlehemite, for I have decided on one of his sons to be king" (1 Samuel 16:1). Remarkably, the storyteller doesn't bother to include anything more detailed about the family and origins of Israel's future king. An ancestry provides evidence that the candidate's family is known and honorable. When Saul was first introduced, the biblical storyteller was unstinting with genealogical details: "There was a man of Benjamin whose name was Kish son of Abiel son of Zeror son of Becorath son of Aphiah, a Benjaminite, a man of substance. He had a son whose name was Saul" (1 Samuel 9:1–2). The prophet Samuel's story began with a reference to his father and his genealogy: "There was a man from Ramathaim of the Zuphitesin the hill country of Ephraim, whose name was Elkanah son of Jeroham son of Elihu son of Tohu son of Zuph, an Ephraimite" (1:1). Given the generous information that is provided about these two figures whose lives are so intertwined with David's, it seems puzzling that news of David's origins is withheld. To be sure, a feeling of incompleteness led to the missing elements being supplied in the book of Ruth, which was written much later, during the Second Temple period. That book ends with a list of the ten generations from Perez son of Judah to David (4:18–22). But our interests lie in the book whose main concern is the life of David, the book of Samuel, and there the lack remains strongly felt.

The story of David and Goliath, which follows the story of David's anointing, once again introduces David's family, though it, too, neglects to supply the missing elements: "David was the son of a certain Ephrathite ['*efrati*] of Bethlehem in Judah whose name was Jesse" (1 Samuel 17:12). Only the detail that David is from an Ephrathite family has been added, but here, as opposed to the term "Ephraimite" in Samuel's genealogy (which is written identically), the reference is not to the tribe Ephraim but to Ephratha, the other name of Bethlehem. (See, e.g., the prophet Micah's words about the Davidic king in the days to come: "And you, O Bethlehem of Ephratha, least among the clans of Judah, from you one shall come forth to rule Israel for Me" [5:1].)

We will discuss the reason for the absence of David's pedigree from the book of Samuel in the course of addressing another source of bafflement: the Bible preserves no account of David's birth. Our astonishment is certainly legitimate, since the Bible describes the births of key figures in the nation's history (as we have already seen in chapters 16, 18, and 21), including that of Perez, the forefather of the Davidic dynasty. Can we offer an explanation for the omission of David's birth story? Is it possible that one explanation will account also for the absence of his genealogy?

On the face of it, one could make the simple claim that a birth story would interrupt plot development. Since David's story is intertwined (at least in its beginnings) with the history of Saul, turning away from Saul at some arbitrary point to observe the birth of a child who would rise onto the stage of history only many years later would be contrived. Even more, one might claim, the narrator-redactor of the book of Samuel is not eager to present David to us until the measure of Saul's transgressions has been laid out and he has incurred God's wrath, as the prophet Samuel tells Saul: "The LORD has this day torn the kingship over Israel away from you and has given it to another who is worthier than you" (1 Samuel 15:28). Only when God comes to regret Saul's kingship (v. 35), this argument continues, is there reason to present

David to the reader, and, at that point, David is already too mature to turn around and tell the story of his birth. Even granting some weight to this argument, there would seem to be another, more decisive reason that explains the missing elements that we have noticed.

The stories of David's youth portray him as a sort of boy Cinderella. Take, for instance, the account of the anointing of David in 1 Samuel 16:1–13. When Samuel arrives to the town, the young David is not invited to participate in the sacrificial ceremony along with his brothers but is, alone, excluded; he remains out with his father's flocks, shepherding. Only when it becomes clear that none of Jesse's other sons are fit to be king and a puzzled Samuel asks, "Are these all the boys?" does Jesse answer, "There is still the youngest; he is tending the flock" (v. 11). It is, in the end, this youngest son who is revealed to be God's chosen, the one to rule over Israel. (As we will see in the next chapter, the story of David's battle against Goliath also contains a similar Cinderella-type picture.)

The Cinderella story type is inherently incompatible with tales of miraculous birth. Cinderella reaches success despite her lack of pedigree and despite her subordinate status within her family. Here, then, we seem to have discovered the cause for our story's two missing elements: David's nonexistent birth story and genealogy in the book of Samuel.

As it is inconceivable that stories of David's birth were not told in Jerusalem and in Judah generally, we must ask whether there is any way for us to glimpse behind the Bible's curtain and eavesdrop on voices that told such tales, even if they have not reached us in written form.

One clue to the nature of that story is perhaps found in the verse that we mentioned above, which introduces Jesse, David's father: "David was the son of a certain Ephrathite of Bethlehem in Judah whose name was Jesse. He had eight sons, and in the days of Saul the man was already old, advanced in years" (1 Samuel 17:12). Why does the verse emphasize Jesse's being an elderly father to his youngest son, David? The elderly father motif is one that appears in other biblical birth stories that are also tales of barren women who miraculously conceive:

the story of Isaac's birth to Abraham (Genesis 18:11–12) and the story of the Shunammite woman to whom Elisha announces the approaching birth of her son (2 Kings 4:14).

Also Boaz was an older man when he married Ruth, a conclusion inferred from his words of praise for Ruth, who did not "turn to younger men, whether poor or rich" (Ruth 3:10). The Rabbis, too, determined that Boaz was older. (See *Tanḥuma Buber* 21:16, where, on the threshing floor, Boaz tells Ruth, "I am eighty years old"; see also *Ruth Rabbah* 6:2: "Boaz was eighty years old and hadn't been granted [a son] and when this righteous woman [Ruth] prayed for him, he was granted [a son].") In fact, Ruth, too, was barren, having been married for ten years to her first husband, Naomi's son, without conceiving (Ruth 1:4), and she has no children with Boaz until God intervenes (4:13).

Does the reference to Jesse's advanced age allude to David being born to a barren woman? If that is the case, then Jesse must have had two wives: the mother of the young David and the mother of his other sons. This theory finds support in a number of the Bible's barren-women stories: Abraham fathered a child through Hagar before impregnating Sarah, Jacob sired numerous sons from Leah and the maidservants before fathering Joseph from Rachel, and Elkanah produced sons from Pnina before Hannah conceived and gave birth to Samuel.

A tradition that told how David had a different mother than Jesse's other sons would also be consistent with the tension the Bible depicts between David and his brothers. This tension is noticeable when, as the threat of war with Goliath looms large, David is sent by his father to check on his brothers' well-being. When he arrives at the battlefield, the eldest, Eliab, angrily accuses him: "Why did you come down here, and with whom did you leave those few sheep in the wilderness? I know your impudence and your impertinence; you came down to watch the fighting!" (1 Samuel 17:28).

The enmity between the youngest son and his older brothers reminds us of the story of Joseph when Jacob sent him (the son of the beloved Rachel, the barren wife who conceived) to check on the well-being of his other sons (from other wives) who were tending the flocks, and they mistreat Joseph (Genesis 37). Joseph and David, youngest sons who were rejected and abused by their brothers, are the sons who will ultimately reach the highest position as one of the king's senior advisors or as king. Moreover, tension between David and his brothers is felt lurking also behind the story of his anointing (1 Samuel 16), where, as we've already mentioned, all the sons are ordered to gather to the sacrificial feast except for the young David, who is brought only after Samuel explicitly orders his attendance.

Let's return to our conjectured story of David's beginnings. As it happens, a story about this hero's birth, though not exactly fitting our expectations of a story of a barren but beloved woman miraculously conceiving a child, is indeed found in Rabbinic literature, in one of the later collections of midrashic traditions, *Yalqut Hamakhiri*. The fact that a story emerges only in a late period does not necessarily attest to the time of its writing. *Yalqut Hamakhiri* copied this tradition from another midrashic source that preceded it but that has since been lost. In fact, a tradition that appears only in a late anthology may be a reappearance of an ancient tradition from biblical times that made its way circuitously through history or of a tradition that responded to another that was lost. The story about David that is found in *Yalqut Hamakhiri* is as follows:

One said: David was the son of a beloved [woman], and one said: David was the son of a hated [woman] . . . and [Jesse] had six older sons, and he avoided his wife for three years. After three years he had a handsome maidservant and he desired her. He said to her: My daughter, fix yourself up tonight. . . . The maidservant went away and said to her mistress: Save yourself and my soul and my lord from hell. She said to her: What is the matter? She told her everything. She said to her: My daughter, What can I do that it is now three years that he has not touched me? She said to her: I will give you advice. Go and fix yourself up, and also I will do so, and in the evening when he says to close the door—you slip in and I will go out. So she did. At evening, the maidservant stood and extinguished the candle, [she] went to close the door, her mistress entered and she left, she spent the whole night with him and conceived David. And from his love for that maidservant David emerged much ruddier than his brothers [apparently, this is based on a folk belief that particularly red babies are the fruit of forbidden desire; see also 1 Samuel 17:42].... After nine months her sons wanted to kill her and her son David because they saw that he was red. Jesse said to them: Leave him alone; he will be our servant and will tend to the flocks. The matter was kept quiet for twenty-eight years, when the Holy One, blessed be He, said to Samuel: "I am sending you to Jesse the Bethlehemite...." [Jesse] told him: "There is still the youngest; he is tending the flock." He told him: "Send someone to bring him." When he came, the oil [this is the oil with which kings are anointed] began to swell and rise up. The Holy One, blessed be He, said to Samuel: ". . . Anoint him, for this is the one." The oil on his head crystallized into jewels and pearls . . . and Jesse and his sons stood in great fear. They said: He did not come but to scorn us and let Israel know that this son is illegitimate. And the mother of David was happy, inside, but sad, outside. When [Samuel] raised a glass, they were all happy. Samuel stood and kissed him on his head and said: "The Lord said to me, 'You are My son'" (Ps. 2:7). At the same time, his mother said: "The stone that the builders [*ha-bonim*] rejected has become the chief cornerstone" (Ps. 118:22). "The sons" [*ha-banim*] is written. [The word *ha-bonim* can be vocalized differently so that it becomes *ha-banim*, and it is the play between these two readings that the midrash makes use of.] She said: You are a son rejected by your brothers and now you have become the cornerstone and you have ascended higher than all. Her sons said to her: "This is the Lord's doing" (Ps. 118:23), therefore "This is the day that the Lord has made—let us exult and rejoice on it" (v. 24). (*Yalqut Hamekhiri* to Psalm 118:22)

It is worth making a number of comments about this tradition:

- While the Bible mentions nothing about David's mother, she stands at the center of this tradition, a typical characteristic of birth stories.
- The question whether David is the son of a beloved or a despised wife returns us to the same biblical stories about barren women in which tension exists between the beloved barren wife and the despised yet fruitful one: Jacob and his wives; Elkanah and his wives; and perhaps also Abraham and his wives.
- The man finds himself engaged in sexual relations not with the woman he desires but with another—a motif found in the story of Jacob and his wives. On his wedding night, Jacob thinks that he is with Rachel but, come morning, learns that it was Leah, her sister (Genesis 29:23–25). The motif of the woman who disguises herself in order to have sexual relations is found also in the story of the birth of Perez, the ancestor of the Davidic line, and Zerah, his brother, where Judah, the tribe's patriarch, has relations with his daughter-in-law Tamar, whom he takes to be a prostitute (Genesis 38:14–16).
- The motif of a desire to kill a woman out of the belief that she became pregnant from adulterous relations is found also in the story of the birth of Zerah and Perez, when Tamar's pregnancy is discovered and Judah orders: "Bring her out and let her be burned" (Genesis 38:24).
- It is possible that the story in *Yalqut Hamakhiri* is indeed a response to an ancient tradition that related how David was the son of another woman from a family of lower origins, a maidservant whom Jesse desired. A story about a father who has relations with a woman of low origins and the tensions that emerge between her son and the man's other offspring can be found in the story of Jephthah: "Jephthah the Gileadite was an able warrior who was the son of a prostitute. Jephthah's father was Gilead; but Gilead also had sons by his wife, and when the wife's sons grew up, they drove Jephthah out. They said to him, 'You shall have no share in our father's property, for you are the son of an outsider'" (Judges 11:1–2). Of course,

in the end it is Jephthah, the son who was rejected and excluded by his half-brothers, who becomes leader and redeemer. We can imagine how, in an attempt to manage a comparable story about David, there began to be told how David was the son of Jesse's one and only wife, the mother of all his sons, and how it was because of Jesse's passing desire for a maidservant that this youngest son was born red, different from the others. For this reason the boy would have been distanced from the rest of the household in order not to invite shame on the family, and this would have been the cause of the antagonism between David and his brothers.

- We cannot exclude the possibility that the midrashic tradition was created as a response to a different tradition that cast doubts on David's origins: a tradition that told how his mother had conceived from a man other than her husband. Such suspicions were aroused concerning the mothers of Samson and Jesus (we saw this regarding Samson's birth in chapter 21) and, in Rabbinic traditions, also regarding Sarah during her stay in the palaces of Pharaoh and Abimelech (we'll deal with this in chapter 25) and even about David's children (see chapter 29).

Even if such stories existed, echoes of which we have tried to find in the late midrash *Yalqut Hamakhiri*, these were certainly not the only tales that were once told about the birth of David. In the circles of his admirers in the Kingdom of Judah many different stories were surely told, stories that were filled with miracles about the birth of the king, and these could not have been more different from the tales told among his rivals in the Kingdom of Ephraim.

Birth stories usually include both an act of naming and a name derivation based on the name's phonological patterns, folk etymologies that often have no scientific basis. An example is the etymology of the name Moses (*mosheh*), which the Egyptian daughter of Pharaoh gives him: "And she named him Moses, explaining, 'I drew him [*meshitihu*] out of the water'" (Exodus 2:10). Because the story of David's birth has been denied us, along with the etymology of his name, we can't exclude the possibility that that story contained a name derivation that explained the name David by way of its relationship to the identically spelled *dod* ("beloved"), *dodim*, or *yedidot* (both abstract nouns meaning "love"), allusions to the father's love for the boy's mother.

Many verses in the first stories about David in the book of Samuel mention love in relation to David, such as Saul's love for David (1 Samuel 16:21), the love between David and Jonathan son of Saul (18:1–3; 2 Samuel 1:26), the love of Michal daughter of Saul for David (1 Samuel 18:20, 28), and the love of "all Israel and Judah" for David (18:16). It is therefore interesting that it is the birth of Solomon, David's son, that finally compensates us for the absence of this etymology of David's name when it points to God's love for Solomon as the reason for Solomon's second name, Yedidiah: "And He sent a message through the prophet Nathan; and he was named Yedidiah at the instance of the LORD" (2 Samuel 12:24–25).

We have seen how, in various layers of Israel's literature, the deficiency that characterizes the story of David's beginnings in the book of Samuel became filled. A genealogical list that supplies the family's roots is provided later, in Ruth 4:18–22 and 1 Chronicles 2:3–17. For a birth story, we must wait even longer, until the late midrashic compilation *Yalqut Hamakhiri*. We found covert name derivations scattered throughout the first chapters of David's life story, and we traced imprints of rejected traditions about David's birth in the official traditions about his youth, in the book of Samuel. All these, joined together, have assisted us in reconstructing what we believe to have been the original story about David's beginnings.

23

Finding the Real Killer of Goliath

Who killed Goliath? There would seem to be no easier question. Even people with the shallowest of knowledge of the Bible somehow remember the tale of the giant Philistine's defeat at the hands of the boy David with his two-pronged stick (1 Samuel 17). David's victory, we recall, brought the demise of the Philistine threat over Israel.

References to the youthful David's wondrous victory can be found also outside of that specific story. When fleeing King Saul and passing through the temple at Nob, David asks Ahimelech the priest for a weapon, and he answers him: "There is the sword of Goliath the Philistine whom you slew in the valley of Elah; it is over there, wrapped in a cloth, behind the ephod" (1 Samuel 21:10). Thus we learn how that oversized enemy's sword was kept in a temple, in the presence of God, as a reminder of God's salvation and as an expression of thanksgiving for God's granting the victory to His servant, comparable to the jar of manna and the staff of Aaron, which were also stored in the presence of God in testimony and tribute (Exodus 16:33–34; Numbers 17:25).

Another reference to David's victory is made when David and Saul return from the battlefield after Goliath's fall and women come out to meet them, singing: "Saul has slain his thousands; David, his tens of thousands" (1 Samuel 18:7). The song becomes famous, known even among the Philistines, as we learn later in the story of David's flight from Saul, when the despairing young hero makes his way to the lion's den itself, to the court of King Achish in Goliath's own city, Gath. The king's courtiers notify him of David's alarming presence: "Why that's David, king of the land! That's the one of whom they sing as they dance, 'Saul has slain his thousands, David, his tens of thousands'" (21:12). Later, when vicissitudes in his relations with Saul push David to return once more to the court of the Philistine ruler, he appears there as one wishing to side with the Philistines against Saul, but the king's ministers counsel the king to take care: "Remember, he is the David of whom they sang as they danced, Saul has slain his thousands; David, his tens of thousands" (1 Samuel 29:5).

David's victory over Goliath is recorded also in Psalm 151, a psalm absent from the Hebrew Bible but included in the Septuagint. The title of the psalm specifies that it was said by David "following his battle with Goliath," and the psalm concludes: "I went out to meet the Philistine, and he cursed me by his idols. But I drew his own sword and cut off his head and took away reproach from the children of Israel" (vv. 6–7). In the *Psalms Scroll* from Qumran, on the other hand, Goliath's defeat is mentioned at the start of another psalm, in the only words of that psalm to have been preserved. The psalm is found directly following the psalm that corresponds to the Septuagint's Psalm 151: "Beginning of David's po[w]er, after God's prophet had anointed him. Then I saw a Philistine threatening from the ran[ks of the Philistines.] I ..." The story is referenced once more in the Septuagint, in Psalm 144 (there numbered as 143), which receives a title that ties it to David's victory over Goliath: "Of David about Goliath." Whoever added this title did so because the psalm indeed offers a blessing to God for preparing the speaker for war: "Blessed is the LORD, my rock, who trains my hands for battle, my fingers for warfare" (v. 1). The poet's enemies, from whose hands he was saved, are "foreigners . . . whose mouths speak lies" (vv. 7–8)—a description that calls to mind Goliath, who "dared defy the ranks of the living God" (1 Samuel 17:26) and who cursed David (v. 23).

The secure position held by the David and Goliath episode in the collective memory of Bible readers can apparently be attributed to two factors. First, there is the legendary aspect of the tale about a simple youth who vanquishes the enemy that threatened Israel, who manages to kill the Philistine giant and thereby win prizes that had been promised to the one who would succeed: "The man who kills him will be rewarded by the king with great riches; he will also give him his daughter in marriage and grant exemption to his father's house in Israel" (1 Samuel 17:25). David, the youngest of Jesse's sons, did not leave for the battlefield with his older brothers but stayed home instead to shepherd his father's flocks. When Jesse sends him to inquire after his brothers' well-being, he witnesses the terror the giant inspires and also learns of the prize that is promised the victor, and he rises to the challenge.

The second explanation for the story's hold on our collective memory is the religious lesson it conveys, the recognition that the power of salvation is the realm of God's, a God who chooses His human messengers for reasons that are hidden from us. Goliath the Philistine is an experienced fighter who is not only massive in size but also massively equipped with a warrior's paraphernalia. The Bible, which generally avoids physical descriptions, here spares no detail: "He was six cubits and a span tall. He had a bronze helmet on his head, and wore a breastplate of scale armor, a bronze breastplate weighing five thousand shekels. He had bronze greaves on his legs, and a bronze javelin [slung] from his shoulders. The shaft of his spear was like a weaver's bar, and the iron head of his spear weighed six hundred shekels; and the shield-bearer marched in front of him" (1 Samuel 17:4–7). Goliath is portrayed as a walking arsenal, more war machine than human being. In his contemptuous challenges to Israel's troops (v. 10), actually to the "God of the ranks of Israel" (v. 45), he leaves no choice to the Israelites but to answer his challenge and dispatch a fighter to meet him in a duel that will decide the war.

When David offers himself for the task, Saul is less than enthusiastic: "You cannot go to that Philistine and fight him; you are only a boy, and he has been a warrior from his youth!" (1 Samuel 17:33). David has to convince the king that he is not only willing but able, and he tells the king of an event that we had not heard about previously: "Your servant has been tending his father's sheep, and if a lion or a bear came and carried off an animal from the flock, I would go after it and fight it and rescue it from its mouth. And if it attacked me, I would seize it by the beard and strike it down and kill it. Your servant has killed both lion and bear; and that uncircumcised Philistine shall end up like one of them, for he has defied the ranks of the living God" (vv. 34–36).

Up to this point, David has attributed his success to himself; his strength and his powerful hands brought him his victories (and note the abundant use of first-person verbs used to describe the youth's deeds). But from the moment that he mentions the God of Israel, whom the Philistine has now challenged, David begins to reflect and is suddenly granted a fresh view of the past. The storyteller marks this new stage in David's recollections by having the young hero open his mouth again—the writer inserts "and David said," even though David's speech has not been interrupted—and then continues: "The LORD who saved me from lion and bear will also save me from that Philistine" (1 Samuel 17:37). David's attribution of the victory to God is what spurs Saul to allow David to face the giant: "Saul said to David, 'Then go, and may the LORD be with you'" (v. 37).

The narrator of our story chooses a number of ways to show readers that the victory has indeed been achieved only with God's help. First, he presents the comic picture of David struggling to dress himself in the king's military uniform, including breastplate and weapons: "Saul clothed David in his own garment; he placed a bronze helmet on his head and fastened a breastplate on him. David girded his sword over his garment. Then he tried to walk; but he was not used to it. And David said to Saul, 'I cannot walk in these, for I am not used to them.' So David took them off" (1 Samuel 17:38–39). The effort fails, and the youthful shepherd soon faces the enemy with only river stones and slingshot. Goliath, the renowned fighter, mocks David, "for he was but a boy, ruddy and handsome" (v. 42), a boy who resembled more a rosy-cheeked girl than a hardened fighter. Goliath calls out, "Am I a dog that you come against me with sticks?" and then "cursed David by his gods" (v. 43).

Goliath blasphemes against David's God and challenges Him, but David, who throws his lot in with God, answers the challenge: "Da-

vid replied to the Philistine, 'You come against me with sword and
spear and javelin, but I come against you in the name of the LORD of
Hosts, the God of the ranks of Israel, whom you have defied" (1 Samuel 17:45). It is not only to Goliath that the young David addresses his
message but also—and, perhaps, chiefly—to his own countrymen:
"And this whole assembly shall know that the LORD can give victory
without sword or spear. For the battle is the LORD's and He will deliver you into our hands" (v. 47). David's speech voices the theme of
the whole story, and even Goliath listens patiently. Once David has
killed the Philistine with his pseudo-weaponry, the storyteller again
emphasizes that "David had no sword" (v. 50), so that it is with Goliath's that David then beheads him (v. 51).

And yet, standing against the force of this story, the important mes-
sages it conveys, and the many echoes of it from other stories, we find
one isolated verse that causes us to question who killed Goliath. At
the end of the book of Samuel (2 Samuel 20:23–24:25) is an appendix
to the story of David's life, placed just before the story of the king's
death and his son Solomon's inheritance of the throne at the start of
the book of Kings. The appendix contains different materials of various literary genres: lists of officials and short anecdotes, longer stories
and bits of poetry and psalms. In the middle we find a succession of
four short stories of heroic deeds ascribed to soldiers who fought for
David and who defeated Philistines (2 Samuel 21:15–22).

The third of these heroic tales deals with the victory over Goliath
from Gath, though it attributes that victory not to David but to another
fighter from Bethlehem: "Again there was fighting with the Philistines
at Gob; and Elhanan son of Jarre oregim [*'orgim*, "weavers," a word
copied here by mistake but that appears also correctly in the text's
continuation] the Bethlehemite killed Goliath the Gittite, whose spear
had a shaft like a weaver's bar" (2 Samuel 21:19). When we recall how
1 Samuel 17, in its description of Goliath (who was, it will be remembered, a Philistine from Gath), also mentioned that "the shaft of his
spear was like a weaver's bar" (v. 7), we begin to realize that, off in the
last verses of the book of Samuel, we find a different tradition about

the name of the hero at whose hands Goliath met his defeat: Elhanan son of Jarre, and not David son of Jesse.

The discrepancy between the main current of traditions, which revolve around the tale told in 1 Samuel 17, and the solitary verse found in the fringes of 2 Samuel generated efforts among ancient writers to sort things out. Early on, the book of Chronicles found a way to rectify the problem when it resolved that "again there was fighting with the Philistines, and Elhanan son of Jair killed Lahmi, the brother of Goliath the Gittite; his spear had a shaft like a weaver's beam" (1 Chronicles 20:5). *Lahmi*, the name of Goliath's brother, was created in order to make peace between the conflicting accounts. The Chronicler fabricated the name from the identification of Goliath as being a Bethlehemite, *beit ha-lahmi*.

A harmonistic solution to the contradiction, following a path often taken in the midrash (which likes to identify anonymous or semi-anonymous figures with those who are known), identifies David with Elhanan: "And there was another battle at Gob with the Philistines and David son of Jesse a weaver ['*oreg*] of the Temple's curtain from Bethlehem [*beit lehem*] killed Goliath the Gittite" (*Targum Jonathan ben Uzziel* on 2 Samuel 21:24). Following this, Rashi wrote: "'Elhan-an'—[this is] David, [who was the] 'son of Yaare oregim,' because his family would weave the curtain for the temple called Yaar." David and Elhanan, according to these explanations, were two names of the same person.

Rejecting these harmonistic midrashic solutions leaves us with the possibility that the victory over Goliath the Gittite was attributed first to Elhanan, a relatively anonymous hero, and only later to David. Principal figures are like stars with great mass whose gravitational pull attracts objects of little mass. Stories that at first were told about marginal characters are joined at a secondary stage to the accumulation of tales told about larger figures. It is, indeed, an example of "a poor man's wisdom is scorned, and his words are not heeded" (Ecclesiastes 9:16), of Elhanan's valiant killing of Goliath becoming attributed to David, a figure of monumental proportions. The appendix to David's life story preserves, therefore, the ancient tradition of Elhanan's feat, while the later tradition, the story of David and Goliath, was the tale that made its way to the very heart of the book of Samuel.

The book of Samuel came to include two accounts of David and Saul's first meeting: the story about David and Goliath in 1 Samuel 17, and the story about the boy, "skilled at playing the lyre," in 1 Samuel 16:14–23, who is brought to play before the troubled king. The narrative turbulence created between these two stories was quieted with the help of the statement that "David would go back and forth from attending on Saul to shepherd his father's flock at Bethlehem" (1 Samuel 17:15). According to this verse, also after he was chosen to play for the suffering king, David did not neglect his familial duties, and so it was possible for him to come to the battlefield from Bethlehem, and not as part of Saul's entourage.

Evidence that the story of David and Goliath was indeed founded on the tale of Elhanan's deed is found in the numerous other connections between 1 Samuel 17 and the rest of the anecdotes about heroes from David's ranks, found in 2 Samuel 21. Those stories, too, provided stones for constructing the David and Goliath story. The first anecdote tells of another Philistine hero whose weapon reminds us of Goliath's: "And Ishbi-benob who was a descendant of the Raphah, his bronze spear weighed three hundred shekels and he wore new armor—he tried to kill David" (2 Samuel 21:16). The fourth anecdote tells of a "giant of a man [*'ish-madon*]" (in 1 Chronicles 6:20 he appears correctly as *'ish-midah*, lit., "a man of size") who taunts Israel (vv. 20–21), as did Goliath (1 Samuel 17:10, 25–26). Yet another, in chapter 23, tells of Benaiah son of Jehoiada, who kills a lion (v. 20) and strikes an Egyptian with the Egyptian's own spear (v. 21), just as was told about David, who killed a lion in his youth and cut off the head of Goliath with the giant's own sword.

The problem of finding the real killer of Goliath cannot, then, come to an unequivocal conclusion, but it seems reasonable to propose that David's victory represents a relatively later version of a tradition about the victory of Elhanan over Goliath, the Philistine from Gath.

24

How a Savior Became a Villain

Jeroboam and the Exodus

Jeroboam son of Nebat, who waves the banner of revolt in David's court and founds the Kingdom of Israel, was the most despised figure in the eyes of the Judahite-Davidic historiographer who was the redactor of the book of Kings. Every king from the Israelite kingdom received an unfavorable judgment from the pen of that redactor, who never missed a chance to mention how this or that king's behavior was like that of Jeroboam. Take, for instance, what he wrote about King Omri: "Omri did what was displeasing to the LORD.... He followed all the ways of Jeroboam son of Nebat and the sins which he committed and caused Israel to commit, vexing the LORD, the God of Israel" (1 Kings 16:25–26). Even regarding Zimri—Omri's predecessor on the throne who managed to rule barely seven days before burning down the royal palace with himself inside—it is written that he died "because of the sins which he committed and caused Israel to commit, doing what was displeasing to the LORD and following the ways of Jeroboam" (v. 19).

In his closing remarks following the demise of the Kingdom of Israel, the redactor refers to Jeroboam's rebellion as the original sin that left the kingdom with meager prospects: "For Israel broke away from the House of David, and they made Jeroboam son of Nebat king. Jeroboam caused Israel to stray from the LORD and to commit great sin, and the Israelites persisted in all the sins which Jeroboam had committed; they did not depart from them. In the end, the LORD removed

Israel from His presence. . . . So the Israelites were deported from their land to Assyria, as is still the case" (2 Kings 17:21–23).

Notwithstanding the Judahite historiography's complete animus toward Jeroboam, it never managed to completely erase that figure's heroic features as they had been portrayed in the kingdom that Jeroboam established, the Kingdom of Israel. In that kingdom, of course, the story of the rebellion would not have been told as it had been recanted in Judah. As we will now see, in Israel Jeroboam was admired and viewed as a "second Moses," as the liberator of the people from their oppressors, and as the kingdom's founder. By reading between the lines of this hostile Judahite tradition, let us try to expose the story's foundations, which were taken from the earlier, Israelite tradition that brimmed with admiration for Jeroboam.

Like Moses leading the Israelite slaves in Egypt, who toiled in construction work, so Jeroboam leads the Israelites who were enslaved by Solomon son of David and who toiled away at colossal building projects in Jerusalem: "This Jeroboam was an able man, and when Solomon saw that the young man was a capable worker, he appointed him over all the forced labor [*sevel*] of the House of Joseph" (1 Kings 11:28). The word *sevel* reminds us immediately of the period of Egyptian slavery: "But the king of Egypt said to them, 'Moses and Aaron, why do you distract the people from their tasks? Get to your labors [*sivloteikhem*]'" (Exodus 5:4, and see also 2:11: "Some time after that, when Moses had grown up, he went out to his kinsfolk and witnessed their labors [*be-sivlotam*]"). Indeed, if Jeroboam is a sort of Moses, then Solomon and his son Rehoboam were perceived by the tribes of Israel, who wanted to remove their oppressive yoke, as new Pharaohs. There are seven further points of comparison, some content-related and some linguistic, between the story of Moses and that of Jeroboam:

1. The Israelites build "garrison cities for Pharaoh" (Exodus 1:11); this is also the purpose of Solomon's enslavement of the Israelites: "This was the purpose of the forced labor which Solomon imposed: It was to build the House of the LORD, his own palace . . . and all of Solomon's garrison towns" (1 Kings 9:15–19).

2. Pharaoh tries to kill Moses, who had killed an Egyptian: "When Pharaoh learned of the matter, he sought to kill Moses" (Exodus 2:15); and Solomon wants to kill Jeroboam, who commanded the rebellion: "Solomon sought to put Jeroboam to death" (1 Kings 11:40).

3. Both Moses and Jeroboam have to flee from their pursuers, Moses from Egypt and Jeroboam to Egypt: "But Moses fled from Pharaoh. He arrived in the land of Midian and sat down beside a well" (Exodus 2:15); "but Jeroboam promptly fled to King Shishak of Egypt" (1 Kings 11:40).

4. When Pharaoh dies, Moses returns to Egypt after God tells him, "Go back to Egypt, for all the men who sought to kill you are dead" (Exodus 4:19), and he appears there before Pharaoh. After learning of Solomon's death, Jeroboam returns to his country and appears before Rehoboam: "Jeroboam son of Nebat learned of it while he was still in Egypt; for he had fled from King Solomon, and Jeroboam had settled in Egypt. [In 2 Chronicles 10:2's version of the story, one word is vocalized differently and another has a different preposition: "and Jeroboam returned from Egypt."] They sent for him; and Jeroboam and all the assembly of Israel came and spoke to Rehoboam as follows" (1 Kings 12:2–3).

5. Jeroboam, like Moses before him, is chosen by God to lead, as is plainly explained by the prophet Ahijah: "For thus said the LORD, the God of Israel: I am about to tear the kingdom out of Solomon's hands, and I will give you ten tribes" (1 Kings 11:31).

6. Moses pleads with Pharaoh: "Thus says the LORD, the God of Israel: Let My people go that they may celebrate a festival for Me in the wilderness" (Exodus 5:1); while Jeroboam petitions Rehoboam, "Your father made our yoke heavy. Now lighten the harsh labor and the heavy yoke which your father laid on us, and we will serve you" (1 Kings 12:4).

7. The appeals of both Moses and Jeroboam result in an increase in the laborers' burden: "That same day Pharaoh charged the taskmasters and foremen of the people, saying, 'You shall no longer provide the people with straw for making bricks as heretofore; let them go and

---

gather straw for themselves. But impose upon them the same quota of bricks as they have been making heretofore; do not reduce it, for they are shirkers; that is why they cry, "Let us go and sacrifice to our God!" Let heavier work be laid upon the men; let them keep at it and not pay attention to deceitful promises'" (Exodus 5:6–9). Rehoboam, following the counsel of his younger advisors, answers the petitioners: "My father made your yoke heavy, but I will add to your yoke; my father flogged you with whips, but I will flog you with scorpions" (1 Kings 12:14).

A glaring illustration of the similarity between the life story of Jeroboam and the story of the Exodus is found also in the golden calves erected by Jeroboam (1 Kings 12:28–30), with which we've already dealt in depth in chapter 11.

This obvious likeness between Jeroboam and Moses becomes even more pronounced in an addition to 1 Kings 12 that is found in the Septuagint immediately following verse 24. Though this passage is not found in the Hebrew Bible's book of Kings, the language of the Greek text betrays the existence of a Hebrew original from which the Greek translator worked:

And there was a man from Mount Ephraim, a servant of Solomon, and his name was Jeroboam and his mother's name was Zeruah, a harlot. And Solomon made him supervisor over the levy of the House of Joseph. . . . It was he who built the Millo with the levy of the house of Ephraim. . . . And Solomon sought to have him killed, and he fled in fear to Shishak, king of Egypt, and stayed with him until the death of Solomon. And Jeroboam heard in Egypt that Solomon had died, and he spoke to Shishak, king of Egypt: "Give me leave to go to my own country." Shishak said to him: "Ask what you will and I will give it to you." And Shishak had given Jeroboam Ano, the sister of Lady Tahpenes, his own wife, for a wife; she had grown up among the king's daughters. And she presented Jeroboam with his son Abijah. And Jeroboam said unto Shishak: "Nevertheless, give me leave to go and I will go." And Jeroboam departed from Egypt.[1]

In its present form, the Septuagint tradition is not particularly sympathetic toward Jeroboam: his father is not identified, while we learn that his mother was a prostitute. It is difficult to ignore the relationship between this element and the tradition about the judge Jepthath, who was "the son of a prostitute" (Judges 11:1) and was forced to flee his native land: "So Jepthath fled from his brothers and settled in the Tob country" (v. 3); he was subsequently called upon to return home to lead his tribe and deliver them from their enemies.

Despite the antagonism toward Jeroboam in this tradition, we can still detect elements there that are from Moses's biography and that a writer used in order to construct Jeroboam's story. It specifies the existence of familial relations between Jeroboam and Shishak that remind us of the relations between Moses and Pharaoh, Moses having been raised in Pharaoh's house as the adopted son of Pharaoh's daughter. Just as Moses marries the daughter of a local priest while he is in exile from Egypt in Midian, so does Jeroboam, exiled in Egypt, marry a woman from the Egyptian ruler's family.

And, too, we find Jeroboam asking the Egyptian ruler, who is related to Jeroboam's wife, for permission to return to his own land, just as Moses asks Jethro, his father-in-law: "Moses went back to his father-in-law Jethro and said to him, 'Let me go back to my kinsmen in Egypt and see how they are faring'" (Exodus 4:18). And just as Moses fathers two sons during his stay in Midian, so does Jeroboam father a son during his stay in Egypt.

Before we draw conclusions regarding the character of the curious tradition in the Septuagint and its relation to traditions told about Jeroboam in the Northern Kingdom, we should examine its relationship with a story that resembles it closely, the tale of Hadad the Edomite, an "adversary against Solomon" who fled Egypt and, following Solomon's death, wanted to return to his own land (1 Kings 11:14–22), this being

1. Translation from Zipora Talshir, *The Alternative Story: 3 Kingdoms 12:24a–z* (Jerusalem: Jerusalem Biblical Studies, 1993).

another story in which the echoes of the Exodus are heard loudly. The beginning of the story is as follows:

> When David was in Edom, Joab the army commander went up to bury the slain, and he killed every male in Edom. . . . But Hadad, together with some Edomite men, servants of his father, escaped and headed for Egypt; Hadad was then a young boy. Setting out from Midian, they came to Paran and took along with them men from Paran. Thus they came to Egypt, to Pharaoh king of Egypt, who gave him a house, assigned a food allowance to him, and granted him an estate. (1 Kings 11:15–18)

The continuation of Hadad's story is presented in comparison with the addition in the Septuagint to 1 Kings 12, which we have discussed already.

The tradition in the Septuagint (1 Kings 12)	The Tale of Hadad (1 Kings 11:19–22)
And Jeroboam heard in Egypt that Solomon had died.	And Hadad heard in Egypt that David had been laid to rest with his fathers and that Joab the army commander was dead.
And he spoke to Shishak, king of Egypt:	Hadad said to Pharaoh:
"Give me leave to go to my own country."	Give me leave to go to my own country.
And Shishak said to him:	22aPharaoh said to him:
"Ask what you will and I will give it to you."	What do you lack with me, that you want to go to your own country . . .
Shishak had given Jeroboam Ano, the sister of	19. . . and gave him for wife the sister of his wife, the sister of
Lady Tahpenes his own wife, for a wife.	Lady Tahpenes.
. . . She presented Jeroboam with his son Abijah.	The sister of Tahpenes bore him a son, Genuvath. Tahpenes weaned him in Pharaoh's palace, and Genuvath remained in Pharaoh's palace among the sons of Pharaoh.
And Jeroboam said unto Shishak, "Nevertheless, give me leave to go and I will go."	22bBut he said, "Nevertheless, give me leave to go."

The Hadad story contains distinctive elements that are particular to it and that connect it with the Pentateuch's story about the Israelites' descent into Egypt, their sojourn there, and their departure under Moses's command.

- Hadad escapes to Egypt when Joab massacres all the males in Edom (1 Kings 11:16), an element parallel to the killing of male children by Pharaoh in Egypt (Exodus 1:16–22).
- Hadad's story mentions a connection with Midian ("setting out from Midian they came to Paran" [1 Kings 11:18]), the land to which Moses flees from Pharaoh (Exodus 2:15). Paran, too, is mentioned in the Exodus tradition (e.g., Numbers 10:12).
- The king of Egypt gives Hadad food ("assigned a food allowance to him" [1 Kings 11:18]), corresponding to what was given to Jacob and his household on their arrival to Egypt, as told to Joseph by Pharaoh: "Tell your brothers . . . come to me; I will give you the best of the land of Egypt and you shall live off the fat of the land" (Genesis 45:18); and as we read later on: "Joseph sustained his father, and his brothers, and all his father's household with bread, down to the little ones" (47:12).
- Pharaoh grants Hadad land in which to settle ("and granted him an estate" [1 Kings 11:18]), parallel to Pharaoh's presenting the Land of Goshen to the Israelites on their arrival to Egypt (see, e.g., Genesis 47:6, 11).
- In the tale of Hadad we read that "Hadad *found great favor with* Pharaoh" (1 Kings 11:19). We can compare this with what is told about Joseph in the Egyptian prison: "The LORD was with Joseph, He extended kindness to him and *made him find favor with* the chief jailer" (Genesis 39:21).
- The unusual name of Hadad's son, Genuvath, may be an echo of Joseph's words about himself in the prison: "For I was kidnapped [*ganov gunavti*] from the land of the Hebrews" (Genesis 40:15).

What can be the significance of this striking resemblance between the Septuagint's tradition about Jeroboam and the tradition about Hadad?

A further question we may ask is why Hadad became the hero of a tradition that carries within it so many elements from the Exodus tradition (as opposed to any other of Solomon's adversaries, e.g., Rezon son of Eliada [1 Kings 11:23–25], about whom nothing is told).

Both questions are related, we propose, and one explanation answers both. It seems likely that a writer from Judah who knew the tradition about Jeroboam, with its many correspondences to the Moses and Exodus story, sought to blur these elements because they presented Jeroboam as Moses's equal. In order to diminish Jeroboam's status, this writer transferred the features from Jeroboam to another, minor figure: Hadad, the enemy of Solomon.

But the writer's efforts did not meet with complete success. The original story about Jeroboam found its way to a manuscript that was later used by a Greek translator who included the tradition in his translation along with the tale of Jeroboam's rebellion, as it appears in the Masoretic Text, and the Hadad story. True, the peculiar tradition had been modified in order to dim Jeroboam's luster—such as by depicting his mother as a prostitute and by deleting some of the common features with the Egyptian enslavement and Exodus traditions—but we can still discern there the admiration that the Israelites felt for Jeroboam: in their eyes he was the founder of the kingdom, a "second Moses" who freed them from bondage under a "second Pharaoh," the king of Judah.

Between the lines of the book of Kings in both the Hebrew and Greek Bibles, we have revealed more than a little of an Israelite tradition about Jeroboam, the man whom the Kingdom of Judah loved to hate. The Judahite tradition became the dominant one in Rabbinic literature, which also linked Moses and Jeroboam, though now it was as antipodes: "He that leads the many to virtue, through him shall no sin befall; but he that leads many to sin, to him shall be given no means for repentance. Moses was virtuous and he led the many to virtue; the virtue of the many depended on him. . . . Jeroboam sinned and he led the many to sin; the sin of the many depended on him" (Mishnah *Avot* 5:18).

4

Relations between Men and Women

25

Sister or Not

Sarah's Adventures with Pharaoh

The story, told in Genesis 12:10–20, of the descent of Abram and Sarai (as Abraham and Sarah are called in this part of Genesis) to Egypt and what befalls them there, reveals little and conceals much. The terseness of the narrative leaves many questions unanswered, including one concerning Sarah during her stay in Pharaoh's palace.

According to the Pentateuch's account, Abraham and his wife descend to Egypt because of a famine in Canaan. Knowing of Sarah's being "a beautiful woman" (Genesis 12:11) and fearing lest the Egyptians kill him and take her, Abraham directs his wife to tell the Egyptians that she is his sister. And indeed, the Patriarch's fears are proven valid: the news of Sarah's exceptional beauty makes it all the way to the king, "and the woman was taken into Pharaoh's palace" (v. 15). After an unspecified period, God afflicts Pharaoh and his household with "mighty plagues" (v. 17), and Pharaoh summons Abraham to him and protests, "What is this you have done to me! Why did you not tell me that she was your wife? Why did you say, 'She is my sister,' so that I took her as my wife?" (vv. 18–19). In the end, Pharaoh sends both Sarah and her husband out of his country.

Did Abraham make the trip to Egypt on God's directive? (Compare God's words to Isaac—"Do not go down to Egypt" [Genesis 26:2]—and to Jacob—"Do not fear to go down to Egypt" [46:3].) Were Sarah and Abraham being truthful when they claimed to be siblings? Did Abraham act in good faith when, after the king took Sarah, Abraham accepted from him "sheep, oxen, asses, male and female slaves, she-asses, and camels" (Genesis 12:16)? Why was the king punished by God when he genuinely believed Sarah to be unmarried and available to him? And how did he finally discover Sarah's real identity as Abraham's wife? These questions, along with the one that will occupy us here, were left unanswered by the biblical author, providing a vast arena in which commentators and translators have long been left to distinguish themselves.

As to the question we have set for ourselves: What happened to Sarah in the king's palace? The simple meaning (*peshat*) of the biblical story appears to assume that Pharaoh took Sarah as his wife and that he lived with her as rulers do with their wives. The verb *l-q-ḥ*, "take," in conjunction with the noun *'ishah*, "woman/wife," relates to marriage and includes sexual relations, as is made explicitly clear in Genesis 25:1–2 ("And Abraham took another wife, whose name was Keturah. She bore him Zimran"), Deuteronomy 24:1 ("A man takes a wife and possesses her"), and many other verses.

True, in this case the verse is ambiguous enough so that the words "the woman was taken into Pharaoh's palace" and "so that I took her as my wife" might convey, to readers who so wished, only that Sarah was *brought* into the royal palace. It appears that the Torah preferred ambiguity to any detail that might prove unpleasant to certain readers. Nevertheless, based on the assumption that the tradition about Abraham and Sarah in Egypt circulated in various forms in ancient Israel, we are certainly entitled to ask whether we can know what else was told, particularly regarding our specific question.

Our search for an answer brings us first to two stories that parallel ours: the story about Abraham and Sarah in Gerar (Genesis 20) and the story about Isaac and Rebekah in Gerar (Genesis 26:1–14), both of which depict a Patriarch who arrives at the court of a foreign king and nervously directs his wife to say that she is his sister. In many ways we should read these two stories, which appear after ours in the book of Genesis, as interpretations of it. The story of Isaac in Gerar even begins with an explicit reference to ours when it mentions "the previous famine that had occurred in the days of Abraham" (Genesis 26:1). The story of Abraham in Gerar also alludes to our story, when Abraham says to the Philistine king, "I said to [Sarah], 'Let this be the kindness that you shall do me: in *every* place we come to, say there of me: He is my brother'" (Genesis 20:13), making it clear that this was not the first or only time that Sarah had made such a claim.

Both of these stories mitigate what is told in our story, each in its own way. For example, chapter 20 in Genesis establishes that Sarah is indeed Abraham's half-sister ("she is in truth my sister, my father's daughter though not my mother's and she became my wife" [v. 12]) and also that the king's gifts were given to Abraham and Sarah only when they left as a form of compensation ("Abimelech took sheep and oxen, and male and female slaves, and gave them to Abraham, and he restored his wife Sarah to him" [v. 14]). Chapter 26 makes no mention of any gifts that the king may have given Isaac, instead claiming that Isaac's newfound wealth was the product of his own success: "Isaac sowed in that land and reaped a hundred-fold the same year. The LORD blessed him, and the man grew richer and richer until he was very wealthy: He acquired flocks and herds, and a large household" (vv. 12–14).

For our purpose, it is important to note how chapter 20 emphasizes that, despite Sarah's being taken to the king's palace, "Abimelech had not approached her" (v. 4), a fact confirmed in God's words to the king: "I knew that you did this with a blameless heart, and so I kept you from sinning against Me. That was why I did not let you touch her" (v. 6). In chapter 26, no contact whatsoever occurs between the king and Rebekah. The king, "looking out of the window, saw Isaac fondling his wife Rebekah" (v. 8), which causes him to chastise Isaac: "What have you done to us! One of the people might have lain with your wife, and you would have brought guilt upon us" (v. 10)—though it remains as only a "might." In this story, it is made unambiguously clear that the only one who gets to touch Rebekah is her husband.

The care taken in chapter 20 to emphasize the absence of any contact between Abimelech and Sarah suggests that the previous tradition told how the foreign king did indeed have relations with Abraham's wife.

The Pentateuch, it seems, tried to uproot that element from the story in various ways, including the use of equivocal language. Nevertheless, some support for its existence in the original tradition is found by comparing Genesis 12:10–20 with the story of Esther.

The book of Esther made extensive use of our story, and the similarities between them are many. Thus, for example, we find that both Genesis 12 and the book of Esther recount how a Jewish or Hebrew man had to leave his own land (Abraham in Genesis 12:10; Mordecai in Esther 2:5–6); in both, he is accompanied by a near relation (Sarah or Esther). Sarah, we are told, is a "beautiful woman" (Genesis 12:11), and Esther, too, is "shapely and beautiful" (Esther 2:7). In both stories the woman is taken to the royal palace, where she conceals her true identity in compliance with the man's request: "Please say that you are my sister" (Genesis 12:13); "But Esther still did not reveal her kindred or her people, as Mordecai had instructed her" (Esther 2:20, and see also v. 10).

In Esther, as in our story, a threat looms over the Jews (or Hebrews), in particular over the woman's close relation, while the man hopes that he and his family will be saved by the woman's words: Sarah announces to Pharaoh that Abraham is her brother, while Esther approaches King Ahasuerus in order "to appeal to him and to plead with him for her people" (4:8). In the end, the king discovers the real identity of the woman and her true relation to the man. In Genesis we read, "What is this you have done to me! Why did you not tell me that she was your wife?" (12:18), and in Esther, "Mordecai presented himself to the king, for Esther had revealed how he was related to her" (8:1). In both stories, the Jews/Hebrews benefit financially from the events. Abraham, as we've already mentioned, acquires numerous assets, while "Mordecai left the king's presence in royal robes of blue and white, with a magnificent crown of gold and a mantle of fine linen and purple wool" (8:15), and the Jews in the Persian Empire are given the right to plunder the possessions of their enemies (8:11).

These many similarities are not coincidental but the result of one tradition having been deliberately shaped on the basis of the other. To them we add the correspondence between the words in our story, "I took her as my wife" (Genesis 12:19), and what is told about Esther's marriage to the king of Persia and Media. In both stories, the ruler's taking the woman is described in almost identical words: "The woman was taken into Pharaoh's palace" (v. 15), and "Esther, too, was taken into the king's palace" (Esther 2:8). This precise parallel suggests that also the story about Abraham and Sarah—whether we speak of a more ancient tradition used by the writer of Esther or only of the way that that author understood the text in Genesis 12—contained the notion that Sarah was taken into the palace for the purpose of marrying Pharaoh in the all-inclusive sense.

By the way, just as the story of Abraham and Sarah was "cleaned up" already within the Bible, so was the story of Esther in Rabbinic literature. There it is claimed that "[Esther] did not listen to [Ahasuerus]," meaning that she refused to have sexual relations with him (*Panim Aherim*, second version 5 [36a]). This tradition perhaps has already been alluded to in "The Prayer of Esther," one of the additions to the book of Esther that is found in the Septuagint, in which Esther proclaims: "I despised lying with an uncircumcised [man]."

Apparently, the writer of Esther allowed himself to preserve this element of the literary pattern since Esther was not Mordecai's wife, making it possible to place her within Ahasuerus's harem. It is interesting to note that the Greek translation of Esther records that she was Mordecai's wife (1:8), as do a number of Rabbinic sources (such as B. *Megillah* 13b). These texts preserve for us the complete literary pattern: the wife of Mordecai arrives to "the bosom of that wicked one" (*Shoher Tov* 22:16), as was the lot of Sarah, Abraham's wife, in Pharaoh's palace.

Another biblical story, that of David and Bathsheba (2 Samuel 11), was also apparently modeled after the story of Abraham and Sarah in Egypt (and its two parallels in Genesis), though in this case the king is Hebrew and the woman a foreigner, the wife of Uriah the Hittite. King David takes a beautiful woman to his palace after seeing her (compare "the Egyptians saw the woman [Sarah]. . . . Pharaoh's courtiers saw her" in Genesis 12:14–15 with "and from the roof he [David] saw a woman bathing" in 2 Samuel 11:2) and lies with her. Each woman's husband faces a threat but, while Abraham manages to overcome it, Uriah finds his death at the king's command. Just as Abraham receives property from Pharaoh, so does Uriah receive his gifts: "a present from the king followed him" (2 Samuel 11:8). The story of David and Bathsheba, in which the woman's arrival to the king's court and bedroom is stated outright, was thus constructed using the same template used by the book of Esther and what we consider to have been the original story of Abraham and Sarah in Egypt. The writer's willingness to disgrace David, and thereby explain the troubles that subsequently visit the House of David in the story's continuation, justified presenting the complete story-pattern without any changes or omissions: David takes another man's wife to his palace and has intimate relations with her. As a consequence, he deserved all the punishments that followed.

Many post-biblical sources also knew the rejected tradition, or at least sensed the interpretative potential, and sought to stifle it in various ways. The *Genesis Apocryphon*, in its retelling of the story of Abraham and Sarah in Egypt, states explicitly that the king "could not get close to her and he did not know her" (col. 20, line 17). Josephus made sure to specify that Pharaoh "was restrained from his lustful intent by a grievous disease inflicted upon him by God and by state troubles" (*Jewish Antiquities* 1.12.1). The Rabbis developed the point: according to them, either Pharaoh became ill with some sort of leprosy that prevented him from having sexual relations (Y. *Ketubbot* 7:10) or an angel descended from heaven and struck Pharaoh every time he attempted to approach Sarah (*Genesis Rabbah* 40 [41]:2). The Rabbis even depicted Pharaoh as acknowledging that "I did not get close to her" (*Targum Pseudo-Jonathan* to 12:19). All these many attempts to insist that nothing sexual occurred between Pharaoh and Sarah cry out for our attention and betray their having been created precisely in order to counter a tradition that claimed exactly the opposite.

Even more can be said. One midrash concludes that Isaac, the son born to Abraham in his old age, bore a close facial resemblance to his father because "when Sarah was being tossed back and forth between Pharaoh and Abimelech and she became pregnant with Isaac, the nations of the world would say: 'Can a child be born to a man one hundred years old?' (Gen. 17:17). Either she has conceived by Abimelech or by Pharaoh" (*Tanḥuma, Toledot* 1). In order to prove false any slanderous insinuations about Sarah, the tradition insists that Isaac resembled Abraham and in this way proves his patrimony.

In this chapter, we have seen how a vulgar folk tradition that did not shrink from acknowledging intimate relations between Sarah and Pharaoh did not suit the Torah, whose writers tried to expunge it, replace it with another, or refute it. Such a tradition satisfied, of course, the human proclivity for relating forbidden relations between men and women (often with great enjoyment) and for describing the shrewd and calculated acts that save ordinary people from the might of powerful rulers. The Pentateuch's efforts to obscure the tradition also allowed us to gain oblique access to it, an ancient story that was impossible to extinguish fully. It seems that, once such stories about forbidden relations were included in the sacred writings, it became necessary to refine them so that, over time, many (such as the story about Reuben and his father's concubine [see chapter 27]) were adapted, refined, and blunted. This was the case with the tradition we have read here, about the events that took place between Sarah and Pharaoh in the royal palace.

26

The Story of Rebekah and the
Servant on the Road from Haran

Of the three Patriarchs, only Isaac never leaves Canaan. Since Canaanite women were forbidden to the Patriarchs, the need arose to send for a wife for Isaac from Haran, from his father's family that lived there. Abraham assigns the task of traveling to Haran and fetching an appropriate wife for his son to "the senior servant of his household, who had charge of all that he owned" (Genesis 24:2). The servant—whom the Rabbis identified as Abraham's steward, Damesek Eliezer, who is mentioned in Genesis 15:2 (see, e.g., *Genesis Rabbah* 59:10)—departs for Haran and performs his task well: Rebekah, the daughter of Bethuel, nephew of Abraham, and the sister of Laban, is identified as the bride-to-be.

Once the servant confirms that Bethuel and Laban agree to the marriage, he hurries to return to his master's home, telling his hosts, "'Do not delay me, now that the LORD has made my errand successful. Give me leave that I may go to my master.' ... Then Rebekah and her maids arose, mounted the camels, and followed the man. So the servant took Rebekah and went his way" (Genesis 24:56, 61).

Nothing is said about the journey back to Canaan. Their meeting with Isaac, on the other hand, is described in detail. Isaac "went out walking" toward evening. "Raising her eyes, Rebekah saw Isaac. She fell off the camel and said to the servant, 'Who is that man walking in the field toward us?' And the servant said, 'That is my master.' So she took her veil and covered herself" (Genesis 24:64–65). Immediately, we are told, "the servant told Isaac all the things that he had done" (v. 66). Isaac takes Rebekah as his wife and brings her into his mother's tent, and "Isaac loved her" (v. 67).

How do we make sense of Rebekah's fall from the camel? And what is the significance of her covering herself with a veil? Can it be that these details signal efforts to polemicize against a different tradition, a folk tradition that the Bible rejected? If so, is it possible to recover that lost tradition?

Indeed, post-biblical sources that deal with the journey from Haran to Canaan and Isaac and Rebekah's meeting seem to strengthen our conjecture that such a tradition hovers below the biblical story. It turns out that these sources contain one of the most amazing and vulgar tales in Jewish literature, in which it is told that Rebekah's fall from the camel caused her to lose her virginity—that from the fall she became a *mukat 'etz* (lit., [a woman] struck by [a piece of] wood), a legal term that describes a girl whose hymen has been accidentally broken (see Mishnah *Ketubbot* 1:3). Isaac discovers Rebekah's state and suspects her and his father's servant of intimacy on the long journey home. Rebekah, however, proves her righteousness and is finally brought to Sarah's tent.

This tradition is found, with slight variations, in at least ten different books that were composed or edited during the Middle Ages in Italy, Germany, and France, including *Yalqut Shim'oni*, *Genesis Rabbati*, and *Midrash Aggadah*. Though they differ in some details, each admits that Rebekah's fall from the camel caused her to lose her virginity, that Isaac doubted her honor, and that she succeeded in proving the veracity of her account. We bring now an example of the tradition brought by a midrash of unknown origins but that is quoted in *Yalqut Shim'oni*, an anthology containing many unique traditions that were otherwise lost:

Since she saw, through the Holy Spirit, that Esau would emerge from her, she was shaken and became a *mukat 'etz*, and the blood of her virginity flowed from her. Immediately, the Holy One, blessed be He, said to Gabriel, "Go down, and preserve the blood so that it won't smell badly, and it will remain intact." Isaac came into her and didn't find her virginity. He suspected Eliezer. He said to her, "Where is your virginity?" She said, "When I fell from the camel, I became a *mukat 'etz.*" He told her, "You lie. Eliezer violated you." So she swore to him that he had not touched her. They went and found the [piece of] wood stained with blood. Immediately, Isaac knew that she was pure. The Holy One, blessed be He, said, "What should I do to this servant who was suspected?" He said to the ministering angels, "Let him enter alive into the Garden of Eden." (*Yalqut Shim'oni* on Genesis, paragraph 109)

All the sources acknowledge Isaac's suspicions concerning Rebekah and the servant and portray Isaac as accusing one or the other. In the end, Rebekah explains what occurred, or the servant suggests the explanation, and Isaac proceeds to the site of the fall, where he discovers Rebekah's blood on a branch or stone. The fresh blood is found preserved—not dried or licked by animals—due to an angel or an animal or a bird, such as a dove or a lion, that guarded it.

This widely circulated tradition was known also to a twelfth-century Christian writer in France, Peter the Venerable, who condemned the Jews for including a tradition in their writings that cast aspersions on the nation's matriarch: "[In the Talmud] it is told about Rebekah who, on hearing from Eliezer that Isaac was his master, hurried to descend from the camel. . . . According to the true Scripture of the Christians—'and she covered herself with a veil,' while according to the false Scripture of the Jews, on alighting, she lost the sign of her virginity."

We are certainly justified in questioning the origins of such a vulgar tradition and how it became linked to Rebekah, one of the four Matriarchs. It turns out that Rebekah's virginity is discussed also in another context, in traditions connected with her father, Bethuel (a name that bears a strong similarity to the Hebrew word *betulah*, "virgin"), who, Rabbinic traditions relate, was the governor of his city and accustomed to demand the right to have sexual relations with every woman on the eve of her marriage—the "right of the first night" (*jus primae noctis*)—including women in his own household. In Rebekah's case, only divine intervention prevented Bethuel from claiming this right (*Yalqut Shim'oni* on Genesis, 109).

It is difficult to know what prompted the creation of this crude tradition, but we offer three suggestions, each more convincing than its predecessor: (1) it is a non-Jewish tradition, created in order to mock the sacred origins of the Jews and their Patriarchs; (2) it is a Jewish tradition, an expansion of the biblical story that follows certain key words and develops them according to traditional methods for interpretation (we will elaborate on this below); (3) in one form or another, it is a more ancient folk tradition that was rejected, for obvious reasons, from the Pentateuch, which offered another tradition in its stead; the original tradition continued to be told, however, and eventually made its way into the literary corpus.

The first possibility is unconvincing. One would be hard-pressed to imagine why Jews would so often repeat a tradition that targeted their religion and Patriarchs as objects of derision.

The second option seems more likely. It is based on the fact that the story about Rebekah, the servant, and Isaac contains a series of words that, through analogy to other biblical stories, might give rise to the creation of such a tradition. We refer, for instance to the fact that Rebekah is first introduced in the story as "a virgin whom no man had known" (Genesis 24:16). A woman is first presented as a virgin in only two other stories in the Bible, both of which contain improper sexual acts: the story of the concubine in Gibeah, in which the host offers his virgin daughter to the townsmen who have gathered at his house (Judges 19:24), and the story of the rape of David's daughter Tamar by her brother Amnon (2 Samuel 13:2). The fact that the servant and Rebekah meet beside a well also points to this option: both of the Bible's other stories about a man and woman meeting beside a well (Jacob and Rachel, Moses and Zipporah) result in marriage. (In the end, Isaac also meets his future wife when he comes "from the vicinity of Be'er-lahai-roi" [Genesis 24:62; *be'er* is "well"].)

And that's not all. The servant asks Rebekah to give him water (Genesis 24:17), reminding us of Sisera's request to Jael in a context containing a number of erotic allusions (Judges 4:19, 5:25; see chapter 28). The servant gives Rebekah a nose ring and bracelets (Genesis 24:2), two pieces of jewelry that the Bible mentions more than once in connection with prostitution and adultery. (See, e.g., Ezekiel 16:11–17, where we read about bracelets and a nose ring [and other items] given by a man to his wife, who takes the ornaments and prostitutes herself; see also Hosea 2:15; Ezekiel 23:42–43.) The erotic connotations of the items were not lost on the Rabbis. *Midrash Aggadah* on the verse records that "when [Laban] saw the nose-ring and the bracelets on his sister's arms he thought [that the servant] had defiled her and ran there to kill him."

Furthermore, Rebekah, on seeing her future husband, covers herself with a veil. The Bible tells of a woman covering herself with a veil in only one other verse, in the story of Tamar. Tamar's veil is part of her disguise as a prostitute in order that Judah, her father-in-law, will have relations with her (Genesis 38:14). Here, too, the Rabbis sensed a connection between the two tales: "Two were they that covered themselves with veils and gave birth to twins" (*Genesis Rabbah* 60:15). Generally speaking, popular myth often attributed the birth of twins to infidelity. This, as we've already discussed (chapter 21), was the case in Greek mythology where Zeus, the supreme god, had sexual relations with Heracles's mother while her husband was on a military expedition, only to be quickly followed in her bed by the husband on his return home. From these two couplings were born twins who were exceedingly different from one another—similar, we observe, to the marked contrast in our story between Rebekah's twins, Jacob and Esau ("The first one emerged red, like a hairy mantle all over, so they named him Esau" [Genesis 25:25]; "Jacob answered his mother Rebekah, 'But my brother Esau is a hairy man and I am smooth-skinned'" [27:11]), an imbalance that could easily have played a part in creating such a tradition of two fathers.

Finally, Isaac and Rebekah meet "in the field" (Genesis 24:63), a place designated for crimes, particularly sexual crimes like rape ("But if the man comes upon the engaged girl in the field, and the man lies with her by force . . . you shall do nothing to the girl. . . . He came upon her in the field; though the engaged girl cried for help, there was no one to save her" [Deuteronomy 22:25–27]). We dealt with this matter in chapter 21, where we discussed the meeting between Manoah's wife and the angel, which likewise took place in the field.

In sum, the use of the term "virgin" and the mention of the encounter at the well, the bracelets and nose ring, the veil, the birth of the twins, and Isaac's coming upon Rebekah specifically in the field—all these elements could have led readers of Genesis 24 to believe that something sexual occurred between Rebekah and Abraham's servant. That story, in turn, would certainly have been challenged, and it could have been in such a context that a tradition about Rebekah losing her virginity from a fall was created. We have here something like a "partial acknowledgment": a polemical technique in which the interpreter admits certain facts while interpreting them otherwise on the basis of a different set of assumptions that suited the interpreter's values.

Another way to deny the conjectured folk tradition is found in the midrash *Pirkei de-Rabbi Eliezer*: "Abraham told his son Isaac: This servant is suspected of these offenses. . . . Bring the girl to my tent. . . . If her virginity is pure then she is yours" (16). The notion that Abraham suspected his servant and that Isaac needed to confirm his wife's virginity must derive from the polemic against that other tradition that told how Rebekah was spoiled as a result of the servant's immoral behavior. In this case, a physical examination of Rebekah proves her chasteness, leaving no room for doubting her or the servant.

The erotic associations awakened by certain key words in Genesis 24 are what led, according to this possibility, to the growth of an aggadic tradition about an incident between Rebekah and Abraham's servant on their way to Canaan, an incident whose reflections we found in Jewish sources by way of either a partial admission or a denial. The allure of this explanation is not insignificant, but it seems to us that the third possible explanation that we will now bring is even more compelling.

This possibility views the origin of the surprising tale of Rebekah's fall from the camel in an ancient and unsavory tale about a servant who deceives his master by violating the master's future wife while the two make their way to him. People have always enjoyed tales of sexual exploits combined with cunning and deceit, especially those in which someone from society's lower ranks outwits his or her superiors. Examples are not hard to find among later writings that were based on older folk traditions—books such as Chaucer's *Canterbury Tales* and Boccaccio's *Decameron* come to mind.

The reverse of that story is found in what is told about Joseph and Potiphar's wife in Genesis 39. In order to heighten our esteem for the slave Joseph, we are told how his married Egyptian mistress tries to seduce him and how he resists her. We readers, who know the popular story type, witness Joseph's moral greatness. See also our discussion of what occurs in the encounter between David, who was Saul's servant, and Abigail, the wife of the wealthy Nabal the Carmelite (chapter 29).

In contrast to a crude folk tradition about Rebekah and the servant, the Pentateuch gives us an innocent story about an honorable meeting in which Rebekah falls from the camel as a sign of respect for the man she is about to marry. We know this from a comparison with what is told about Achsah, the daughter of Caleb, in Joshua 15:18 (= Judges 1:14), where a quick dismount from an animal signals a daughter's deference toward her father, and also in 1 Samuel 25:23, where Abigail quickly dismounts an ass when she meets David. Rebekah even covers herself with a veil, which can now be interpreted as an expression of her exceptional modesty. The assertion that the servant told Isaac "all the things that he had done" now means that he has hidden nothing from him and that there is nothing to hide. The words that convey erotic connotations did not, according to this scenario, stimulate the creation of a folk tradition but are only the distant and bland echoes of such a tradition that became incorporated into a seemingly innocent story in such a way as to effectively remove their sting.

27

Reuben, Bilhah, and a Silent Jacob

Following the story of Rachel's sudden death while giving birth to Benjamin (Genesis 35:16–20) and before listing all twelve of Jacob's sons along with their mothers ("Now the sons of Jacob were twelve in number. The sons of Leah: Reuben—Jacob's first-born—Simeon, Levi . . ." [vv. 22b–26]), the Bible inserts a very short story about the family's move to a new home ("Israel journeyed on, and pitched his tent beyond Migdal-eder") and an incident there involving Reuben: "While Israel stayed in that land, Reuben went and lay with Bilhah, his father's concubine" (vv. 21–22a). The event is left without any real response from Jacob, about whom it is only said: "and Israel heard."

By all accounts, the list of Jacob's sons should have been brought directly after the story of Benjamin's birth (i.e., after verse 20), Benjamin being Jacob's youngest son. We therefore must ask: Why was the continuity between the story of Benjamin's birth and the list of sons interrupted by the story of Reuben and Bilhah? Evidently, the story's insertion at this point can be explained by the juxtaposition it creates between Rachel's death and Reuben's intimate relations with Bilhah: after the death of Rachel, who was his mother's nemesis, Reuben (Leah's firstborn) seeks to dissolve any ties between his father and the memory of his father's favorite wife by defiling her maidservant, Jacob's concubine Bilhah. Now that Rachel has died and Bilhah is defiled, Leah can emerge as the family's matriarch, with no one to challenge her status.

A son who sleeps with his father's concubine, thereby making her forbidden to the father, is found also in the story of David's concubines who were defiled by his son Absalom (2 Samuel 16:21–22). Absalom, following the advice of Ahithophel, did what he did publicly in order to strengthen his own position. Absalom's act signified his determination to mount a rebellion against his father and to fight to the end, but Reuben's act is for the sake of his mother and her honor. This was noted already by the Rabbis: "His mother's revenge he [Reuben] sought, since, for all the days that Rachel lived, her bed was near the bed of our father Jacob. When Rachel died, our father Jacob took Bilhah's bed and placed it near his bed. [Reuben] said: Is it not enough that my mother was jealous of her sister during her lifetime, but even after her death?" (*Genesis Rabbah* 98:4). This is the reason Reuben did what he did. The idea that Reuben's act caused Jacob to desist from having relations with Bilhah is stated explicitly in two apocryphal books, *Jubilees* ("And Jacob no longer came near to her because Reuben had defiled her" [33:9]) and *Testament of Reuben* ("and her, he [Jacob] no longer touched" [3:15]).

An extra-biblical parallel that tells of a son having sexual relations with his father's concubine for the sake of his mother's honor is found in Homer's *Iliad*, which relates how Phoenix had relations with his father Amyntor's concubine in compliance with his mother's request:

[I was then] fleeing from strife with my father Amyntor, son of Ormenus; for he was enraged with me because of his fair-haired concubine, whom he himself ever loved, and scorned his wife, my mother. So she begged me by my knees continually, to sleep with his concubine first myself, so that the old man might be hateful in her eyes. I obeyed her and did the deed, but my father learned of this immediately and cursed me mightily, and invoked the dire Erinyes, that he should never set on his knees a dear child begotten by me; and the gods fulfilled his curse, Zeus of the nether world and dread Persephone.[1]

1. Homer, *Iliad*, trans. A. T. Murray, rev. W. F. Wyatt (Cambridge MA: Loeb Classical Library, 1999), 9.448–457.

In Homer the father discovers his son's treacherous act and curses him strongly, while in our story, as we've already remarked, we find only the words "and Israel heard." This is followed by a midverse break, a space of a few letters that was left empty in the manuscript between these words and "Now the sons of Jacob were twelve in number . . .," and so on. Such breaks, which occur periodically throughout the Bible, are always meaningful. The significance of this midverse break and the question of Jacob's reaction to his son's act are the subject of this chapter.

The midverse break in our verse has been viewed by some as reflecting the intentional deletion of several words that contained Jacob's response. Some of the ancient versions filled the narrative gap, and from their additions we might be able to conjecture what may have been erased in the masoretic version. Thus, in the Septuagint we find, following "and Israel heard," the expression "and it was evil to him," words unflattering to Reuben in their depiction of Jacob as responding to his son's betrayal with noticeable bitterness, though no verbal or physical expression of that bitterness is described. This expansion appears also in *Targum Pseudo-Jonathan*, where Jacob also expresses fear lest, among his sons, too, there is a bad apple, like Ishmael for Abraham and Esau for Isaac, but the Holy Spirit assures him that it is not so. The writer of *Jubilees* relates that "Jacob was enraged at Reuben that he had lain with Bilhah" (33:8), though it doesn't say how Jacob expressed that anger. These three sources thus fill the deficiency of the verse in similar ways, and we cannot help but suspect that the verse has indeed been broken off and that part of it was deleted; however, the missing words are not necessarily those found in these sources.

The missing part of our verse can perhaps be completed with the help of other verses that address Reuben's act. Take, for instance, what Jacob tells his son at the end of his life: "Reuben, you are my first-born, my might and first fruit of my vigor, [you deserve] exceeding rank and exceeding honor. Unstable as water, you shall excel no longer; for when you mounted your father's bed, you defiled my couch, you mounted!" (Genesis 49:3–4). According to the rule of the firstborn, Reuben's sta-

tus granted him "exceeding rank and exceeding honor," but his transgression with Jacob's concubine, though described in the somewhat
restrained and euphemistic terminology of "[mounting his] father's
bed" and "defiling," nevertheless causes Jacob to rebuke him as being
"unstable as water" and to take from him the advantages that his birth
had granted: "You shall excel no longer." (Jacob's words to his next
two sons, Simeon and Levi, are also full of reproach, the effect being
to emphasize that it is the fourth son, Judah, who will be accorded
primacy over his brothers.) According to this tradition, the Patriarch
curses his wrongdoing son only at this point, on his deathbed, and
perhaps for this reason it was necessary to remove the curse or bitter
reaction that was initially part of the story in Genesis 35 in order to
avoid duplication. The curse Jacob pronounces over Reuben on his
deathbed, when Jacob also curses Simeon and Levi, is enough. (See
also 1 Chronicles 5:1, where the author associates Reuben's act "when
he defiled his father's couch" with the loss of his firstborn rights and
their transfer to the sons of Joseph, following the spirit of Jacob's blessing in Genesis 49.)

   If indeed the story of Reuben and Bilhah originally included a curse
directed at Reuben, it may have involved the curse of losing his firstborn rights (as we find in Genesis 49) and perhaps even a death curse,
an echo of which we find in Moses's blessing to the tribe of Reuben:
"May Reuben live and not die, though few be his numbers" (Deuteronomy 33:6). The redundancy between the words "may Reuben live"
and "not die" might represent an attempt to cancel a death sentence
that had been pronounced following Reuben's relations with Bilhah.
It is reasonable to think that Moses's blessing responds to some version of our verse and not to Jacob's deathbed blessing, since there is no
mention there of any death curse. *Midrash Tannaim* to Deuteronomy
33:6 sensed this connection and determined that "may Reuben live"
was uttered in response to Reuben's noble behavior during the sale of
Joseph, when he had prevented his siblings from killing their young
brother (Genesis 37:21–22), while "not die" was directed at his affair
with Bilhah.

The late midrashic compilation *Sekhel Tov* to our verse challenges the notion that Reuben was cursed for his actions with Bilhah: "And Israel heard—he heard what Reuben had done, overcame his anger, and did not curse him, neither him nor his descendants." This certainly sounds as though it were disputing a flow of traditions that contended how Jacob had indeed cursed his eldest son. It joins a long list of post-biblical sources that supposed Jacob's reaction to have been a prayer for his son (e.g., *Testament of Reuben* 4:4: "And my father consoled me and prayed to God on my behalf") or an ill-founded concern that there was a bad apple among his offspring (see above) and that attempted, in a variety of ways, to understand Reuben's act not according to the simple meaning of the Hebrew words (the *peshat*) but through a process of refinement and mitigation. What is significant for us is our contention that echoes of what is missing from our verse (following the words "and Israel found out") can be heard in other verses in the Pentateuch and also in post-biblical texts. Together, these sources help us to imagine the original contours of the Reuben and Bilhah tradition.

28

Seduction before Murder

The Case of Jael

Folklore studies have often shown how sexual motifs disappear when stories are incorporated into socioliterary contexts in which such references have been deemed inappropriate. Early versions of Sleeping Beauty, Snow White, Rapunzel, and Cinderella were not so innocent as we have come to know them from fairy tale collections and Walt Disney movies, which are geared to family entertainment. We have already seen, in our discussions of Sarah in Pharaoh's palace (chapter 25) and Rebekah and Abraham's servant (chapter 26), how traditions became gradually refined in a process that included discarding erotic elements between men and women. With this in mind, we turn now to the Bible's two versions—one in prose and one in poetry—of the encounter between Jael, the heroine whose cunning and courage save the Israelites, and Sisera, the army commander of King Jabin of Hazor.

The story, in Judges 4:17–22, reports how the enemy general Sisera had fled the battlefield after his army's crushing defeat at the hands of Barak son of Abinoam and arrived to the tent of Jael, who coaxes him to enter. Jael coddles the enemy general. She covers the weary fighter with a blanket and brings him milk to drink instead of the water he requested, and when he finally falls asleep, she plunges a stake into his temple, killing him. Though Jael is alone with Sisera in her tent, nothing sexual occurs between the two.

However, when we compare this prose version with its poetic counterpart in the Song of Deborah in Judges 5, the victory poem that abuts

it, we discover a small bit of what the prose conceals. The poem alludes
to sexual relations between Jael and Sisera, during which she kills the
enemy commander, who had unwisely abandoned himself (and all
caution) to lovemaking.

Most blessed of women be Jael,
wife of Heber the Kenite,
most blessed of women in tents.
He asked for water, she offered milk;
In a princely bowl she brought him curds.
Her [left] hand reached for the tent stake,
her right for the workmen's hammer.
She struck Sisera, crushed his head,
smashed and pierced his temple.
Between her legs he kneeled, he fell, lay,
between her legs he kneeled, he fell;
Where he kneeled, there he fell—destroyed. (Judges 5:24–27)

This last verse is the decisive one. Although the expression *bein
ragleiha* has often been translated with "at her feet," its meaning as
"between her legs" is unambiguously clear from the expression's only
other appearance in the Bible, where it appears in the context of childbirth: "the afterbirth that issues from between her legs" (Deuteronomy
28:57). The Rabbis laid bare the true meaning of the poetic verse when
they wrote: "'Between her legs' [this is] a euphemism. Rabbi Yochanan
said: seven times did that wicked one possess her on that day, as it is
said, 'between her legs he kneeled, he fell, he lay, between her legs he
kneeled, he fell, where he kneeled there he fell, destroyed'" (B. *Yevamot*
103a; see also *Horayot* 10b; *Nazir* 23b). Yochanan's "seven possessions"
correspond to the seven verbs in the verse—Sisera "kneeled, fell, lay
... kneeled, fell ... kneeled ... fell." The sages' emphasis on the sexual
component draws our attention because it is atypical: they were usually keen to obscure or diminish anything that might sully a hero's
reputation or otherwise tarnish the sanctity of the Bible. When the

Rabbis do stress a sexual component, the likelihood is great that the biblical storyteller indeed alluded to it, and the sages have only made explicit the Bible's implicit agenda.

In their exegesis, the sages attribute erotic significance to each of the verbs "kneeled," "fell," and "lay." As is their custom when interpreting words that seem redundant, they view each verb as representing a distinct action. And truly, while these verbs ostensibly describe Sisera's collapse and death, they nonetheless carry within them also intimations of the story's erotic character. There is no need to bring examples of the possible sexual connotations of the root *sh-kh-v*, "lay." The root *k-r-ʻ*, "kneel," is found with erotic meaning in the words of Job: "May my wife grind for another, may others kneel over her" (31:10); and *n-f-l*, "fell," which marks Sisera's death in both story and poem, is used in a plainly erotic context in the book of Esther (in a tradition we will soon discuss in detail), where Haman's behavior arouses the king's anger and suspicion that Haman was about to rape the queen: "When the king returned from the palace garden to the banquet room, Haman had fallen on the bed on which Esther reclined. 'Does he mean,' cried the king, 'to ravish the queen in my own palace?'" (7:8).

All of this leaves us with the distinct impression that the story of Jael and Sisera in Judges 4 confronts and grapples with an erotic tradition and, indeed, was formulated in order to moderate it. In order to uncover the components of the ancient tradition, we should first remind readers of three other stories that share a similar plot with ours, stories in which a man is seduced by a woman at whose hands he finds his death: (1) Delilah, who maneuvers Samson's submission and turns him over to his Philistine enemies (Judges 16:4–22); (2) Queen Esther, who maneuvers Haman's surrender and exposes him to the king's anger during the royal banquet (see especially Esther 7:8); (3) and Judith, the eponymous heroine of the apocryphal book that relates how she kills the Assyrian general Holophernes at the moment he believes her to have surrendered herself to his sexual desires (Judith 10–13).

In contrast to the stories about Jael, Esther, and Judith, where the reader's admiration swells around the heroines who save their people from a foreign champion, in the story of Samson and Delilah we stand on the side of the bested hero who discloses his secret to the seductress. This story may in fact be rooted in a Philistine tradition that. originally glorified Delilah for her success in toppling Samson. Turning the conjectured Philistine story into a Hebrew one involved a number of changes: the woman acts not out of patriotic motives but, instead, for monetary gain (Judges 16:5), and the hero's ruin is neither final nor complete: he will yet be given the opportunity to strike his enemies before he dies. Each of the stories that we have mentioned refines the plotline's erotic elements for the same reason that these elements were removed from our story: the desire to include the story in Scripture.

Another appearance of this story type is found in the book of Proverbs' warning to the wise man not to go astray after a foreign woman, a seductress. It describes a picture in which the woman entices an innocent youth to come into her home and take delight in the pleasures of love, a diversion that will inevitably end with his death (7:5–27). Since Proverbs is not concerned with the glorification of Israel's heroes, and since its goal is precisely to warn against men falling into the trap of a woman's seductions, it cannot help but clearly articulate the story-type's erotic elements. Similar motifs reappear in the seductive words that are spoken by Wisdom and the "stupid woman bustling about" (9:1–5, 13–18)—the two female personifications of these characteristics.

To compare the story of Jael and Sisera with its parallel stories, we will divide it into five components, following the plot's stages: (1) Sisera is invited to enter Jael's tent; (2) Sisera drinks; (3) Jael covers Sisera with a blanket; (4) there is contact between them; (5) Sisera sleeps. Let us now compare the stories component by component.

1. Sisera Is Invited to Enter Jael's Tent

The scene of Jael leaving her tent, approaching Sisera, and inviting him to enter with the words "Enter, my lord, enter here, do not be afraid" (Judges 4:18), brings to mind what is told of the foreign woman in Proverbs, who "comes toward him dressed like a harlot, with set purpose" (7:10). In Proverbs 9, Wisdom says, "Let the simple enter here" (v. 4), and these exact words are later repeated by "the stupid woman who bustles about" (v. 16). In the book of Esther, too, Haman arrives—twice—to feasts in response to Esther's invitations (5:4, 8).

2. Sisera Drinks

Although Sisera asks Jael to bring him water to drink, she gives him milk in order to gain his trust and his belief in her good intentions. And yet water and milk can also be construed as conveying erotic meaning. The stupid woman in Proverbs 9 compares forbidden love with stolen waters: "Stolen waters are sweet, and bread eaten furtively is tasty" (v. 17); milk appears together with wine in the Bible's love poetry (e.g., Song of Songs 5:1: "I have come to my garden, My own, my bride; I have plucked my myrrh and spice, eaten my honey and honeycomb, drunk my wine and my milk. Eat, lovers, and drink: Drink deep of love!").

The sages, perceiving the erotic allusions in Jael and Sisera's tale, identified the milk she gave him as breast milk (B. *Niddah* 55b), but in another place they felt that the drink was meant to get him drunk: "'She opened a skin of milk and gave him some to drink'—to ascertain whether or not his wits were about him. He drank and became drunken and he tried to have his way with her" (*Midrash ha-Gadol* to Genesis 23:1). *Biblical Antiquities*, in its telling of the tale, explicitly mentions wine when it cites the biblical verse that speaks about milk: "And Jael took wine and mixed it with milk" (31:6).

To this we must compare the other stories of seduction. In *Jewish Antiquities*, Flavius Josephus writes that Delilah gave Samson wine to drink so that she would be able to tie him up—"in his being in a drunken state she bound him with vines" (5.8.11)—a detail not mentioned in Judges, where we are led to believe that, of his Nazirite vows (including the ban on drinking alcohol), Samson broke only the prohibition against cutting his hair, which led to the loss of his strength. In the book of Judith, it is stated explicitly that Holophernes was given wine on his last night:

"And he drank more wine than he had ever drunk in one day since he was born . . . and Holophernes . . . kneeling on his bed because he was soaked with wine" (12:20–13:2). The commander's deep, drunken sleep made it possible for Judith to kill him. In the book of Esther, the picture that arouses the king's anger occurs during the wine banquet that Esther hosts for him and Haman (7:1–7), and in Proverbs' descriptions of seductions, Wisdom turns to the fool and invites him, "Come, eat my food and drink the wine that I have mixed" (9:5).

3. Jael Covers Sisera with a Blanket

In the story of Jael and Sisera, the blanket with which Jael covers the army commander is used as evidence that no physical contact between them occurred, prompting the verbal phrase "and she covered him" to appear twice (Judges 4:18, 19). The term used for blanket, *smikhah*, makes its single appearance in the Bible here, a fact that made it possible for the Rabbis (following one of their hermeneutic principles, called *notariqon*) to divide the word into two halves: "*shmi koh* [lit., My name is]: My name testifies for her that that villain did not touch her" (*Leviticus Rabbah* 23, 10; the letters of both *smikhah* and *shmi koh* are identical). Sensing the erotic bombshell concealed in the story's plot, the Rabbis sought to claim that nothing of the sort transpired.

The covering motif would appear to be the inverse of the motif of offering a bed, cushioning it with pillows, and perfuming it, which we find in the words of the foreign seductress in Proverbs: "I have cushioned my couch with covers of dyed Egyptian linen; I have sprinkled my bed with myrrh, aloes, and cinnamon" (7:16–17). Also in Judith, the heroine's maidservant prepares her mistress's bedding next to Holophernes's in the evening when he expects to satisfy his lust (12:15–16). In *Biblical Antiquities* it is specified that Jael's bed is covered with lilies (31:3). (Compare Song 2:5: "Sustain me [*samkhuni*; this is similar to the root *s-m-kh*, "cover"—the letters *samekh* and *sin* are often interchangeable in biblical Hebrew] with raisin cakes, Refresh me [*rapduni*; the root *r-p-d* is similar to *r-v-d*, which is used elsewhere to describe adding cushions, such as in the verse we cited above from Proverbs, "I have *cushioned* my couch"—the letters *pe* and *bet* are also often inter-changeable in biblical Hebrew] with apples, For I am faint with love.")

4. There Is Contact between Them

What was left obscure in the story is expressed more clearly in the po-etic version, in the Song of Deborah (Judges 5:27), and is explicitly stated in the midrash. Sexual relations are not overtly referred to in the Samson and Delilah story, where the writer of Judges records only that Delilah lulled Samson to sleep on her knees (16:19), but the Septua-gint specifies "between her knees" (compare "between her legs" in the Song of Deborah). The sages revealed sexual relations between Samson and Delilah in their interpretation-explanation of a singular word in that story, *va-te'altzehu*, in the verse "Finally, after she had nagged him and pressed him constantly [*va-te'altzehu*], he was wearied to death" (16:16), saying: "What is [the meaning of] *va-te'altzehu*? Rabbi Isaac of the school of Rabbi Ammi said: At the moment that he reached or-gasm, [Delilah] detached herself from under him" (B. *Sota* 9b).

As we've already mentioned, in Esther we find also the motif of the bed during the course of the king's mistaken suspicion that Haman had tried to have relations with Esther (7:8). The matter is even more pronounced in the book of Judith, where we find, for example, Holo-phernes saying: "For it will be a disgrace to us if we let such a woman go without enjoying her company" (12:12). And when Judith arrives to the commander's tent it is said: "And he was moved with great de-sire to possess her; for he had been waiting for an opportunity to se-duce her, ever since the day he first saw her" (v. 16). Judith dresses in her fine clothes and jewelry in order to make the false impression that she means to yield to Holophernes's desires. Sexual temptation is stated openly in the seductress's words in Proverbs: "Let us drink our fill of love till morning; Let us delight in amorous embrace" (7:18). A comparable scene of seduction is supplied to our story by the author of *Biblical Antiquities*, who writes that "Jael the wife of the Kenite or-namented herself with ornaments and she came out to him and the woman was very beautiful" (31:3).

5. Sisera Sleeps

In Judges 4:15, Sisera is depicted as falling asleep from exhaustion, having fled on foot from the battlefield. In the story of Samson, it is said that Delilah lulls him to sleep (16:19), which allows Delilah to overcome him and deprive him of his strength. Only in the story of Judith does the storyteller place the hero's sleep together with wine drinking: "For everyone was tired from all the drinking ... and Holophernes ... kneeling on his bed because he was soaked with wine" (13:2). His sleep makes it possible for Judith to behead him and escape undetected.

Our comparison of the story of Jael and Sisera with its poetic parallel, on the one hand, and with the other expressions of this story type about the murdering seductress, on the other, reveals the aim of the biblical author to maintain a level of propriety that befits the story's biblical home. For this reason, he left only faint impressions and weak echoes of the erotic tradition that lies at the crux of his work. Postbiblical generations could not help but reassert it.

29

No Innocent Death

David, Abigail, and Nabal

In his escape from King Saul, David arrives in the Judean Desert with an unruly band of men in tow: "Everyone who was in straits and everyone who was in debt and everyone who was desperate joined him, and he became their leader" (1 Samuel 22:2). During his stay, David extends his protection to the region's inhabitants—farmers and shepherds—against outlaws, services for which he demands payment (even though he was never asked to perform them). Chapter 25 of 1 Samuel tells about one of the wealthy men in the region by the name of Nabal the Carmelite, who celebrates the festival of the shearing of the sheep at a feast with his shearers (another such shearing feast is mentioned in 2 Samuel 13:23–28). David dispatches his men to Nabal with a request that he award David goods for his services. Nabal refuses, and in his reply he refers to David and his band as fugitives fleeing the law: "Who is David? Who is the son of Jesse? There are many slaves nowadays who run away from their masters. Should I then take my bread and my water, and the meat that I slaughtered for my own shearers, and give them to men who come from I don't know where?" (1 Samuel 25:10–11). Enraged by Nabal's ungratefulness, David sets out at the head of his army to take revenge (v. 13), ready to wipe Nabal, his people, and all Nabal's property from the face of the earth.

David would have succeeded were it not for the intervention of Nabal's wife, Abigail, who acts quickly to calm David's fury. Without her husband's knowledge, the "intelligent and shapely" Abigail

(1 Samuel 25:3) sets out to meet David with donkeys heavily laden with provisions, a gift to David and his men (vv. 18–20). Upon reaching them, she throws herself down before David, soothing his temper with a perfectly formulated speech. Abigail does not hesitate to characterize her husband as a scoundrel, as one who "is just what his name says: His name is 'villain' [*naval*] and he is vile [*nevalah*]" (v. 25). She explains to David that she had not been aware of his messengers' arrival and that the moment she learned of their visit she set out to meet him. She further takes an oath—on his life—that he will not exact Nabal's judgment with his own hands, hinting that God will be the one to deliver Nabal's punishment: "I swear, my lord, as the LORD lives and as you live—the LORD who has kept you from seeking redress by blood with your own hands—let your enemies and all who would harm my lord fare like Nabal!" (v. 26).

Abigail foretells David's victory over Saul and his ascension to kingship over Israel and, accordingly, she entreats him to avoid spilling blood so that his throne will be unstained (1 Samuel 25:30–31). In the same breath, she asks also that he "remember your maid," meaning that when he rules over Israel he can repay the favor Abigail did for him. David thanks Abigail for preventing him from killing Nabal, and he accepts her gifts (vv. 32–35).

The following day, with the hungover Nabal recovering from the previous evening's revels, Abigail relates to him "everything that had happened," and Nabal takes it hard: "His courage died within him and he became like a stone" (1 Samuel 25:37). God even intervenes directly and delivers the evildoer his due: "About ten days later the LORD struck Nabal and he died" (v. 38), thus fulfilling Abigail's prophecy. David praises God, who fights his enemies (v. 39), and hurries to send his youths to Abigail to take her as David's wife. Her compliance is instant: "She immediately bowed low with her face to the ground and said, 'Your handmaid is ready to be your maidservant, to wash the feet of my lord's servants.' Then Abigail rose quickly and mounted an ass, and with five of her maids in attendance she followed David's messengers; and she became his wife" (vv. 41–42).

A comparison of this story with another, similar story from David's biography, the tale of David's taking Bathsheba from her husband, Uriah (2 Samuel 11), leaves the impression that, in his telling of the story, the writer of 1 Samuel 25 wrestled with a previous version of the tale that did not paint David and Abigail and the relations between them as being so honorable. Both stories open with David dispatching a delegation: ten young men to Nabal in the first, and Joab and his men to fight the Ammonites in the second. Both of the women are said to be beautiful: about Abigail, "the woman was intelligent and shapely [*yefat to'ar*]" (1 Samuel 25:3), and about Bathsheba, "the woman was very beautiful [*tovat mar'eh*]" (2 Samuel 11:2). Each woman returns to her home after her first meeting with David (1 Samuel 25:36; 2 Samuel 11:4).

In each story, David takes the woman as his wife after the death of her husband. The phrasing used to describe this is similar: "David sent messengers to speak for Abigail [i.e., to propose marriage], and to take her as his wife" (1 Samuel 25:39); "David sent and had [Bathsheba] brought to his house and she became his wife" (2 Samuel 11:27). In both stories, the drinking of wine until drunkenness is mentioned in connection with the woman's husband: Nabal gets drunk before being informed of his having awakened David's fury (1 Samuel 25:36), while David gets Uriah drunk so that the latter will return home and sleep with his wife, part of David's scheme to conceal his own sexual relations with Bathsheba (2 Samuel 11:13).

Along with these many correspondences between the two stories, we must also point to the huge difference between them. In the story of David and Bathsheba, Uriah, Bathsheba's husband, finds his death at David's command, while in the first story it is God who takes revenge on Nabal. (The possibility that in a more ancient version of the story it was David who killed Nabal is not unthinkable, though we find no evidence of such a tradition apart from the similar motif in the parallel tradition about Uriah.) That isn't the only difference between the two episodes: in the story about Abigail as we have received it, David does not try to have relations with Abigail until her husband has died and she has become his wife, while in the story of Bathsheba, David seeks to immediately satisfy his lust and has relations with her, fully knowing that she is a married woman.

The placement of the Abigail story in its present form before the story of Bathsheba and the lines of resemblance between the two stories are meant to convey the notion that David's sin with Bathsheba was a one-time misstep. *Look* (it tells us), *also in the past he married someone who had been another man's wife, but that was different.* It was not his desire for Abigail that caused her husband's death, a divine act brought about by that man's sinning, and David married Abigail out of gratitude for her having prevented his killing Nabal. The writer of the book of Samuel needed one story about David doing wrong in order to justify the misfortunes that would subsequently befall David and his family: the death of a son, a son's murder by a brother, the rape of a daughter by her brother, and a son's mounting a rebellion against David.

Nevertheless, the lines of resemblance between the David and Bathsheba affair and that of David and Abigail lead us to consider another possibility: that initially these were similar stories about the snatching of a woman from her husband's grasp while the husband still lived, with David and the woman equal conspirators in the act. These two stories together present an unfavorable rendering of David as one who collects women without thinking twice about disposing of any husbands who stand in his way. David appears as an impulsive and callous man for whom basic laws of morality carry little weight.

It is interesting to note one other story in which David claims another man's wife as his own: the story of Saul's daughter Michal, who was married to Paltiel son of Laish (2 Samuel 3:12–16). According to the book of Samuel, Michal was first married to David (1 Samuel 18:27), but after David fled from her father, she was given to Paltiel (25:44). When David finally ascends the throne, he wants Michal returned to him as a sign of his right to succeed Saul. It may be, however, that behind this story hides another, about a woman taken from her husband by David, a tradition that the writer of Samuel tried to disguise with the claim that David was only seeking to reclaim what had been previously stolen from him. Whatever is the case, evidence for the existence of a story about Abigail being unfaithful while still married to her husband emerges not only from the resemblances still apparent between the present story and the story of David and Bathsheba but also from traditions told by the Rabbis, where the encounter between David and Abigail is depicted in the most immodest light.

The Babylonian Talmud counts Abigail among the "four most beautiful women in the world: Sarah, Rahab, Abigail, and Esther" (*Megillah* 15a; in another opinion there, Vashti is also included). The Bible speaks only about the beauty of Sarah (Genesis 12:11), Abigail (1 Samuel 25:3), Esther (Esther 2:7), and Vashti (Esther 1:11). The addition of Rahab, the prostitute from Jericho (Joshua 2:1), changes completely the complexion of the list. We remember that Sarah's beauty is mentioned in the context of her being taken into Pharaoh's palace while still Abraham's wife (see chapter 25), while Esther's beauty is referred to in the course of her being take to Ahasuerus after already being married, according to the midrash, to Mordecai (see chapter 25). We've already seen how, in their biblical versions, the story about Sarah and Pharaoh and that of Esther and Ahasuerus reveal clear literary connections to the David and Bathsheba story, to which, as we've already said, our story is connected. The Babylonian Talmud's list of beautiful women thus awakens the possibility that the author of the list was aware of the similarity or even of the connection between the story of Abigail and the other stories about women being taken from their husbands by a king (or one who claims the kingship).

Moreover, about two of the women, along with two more (Saul's daughter Michal, and Jael, another woman who slept with a foreign ruler while still married; see chapter 28), the Talmud states: "Rahab caused lust [lit., she whored] with her name, Jael with her voice, Abigail with the recollection of her, Michal daughter of Saul with her appearance" (*Megillah* 15a). The Talmud explains only the first part of the passage: even the mention of Rahab's name was enough to cause men to ejaculate, due to the prostitute's pronounced sexuality.

The references to Jael, Abigail, and Michal require a different explanation. Jael behaved improperly with her voice when she invited Sisera into her tent; Michal committed a grave transgression when she despised David as she watched him dance before the Ark, "Michal daughter of Saul looked out of the window and saw King David leaping and whirling before the LORD; and she despised him for it" (2 Samuel 6:16); while the reference to "Abigail with the recollection of her" alludes to Abigail's words to David: "And when the LORD has accomplished for my lord all the good He has promised you, and has appointed you ruler of Israel . . . and when the LORD has prospered my lord, remember your maid" (1 Samuel 25:30–31). Abigail's request to David that he remember her when he ascends the throne represents a betrayal of her husband. Her request was viewed by the Jerusalem Talmud as shameful: "It teaches that she behaved immodestly, and since she behaved immodestly the verse [records] defectively, 'David said to Abigail [written "Abigal"]'" (1 Samuel 25:32). The Talmud attributes the writing of the name "Abigail" with one letter missing to the Bible's disapproval of her disgraceful behavior.

Regarding David and Abigail's meeting, the Jerusalem Talmud recounts how, as Abigail stood before David and his men, "they all ejaculated," while the Babylonian Talmud claims that "[Abigail] uncovered her thigh and [David] walked by its light three *parsa'ot* [about seven and a half miles]" (*Megillah* 14b). A later midrash combines the two traditions: "Her thigh was uncovered and they all ejaculated" (*Midrash Samuel* 23:11 [59a]). These traditions speak both to the woman's immodesty and to the extreme reaction by the men, which together lend a vulgarity to the meeting. The Babylonian Talmud goes so far as to put into David's mouth the explicit command, "Obey me!"

As if this were not enough, the Babylonian Talmud further relates how Abigail spoke with David about an intimate female matter, "about matters of blood, which come from secret parts. She took blood and showed him. He said to her, 'does one show blood at night?' She said to him, 'and are matters of life and death decided at night?'" (*Megillah* 14a–b). Abigail consults with David concerning the particulars of a stain of "[menstrual] blood" that she had found (see Rashi's commentary there), and suggests that, just as rabbis do not rule on matters concerning such stains during the nighttime, so too should David refrain from exacting judgment against Nabal at night. For this David blesses Abigail, saying, "And blessed be your prudence, and blessed be you yourself for restraining me from seeking redress in blood by my own hands" (1 Samuel 25:33), and the Talmud, addressing the verse's plural form of the word for blood, *damim*, expounds: "blood in both its meanings" (Rashi explains: menstrual blood and bloodletting).

It becomes apparent that David, according to the story known to the Talmud, demanded that Abigail have relations with him, and it was only her exemplary behavior that prevented him from sleeping with a menstruating woman (an act forbidden by Jewish law). In this regard, it is interesting to note that in the parallel story about David and Bathsheba, it is mentioned explicitly that, previous to the king's coupling with Bathsheba, "she had purified herself after her period" (2 Samuel 11:4).

Altogether, these motifs—Abigail's rebuke for immodest behavior, the statement that she "caused lust with the recollection of her," her appearance in the same passage with Rahab the prostitute, the notion that she exposed her thigh and caused ejaculation among David's men, David's demand that she lie with him, her discussing menstrual blood with David—present the meeting between David and Abigail in a distinctly brazen light, and it seems likely that the writers of these traditions sensed that they represented what the Bible, in its war against ancient beliefs, had sought to temper. The resemblance between the story of David and Abigail and that of David and Bathsheba, despite all the differences between them, lends further weight to this conjecture.

Further support can be brought from a midrash that focuses on the book of Samuel's presentation of David's son Chileab: "Sons were born to David in Hebron: His first-born was Amnon, by Ahinoam of Jezreel; his second was Chileab, by Abigail wife of Nabal the Carmelite; the third was Absalom son of Maacah, daughter of King Talmai of Geshur" (2 Samuel 3:2–3). The identification of Abigail as the "wife of Nabal the Carmelite" in the same breath as naming her the mother of Chileab son of David requires explanation, and the midrash delivers:

After he had brought her [Abigail], David withdrew from her for three months in order to ascertain whether she was pregnant from Nabal or not. After three months he came to her and she conceived by him, though the mockers of the generation would mock him and say [that] from Nabal she had conceived. What did the Holy One, blessed be He, do? He commanded the angel assigned to the creation of newborns and to their appearance and he said to him, "Go and create him in the image of David his father in order that all will testify that David is his father" . . . Chileab [kil'av]—[that he] was wholly [his] father [kulo-'av; this is a covert name derivation] that anyone who sees him says, "David is that one's father." (Tanḥuma, Toledot 6)

It is not clear what the "mockers" were ridiculing. Were they insinuating that Abigail slept with David while pregnant with her former husband's child? And if so, what is there to ridicule? The solution would seem to come from a comparison between this tradition and another midrashic tradition about the ridicule directed at Sarah after her stay in the palace of Pharaoh or Abimelech (see chapter 25), where she was suspected of having conceived from the foreign king and not from her husband. It is quite possible, therefore, that the Tanḥuma's tradition about Abigail is a new version of another, in which the mockers of the generation ridicule Abigail, the wife of Nabal, for being pregnant with David's child, thus explaining the verse that presents Chileab as the son of David from "Abigail wife of Nabal the Carmelite"!

Incidentally, it seems likely that a similar motive—a desire to remove the suspicion that one of David's sons was not, in fact, his own—stands also behind the story of the death of David's first son with Bathsheba (2 Samuel 12:14–23), after which is related the birth of Solomon (vv. 24–28). Even if one were to suspect that that first child was in fact Uriah's offspring, there is no room for casting doubt on David's having fathered Solomon. It is in this spirit that we should understand perhaps also the Bible's insistence that Bathsheba had come to David only after having purified herself following her menstrual period (2

Samuel 11:4), and if that is the case, we have before us two separate attempts to cut off all connections between Uriah's and David's offspring.

An early story about David and Abigail, a story about a passionate meeting between an impulsive warrior and a married, unfaithful woman, became transformed in the Bible into a story about a wise woman and a hero who conquers his impulsive passions. The sensitive readings of generations of interpreters and exegetes of the Bible have helped us to bring the ancient tradition, more or less, to light.

30

Not Just Riddles

Solomon and the Queen of Sheba

The episode about the queen of Sheba's visit to Solomon's palace in 1 Kings 10:1–13 illuminates and substantiates what is told elsewhere in the book of Kings about Solomon's wisdom and wealth. The stories on either side of the episode report Solomon's economic relationships with other kingdoms and the sources of his wealth. The gifts brought by the queen of Sheba—"She presented the king with one hundred and twenty talents of gold, and a large quantity of spices, and precious stones. Never again did such a vast quantity of spices arrive as that which the queen of Sheba gave to King Solomon" (v. 10)—increase the king's fortune.

With regard to the king's wisdom, the book of Kings contains divergent views about its nature: vast knowledge of the universe, on the one hand, and a thorough command of the law and the wisdom to execute justice, on the other. In accordance with the first notion, the king's wisdom is manifested in his vast literary output and encyclopedic knowledge of the world, its flora and fauna:

Solomon's wisdom was greater than the wisdom of all the Kedemites and than all the wisdom of the Egyptians. He was the wisest of all men: [wiser] than Ethan the Ezrahite, and Heman, Chalkol, and Darda the sons of Mahol. His fame spread among all the surrounding nations. He composed three thousand proverbs, and his songs numbered one thousand and five. He discoursed about trees, from the cedar in Lebanon to the hyssop that grows out of the wall; and he discoursed about beasts, birds, creeping things, and fishes. (1 Kings 5:10–13)

The king's wisdom awakens great wonder: "Men of all peoples came to hear Solomon's wisdom, [sent] by all the kings of the earth who had heard of his wisdom" (1 Kings 5:14). We read, too, in 10:24–25: "And all the world came to pay homage to Solomon and to listen to the wisdom with which God had endowed him; and each one would bring his tribute—silver and gold objects, robes, weapons and spices, horses and mules—in the amount due each year."

The queen of Sheba's journey to hear Solomon's wisdom and to augment his coffers is therefore no different from the actions of other sovereigns who came from near and far to the Jerusalem king's court: "The queen of Sheba heard of Solomon's fame, for the sake of the LORD's name, and she came to test him with hard questions" (1 Kings 10:1). The queen intended to test Solomon's wisdom, since a knowledge of riddles and their solutions was a sign of a wise person, as we read in Proverbs: "The wise man, hearing them, will gain more wisdom; the discerning man will learn to be adroit; for understanding proverb and epigram, the words of the wise and their riddles" (1:5–6).

One cannot help but notice the awkwardness in 1 Kings 10:1, the opening verse to the queen of Sheba episode. Much smoother is the verse's parallel in 2 Chronicles, which knows nothing of the words *le-shem 'adonai*, "for the sake of the LORD's name": "The queen of Sheba heard of Solomon's fame, and came to Jerusalem to test Solomon with hard questions" (2 Chronicles 9:1). It seems that the words *le-shem 'adonai* (i.e., for the sake of Solomon's God and His glory) were an addition that was meant to be inserted either after "and she came" or at the end of the verse. Whoever added these words was uncomfortable with the notion that the queen's visit had been inspired by the glory of a man and his wisdom and not the glory and wisdom of God.

And indeed, though God is the source of the king's wisdom—"The LORD endowed Solomon with wisdom and discernment in great measure, with understanding as vast as the sands on the seashore" (1 Kings 5:9)—the pilgrimage to witness the wonder of Solomon's wisdom does place the king on a rung closer to the giver of wisdom, that is, God, the creator of the universe who knows its orders and all its secrets (an idea expressed, e.g., in Job 28). In order to mitigate the impression that a human's knowledge could be boundless and approach that of God's, the book of Kings wished to emphasize that Solomon's knowledge was primarily of a different character: the wisdom to judge his people with fairness (1 Kings 3:9–28). In this spirit, a verse was added into the queen's words of tribute: "Praised be the LORD your God, who delighted in you and set you on the throne of Israel. It is because of the LORD's everlasting love for Israel that He made you king to administer justice and righteousness" (1 Kings 10:9). In other words, a story that previously spoke about a human's encyclopedic knowledge was supplemented with new layers that shifted the bulk of veneration to God. God gave Solomon his wisdom, a wisdom that related to laws and justice, and it was for the glory of God, the giver of wisdom, that the queen of Sheba traveled to Jerusalem.

And still, notwithstanding the removal of this secondary element and our evaluating the story's core—that the king's wisdom was what drew foreign rulers, including the queen of Sheba, to make pilgrimages to Jerusalem and to bestow their gifts upon him—we are left with the sense that a bit of the story's truth has been revealed, while its most essential element remains hidden: an erotic encounter between the king and his esteemed visitor. Support for this conjecture can be brought from both the story itself and post-biblical sources.

The queen of Sheba tests Solomon with riddles—an activity typical of wedding celebrations, as we know from the story of Samson and the Philistine woman Samson married in Timnah: "Then Samson said to them, 'Let me propound a riddle to you. If you can give me the right answer during the seven days of the feast, I shall give you thirty linen tunics and thirty sets of clothing'" (Judges 14:12). Like the Philistines who were challenged with Samson's riddle, so is Solomon challenged to solve the riddle posed by the queen of Sheba (in 1 Kings 10:3), and just as Samson was forced to reward those who solved his riddle and give them their due (Judges 14:19), so does the queen give Solomon payment for solving hers (1 Kings 10:10).

The argument for a covert eroticism at the base of the story of the queen's meeting with Solomon finds its main support in the story's closing verse: "King Solomon, in turn, gave the queen of Sheba everything she desired [*heftzah*] and asked for, in addition to what King Solomon gave her out of his royal bounty. Then she and her attendants left and returned to her own land" (1 Kings 10:13).

Aside from the verse's verbosity, which cries out for explanation, it is of note that, in the biblical lexicon, the root *h-f-tz*, "desire," is often used in the context of male-female relations, as in a verse about Shechem son of Hamor in Genesis 34: "For he desired Jacob's daughter" (v. 19). We find it used also in the law regarding the treatment of beautiful female captives whose captors had married them but who have had a change of heart: "Then should you no longer desire her, you must release her outright" (Deuteronomy 21:14); and see also Song of Songs 2:7: "I adjure you, O maidens of Jerusalem . . . Do not wake or rouse love until it desires" (see also 3:5, 8:4). The long-winded phrase in 1 Kings 10:13 ends with the words "out of his royal bounty [*ke-yad ha-melekh*]," which remind us of verses in the book of Esther where it appears, first, in the description of the king's banquet (1:7), when the king wished to display the beauty of his wife, Vashti, before the guests, and, again, in the description of the banquet he gives in honor of his wedding to Esther: "The king gave a great banquet for all his officials and courtiers, 'the banquet of Esther' . . . and [he] distributed gifts out of the royal bounty" (2:18).

Moreover, the chapter that follows the episode of the queen's visit relates Solomon's marriages to foreign women: "King Solomon loved many foreign women in addition to Pharaoh's daughter—Moabite, Ammonite, Edomite, Phoenician, and Hittite women" (1 Kings 11:1). It is thus conceivable that the juxtaposition of this chapter with our story, which tells about the visit of a foreign queen, is one more allusion to the story's previous, erotic character.

Furthermore, we cannot exclude the possibility that the redactor responsible for ordering the poems in Song of Songs was aware of an intimate relationship between Solomon and the queen of Sheba. Immediately before the poem in Song of Songs that tells about Solomon's wedding bed—"There is Solomon's bed, encircled by sixty warriors of the warriors of Israel" (3:7–11)—the redactor-arranger planted an isolated poetic fragment: "Who is she that comes up from the desert like columns of smoke, in clouds of myrrh and frankincense, of all the powders of the merchant?" (v. 6). This perfumed young woman who comes from afar, from the exotic desert, awakens associations of the visit of the queen of Sheba, who brought perfumes to the king (1 Kings 10:10). The juxtaposition of these two poems suggests that it was the queen of Sheba who came to the king's bed. And, anyway, the mention of perfumes in the Bible is more often than not in blatantly erotic contexts: Esther's preparations for her first meeting with King Ahasuerus ("six months with oil of myrrh and six months with perfumes and women's cosmetics" [2:12]); the seductress's words in Proverbs ("I have sprinkled my bed with myrrh, aloes, and cinnamon. Let us drink our fill of love till morning; Let us delight in amorous embrace" [7:17–18]); and, most often, in Song of Songs (e.g., "I have come to my garden, My own, my bride; I have plucked my myrrh and spice" [5:1]).

The Rabbis apparently felt that the biblical story about the meeting between Solomon and the queen of Sheba was trying to obscure an erotic core, and they fortified the effort with their assertion, apparently in relation to verse 13, that "anyone who says that 'the queen of Sheba' was a woman is wrong. What is 'the queen of Sheba'? [It should be read] the kingdom of Sheba" (B. *Bava Batra* 15b). According to this explanation, the biblical story refers not to a woman but to a male representative of the kingdom of Sheba, leaving no room for any sort of story of male-female intrigue.

That said, the queen's riddles, according to the Rabbis and those who followed them, have a strongly erotic scent. According to *Midrash Mishlei* 1, the queen asks Solomon two questions and tests him with two tests. The first question asks: "Seven go out and nine enter, two pour and one drinks?" And the answer: "The seven days of separation during a woman's menstrual period, [at the end of which the woman can become pregnant, at which point begin] the nine months of pregnancy, two breasts, and the one infant who suckles from them." The second question asks: "Who is the woman who tells her son: Your father—[he is] your elder [and] my husband, you are my son and I am your sister?" The answer: this was what the daughters of Lot told their sons, since they became pregnant from their father (see Genesis 19:30–38). Following these two questions, which touch on impregnation, birth, and breastfeeding as well as on a biblical story about incest between daughters and their father, the queen of Sheba asks Solomon to distinguish between young boys and girls who are dressed identically and then between circumcised and uncircumcised men—two acts of differentiation that focus entirely on gender and genitalia.

In another work, *Midrash ha-Ḥefetz* (1:406–407), the story includes nineteen more riddles. A few of these also deal with the realm of male-female relations, referring to a woman's uterus and the story of Judah and Tamar ("[identify the] woman who married two [men] and gave birth to two sons, all four of whom had one father" [Genesis 38]). The selection of riddles from the sexual realm substantiates our sense that intimate relations between a man and a woman rest at the foundation of our story.

Other sources also restore the story's rejected erotic base and bring it to the surface. Before turning to Jewish texts, we'll look at Muslim and Ethiopian sources since, chronologically, they supply the link between the Bible and later Jewish sources.

The Qur'an (sura 27, the "Ant Sura," 43–44) tells about the visit of the queen of Sheba to Solomon's palace: "She was invited to enter the palace, but when she saw the floor she thought it was a pool of water, and she [lifted her dress so as not to get it wet and] exposed her thighs." The queen's bared thighs—compare "strip off your train, bare your leg, wade through the rivers, your nakedness shall be uncovered" (Isaiah 47:2–3) and "a woman's leg is a sexual incitement" (B. *Berakhot*

24a)—add the eroticism of a woman's body being uncovered before a man. Early Qur'an exegetes related how, when the queen laid bare her legs, it became apparent that they were excessively hairy, due to her being the queen of the demons, and that Solomon instructed her how to remove the hair (see, e.g., al-Tabari). This tradition lets us understand better what we found in the Qur'an: the palace's floor had intentionally been constructed from glass, with water flowing underneath, in order to establish whether the queen's legs were as hairy as had been reported. In the end, report the Muslim writers, King Solomon slept with the queen, who is called by the name Bilkis (perhaps derived from the Hebrew *pilegesh*, "concubine"?), after which she returned to her own land.

The Ethiopian national epic *Kebra Nagast*, the Book of the Glory of Kings, reports of the travels of Makeda, the queen of Sheba, to Jerusalem, and it describes also the result of that meeting: Menelik I, the child conceived from the queen's meeting with Solomon, who was the king of Ethiopia and true heir to the Israelite monarchy. Up until the 1970s, when the Ethiopian monarchy was abolished, the emperors there viewed themselves as descendants of Menelik I.

The meeting between King Solomon and the queen of Sheba is discussed also by Jewish sources. *Targum Sheni* to the book of Esther (on verse 1:3, "in the third year of his reign") relates in detail how, when the queen came to Solomon, she first met Benayahu ben Yehoiada, whose beauty impressed her greatly. She turned to her servants and remarked that, if Solomon's servant possessed such beauty, who knew how the king himself must look—a comment that suggests the queen's physical interest in her host. The *Targum* tells also about the queen's hairy legs and about the trick used to reveal this to Solomon.

Other texts are more explicit and relate outright how Solomon had relations with the queen of Sheba and how, as a result, Nebuchadnezzar, the destroyer of the First Temple, was born (so reports, e.g., the Alphabet of Ben Sira). In a comment incorporated into Rashi's commentary on 1 Kings 10:13 ("King Solomon, in turn, gave the queen of Sheba everything she desired and asked for"), it is said: "He came to her and there was born from her Nebuchadnezzar." The writer of *Shalshelet ha-Kabbalah* refers to a midrash according to which the union between Solomon and the queen of Sheba resulted in the birth of a daughter, from whom was subsequently born Nebuchadnezzar.

The fact that we find explicit references to sexual relations having taken place between Solomon and the queen of Sheba in Jewish literature only in later and peripheral texts suggests that the official sources such as the Talmud and early midrashic works were uncomfortable with the ancient tradition and avoided any allusion to it. The later identification of the resulting offspring as being Nebuchadnezzar further reflects Jewish hostility to the tradition: if indeed a sexual relationship did take place, its consequences were detrimental in that it produced the person responsible for the destruction of the Kingdom of Judah. If, according to the book of Kings, Solomon's marriages to foreign women were the cause of the kingdom's breakup (1 Kings 11), his meeting with the queen of Sheba, according to this tradition, had even graver consequences.

In Closing

We had a single aim in writing this volume: to open a window through which readers might glimpse traditions that existed before the Bible came into being. In this way we hope to give readers the ability to appreciate the varied strategies that the biblical writers used to cope with the traditions known to them. These traditions needed to be adapted and refined in order to make them suit the lofty ideals of monotheism, to elevate them to the morals and value system that the Bible sought to instill in its readers.

The ancient traditions dealt primarily within the realm of myth (e.g., the creation of the world; the origins of manna, the food of heavenly beings), cult and holy places (the origins of Shechem's sanctity; the reason for eating matzah), the biographies of central and even holy figures (Abraham's origins; the births of Samson and David; the death of Moses; the biography of Jeroboam), and affairs between men and women (Jael's relationship with Sisera; the queen of Sheba's ties with King Solomon). The Bible, unable to ignore popular traditions, offered alternate versions of these stories or revised them in ways that would dull the sharper elements that it could not tolerate.

Is it conceivable that the Bible did not faithfully transmit events as those events occurred? That it allowed itself to alter what had been recounted in our forebears' homes about the history of Israel and its heroes and even about the acts and pronouncements of God? To each of these questions we answer yes. Indeed, it was not the chronological reporting of events, of recording facts as they occurred, that constituted the chief interest of the biblical writers. These writers served a much loftier aim in their enterprise: to educate a nation, purify its beliefs, cleanse it of the dust of idolatry and myth, and wash it of vulgar expressions and faulty morality. Metaphorically speaking, the chain of events that stretches from "in the beginning" onward can be understood as a long line of railway cars that securely convey values, concepts, beliefs, and ideas. It is not the individual cars that are of consequence but the priceless cargo they carry.

Even readers who are determined to cling to the biblical stories as they are will reluctantly admit that, already within the Bible itself, we sometimes find interchangeable traditions that convey distinct and conflicting interpretations of a single event (such as the two stories about the Creation, or the different accounts of the identity of Goliath's killer). Moreover, generations upon generations of readers allowed themselves—perhaps even saw it as necessary—to deviate from the biblical story, to add to or omit from it, according to their religious beliefs, moral convictions, and worldviews. As an example, we can look at the story of the Binding of Isaac, which underwent profound transformation between the Bible and Rabbinic traditions. These turned Isaac into a martyred hero and even involved Sarah in the story, recounting how she died as a consequence, and also how Satan(!) tried tenaciously to prevent Abraham from carrying out the divine command. The book of Esther, too, where God is never mentioned, could not provide a starker contrast to the tale of Esther as told in the Additions to Esther in the Septuagint or in Rabbinic literature, where prayers to God seem to be recited endlessly and God is repeatedly and explicitly mentioned. Equally stunning is the contrast between the Bible's silence at Abraham's origins in comparison with the lavish traditions preserved in the Pseudepigrapha and Rabbinic texts about a youthful Abraham's spirited fight against idolatry. And what the Bible doesn't want to tell us about the circumstances of Sisera's death we find told in great detail in Rabbinic literature, where it is described quite clearly as having occurred during the sexual act.

It has become apparent that what we know to have been acceptable to generations of readers and writers who returned to the Bible's pages and reinterpreted its verses again and again in order to preserve its relevance and meaning for their generations was true, too, for the biblical writers. In fact, it seems that it was easier to adjust the contours of an ancient tradition or story *before* it was first committed to writing than to change them once they had already been inscribed by the Bible's scribes.

When we took up the role of literary archaeologists and applied ourselves to reconstructing pre-biblical traditions, we suddenly found ourselves in the realm of extra-biblical writings—those that preceded the Bible (the literature of the ancient world, e.g., Babylonia and Canaan) and those that postdated it by many hundreds of years (our quest sometimes led us all the way to the Middle Ages). We set out looking for signs of pre-biblical traditions, knowing that they could be hiding in a vast array of literary genres from different civilizations—from ancient Babylon (such as the Creation epic *Enuma Elish*) to the classical world that thrived across the Mediterranean Sea (e.g., Hesiod's *Shield of Heracles*).

Happily, the most significant literary harvest came to us from home, from Jewish writings throughout the generations. We found allusions scattered about in the biblical corpus itself that shed light on a passage under our scalpels, as well as in extra-biblical writings (such as Judith, Ben Sira, *Jubilees*, and *Testaments of the Twelve Patriarchs*). We plucked them from the ancient translations of the Bible (the Greek Septuagint, Latin Vulgate, Aramaic *Targum Pseudo-Jonathan* to the Torah, and others), the Samaritan version of the Pentateuch, and Jewish Hellenistic literature (the writings of Artapanus and Flavius Josephus). We uncovered them in the various and varied scrolls found in caves in the Judean Desert and, chiefly, in the writings of the Rabbis and those who followed in their path. Here we discovered rich sources in the Mishnah and Tosefta, the Talmuds and midrashim of the *tannaim* and *amoraim*, the Passover haggadah and *piyyutim*, the writings of the medieval commentators (Rashi, Rashbam) and others of their time (the Zohar and later midrashic anthologies such as *Yalqut Hamakhiri*).

We reached beyond our borders, outside the Jewish world, knowing that pre-biblical traditions also found their way there. We read from the New Testament and Christian writers such as Peter the Venerable, on the one hand, and from the Qur'an and its exegetes (e.g., al-Tabari), on the other. All of these and many more have preserved, in a variety of ways, something from the traditions of the ancients that we seek. From this volume's glossary, in which each of these sources is given a brief description, the reader can gain an appreciation of the extraordinary diversity of sources that have helped us shape our arguments.

The two-way journey from the Hebrew Bible to the writings that were earlier, later, and contemporary to it and then back to the pages of the Bible convinces us that, while it is good to study one body of literature in depth, that study cannot be in isolation: the many cultures and literatures that influenced it must also be taken into consideration. Students who limit themselves to the province of the Hebrew Bible or to a limited group of interpreters (such as a selection of Rabbinic midrashim) cannot possibly achieve a profound understanding of the text's significance. Only by examining the entire mosaic, including each stone and its color, shade, and hue, will we be able to fully understand this extraordinary work as well as to reveal subterranean streams that connect it with cultures that are distant in both time and place.

Thirty short chapters have been included here, but they are thirty appetizers only. No doubt there are many other examples of deliberate changes and subtle refinements in the ancient stories that became the Bible. We invite others to dig deep and wide in order to reveal even more.

Glossary of Extra-Biblical Sources

*An asterisk before a name or title within an entry indicates
that a separate entry exists for that source.*

Abarbanel, Isaac

Bible commentator, philosopher, and statesman (1437–1508) who lived in Portugal,
where he served as the foreign minister in the king's court. Following the expulsion
of the Jews from Portugal, he lived in Italy. His work reveals extensive knowledge
of Greek and Roman literature, philosophy, and theology. His commentary on the
Bible—which takes the shape of questions and answers and which reflects great literary sensitivity—reveals also Abarbanel's particular interest in matters of state and
society. Among his writings we find essays dealing with messianism in Israel and
polemical writings that defend Judaism against Christianity's attacks.

Acts of the Apostles. *See* New Testament

Additions to Esther

In the *Septuagint version of the book of Esther, we find seven lengthy aggadic additions that expand and complete the narrative along a number of lines. These additions give the book a more religious character by including God's name (missing
from the original) and also by mentioning prayers, dreams that foreshadow the future, and the like. Some of the added material appears to have been translated from
a Hebrew version of the biblical book. One represents a long prayer voiced by Esther, in which she expresses her utter confidence in the God of Israel and describes
her internal struggle between concern for her own safety and the responsibility she
feels for the fate of her people. It is reasonable to say that the additions were written
in the first century BCE and first century CE.

Alphabet of Ben Sira

A short book that tells the story of a fictional figure, Ben Sira, son of the prophet
Jeremiah, who discusses many topics with the Babylonian king Nebuchadnezzar.
(He should not be confused with the priest Ben Sira, whose *Book of Ben Sira dates

to the second century BCE.) The king asks Ben Sira twenty-two questions (such as "Why were the hornets and mice created?"), and Ben Sira responds, incorporating stories and fables into his answers, some of them of a vulgar character. It is assumed that the book was written in Babylonia in the ninth and tenth centuries, and it gives expression to narrative traditions that were popular among the Babylonians at that time.

al-Tabari, Abu Ja'far Muhammad Ibn Jarir. *See* Tabari, Abu Ja'far Muhammad Ibn Jarir al-

Apocryphon of Joshua

Two incomplete, fragmentary copies of this work were discovered in Cave 4 at Qumran and have been given the name *Apocryphon of Joshua* by modern scholarship. It is an essentially narrative work that relates anew and expands on stories from the book of Joshua, such as the story about the curse of any person who rebuilds Jericho (Joshua 6:26). The work's general character is reminiscent of that of **Jubilees*, and it appears to have been written close to the beginning of the first millennium.

Aramaic Targum to Psalms

In addition to the Aramaic Targumim (translations) to the Torah and **Targum Jonathan ben Uzziel* to the Prophets, we have also Aramaic translations to most of the books of the Writings, the third section of the Hebrew Bible. The Aramaic Targum to Psalms, which scholars have dated to the fifth–eighth centuries (the later dating being the most likely), translates many verses literally, though numerous aggadic traditions are also included, some of which are unparalleled in other sources.

Artapanus

A Jewish-Hellenistic writer who lived in Alexandria during the second century BCE. Artapanus's writings have reached us only fragmentarily, second- and thirdhand, primarily from several church fathers. In his most important work, *Concerning the Jews*, he sought to prove that the foundations of human culture were all established by the Israelite Patriarchs: Abraham, Jacob, Joseph, and, particularly, Moses. Artapanus's essay is a Jewish response to Hellenistic anti-Jewish polemics, which blamed the Jews for, among other things, laziness and separatism.

Avot de-Rabbi Natan

The Mishnah's Tractate *Avot* (known also as *Pirkei Avot*), which deals with matters of ethics and moral behavior, is among its most famous. It is not treated systematically by either the Babylonian Talmud or Jerusalem Talmud, and the **Tosefta* does not provide a corresponding tractate. *Avot de-Rabbi Natan* fulfills this function of

Tosefta and the Talmuds for Tractate *Avot*, and it includes additions, expansions, interpretations, and completions of a good many of its parts. Some attribute it to the Babylonian rabbi Natan (a sage contemporary with Rabbi Judah ha-Nasi, who compiled the Mishnah). Its present form appears to include additions and expansions inserted over a long period of time.

Biblical Antiquities (also known as Pseudo-Philo)

A book written at the end of the Second Temple period or beginning of the mishnaic period, it was preserved only in its Latin translation and erroneously attributed to the first century CE Alexandrian philosopher Philo. It tells the history of the world from its beginnings until the death of King Saul, with the biblical account accompanied by numerous aggadic traditions, some of which are unique. Others are known to us from Rabbinic literature.

Book of Ben Sira (also known as Sirach or Ecclesiasticus)

One of the books written during the Second Temple period that were included in the *Septuagint, thereby becoming part of Christian Scripture. Written by a priest from Jerusalem by the name of Shimon (or Joshua) Ben Sira at the beginning of the second century BCE, the Book of Ben Sira consists of wisdom sayings in the spirit of biblical wisdom literature such as the book of Proverbs. It includes a number of hymns but is mostly comprised of short sayings written in biblical language and designed to direct the reader onto a moral path. In the book's final section, titled "Praise of the Ancestors," the author describes biblical heroes in chronological order from Enoch to Shimon, the High Priest in the author's time, and also adds aggadic traditions. The Book of Ben Sira is mentioned in Rabbinic literature, with some Rabbis regarding it as part of the canon. The book should not be confused with the much later *Alphabet of Ben Sira. The Hebrew text of Ben Sira, which was translated into Greek during the second century BCE, was discovered more than one hundred years ago in the Cairo Genizah, and parts of it were found also on Masada and at Qumran.

Canterbury Tales, The

This famous work of the English poet Geoffrey Chaucer (1342–1400) contributed much to the development of English literature and language. *The Canterbury Tales* is a collection of stories told by pilgrims—including a knight, miller, cook, monk, and nuns—on a pilgrimage to Canterbury. The stories convey the spirit and sounds of English society and include stories of adventure and love, popular jokes, morality tales, and more.

Chronicles of Moses Our Teacher, The

A short narrative written during the tenth or eleventh century that tells the life story of Moses using pseudo-biblical language and relying on Rabbinic sources and perhaps even the writings of Flavius Josephus (*Jewish Antiquities*). The writer clearly wished to present his readers with a captivating adventure story that would distinguish itself from the biblical story, and he embellished it with descriptions of battles and love intrigues.

David ben Abraham ha-Nagid

The grandson of Maimonides, born in Cairo in 1212 (d. 1300), he was appointed official head (*nagid*) of the Jewish communities in Egypt, Syria, and the Land of Israel after the death of his father, Abraham, who had filled the position before him. To Rabbi David is attributed a number of Arabic writings, including a volume of sermons and interpretations on the Torah and a commentary on the Mishnah's Tractate *Avot*.

Decameron

The most famous work of the Italian writer and poet Giovanni Boccaccio (1313–1375), the *Decameron* is considered one of the all-time masterpieces of Italian literature. It tells the story of ten young women and men who flee Florence due to the plague and make their way to a lush, rural area where, over the course of ten days, each tells ten stories on subjects including nobility of spirit, disastrous love, and the rescue of a person in danger. Most of the stories draw from popular tales, but their vivid adaptation has made this one of the most famous story anthologies of the Western world.

Deuteronomy Scroll (4QDeutʲ)

4QDeutʲ is one of a number of copies of Deuteronomy whose remnants were discovered in Cave 4 at Qumran. The scroll, which differs in some of its readings from the Masoretic Text, is from the late Hasmonean period (100–50 BCE).

1 Enoch

One of the books written during the Second Temple period, apparently during Hasmonean rule, it survived in Ge'ez, the language of the Ethiopian Church, as part of that church's Scriptures. In it is described the miraculous figure of Enoch son of Jered (Gen 5:18–24), and, along with other ancient works dedicated to him, it describes primarily the secrets of the world that were revealed to Enoch on his journeys through heaven, visions of the Days to Come, and the fate that awaits in the upper worlds.

Enuma Elish

The ancient Babylonian Creation epic that was found written on seven clay tablets and is named for its two opening words, *enuma elish*, "when on high." Scholars believe it to have been composed toward the end of the second millennium BCE and to have played a central role in the Babylonian New Year celebrations. Its plot centers on the battles between gods and the forces of light and of the abyss. In the epic, Marduk, father of the gods, wars against the goddess-monster Tiamat, whose corpse he then uses to form the world.

Epic of Gilgamesh

The Babylonian heroic epic that recounts the history of the Sumerian king Gilgamesh, the complete version was inscribed onto twelve tablets that initially contained some three thousand lines of poetry. The poem was discovered in the library of the seventh century BCE King Ashurbanipal in Nineveh, modern-day Iraq. This version is apparently from the end of the second millennium BCE. The original version appears to have been written during the early Babylonian period (1800–1700 BCE). The principal focus of the work is humankind's aspiration to immortality. Gilgamesh survives countless dangers in his pursuit of the elixir of life, though he fails, finally, and his end is like that of all men.

Exodus Rabbah

A midrash, or exegetical work, on the book of Exodus. Its first section (*parashot* 1–14) deals with Exodus 1–10 and is rich with aggadic traditions from a variety of sources, including the Babylonian Talmud. This section dates to the ninth or tenth century CE. The second section, which deals with the remaining chapters of Exodus, is very similar to the *Tanḥuma*, both linguistically and in its literary forms, leading some scholars to view it as a *Tanḥuma*-like midrash that focuses on selected verses from the book of Exodus and, around them, develops lengthy exegesis. The date of this section is unknown, possibly the sixth or seventh century. It is thought that the two parts were joined into one work after the tenth century.

Flavius Josephus. See *Jewish Antiquities*

Genesis Apocryphon

One of the Dead Sea Scrolls written in Aramaic that (in those parts we are able to decipher) retells stories from the book of Genesis that deal with Lamech, Enoch, Noah, and Abraham. The story of Abram and Sarai in Egypt (Genesis 12) is narrated, at great length and in a first-person account, by Abraham. The scroll retells the biblical stories and supplements them with many expansions and additions that are rich and varied, some of which are known to us also from the apocryphal and pseudepigraphal literature and from the midrash. The scroll seems to have been authored during the first century BCE, or a little earlier, in the Land of Israel.

Genesis Rabbah

One of the most important and most extensive of the midrashim (exegetical works) of the *amoraim* (Rabbinic sages who lived during the third–fifth centuries CE and whose teachings were collected in the Talmud). It was compiled in the Land of Israel during the fifth century. *Genesis Rabbah* follows the book of Genesis verse by verse, bringing a wide variety of aggadic material to almost every verse, with no specific agenda apparent. It seems that the anonymous editor considered important the act of assembling and preserving aggadic traditions representing a wide range of sources and literary genres—midrashim, stories, fables, and more—that had reached him both in written and in oral form. The language of the volume is Hebrew mixed with Palestinian Aramaic and is sprinkled with Greek and Latin.

Genesis Rabbati

An aggadic midrash based on the teachings of Rabbi Moshe ha-Darshan, one of the sages of Narbonne, France, during the first half of the eleventh century. The work contains a multitude of midrashim following the order of the book of Genesis, some of which are familiar to us from earlier Rabbinic texts (such as *Genesis Rabbah*) and some drawn—in ways yet unclear—from apocryphal and pseudepigraphal literature of the Second Temple period (such as the *Testaments of the Twelve Patriarchs*). The work contains unique aggadic traditions.

Gospels (of Matthew, Mark, Luke, John). *See* New Testament

haggadah (the Passover haggadah)

The Passover haggadah is the text read during the seder on Passover night, which begins the Passover holiday. It is a collection of blessings and psalms, biblical verses and prayers, midrashim and stories that have been told and collected over the course of many generations. The core text is the story of the Israelites' enslavement in Egypt and their escape to freedom—the Exodus—the telling of which fulfills the biblical injunction, "And you shall tell your son" (Exodus 13:8). The origins of the haggadah reach as far back as the Second Temple period, to the days in which the eating of the passover offering still constituted the holiday's main activity. It developed and was expanded after the destruction of the Temple by the Romans in 70 CE, until it reached its final form in the gaonic period, apparently in the eighth century CE. Over the centuries, *piyyutim* (liturgical prayers) and other pieces were added. After the Bible, the haggadah is the most widely read Jewish book and has been printed in thousands of editions.

Hesiod

An early Greek poet who, it is believed, lived during the ninth or eighth century BCE. His writings are of a diverse nature, including the epic *Works and Days* (a poem of eight hundred or so verses that addresses the day-to-day life of ancient Greece and praises the life of honest labor) and *Theogony* (describing the creation of the gods and the origins of the world). The poem *The Shield of Heracles* (believed by some to be falsely attributed to Hesiod) tells about the life of the mythological hero Heracles and the battles he fought.

Iliad

A Greek epic poem, among the premier literary works of the ancient Greek world and one of the works that shaped Western culture, values, and literature. The epic is attributed, according to tradition, to Homer, the chief poet of ancient Greece (eighth century BCE). The *Iliad* recounts the story of the Greek war against the city of Troy as well as other subjects from Greek mythology. The *Iliad* finds its sequel in another epic, the *Odyssey* (also attributed to Homer), which tells the story of the hero Odysseus and his return home from the war.

Jewish Antiquities by Flavius Josephus

Flavius Josephus (known also by his Jewish name, Yosef ben Matitiahu) lived during the first century CE. He was commander of the Galilee in the Great Revolt against the Romans. Later, toward the end of the century, in Rome, Josephus wrote numerous volumes in Greek in order to introduce the religion of Israel to the Greco-Roman world, which was rife with anti-Semitism. His largest work, *Jewish Antiquities*, laid out the history of the world and of the people of Israel in twenty volumes, from the Creation until the generation preceding the destruction of the Second Temple. The book follows the biblical account but is embellished by Josephus's own expansions, additions, changes, and abbreviations, all designed to promote his particular point of view. Josephus integrates into the biblical account traditions borrowed from the Hellenistic world and a writing style reminiscent of the historiographic works of the contemporary Greco-Roman world.

Jubilees

One of the books that were apparently written during the Hasmonean period in Hebrew by a Jewish writer but that survived only as part of the sacred writings of the Ethiopian Church in Ge'ez, the ancient Semitic language that developed in that region. Fragments from sixteen Hebrew manuscripts were discovered also among the scrolls at Qumran. The book tells the history of the world from the Creation until the Giving of the Torah, in a greatly expanded version, as narrated by an angel to Moses during the forty days Moses spent on Mount Sinai. The book takes its name from its custom of reckoning years according to seven-year cycles and jubilees (the jubilee year follows seven seven-year cycles). It follows a solar calendar (whereas current Judaism follows a lunar calendar). The author incorporates laws and commandments into his narrative as well as numerous aggadic traditions known to us from no other source. It is possible that the book originated in circles that were close to one of the sects that thrived during the Second Temple period.

Judith

Written during the Second Temple period, it is one of the books included in the *Septuagint and thus came to be part of Christian Scripture. It can be dated to the Persian or early Hellenistic period. The book tells the story of Judith, the beautiful and gracious widow who, with great cunning, managed to kill the enemy general Holophernes, effectively removing the threat of Assyrian occupation from her city and land. The book exhibits many principles of faith, such as confidence in God, and valuable knowledge of Jewish law from the time in which the book was written.

Kebra Nagast (Book of the Glory of Kings)

The central text of the Ethiopian Church, the core of which is the story of the queen of Sheba, including the story of her visit to Solomon's court, her conversion, the birth of their son (Menelik), and the son's visit to his father. That visit concluded with the Ark of the Covenant being taken from Jerusalem to Aksum, the capital of the ancient Ethiopian kingdom.

Leqaḥ Tov

A collection of midrashim covering the five books of the Torah and the *megillot* (Ecclesiastes, Song of Songs, Ruth, Lamentations, Esther), it was written by Rabbi Tuvia ben Eliezer, an eleventh-century Greek Jew. The author generally follows the order of the biblical verses and discusses them using a combination of aggadic and legal traditions, with linguistic explanations and rather literal interpretations. In many ways, the volume can be viewed as a transitional stage between midrashic literature and the works of medieval commentators (such as the exegetical work of Rashi and others).

Leviticus Rabbah

A midrash written most likely during the first half of the fifth century CE in the Galilee. Its anonymous compiler was faced with the difficult challenge of writing an aggadic midrash on the biblical book of Leviticus, which is filled with subjects such as sacrifices, skin diseases, and so on. He constructed his work around selected verses, the thirty-seven that served as the opening verses of the weekly Torah readings according to the triennial reading cycle (when the Torah is read not in one year but three). On the basis of each verse he formed a lengthy chapter of set structure that discussed it fully; for example, the drinking of wine or the reason for the commands (*mitzvot*). The book is written in Galilean Aramaic with a smattering of Hebrew, Greek, and Latin, and it includes many stories, making it one of the most interesting midrashim in Rabbinic literature.

Life of Adam and Eve

One of the books written in Hebrew during the Second Temple period that did not survive in Hebrew but survived in Greek and other translations. The story

deals with the sin in the Garden of Eden and the history of Adam and Eve until
their deaths, greatly expanding the biblical story. Over time, additions were made
to some versions of the book by Christians, but the secondary nature of these elements—that they are not original to the text—is evident.

Mekhilta de-Rabbi Ishmael

An early tannaitic composition (edited during the third century CE) on the book of
Exodus. Written in Hebrew, it follows the sequence of the biblical verses, augment-
ing many of them with halakhic and aggadic traditions. (Due to the considerable
amount of halakhic material, the book is sometimes referred to as *Midrash Hal-
akha*.) Its attribution to Rabbi Ishmael (who lived during the first to second centuries) likely testifies to the book's connection with the school of that sage, analogous
to the *Mekhilta de-Rabbi Shimon ben Yoḥai*, which is attributed to the school of his
colleague Rabbi Akiva.

Mekhilta de-Rabbi Shimon ben Yoḥai

An early tannaitic midrash on Exodus that deals with many of that book's verses,
beginning with Exodus 3, the story of the burning bush. It brings many pertinent
halakhic and aggadic traditions, almost all in Hebrew. The work is attributed to one
of the students of Rabbi Akiva, an attribution that might indicate the book's connection with the school of Rabbi Akiva and attest to the book's being compiled during the third and fourth centuries.

Mendelssohn, Moses

A Jewish-German philosopher (1729–1786) and one of the outstanding proponents
of the Haskalah (Jewish Enlightenment) in Europe, Mendelssohn is considered the
forefather of modern Jewish thought. Alongside his philosophical and theological
writings, he directed his energies to a translation and commentary of the Pentateuch in German, through which he sought to instill the values of the Haskalah in
European Jewish society. The commentary, which he wrote in collaboration with
a number of scholars, tends toward the *peshat* (literal meaning of the biblical text)
and gives attention to grammatical questions. Aesthetic interpretations (matters of
style and literary devices) are prominent, while philosophical issues are sometimes
discussed, too.

Midrash Aggadah

A midrash on the whole Torah, published by Shlomo Buber on the basis of a single
manuscript (Vienna, 1894); Buber also gave the work its name. Its author amassed
numerous midrashic traditions and arranged them in the order of the books of the
Torah. Some of the traditions are unparalleled in Rabbinic literature. The volume
seems to have originated in the school of Rabbi Moshe ha-Darshan (*Genesis Rabbati*), giving it a date not earlier than the eleventh century.

Glossary of Extra-Biblical Sources

Midrash ha-Gadol

Midrash ha-Gadol ("The Great Midrash") is an exhaustive midrash on the five books of the Torah. It is the work of Rabbi David ben Amram Ha-Adani, a twelfth- or thirteenth-century Yemenite Jew. The compiler collected numerous traditions from the vast number of sources that were available to him, though he did not note his sources but joined them together, to a large extent rewriting them, thus creating a new midrashic work that is mostly in Hebrew. Among his sources were also very early works that have not survived, lending the Midrash ha-Gadol further importance.

Midrash ha-Ḥefetz

A compilation of midrashim about the Torah, Midrash ha-Ḥefetz was written by Zekharia ben Shlomo ha-Rofe in Yemen during the fifteenth century. Partly in Arabic, most of the traditions found here are known to us from other works, primarily *Midrash ha-Gadol. The author occasionally brings homilies unknown to us from other sources.

Midrash Mishlei (Midrash Proverbs)

A midrash on the book of Proverbs that follows the order of verses in that book and elaborates on them with a variety of aggadic traditions, with no clear or obvious agenda. Some of its traditions are unique. It seems to have been formed during the ninth century.

Midrash Samuel

A midrash on the book of Samuel that follows the order of the biblical story and elaborates on it with a variety of midrashic traditions, observing no particular agenda. Its anonymous editor lived, as far as we can tell, during the ninth or tenth century.

Midrash Tannaim (to Deuteronomy)

When *Midrash ha-Gadol was discovered, scholars realized that embedded in it were pieces from very early midrashic works that had been lost, among them pieces from a midrash on Deuteronomy that differed from Sifre Deuteronomy (*Sifre). The scholar David Tzvi Hoffman collected these pieces and published them under the name Midrash Tannaim (Berlin, 1908). The fragmentary state of the compilation prevents any definitive estimation of its date or place of origin, though the core of the material is clearly tannaitic.

Mishnah

The foundational book of the Oral Torah. Rabbi Judah ha-Nasi (Galilee, beginning of the third century CE) redacted the Mishnah, gathering into his work numerous halakhic and aggadic traditions that had been circulating orally (or that had already been collected into previous compilations) and compiling them into six orders (main divisions) that are dedicated to different spheres of social and national life. Material that he did not see fit to bring, or materials that he did not know, eventually found their way to the *Tosefta. The different orders (*sedarim*) of the Mishnah deal with earthbound mitzvot (*Seder Zera'im*), the Jewish calendar year (*Mo'ed*), relations between a man and his wife (*Nashim*), civil and criminal law and the proper functioning of society (*Neziqin*), sacrificial and Temple rites (*Qodashim*), and matters of purity and impurity (*Teharot*). Each order is divided into tractates according to their subjects, which are, in turn, organized by chapters and *mishnayot* (individual sayings). The Mishnah became the focus of much exegetical work in the centuries that followed its redaction, that is, in the period of the *amoraim*, by the Rabbinic sages who wrote the *Talmuds (Babylonian and Jerusalem) both in the Land of Israel and in Babylonia. Over the centuries, many commentaries to the Mishnah have been written.

Moshe ha-Darshan, Rabbi. See *Genesis Rabbati*

New Testament

The foundation text of Christianity, it was created and formed as the continuation and completion of the Hebrew Bible (called the Old Testament in the Christian world). The New Testament, written in Greek, though the original language of some parts may have been Aramaic or even Hebrew, took shape for the most part over the first and second centuries CE. It is comprised of several parts. First, the Gospels of Matthew, Mark, Luke, and John narrate, in different ways, the life story of Jesus from his birth until his crucifixion and resurrection. Following the Gospels is the book of Acts, which begins where the Gospel of Luke ends, and gives the history of the spread of Christianity. Next come more than twenty epistles (the Epistle to the Romans, the Epistle to the Corinthians, etc.), written by the leading figure in the formation of the new religion, Paul (who was known, before his conversion, by his Hebrew name, Saul), or attributed to him by the early church. The Epistles demonstrate Christian theology's early development and reveal its institutional organization. The volume closes with the book of Revelation, written in the form of apocalyptic prophecies describing the End of Days.

Panim 'Aḥerim

A midrashic work on the book of Esther that discusses many of its verses and follows the order of that book. The manuscript was published by Shlomo Buber (as part of *Books of Aggadah on the Scroll of Esther* [Vilna, 1887]) in two recensions. It appears to be a late midrash from the ninth or tenth century, with large sections borrowed from other Rabbinic works. The name was given by Buber from the book's opening words, which state that it is *panim 'aherim*, that is, "another version" of a midrash to the *Scroll of Esther*.

Peshitta

The earliest Syriac translation of the Hebrew Bible and the Christian Bible (the New Testament), its name means "the simple [translation]." Syriac was an Aramaic dialect that was spoken chiefly in the area known today as Syria. The translation, the work of Jews or Christians, was influenced also by early Rabbinic midrashim and by the *Septuagint. Scholars estimate that the Peshitta to the Torah was written in the second and third centuries CE. From the third century on, the Peshitta became the standard version of the Bible used by the Syrian Church.

Peter the Venerable

Abbot of the Benedictine abbey of Cluny and writer (1094–1156) who dedicated his life to fighting Muslim and Jewish heretics and heresy. In his writings (primarily *Adversus Judaeorum inveteratam duritem*) he condemns Judaism as a false religion that desecrates God. But he also writes of aggadic traditions that he knows and so is considered a reliable witness for the history of Jewish traditions in medieval France. The war Peter waged against the Talmud gained him fame in the Christian world and played an important role in medieval Jewish-Christian polemics.

Philo of Byblos (also known as Philo of Gebal)

A Phoenician writer born in 64 BCE. Parts of his book on the religion of the Phoenicians were preserved in the writings of the church father Eusebius. They help us to learn about the religions of Canaan while also shedding light on a variety of biblical topics.

Pirkei de-Rabbi Eliezer

A midrash of distinct literary character in that it retells the biblical narrative—with multiple additions, expansions, and omissions—from the Creation to the Israelites' history in the wilderness. (It is unclear whether the work has reached us in its entirety or whether it has been truncated near its end.) It appears to have been written during the eighth century, since it contains a noticeable anti-Muslim polemic, but its sources are often much older. Tradition attributes its writing to Rabbi Eliezer ben Hyrcanus, a *tanna* from the first century CE, though the attribution is unreliable. The writer of the book, who wrote in Hebrew, knew many Rabbinic sources and merged them with oral folk traditions and with traditions borrowed from extra-biblical compositions from the Second Temple period.

piyyutim (liturgical poems) in the Aramaic Targumim

During Rabbinic times it was customary for the Torah to be read aloud in Hebrew, followed by a translation into the vernacular, which, in the Land of Israel and Babylonia, was Aramaic. The versions of the Aramaic translations (Targumim) that are known to us (e.g., *Targum Onqelos*, *Targum Neofiti*) originated in this context. Moreover, the translators would often incorporate liturgical poems (*piyyutim*) into their Aramaic renderings of the Hebrew text with the aim of heightening the reading's impact. These poems were inserted close to the climactic scenes in the weekly readings, such as the story of the Sacrifice of Isaac or the Crossing of the Sea of Reeds. *Piyyutim* have been preserved in manuscripts of the Targumim that originated in the Land of Israel.

Prayer of Manasseh

A Greek work that has reached us via the Christian *Didascalia Apostolorum* and was apparently written during the second or third century CE. It presents itself as the prayer that is referred to by the Chronicler (2 Chronicles 33:18–19), who mentions a prayer offered by Manasseh, king of Judah, when he was held captive by the king of Assyria. It consists mainly of praise for God and pleas for forgiveness of sins and transgressions.

Psalm 151

At the end of the book of Psalms in the *Septuagint there is an extra psalm, Psalm 151, the superscription of which reads: "This psalm, though supernumerary, is truly written by David when he single-handedly fought Goliath." In the psalm, which is written as if by David himself, David recounts his youth, his fashioning of musical instruments, and his victory over the Philistine giant. A Hebrew version of the psalm was discovered in the Qumran *Psalms Scroll*, whose beginning reads: "A Hallelujah of David the son of Jesse."

Psalms Scroll (11QPsª)

This partially preserved scroll of Hebrew psalms was discovered among the Dead Sea Scrolls in Cave 11 at Qumran. In addition to canonical psalms, it includes seven psalms that do not appear in the Hebrew Bible, one of which parallels Psalm 151 of the *Septuagint. Four more have been preserved in the Syriac translation of Psalms.

Qur'an

The sacred book of Islam, it is held by Muslims to be the eternal word of God and to provide the foundation of their religion and laws. According to Islamic tradition, the Qur'an was revealed to Muhammad while he was occupied in communal-religious activities during the early part of the seventh century CE in order to shape the true monotheistic religion that was to replace its predecessors, Judaism and Christianity. The Qur'an is comprised of 114 chapters (called suras, such as the "Joseph Sura" and the "Ant Sura"), arranged from the longest to the shortest. Over the centuries, many commentaries on the Qur'an have been written, dealing both with laws that are binding on Muslims and with matters of beliefs and ideas. A good portion of the Qur'an is dedicated to traditions that deal with the Hebrew Bible and biblical characters, in which a familiarity with midrashic traditions is noticeable.

Rashbam

An acronym for Rabbi Shmuel (Samuel) son of Meir. One of the most eminent commentators of the Bible and Talmud, Rashbam lived in France during the twelfth century (ca. 1080–1160). He was a grandson of *Rashi through his mother. His literary works covered an enormous range: commentaries on many of the biblical books (his commentaries on the Torah have survived, along with parts of his commentaries on the prophetic books and commentaries on Ecclesiastes and Job) and on parts of the Babylonian Talmud, as well as halakhic rulings, Responsa, exegesis of *piyyutim*, and a treatise on Hebrew grammar. In his commentary on the Bible he follows strictly the *peshat* (the plain meaning of the text) and bases his interpretations primarily on linguistic and grammatical elements in the text.

Rashi

An acronym for Rabbi Shlomo (Solomon) Yitzhaki (1040–1105), the most important talmudic commentator of all times and one of the most important of the biblical commentators, a *dayyan* (religious judge), and a liturgical poet. Rashi lived in Troyes, in northern France, but his work gained him fame throughout the Jewish world. His biblical commentaries are concise, based on linguistic-grammatical elements, but they are also packed with Rabbinic midrashim that are adapted to their new context. His commentary on the Talmud became the primary and paramount interpretation of that text. Many commentaries, and commentaries of those commentaries, have been written about Rashi's interpretations of the Bible and Talmud; they, too, testify to his widespread popularity and the unparalleled position his work occupies in Jewish tradition.

Revelation. *See* New Testament

Ruth Rabbah

An aggadic midrash about the book of Ruth that was written in the Land of Israel. The book, written in Galilean Aramaic mixed with Hebrew, dates, apparently, to the sixth or seventh century CE. The midrash proceeds through each of the biblical book's verses, in order, and brings to them a wide range of aggadic traditions that are frequently embedded with stories and proverbs.

Glossary of Extra-Biblical Sources

Samaritan Pentateuch

The Samaritan community views the Torah of Moses—the Pentateuch—as Scripture, though it does not extend sacred status to the Prophets and Writings. The version of the Torah that the Samaritans use differs from the Masoretic Text in thousands of variants, some minor, some of great significance. Some of these differences stem from Samaritan theology, principally around its emphasis on the centrality and sanctity of Mount Gerizim, in Shechem. Written in ancient Hebrew script, the Samaritan Pentateuch is an invaluable witness to the history of the text of the Pentateuch.

Seder 'Olam Rabbah

A work attributed to the *tanna* Rabbi Yossi ben Halafta (middle second century CE) in which is recorded the history of the world and the people of Israel from its beginnings until the Bar Kokba revolt (132–136 CE). The book supplies dates and time spans, presenting events in chronological order and interweaving a variety of aggadic traditions. The aim of the work appears to have been a firm chronological-historical picture that removed any contradictions from the biblical account and that recorded post-biblical events in chronological order, perhaps in reaction to similar compositions from the Greco-Roman world.

Sekhel Tov

A compilation of homilies and interpretations that follow the order of the verses in Genesis and Exodus. The author—Rabbi Menachem ben Shlomo, who lived in Europe during the twelfth century—incorporated Rabbinic traditions, flavoring them with interpretative-linguistic comments in the spirit of the medieval exegetes. From this perspective, the book is like Midrash *Leqaḥ Tov*, it, too, exemplifying the transition from late midrashic literature (primarily compilations) to the exegesis of the medieval period.

Septuagint

The Greek translation of the Hebrew Bible, the Septuagint is the oldest translation of the Bible that has reached us. The translation seems to have been completed in stages, beginning with the Torah and only afterward the rest of the Bible, including also such books as the *Book of Ben Sira and *Judith. It was written in Alexandria, Egypt, beginning in the third century BCE and was produced for the Greek-speaking Jewish community there, whose members were no longer able to read the Hebrew original. According to legend, the Torah was translated by seventy elders, who, following the request of the then-king of Egypt, Ptolemy II, completed their work with exceptional speed; it was for this reason that it came to be known as the Septuagint ("of the Seventy"). The order of the biblical books in the Septuagint differs from that in the Masoretic Text: first, the historiographical books, poetic and wisdom literatures, and, lastly, books of prophecy. In general, the translators tried to remain loyal to the Hebrew version. The translation's ultimate importance derives both from the information it provides on the history of the biblical text and its interpretation in the ancient world and from its influence on the Greek and Latin literature that followed it, primarily in the Christian Church. See also Additions to Esther.

Shalshelet ha-Kabbalah

The work of Gedaliah Ibn Yachya (1515–1587), descendant of an Italian Rabbinic family. The book is primarily a survey of the history of the Jewish people, but it includes also a discussion of the chronology of the world and other topics from the realm of natural science, medicine, and magic.

Shoher Tov

A midrash on the book of Psalms, named for the first two words from Proverbs 11:27, with which it opens ("The one that seeks good"), and known also by the name *Midrash Tehillim*. Written for the most part in Hebrew, it contains a relatively early section (until Psalm 118) and a much later one (until the end of the book). The former seems to have been composed before the seventh century. The book systematically addresses the verses in Psalms, one after the other, and harbors numerous aggadic traditions that are unique to it.

Sifre

The name is shared by two tannaitic volumes of midrashim, one that deals with Numbers, the other Deuteronomy (*Sifre Numbers* and *Sifre Deuteronomy*). Both follow the order of the biblical text and incorporate homilies that deal with halakhic and aggadic materials. The books were composed during the third and fourth centuries and were written primarily in Hebrew. *Sifre Numbers* is usually attributed to the school of Rabbi Ishmael and *Sifre Deuteronomy*, or at least the bulk of that volume, to the school of Rabbi Akiva (compare the entries for *Mekhilta de-Rabbi Ishmael* and *Mekhilta de-Rabbi Shimon ben Yohai*).

Tabari, Abu Ja'far Muhammad Ibn Jarir al-

One of the greatest Muslim thinkers and historians (b. 839, Iran; d. 923, Baghdad). Al-Tabari worked in a variety of fields in science and history and gained fame primarily for his extensive commentary on the Qur'an ("Tafsir")—a commentary that is considered a classic in Muslim literature because of its scope, independence of thought, and precision. His substantial historical work (*The History of the Prophets and Kings*) became a model for later Muslim historians.

Talmud, Babylonian

The Talmud is a work in which were collected—in Babylonia and in the Land of Israel—the halakhic traditions of the *amoraim*, sages who lived in those two centers of Jewish life from the third century on. The bulk of the Talmud revolves around the *Mishnah and the discussions that that book precipitated. Each center produced its own Talmud; for the Talmud produced in the Land of Israel (called the Yerushalmi, or Jerusalem Talmud), see the next entry.

A work of vast breadth, the Babylonian Talmud includes *halakhah* and *aggadah*, Jewish thought and morality, history, theology, and other realms of human knowledge. Its structure follows the order of the Mishnah, which it examines, expanding and discussing matters as necessary. Though written in Babylonian Aramaic, the vernacular in Babylonia between the third and sixth centuries, the Talmud's pages are embedded also with Hebrew traditions from the Land of Israel. It is generally accepted that the Talmud came into being over hundreds of years until it was finally sealed more or less at the beginning of the sixth century. Scholarship has revealed its serpentine history in the layers upon layers of traditions that it contains.

Not all of the Mishnah is discussed in the Babylonian Talmud in a systematic and consistent fashion. The focus is primarily on four of the Mishnah's orders: *Mo'ed, Nashim, Neziqin,* and *Kodashim,* and even that incompletely. It seems likely that only these orders were studied regularly in the Babylonian yeshivot (Rabbinic academies). That said, the endless commentaries, innovative interpretations, *pilpul* (sharp analysis and exacting explanations of contradictions in the talmudic text), and expansions that have been written on the Talmud since the time of the *ge'onim* until today have made it the central and primary text of the Oral Torah, which has shaped the language, literature, law, and thought of Jews to an extraordinary extent. The Talmud was first printed in a complete version in Venice in 1520–1523. In this volume, references to the Babylonian Talmud use the abbreviation "B." along with the name of the specific tractate.

Talmud, Jerusalem (Yerushalmi)

The Jerusalem Talmud, known also as the Talmud of the Land of Israel, contains the teachings of the *amoraim* of the Land of Israel who lived during the third–fifth centuries (compare the Babylonian Talmud, above). It includes assorted discussions of some forty tractates from four of the Mishnah's orders: *Zera'im, Mo'ed, Nashim,* and *Neziqin,* these apparently comprising the orders that were regularly studied by the sages in the Land of Israel. The Yerushalmi is written in Galilean Aramaic, and it was mostly there, in the Galilee, that it took shape, reaching its final form during the first third of the fifth century CE.

The fate of the Jerusalem Talmud was not as favorable as that of the Babylonian. It was studied by relatively few, and, in consequence, its text became corrupted and was the subject of only a handful of commentaries. In recent years there has been a renewed interest in the Jerusalem Talmud, mostly due to the formation of the State of Israel and the subsequent observance of *halakhah* that is specific to life there. Thus, for instance, the order *Zera'im* ("seeds") receives treatment in the Jerusalem Talmud but not the Babylonian Talmud, since its primary interest is laws pertaining to the Land of Israel such as *shmita* (sabbatical year) and the offering of firstfruits. In this volume, the Yerushalmi is referred to using the abbreviation "Y." along with the name of the individual tractate.

Tanḥuma, Tanḥuma Buber

A midrash that deals with all five of the Pentateuch's books and takes its name from the name of Rabbi Tanḥuma bar Abba, one of the homiletic masters in the Land of Israel during the *amoraic* era (though he apparently was not the only or even the primary author). The midrash is constructed around lengthy homilies that are founded on the opening verses of the weekly Sabbath readings of the Torah according to the triennial reading cycle (see *Leviticus Rabbah*). Since Rabbi Tanḥuma is often mentioned in relationship to the book, it became customary to refer to it by his name. The *Tanḥuma*, written mostly in Hebrew and distinguished by its unique literary structure, was composed in the Land of Israel, though the time of its writing has not been determined. It contains numerous layers of authorship and is thought to have achieved its final form during the sixth or seventh century.

We have two versions of the midrash: one has been printed many times since the sixteenth century and is referred to simply as *Tanḥuma*; the other was published by Shlomo Buber in 1884 from manuscripts that he found. This version is referred to as *Tanḥuma Buber*. There is strong similarity between the two versions. The second section of *Exodus Rabbah* reflects similar hermeneutics and is likely the product of the same midrashic school.

Targum Jonathan ben Uzziel to the Prophets

In addition to the Targumim (Aramaic translations) to the Torah, we have *Targum Jonathan ben Uzziel* to the Prophets, some of which were read as haftarah readings in synagogues in ancient times. According to tradition, this translation was written by the *tanna* Jonathan ben Uzziel, a disciple of Hillel the Elder. The translation was probably written during the second or third century in the Land of Israel, but—as with its elder cousin, *Targum Onqelos*—it arrived in Babylonia, where it became established as the most reliable and authoritative translation of the prophetic books. In both language and tendencies it is similar to *Targum Onqelos*, and they seem to have been created around the same time.

Targum Neofiti

In the middle of the twentieth century, a previously unknown Aramaic Targum to the Torah was discovered in the Vatican's Neofiti Library. It became clear that the found manuscript contained a work from the Land of Israel from the fifth and sixth centuries (though some scholars date it much earlier), a translation that reflects the manner in which the Torah was interpreted and its traditions elaborated on in the synagogues in the Land of Israel toward the close of the *amoraic* period. In most verses the Targum takes a literal approach, but in some it breaks off into particularly lengthy expansions that may have originated in sermons. In the Targum's margins, scribes recorded other versions of Aramaic translations that were known during the Middle Ages—many of which have been otherwise lost—something that further heightens the importance of the work.

Targum Onqelos

The most authoritative and well known of the Aramaic translations of the Torah. According to Jewish sources, Onqelos was a convert to Judaism who lived in the Land of Israel at the end of the first century CE and the beginning of the second. Some suspect that "Onqelos" is a corruption of "Aquila," a name known to us as that of one of the Greek translators of the Bible, but the matter has not been proved. *Targum Onqelos* made its way from Israel to Babylonia, where, during the talmudic period, it was edited, reworked, and became celebrated as the principal and most reliable interpretation of the Torah (and was even printed on the side of every traditional edition of the Torah). The translation tends toward the literal, but it contains also aggadic and halakhic expansions, where its underlying interest—alongside clarification of the biblical verse—is its desire to protect the honor of the nation's Patriarchs and leaders and to avoid personifications of God.

Targum Pseudo-Jonathan to the Torah

An Aramaic translation of the Torah that was mistakenly attributed to the *tanna* Jonathan ben Uzziel (who composed the *Targum Jonathan ben Uzziel* to the Prophets), apparently due to the initials *T.Y.*, which originally referred to *Targum Yerushalmi* (Jerusalem Translation) but which were interpreted otherwise. The translation brims with thousands of aggadic traditions, both short and long, early and late (reaching until the Islamic period), to the point that it often seems to resemble more a paraphrase of the Torah than a translation of it. It appears likely that the book was completed only during the eighth century and that its origin was in the Land of Israel or its environs. *Pseudo-Jonathan* is remarkable in its many aggadic traditions that have no other witness in all of Rabbinic literature. Many of these seem to have been collected from folk traditions that were circulating orally at the time.

Targum Sheni to the Book of Esther

The book of Esther was translated into Aramaic a number of times. One of these translations, dubbed *Targum Sheni* ("second translation"), is actually a broad paraphrase of the book in Aramaic. Indeed, the translation barely resembles the verses being translated, since the compiler inserted many aggadic traditions. Most of these are known to us from elsewhere in midrashic literature, though some were apparently drawn from traditions that were circulating orally, including Muslim traditions, a fact that helps us to date this translation to the eighth century.

Testament of Joseph. See *Testaments of the Twelve Patriarchs*

Testament of Reuben. See *Testaments of the Twelve Patriarchs*

Testaments of the Twelve Patriarchs

One of the books written during the Second Temple period, apparently during the second century BCE. The book survived mainly in the Christian Church, in Greek and other languages (a very few fragments were preserved in Hebrew), and its subject matter is the individual testaments of each of Jacob's twelve sons. Each son, in his own composition, tells the history of his life, confesses his transgressions, praises his good deeds, moralizes to his own sons, and prophesies their future. The book was copied numerous times by Christian scribes, who inserted Christian elements into it, predominantly in prophecies that they added to the original work. The *Testament of Reuben* deals to a great extent with the sin of Reuben with Bilhah (Genesis 35), and the *Testament of Joseph* dedicates much space to the story of the hardships Joseph suffered in Potiphar's house (Genesis 39).

Tosefta

A work that seeks to complete the *Mishnah by collecting tannaitic materials that were not included in the Mishnah. The Tosefta follows the mishnaic model (orders and tractates), and its relationship with the Mishnah varies: sometimes it explains the Mishnah, sometimes it contradicts it, still other times it elaborates on topics that the Mishnah discusses. (Recent scholarship has raised the opinion that the core of the Tosefta preceded the Mishnah, but this remains a subject of scholarly debate.) It is written in the Hebrew of the *tannaitic* period, and it is generally accepted that it took shape and was edited in the Land of Israel close to the time of the final redaction of the Mishnah.

Vulgate

The Latin translation of the Hebrew Bible, written by the church father Jerome in Bethlehem around the year 400 CE. Jerome was a theological authority and one of the prominent figures of the early church. For the most part, the translation follows the Hebrew text literally. Yet it seems apparent that Jerome was familiar also with some Rabbinic traditions, since he relates how Jewish teachers helped him in his work. Jerome's translation, which was based on a Hebrew version of the Bible that is almost identical with the Masoretic Text, was accepted as the official version of

Scripture by the Catholic Church of the Middle Ages. The Vulgate also provided the basis for many translations of the Bible into other languages.

Wisdom of Solomon

Among the books written during the Second Temple period that came to be included in the *Septuagint and, therefore, in the Scriptures of the Christian Church. The book seems to have been composed during the second century BCE, apparently in Egypt, and was attributed to King Solomon in order to increase its importance. It is written in Greek and treats topics typical of Wisdom literature: the righteous and the wicked, the character and greatness of wisdom, the importance of faith, ethical matters, and more. The last part of the work is a sort of midrash on the story of the Exodus from Egypt.

Yalqut Hamakhiri

A compilation of midrashim on biblical books composed during the fourteenth century in southern France by Makhir ben Aba Mari. Using the vast resources of Rabbinic literature—Mishnah, Talmud, midrashim—the editor created an anthology of traditions (with the addition of a few from sources that have not reached us) that were dedicated to the books of Isaiah, Psalms, the Minor Prophets, and Proverbs. The book is important for the evidence it provides of the widespread distribution of midrashim during the Middle Ages and for the few traditions it brings whose sources have not survived.

Yalqut Shim'oni

An immense compilation of midrashic traditions to the entire Bible, drawn from some fifty sources and following the order of the biblical text. The compilation (*yalqut*) was produced by Rabbi Shimon ha-Darshan from Ashkenaz (Germany) during the thirteenth century with the aim of collecting into one book midrashic traditions and texts from vastly scattered and disparate sources. The editor recorded the source of each passage in the margins, allowing us to appreciate the extensive library of which he availed himself. Among his sources were some that have not survived (such as *Deuteronomy Zuta*), which grants *Yalqut Shim'oni* its particular importance. It also provides testimony on the distribution of midrashim and their different versions.

Zohar

This central text of Jewish mysticism, written in Aramaic, takes the shape of a midrash and covers most of the weekly readings from the Torah and some from the *megillot*. Tradition ascribes the Zohar to the early Rabbinic sage Rabbi Shimon ben Yohai and his students (who lived during the second century CE), though most of it was composed during a much later period, in the time of Rabbi Moses de León

(Spain, thirteenth century). An anthology of discrete compositions, the book concerns mysticism and matters of the upper realms. It is written in obscure, enigmatic language and is embedded with both short stories and long discourses on a variety of subjects. Despite emerging from mystical circles, the Zohar preserves aggadic traditions that were not included in earlier writings with the addition of what appear to be original materials. The wide distribution of the Zohar from the thirteenth and fourteenth centuries on made it an important force in the development of various mystical doctrines (such as the Kabbalah, which was developed in Safed during the sixteenth century in the days of Rabbi Isaac Luria). The influence of the Zohar reaches into the spheres of *halakhah*, ethics, and theology.

Index

Aaron: and the Cushite woman, 176; making the golden calf, 101, 102; and Sea of Reeds, 38; sons of, 104

Abarbanel, Isaac: description, 271; Samson's birth, 190–91

Abigail: beauty of, 254; betraying husband, 255; compared to Bathsheba, 252–53, 256; immodest behavior of, 255; and menstrual blood, 255–56; pleading with David, 250–51; possibly pregnant by Nabal, 257; and relations with David, 254

Abimelech, 225, 229

Abraham: birth and youth of, 138; burning house of idols, 144; compared to Mordecai, 226; in Gerar, 224–25; presenting Sarah as sister, 223; reasons for journey to Canaan, 139–43; rescued from furnace, 144, 146–47, 148; sending servant to find wife for Isaac, 230; suspecting servant defiled Rebekah, 235; ten tests of, 140, 143, 147

Abram. *See* Abraham

Absalom, 238

Additions to Esther: description, 271; Esther and Ahasuerus, 227

Alphabet of Ben Sira: description, 271; Solomon and queen of Sheba, 265–66

Amnon and Tamar, 233

angels: conceiving Samson, 189–92; re-

quiring nourishment, 52–53; in Sodom and Gomorrah, 133–34; weeping, 79, 80

Apocryphon of Joshua: description, 272; Moses's birth, 169; Moses's stopping sun, 59

Aramaic Targum to Psalms: 'abirim, 14; description, 272; sea dragons, 14

Araunah, 69, 127–28

Artapanus: description, 272; Moses in Ethiopia, 173–74, 175, 177

Avot de-Rabbi Natan: Abraham's ten tests, 140; description, 272; God as judge, 32

Baal: and creation story, 10; and Elisha, 184

barren women, 138, 165, 189, 195, 199–200, 203

Bathsheba: compared to Abigail, 252–53, 256; possibly pregnant by Uriah, 257–58

Beit Shemesh, 193

Benjamin, etymology of name, 82

Bethel: as cultic center, 69, 78, 79, 103, 120–21; as gate to heaven, 66–69; Jacob wrestling with God in, 78; as Jerusalem, 69–70; names of, 78–79

Bethlehem, site of Rachel's burial, 84–87

Beth-on, 78–79, 82, 83

Bethuel, 232–33

Bible: allowing multiple interpretations, 136, 186, 224; duplicate traditions in, 7–8; modified in post-Biblical literature, 268; as monotheistic manifesto, 1, 267; pagan traditions in, 8, 267; purpose of, 1, 5, 267–68; suppressed meanings, sources of, 269–70

Biblical Antiquities: and Abraham's rescue from fire, 144; description, 273; Jael, 246, 247, 248; Moses at Marah, 94; Moses's birth, 167, 169

Bilhah, 237–41

birth stories, motifs of, 165–66, 199–200

Bokhim, 79–80, 83

Book of Ben Sira: description, 273; Elisha's grave, 186; Joshua's stopping sun, 57–58, 60

bread of affliction, 97, 98–99

calves: compared to cherubim, 105; idols of, as legitimate worship, 103–8; and Jeroboam, 103–6, 108; as part of covenantal ceremonies, 107–8. *See also* golden calf

Canaan, punishment of, 132

Canaanites, sexual vilification of, 132–33, 136

The Canterbury Tales, 236, 273

castration, 135–36

Chenephres, 173–74

cherubim: and calf idols, 105; and serpents, 22

Chileab, 256–57

Chronicles: genealogies in, 157; reflecting Patriarchal stories, 157–60

Chronicles of Moses Our Teacher: description, 273; Moses in Ethiopia, 175

commandments, reasons for observing, 109

creation story: Babylonian/Ugaritic version of, 10; as creating boundaries, 27;

and Moses's birth, 169

cults, biblical opposition to, 6

Cushite woman (Moses's wife), 175–78

Damesek Eliezer, 230–32, 233–36

Dan: conquest of, as mini-Exodus, 124–25, 127; as cultic center, 103, 121, 126; and lack of divine selection, 128; naming of, 125; priests at, 125

Daniel, friends of, in furnace, 145

Danites, idolatry of, 121–23

David: compared to Joseph, 200–201; demanding relations with Abigail, 256; and Elhanan, 211–12; etymology of name, 204–5; fleeing Saul, 206–7; genealogy of, 1–2, 198; lack of birth account of, 198–99; missing genealogy of, 197–98; punishment of, 253; slaying Goliath, 206–10; stealing kingdom from Saul, 152; taking married women, 227–28, 253; threatening Nabal, 250–51

death, nature of, 180

Deborah (Rachel's wet nurse), death of, 82

Decameron, 274

deification of mortals, avoiding, 38, 40, 62

Delilah, 245, 246, 248, 249

Deuteronomy Scroll (4QDeutʲ), 274

drunkenness, 131, 134, 137, 252

Ecclesiasticus. *See* Book of Ben Sira

Edom, 152

Egyptians, sexual vilification of, 132–33, 136

El (Canaanite god), 28

Elhanan son of Jarre, 210–12

Eliezer (Abraham's servant), 230–32, 233–36

Elijah: ascending to heaven, 180, 182–84,

185; and calf worship, 105; compared
to Moses, 182–83, 184–85; parting of
Jordan River, 41–42; provided bread
and meat, 54–55
Elim, 92
Elisha: and calf worship, 105; death and
burial of, 185; grave of, and resurrection, 185–86; parting of Jordan River
by, 41–42; promising food, 49; resurrection of, 186; succeeding Elijah, 184
Enoch, death of, 179–81
Enuma Elish: description, 274; Marduk,
10, 66, 275; Tower of Babel, 66
ephod, 121, 122
Ephraim: etymology of name, 160; fighting Philistines, 162–63; genealogy of,
157–58; mourning sons, 158–59
Ephratha, 198, 199
Epic of Gilgamesh: description, 275;
snake, 24
Esau: birth of, 149, 152; relinquishing
birthright, 156
Esther: in Ahasuerus's harem, 226–27;
beauty of, 254; compared to Sarah,
226–27; seduction motif, 244, 245
Exodus: meaning of, 15, 100, 161–62; Moses's absence from, 38
Exodus Rabbah: description, 275; Miriam's age, 166; Moses's birth, 167, 168,
169; Pharaoh killing male babies, 168;
waters during creation, 13

fasting, 98
fathers, elderly at birth of children,
199–200
fields, as venue for crimes, 191, 234–35
Flood, sexual perversions before and after, 131, 133–34
food, descending from the skies, 49–50.
See also manna

Garden of Eden: meaning of, 19; and
Temple, 20; and Tower of Babel, 28.
See also serpent
gematria, 182
genealogies, in Chronicles, 157
Genesis Apocryphon: description, 275;
Moses's birth, 169; Sarah and Pharaoh, 228
Genesis Rabbah: Abraham rescued from
fire, 144–45, 147; description, 275;
Eliezer and Rebekah, 230, 231; Enoch,
181; Lot's daughters, 134; Moses's
death, 182; Noah and Ham, 136; ravens sustaining Elijah, 54; Reuben
and Bilhah, 238; Sarah and Pharaoh,
228; serpent, 21; sons of god, 32;
Tower of Babel, 72; twins, birth of,
151, 234
Genesis Rabbati: description, 276; Joshua's stopping sun, 61–62
Gilgamesh, 24, 275
God: attendants of, 30; burying Moses, 181; choosing cultic sites, 127–28;
fighting enemies at creation, 11–14;
as healer, 92–93; manipulating creation, 47; man surviving view of,
74–75; mercy of, 140–41; and parting
of Jordan River, 40–42; parting Sea
of Reeds, 35–39, 43; pulling people
from waters, 43–44, 45; as savior,
208–10; as source of Solomon's wisdom, 260–61; stopping the sun, 56,
59–62; sweetening water at Marah,
91–95; term for, as judge, 32–34; testing Abraham, 140–41, 143, 147; testing
Israel, 92; weeping, 80
gods, having relations with mortals,
28–29, 195
Gog and Magog, 14
golden calf: Aaron's construction of, 101,
102; and adultery, 102; and Kingdom